Savannah

A wave of pain rose up to slam into my stomach and chest, wiping the smile right off my face. This was an ache I knew far too well. It hit me every time he came within a hundred yards of me, usually before I even saw or heard him.

Michelle let out a dreamy sigh, confirming what my body already knew.

"Please let me trip him," Anne muttered once she'd glanced back over her shoulder and spotted him, too.

I kept my gaze on Michelle, though the tiny blonde's moonstruck expression was tough to watch. Anything to keep me facing forward.

Just a few more seconds and he'd pass right behind me. I told myself I didn't care, even as my skin tingled with some secret knowledge all its own that he was drawing closer.

I groaned inside my head. How did he *do* this to me?

Tristan

Even in the middle of a noisy mass of students, one girl's laugh grabbed my attention.

I couldn't figure out how she did it. The hallway was loud, with at least a hundred students all talking and yelling in a space only a few yards wide and a hundred yards long. But every time Savannah Colbert laughed, the husky sound somehow managed to reach out and twist up everything inside me.

I and all the rest of the descendants of the Clann had been forbidden to have anything to do with Savannah. Supposedly she was a dangerous influence or something. Whatever she was, she was definitely on the Clann's list of social outcasts. And Mom made sure I knew it, too, constantly pounding it into my head for the past five years to "stay away from that Colbert girl."

And yet I couldn't stop myself from turning to look at her now.

THE CLANN

CRAVE

Melissa Darnell

HARLEQUIN®TEEN

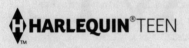

H HARLEQUIN®TEEN
TM

ISBN-13: 978-0-373-21035-0

CRAVE

Recycling programs
for this product may
not exist in your area.

This edition published by arrangement with Harlequin Books S.A.

For questions and comments about the quality of this book please contact us at Customer_eCare@Harlequin.ca.

® and TM are trademarks of the publisher. Trademarks indicated with ® are registered in the United States Patent and Trademark Office, the Canadian Trade Marks Office and in other countries.

www.HarlequinTEEN.com

Printed in U.S.A.

Dedication

As always, thanks goes out first to my hubby, Tim…
not just for being my soul mate in every sense of the word,
but also for being my best friend, the bouncing board I run
all my plot ideas by, my confidant and therapist, the best short-order
cook I've ever seen, the ultimate beta reader, not to mention so
romantic you put me to shame and inspire me daily to write another
story! Thank you for showing me just what a true romantic hero should
be like! I thank God every day for bringing us into each other's lives.

To my boys, Hunter and Alex…you gift me with tons of laughter
and smiles and hugs every single day, fueling me to keep on keeping on.
I hope that I can make you proud of your mother. I love you guys!

A huge THANK YOU also goes out to my editor, Natashya.
You are truly one of the great unsung heroes in the publishing world,
and this story would not be even half what it is without you! Thank you
for believing in me and my characters and helping make them so much
better. If they live on in even one reader's mind, it is because of you and
your genius suggestions! Also, thank you to everyone at Harlequin TEEN
for your awesome ideas and creativity and support for this series!

Thank you to my agent, Alyssa Eisner-Henkin, for your enthusiastic
support and all your hard work. You are an amazing and tireless
warrioress for authors, and I am truly blessed to get to work with you!

To my friends Melissa, Mandi and Corrie…you have shown me the
true meaning of lasting friendship over the years, no matter how
much or little we had in common (or how bad I stank at sports!), and
regardless of how time and miles and crazy schedules have separated us.
I miss hanging out with you guys and think about y'all every single day.

And last, but NEVER least…thank you to my family. You have taught me
how to be strong, have faith and have the courage to keep reaching for
my dreams. Thank you for your love and your support!

PROLOGUE

Savannah

I edged closer to my unconscious boyfriend cuffed to a chair nearby.

My judges gathered in a tight half circle a few feet away. Probably so they could see me better as I failed their test.

The guard's face looked bored, as if to say this was nothing personal. Which was a lie. This was totally personal. And all my fault.

He reached inside his inner jacket pocket and took out two items…a syringe and a scalpel. Their clear plastic protectors made loud snicks as he removed them.

I gulped, the air rushing in and out of my lungs in noisy gusts I couldn't hide within the silence of the cold cement room.

The guard stepped closer to us. My thigh muscles tensed, the instinct to fight pulsing through me, and the guard's eyes grew cautious. He knew I was desperate. But that didn't make me stupid. The guard was big, built like a linebacker beneath his badly fitted suit. And even if I could somehow fight him off, my audience of judges would step in to stop me.

I struggled to breathe, calm down and think straight. Time for logic, not emotion.

Okay. So we were in deep this time. But we weren't totally doomed. Yet. The judges had promised that I had only to pass one test, and then my boyfriend could go free.

An innocent boy who wouldn't even be here if I hadn't fallen in love with him. My fault he was in danger...

No, no time for a guilt trip right now. I had to focus on passing this test so we could go home.

Just one test to pass.

A test I was genetically destined to fail.

CHAPTER 1

Savannah

The last day I was fully human started off like any other April Monday in East Texas. Oh, sure, there were all kinds of warning signs that my entire world was about to come crashing down around me. But I didn't recognize them until it was too late.

I should have known something major was wrong when I woke up that morning feeling like utter crap, even though I'd just snagged a full nine hours of sleep. I'd never been sick before, not even with the flu or a cold, so it couldn't be anything like that.

"Good morning, dear. Your breakfast is on the table," Nanna greeted me as I shuffled into the kitchen. As usual, she was the ultimate in contradictions, her voice and smile a Southern mixture of sweetness and steel. Like your favorite old baby blanket wrapped around a mace. "Eat up. I'm going to go find my shoes."

I nodded and plopped down into one of the creaky chairs at the table. When it came to cooking, Nanna rocked. And she made the absolute best oatmeal in the world, maple and brown sugar with a ton of butter just the way I liked it. But it tasted like flavorless mush today. I gave up after two bites and dumped it in the trash can under the sink seconds before she came back.

"Finished already?" she asked before slurping her tea. The sound grated over my nerves.

"Um, yeah." I set the bowl and spoon in the sink, keeping my back turned so she couldn't see the blush burning my cheeks. I was a horrible liar. One look at my face and she'd know I'd just thrown out the breakfast she'd made me.

"And your tea?"

Oops. I'd forgotten my daily tea, a blend that Nanna made just for me from the herbs she spent months growing in our backyard. "Sorry, Nanna, there's no time. I still have to fix my hair."

"You can do both." She held out my mug, her cheeks bunched into a bright smile that didn't do much to disguise the snap in her eyes.

Sighing, I took the cup with me to the bathroom, setting it on the counter so I could have both hands free to do battle with my wild, carrot-colored curls.

"Drink your tea yet?" she asked ten minutes later as I finished taming my hair into a long ponytail.

"Nag, nag, nag," I mumbled.

"I heard that, missy," she called out from the dining room, making me smile.

I chugged the cold tea, set down the empty mug with a loud thump she'd be sure to hear, then headed for my bedroom to grab my backpack. And nearly fell over while trying to pick it up. Jeez. I must have forgotten to drop off a few books in my locker last week. Using both hands, I hefted a strap onto my shoulder and trudged back down the hall.

Nanna was at the dining table digging through her mammoth purse for her keys. That would take a while.

"Meet you at the car?" I said.

She gave an absentminded wave, which I took for a *yes,* so I headed through the living room for the front door.

As usual, Mom had been on the couch for hours already, talking on her cell phone while drowning in stacks of paperwork and pens she'd be sure to lose under the sofa cushions by the end of the day. Why she couldn't work at a desk like every other safety product sales rep was beyond me. But the chaos seemed to make her happy.

Even as she ended one call, her phone squalled for attention again. I knew better than to wait, so I just waved goodbye to her.

"Hang on, George." She hit the phone's mute button then held out her arms. "Hey, what's this? No 'good morning, Mom,' no hug goodbye?"

Grinning, I crossed the room and bent over to hug her, resisting the urge to cough as her favorite floral perfume flooded my nose and throat. When I straightened up again, my back popped and twinged.

"Was that your back?" she gasped. "Good grief, you sound worse than your nanna today."

"I heard that," Nanna yelled from the dining room.

Smothering a smile, I shrugged. "Guess I practiced too much this weekend." My beginner ballet and jazz classes would be performing in Miss Catherine's Dance Studio's annual spring recital soon. As the days ticked down to my latest impending public humiliation, I'd kind of started freaking out about it.

"I'll say. Why don't you take it a little easier? You've still got two weeks till the recital."

"Yeah, well, I need every second of practice I can get."

That is, if I wanted to improve enough to avoid disappointing my father yet again.

"You know, killing yourself in the backyard isn't going to impress your father, either."

I froze, hating that I was so transparent. "Nothing impresses him." At least, not enough to earn a visit from him more than twice a year. Probably because I was such a screwup at sports. The man moved like a ballroom dancer, always light and graceful on his feet, but I didn't seem to have gotten even a hint of those genes in my DNA. Mom had tried enrolling me in every activity she could think of over the years to help me develop some grace and hand-eye coordination…soccer, twirling, gymnastics, basketball. Last year was volleyball. This year it was dance, both at Miss Catherine's Dance Studio and at my high school.

Apparently my father was fed up with my lack of athletic skill, judging by Mom's argument with him over the phone last September when I began dancing. He really didn't want me to take dance lessons this year. He must have thought they were a waste on someone as uncoordinated as me.

I was out to prove him wrong. And so far, failing miserably.

Mom sighed. "Oh, hon. You really shouldn't worry so much about making him happy. Just dance for yourself, and I'm sure you'll do fine."

"Uh-huh. That's what you said last year about volleyball." And yet, in spite of taking her advice to "just have fun," I'd still ended up hitting a ball through the gym's tile ceiling during a tournament. When the broken pieces had come crashing down, they'd almost wiped out half my team. That had sort of ended the fun of volleyball for me.

Mom bit her lip, probably to keep from laughing at the same memory.

"Found 'em!" Nanna sang out in triumph from the dining room. "Ready to rock and roll, kid?"

Sighing, I pulled up my backpack's slipping strap onto my shoulder again. It scraped at my skin through my shirt, forcing a hiss out of me. Youch. "Maybe I should grab an aspirin before we go."

"Absolutely not." Nanna strode into the room, keys jingling in her hand. "Aspirin's bad for you."

Huh? "But you and Mom take it all the t—"

"But *you* don't," Nanna snapped. "You've never taken that synthetic crap before, and you won't start polluting yourself with it now. I'll make you more of my special tea instead. Here, take my purse to the car and I'll be right there."

Without waiting for a reply, she shoved her forty-pound purse into my hands and headed for the kitchen. Great. I'd be late for sure. Again.

"Why can't I just take an aspirin like everyone else in the world?"

Mom smiled and picked up her phone.

Four very long minutes later, Nanna finally joined me in the car. She thrust a metal thermos into my hand. "There, that ought to fix you right up. Be careful, though. It's hot. I had to nuke it."

I bit back a groan. Nanna hated the microwave. The only button she'd learned how to use was the three-minute auto-heat. I'd be lucky if the tea cooled off at all before we reached my school, even if it was a ten-minute drive.

We lived in a small, somewhat isolated nest of houses five miles outside of town. As I blew on my tea to cool it, I watched the rolling hills pass by, dotted here and there with solitary houses, big round bales of hay, and cows in all shades of red, brown and black. Out here, the thick pine trees that had once covered all of East Texas had been cut back to make room for ranches that were now broken only by rows of fences, mostly of barbed wire, sometimes wide slats of wood turned gray by time and the weather. You could breathe out here.

But as we neared the city limits, the strips of trees became thicker and showed up more often, until we passed through a section of nothing but pines just before reaching the junior high and intermediate schools. The first traffic-light intersection marked the start of downtown Jacksonville, where all of a sudden it became nothing but streets and business after business, mostly single-story shops and a few three- and four-story buildings for the occasional bank, hotel or hospital. And more pines winding around and through every area of housing large and small, even butting up against the edges of the basket factory and near the Tomato Bowl, the brownstone open-air stadium where all the home football and soccer games were held.

I used to love my hometown with its cute boutiques and shops full of antiques where Nanna sold her crocheted designs. I even used to love the town's ribbons of pines and the way the wind in the trees added a subtle sighing to the air. When the fields of grass and hay turned brown and dead in the winter, you could always count on the pines to keep Jacksonville colorful all year long.

But the town's founding families, locally referred to as the Clann due to their Irish ancestry, had ruined it for me. Now when I heard the wind in the trees, it sounded like whispering, as if the trees themselves had joined the town's grapevine of gossips. Those gossips had probably produced the long line of famous actors, singers, comedians and models that Jacksonville's relatively small population of thirteen thousand residents was so proud of. Growing up here, where everybody talked about everybody else, either made you want to live here forever or run away and become something special just to prove the gossips and the Clann wrong.

I wasn't sure I wanted to be famous. But I definitely wanted to run away.

We made the daily turn through the neighborhoods that led to Jacksonville High School, the drive made shady by still more pines and a few hardwoods that lined the modest streets. And then the blue-and-yellow home of the JHS Indians exploded into view, its perimeter choked by woods thick and shadowed, and I felt my shoulders and neck tense up.

Welcome to my daytime prison for the next four years, complete with a guard shack and a guard who lowered a heavy metal bar across the driveways on the dot of 8:00 a.m. every weekday, forcing you to accept a tardy slip in order to gain entrance when you were late. Unlike a teacher who might be convinced to let you slide, the guard was notoriously without mercy, ruling our school's entrance as if it were the gates to some medieval castle.

If JHS were a castle, then its royalty would definitely be the twenty-two equally merciless Clann kids who ruled the rest of the campus.

The Clann kids had probably learned their bullying tactics from their parents, who ran this town and a good portion of Texas, inserting themselves into every possible leadership role from county and state even to federal government levels. Local rumor had it that the only way the Clann could do this was by using magic, of all things. Which was total bull. There was nothing magical about the Clann's power-hungry methods. I should know. I'd had more than enough of their kids' idea of "magical" fun at school. After graduation, I was so out of here.

While Nanna pulled up to the curb by the main hall doors,

I sucked down a quick slurp of tea, adding a burnt tongue to my list of pains for the day.

"Better take that with you." Nanna nodded at the thermos. "You should feel it kick in pretty soon, but you might need more later."

"Okay. Hey, don't forget, today's an A day, and I have algebra last period, so—"

"So pick you up in the front parking lot by the cafeteria. Yeah, yeah. I'm old, not senile. I think I can keep up with your alternating A-B schedule." Her twinkling green eyes nearly disappeared as her plump cheeks bunched higher into a wry smile.

The front parking lot was closer to my last class on A days. The first class in five years that I'd shared with Tristan Coleman...

"Savannah?" She shifted the car into Drive then looked at me with raised eyebrows, a silent prod to get moving. I climbed out into the pine-scented warmth of the morning, shut the door and gave her a wave goodbye.

Tristan...

His name echoed through my head, fuzzing up my mind with old memories and emotions. An answering tingle rippled up the back of my neck and over my scalp. Ignoring it, I stuffed the forbidden thoughts back into their imaginary box and turned to face the main hall doors. The day was sure to be miserable enough without my stewing over backstabbing traitors like him.

Sure enough, I shoved through the main hall's heavier-than-normal glass front doors and slammed right into the Brat Twins, two of the Clann's worst members. Yep, the perfect start to a fabulous day.

"Watch where you're going, idiot!" Vanessa Faulkner said,

brushing off imaginary dirt from her latest Juicy Couture purse.

"Yeah, try looking before you just barrel in," Hope, her mirror-image sister, added. She reached up and patted her perfect platinum curls, the tiny mole to the left of her smirk the only difference between the two sisters.

I glanced around. We already had an audience for my daily humiliation. Great. My hands itched to try and smooth my own wild curls as my stomach twisted into knots. *Why* did the Brat Twins have to treat me like this? Just because I couldn't get a tan? Because my hair was the wrong color, too frizzy, not shiny enough?

"Well? Aren't you at least going to say you're sorry?" Vanessa demanded.

For a moment, the anger drowned out everything else. What would happen if I slapped that smirk off her face? She couldn't go crying to her precious Clann for the usual revenge. Nanna was retired, Mom worked for a Louisiana-based company and my father owned a national historical-home restoration business. The Clann couldn't touch my family.

Or could they? Several members of the Clann were politicians at the federal level. And Louisiana was within easy reach of East Texas. So maybe they did have enough connections to at least get Mom fired. Crap.

My backpack's strap bit into my hands as I swallowed down all the things I wanted to say and instead muttered, "Sorry."

"Yeah, you are," Vanessa said. She and her sister laughed like hyenas high on helium and turned away.

I should have just let them go and been grateful to get away from them. But a headache pounded at my temples now, and all I could think about was how different things were when we were kids. Back when these girls were my best friends.

As soon as my hand touched her shoulder, Vanessa hissed.

Both sisters whirled around to face me again. Shocked by the fury on Vanessa's face, I stepped backward until the wall of lockers stopped me. Whoa. This was nuts.

"Van, why are you being like this?" I made a point of using my old nickname for her. "We used to be friends. Remember Valentine's Day, fourth grade? We held that pretend wedding, and you two were my bridesmaids?" That was the last day we'd all played together, and it was one of my favorite childhood memories. The twins and I had prepared for the ceremony by sitting in a circle on the merry-go-round and braiding flowers into each other's hair. While my first and only boyfriend, Tristan Coleman, had stood beneath the nearby oak tree watching us, waiting for me.

Waiting to give me my first and only kiss...

Everything about that half hour had seemed so sweet, almost magically perfect. But I must have been the only one who'd thought so. Because the next day, all of the Clann's kids had refused to talk to me, not even long enough to tell me what I'd done to upset them. Including Tristan. Ever since, the only time anyone from the Clann spoke to me was when the Brat Twins called me names or "accidentally" shoved me in the hallways.

"We braided daisies into each other's hair," Hope whispered, almost smiling.

She remembered. I nodded, daring a small smile of my own, and eased away from the lockers.

Vanessa's eyes softened for a few seconds, transforming her into the girl I used to know, like she was remembering our former friendship, too. But then her expression darkened again, twisting with hatred. "That day was a huge mistake. *Your* mistake, for thinking a freak like you could actually be friends with anyone in the Clann. And especially for thinking you could even pretend to marry someone like Tristan."

"Yeah. The Clann does *not* hang out with freaks like you," Hope added.

So much for remembering the good old days.

I sighed, defeat making me even more tired. "I don't get you two. Or Tristan. You guys used to be my best friends. What did I ever do to—"

Vanessa closed the distance between us so fast I didn't have time to react, her nose nearly touching mine. "You were *born,* freak. That's more than enough reason to make every member of the Clann hate you for the rest of our lives. Now get. Out. Of our. Way!" Using both hands, she slammed me against the lockers then stalked off, Hope tagging along in her footsteps.

I shouldn't have been stunned. I should have known the past was over and done with and there was no going back. But still, it took a few seconds before I could make my feet move again. My throat and eyes burning, I tried to ignore the way everyone was staring at me and headed for my locker at the other end of the hallway, my chin lifted, as if the encounter had been no big deal.

Three hours later, I flopped into my seat at my friends' table in the cafeteria.

Carrie Calvin's eyebrows shot up beneath her long blond bangs. "A little early in the day to be so tired, don't you think?" She flicked her shoulder-length hair behind her.

I managed a grunt and focused on unscrewing the cap of my tea thermos. Time for another dose of homegrown medicine. Hopefully it wouldn't take too long to kick in this time. Or maybe I should open a vein in my arm and pour it in directly.

As promised, Nanna's special tea had helped during first-period English. But climbing the sports and art building's two flights of stairs to second period pre-drill class, followed by an hour and a half of dancing, had set back my recovery. I felt worse than ever.

"Oh, she's just worn-out from all that dancing she's taken up," Anne Albright said. "You know, twirling with the frou-frou tutus at Miss Catherine's Dance Studio. Kicking it in pre-drill with all those sad Charmer wannabes." She tightened her thick, chestnut-brown ponytail and grinned, apparently unable to resist stirring up a little excitement for lunch.

I chucked a French fry at her. She was lucky she was my best friend, or I'd be tempted to dump her soda over her head instead. She knew Carrie and Michelle were still annoyed that I'd picked dance lessons instead of playing volleyball again with them this year. To them, even sucking at volleyball was better than dancing.

Michelle Wilson turned her big hazel eyes toward me. "Are you going to try out for the Charmers, Sav?"

It took me a few seconds to understand. Then I remembered. Most students only took pre-drill as a required class so they could audition for the JHS Cherokee Charmers Dance/Drill Team in May.

"Of course she isn't," Anne jumped in before I could reply. "Pre-drill is just her mom's idea of fulfilling her P.E. credit without embarrassing herself again like last year."

"Gee, thanks," I said. But I couldn't really be mad. Anne was only saying the truth, as usual. I *had* taken pre-drill for the P.E. credit, and because it had no audience or competitions for me to doom a team at. Trying out for the Charmers was the last thing on my mind.

"Sorry," Anne muttered, both looking and sounding sincere.

Between desperate gulps of tea, I gave her a half grin to show I wasn't really upset. She'd been my best friend for over two years now, and I'd gotten used to her blunt style. In a way, it was even comforting. At least I could always count on her to be honest, no matter what.

A new wave of pain rose up to slam into my stomach and chest, wiping the smile right off my face. This was an ache I knew far too well. It hit me every time *he* came within a hundred yards of me, usually before I even saw or heard him.

Michelle, who sat across from me, let out a dreamy sigh, confirming what my body already knew.

"Please let me trip him," Anne muttered once she'd glanced over her shoulder and spotted him, too.

I kept my gaze on Michelle, though the tiny blonde's moonstruck expression was tough to watch. Anything to keep me facing forward. Tristan had to either walk along the outer wall of the cafeteria or cut across the center by our table on his way to the food lines. Most people cut across. No doubt he would, too.

Just a few more seconds and he'd pass right behind me. I told myself I didn't care, even as my skin tingled with some secret knowledge all its own that he was drawing closer.

And then I heard it…a low whistling, the notes so quiet I could almost have believed I'd imagined them if not for my sensitive hearing. Sugarplum music, as plain as if he'd whistled the notes right against my ear.

Ever since he'd seen my ballet slippers fall out of my backpack during algebra earlier this year, Tristan had started whistling *The Nutcracker*'s "Dance of the Sugar Plum Fairy" song every time he saw me. I remembered his sense of humor, how his mind worked. This was his wordless way of teasing me about wanting to be a ballerina, without having to actually bother to talk to me. Because of course a klutz like me couldn't ever become a decent dancer, right?

I felt a blush flood my cheeks and neck with heat, adding to my frustration. I must look like a strawberry…red face, red hair, red ears. But no way would I duck my head. I would not give him the satisfaction of any reaction I could control, at least.

"Oh, I am so gonna trip him," Anne hissed, turning her chair toward him. Apparently she got his sense of humor, too, even if she didn't approve of it.

"No, you can't!" Michelle reached over the edge of the round table, grabbed Anne's arm and yanked her sideways half out of her seat. By the time Anne recovered, he was past our table.

"He's a member of the Clann. You know how all those witches treat Savannah," Anne said.

"Tristan Coleman isn't like them. He's nice," Michelle said. "The whole witchcraft thing is just a rumor. And a stupid one, at that."

Carrie, Anne and I all shared a look.

Michelle sighed. "Tristan is so not a witch! Or warlock, or whatever they're called. His family goes to my church. And he's too nice to sacrifice small animals. Remember how he saved me last summer at that track meet? None of the others would have done that, but he did."

Carrie and Anne both groaned out loud. We'd heard this story countless times this year, until Anne had finally threatened to beat Michelle to death if she told it one more time.

I just groaned inside my head. I was too busy forcing air in and out of my lungs past the tightness in my chest. How did he *do* this to me?

"'Saved' is a little much," Carrie said. "And for the record, witches don't sacrifice animals."

"Yeah, Michelle," Anne said. "All he did was help you off the track after you got shin splints."

"Exactly!" Michelle retorted. "Those shin splints hurt *so*

badly. And he was the only one to come and help me. And he didn't even know me!"

Carrie sighed and dropped her chin into a propped-up hand.

"Michelle, get a grip. He just did that to make himself look good for everyone at the track meet." Anne chugged the rest of her soda then burped. She didn't bother to say *excuse me.* "He's nothing more than a glorified spoiled rich kid."

"That's not true. And he doesn't need to try and make himself look good. He already looks good. Did you see that chest? Those huge shoulders?" Michelle sighed again. "Thank you, God, for growth spurts. I swear he's grown half a foot taller this year. And that new voice. Oh, yum."

"Oh, gag me," Anne said. "I'll bet his ego grew right along with the rest of him. He thinks every girl on the planet should be eager to drool over him. And what do you mean, 'that new voice'? You got a class with him or something?"

It was Michelle's turn to blush. "No. He stops by the front office before first period on A days sometimes to talk to me and the other office aides."

"And I'll bet you just love chatting him up, don't you?" Anne glared at her.

"Well, it...it's the least I can do, since he saved me."

"Ugh, I'm gonna hurl." Anne gathered up her books.

"Me, too. I can't believe you talk to a Clann member," Carrie said, picking up her things despite her still half-full salad bowl. "Especially one who thinks he owns all of East Texas."

I stared down at my untouched chili cheese fries. My comfort food looked anything but comforting today. "I think I'm done, too."

"Aw, guys. Don't be mad." Michelle jumped up and grabbed her stuff. "Y'all are way too hard on him. He's really very nice once you get to know him."

"Puh-lease." Anne proceeded to explain the difference between being nice and being a total player as we all headed for the trash cans then the rear exit. I followed but tuned them out, tired of hearing about Tristan Coleman's infamous reputation with the girls. But my traitorous gaze still slipped over to the Clann kids' table long enough to see that the prince of Jacksonville needed another haircut. Tristan's golden curls had grown long enough to brush the collar of his polo shirt again.

Later that afternoon before fourth period, the foot traffic streamed around me like a human river flowing through the main hallway. I sighed, tired and achy and cranky, trying to ignore the claustrophobic feeling from the swarm of people all around me while I squatted in front of my bottom-row locker. I still hadn't gotten used to how many students were packed into this campus every day. The junior high had only three grades and much bigger hallways, so when someone had bumped into me there last year, it had been a personal message. Here, students nudged against me every couple seconds as I struggled to find a pencil inside the chaos of my locker for my last class. Stupid algebra. It was my toughest subject, and the only class that required a pencil.

It was also the only one I had with any Clann members. And with the worst one of them all, too.

Thank goodness at least Anne was in the same class. She was a genius at anything to do with numbers.

She wasn't great at waiting for me, though.

"Hey, slowpoke, you're gonna be late. As usual." Anne leaned against the lockers next to mine and gave me a friendly punch on the shoulder, hard enough to make me wobble. I righted myself and winced, guessing I'd probably have a bruise on my shoulder for a day or two.

"And what does a female jock care about being late to class?" I teased while I wearily continued to dig through books and supplies. Where the heck had that pack of pencils gone? If I had to borrow a pencil from Anne, I'd never hear the end of it. She'd use loaning me a pencil as an excuse to launch yet another tirade about how I needed to get organized.

She snorted and squatted down beside me. "Obvious answer. If volleyball doesn't pan out for a scholarship, the grades will have to do it for me instead. Harvard costs a butt load, or haven't you heard?"

"I still don't understand why you need to go to Harvard just to become a CPA. Can't you go to any college to do that?"

"And I still don't understand why you can't keep a locker clean." She reached forward as if to start tidying up the pile. I swatted her hand away with a smile.

Suddenly someone rammed into my back. I threw one hand against the lockers and the other hand to the floor to catch myself as my backpack slid off my shoulder and thudded on the floor at my feet. My entire body vibrated from the impact, as if my bones were hollow and echoing from the hit like metal pipes. Then everything came cascading out of my locker in a mini avalanche, hitting my shoulder on the way down. That was definitely going to leave a bruise.

I glanced up in time to see Dylan Williams, another member of the Clann and one of my most loyal tormentors, saunter away with his usual braying laugh. Sometimes I had nightmares about that laugh of his. I shuddered.

"Oh, he did *not* just do that! I am so gonna kick his—" Anne jumped up, grabbed her chestnut ponytail in two thick handfuls and yanked the halves in opposite directions to tighten her rubber band. The same way she always tightened her ponytail before smacking one of her lethal power serves during a volleyball game. Was she about to smack Dylan a power serve to the head?

While the image was tempting, I didn't want to know what the consequences would be if she actually did it. I grabbed her ankle and tugged just enough to direct her attention back to me.

"Anne, don't, he isn't worth it. Some people never change. Dylan's been knocking books out of my arms and popping my bra for years." I started grabbing things off the floor and stuffing them into my locker.

Grumbling, she bent down to help me. "Why don't you pop him one?"

"Don't worry, if he gets too bad, I'll handle it." Somehow. And definitely on a day when I didn't feel so bad. "He's just another spoiled brat from the Clann. Why give him the satisfaction of a reaction?" At least, that's what my mother and grandmother kept telling me. So far, their theory that I should ignore the Clann bullies hadn't been much of a success.

Anne frowned, but at least she didn't go after the jerk.

As we fit the small mountain of papers and books back inside the too-small locker, a bright bit of yellow in the pile caught my eye. I reached beneath the jungle of stuff and snatched out a pack of pencils. "Yes, found them!"

"Finally. I am so cleaning that locker if you don't."

"Ha! Be my guest." Everything now in its disorganized place, I stood up and shoved the locker door shut, having to use both hands to get it closed enough for the latch to click. "Just don't blame me if something in there bites you."

At Anne's furtive glance toward the locker door, I couldn't help but laugh. She wouldn't hesitate to start a fight with a member of the Clann, but my messy locker scared her?

The laugh died as quickly as it had begun as a strange yet

familiar ache welled up in my stomach and chest. I nearly
moaned out loud. *Not again.*

Even knowing the cause for the weird ache couldn't stop
me from turning and looking down the hall. My gaze immediately collided and locked with the sensation's green-eyed
source towering over most of the other students.

Tristan

Even in the middle of a noisy mass of students, one girl's
laugh grabbed my attention.

I couldn't figure out how she did it. The hallway was loud,
with at least a hundred students all talking and yelling in a
space only a few yards wide and thirty times as long. But every
time Savannah Colbert laughed, the husky sound somehow
managed to reach out and twist up everything inside me.

Part of me wished I never had to see or hear her again. Life
would be a lot easier if I didn't. The way I felt about Savannah
was all mixed-up. Once, she'd been my best friend. And the
first girl I'd ever kissed.

Then I'd made the mistake of telling my older sister,
Emily, about pretending to marry Savannah during recess in
the fourth grade. Emily had blabbed to our parents. Mom had
blown a gasket and called the school to get me yanked out of
Savannah's class. Dad had turned purple in the face and gone
all silent and scowling. And I'd known I was in big trouble.

Ever since, I and all the rest of the descendants of the Clann
had been forbidden to have anything to do with Savannah.
Supposedly she was a dangerous influence or something.
Whatever she was, she was definitely on the Clann's list of
social outcasts. And Mom made sure I remembered it, too,
constantly pounding it into my head for the past five years to
"stay away from that Colbert girl."

And yet I couldn't stop myself from turning to look at her now.

From this distance, I couldn't see Savannah's eyes in detail. But I remembered them way too clearly. Their color changed from gray to slate-blue to blue-green depending on her mood. *Wonder what color they are now?* I thought, vaguely aware of my hands tightening around my books.

A heavy arm draped over my shoulder. "Hey, Tristan. Ready to hit the weights after school?"

My best friend, Dylan Williams, shook me, breaking my focus. I met his usual cocky grin with a frown of my own. "Yeah, sure. Though you might want to try showing up on time today, or Coach Parker is gonna be ticked."

He laughed. "We're descendants. What's he gonna do to us?"

I shot a glance around to see if anyone was listening, then glared at him. "Dude, ever heard of the word 'discretion'?" I lowered my voice, trying to set an example for the dumb blond. "You know we're not supposed to talk about that stuff in public. And Coach Parker isn't a descendant, so he's still going to be ticked if you're late again. Or do you actually like running laps?"

Dylan's smile hardened as his chin rose a notch. "We'll see who runs laps. No one messes with a descendant. Not even a football coach."

"Even descendants have to play by the rules, Dylan. We always have, always will."

He shook his shaggy bangs out of his eyes. "Maybe, for now. Or maybe we'll be the descendants who make some changes."

"Make some changes? Like what?"

He shrugged. "We founded this town. Don't you think it's past time we were running it the way we should be?"

I rocked back on my heels. "Oh, yeah? And how should we be running things?"

"I don't know…more out in the open about it?"

I scowled at him, hoping he was just joking around. But something about the set of his jaw and the dark look in his eyes said otherwise. "You're not suggesting coming out about the Clann's abilities?"

He shrugged again. "Why not? This is the modern world. All the books and movies say we're cool. Why not own up to it, let everyone know what we can—"

Sudden and total fear had me grabbing his shoulder at the base of his neck without thinking. I pulled his face close and growled, "Are you out of your freakin' mind? If any other descendant heard you talking like that and told the elders, you'd be history."

He stiffened under my grip, his chin hiking up again so he could meet my stare head-on with a glare of his own. He actually opened his mouth like he was going to argue.

But after a tense moment, he took a deep breath and chuckled. "Hey, man, ease up! I was just messing around. Forget about it."

"Dylan—"

"I said I was just kidding! Man, can't you even take a *joke?*"

I stared at him a few seconds longer, trying to figure out what was going on with him lately. Even joking around about stuff like that was dangerous, and he knew it. So why do it?

The warning bell rang, making me swear under my breath. I had less than a couple minutes now to get all the way across campus to the math and home-ec building. "All right. Are we cool?"

"Yeah, sure." He lifted his head and smiled, but it didn't reach his eyes. "You're just looking out for me, right?" He turned away, yelling "Later" over his shoulder as he headed in the opposite direction.

I watched the blond as he strutted off like he owned the world. Then I turned and headed for algebra class. Even if he'd been serious, Dylan was just a hothead with a big mouth. Being the star quarterback for the junior varsity team this year despite only being a freshman hadn't improved his ego much, either. Hopefully he would come to his senses soon...*before* the elders had to step in. What he was talking about—the movies, the books—that was Hollywood. People liked the idea of magic. But no way would magical abilities fly in the real world, especially in Jacksonville, Texas. This was a Bible Belt town with conservative, old-school beliefs about religion and magic. Even if descendants held key positions in government and business here, if everyone found out just how powerful most descendants were, they would assume we were a bunch of Satan-worshiping baby murderers or something and run us out of the very town we founded. Dylan needed to remember that the Clann's power came from the secrets we kept.

Well, one thing was for sure...if Dylan kept screwing around and being late all the time for practice, at least Coach Parker would be willing to help him regain his memory. The head coach had zero tolerance for tardy players, Clann or otherwise, on his teams. He'd probably make Dylan run laps after practice as punishment. That ought to take Dylan's ego down a notch or two, and would totally serve the idiot right.

Sometimes I honestly couldn't remember why I still considered him my best friend.

I headed down the hall toward the last class of the day. And toward Savannah. Her flame-bright hair and pale skin were easy to spot in the boring sea of tanned brunettes and blondes. A couple girls called out "Hey, Tristan!" to me, and one of the sophomore cheerleaders even touched my arm and grinned up at me. But I didn't have time to stop and talk. I was much more interested in watching that redhead. Something about looking at Savannah calmed me down today.

I exited the air-conditioned main building and headed through the sticky spring-afternoon heat along the metal-awning-covered cement catwalk that stretched over the lower outer walkways, connecting the main building to the math building on the far side of the campus. Savannah and her friend were several yards ahead of me. Neither looked back. And yet something about the way Savannah's shoulders rose up as soon as I saw her...I could almost swear she knew I was watching her. Not for the first time, I wondered if she could somehow sense the focus of my attention. But that was impossible. She wasn't a descendant, and the Clann would know about any outsiders with special abilities like that.

Except...no normal girl had ever stuck in my mind like she did.

Then again, no girl, normal or otherwise, seemed to mess with my thoughts quite like Savannah did. So maybe I was just desperate to find any reason besides my own weakness to blame for the crazy hold she had on me.

At least she made algebra interesting.

Savannah

"You look like crap," Anne whispered halfway through class, distracting me from the foggy circle my mind kept whirling around in.

I couldn't even force a smile to reassure her. Nanna's special tea hadn't made a dent in the pain this time. It was all I could do not to bawl like a baby. This was way beyond simple soreness from dancing. Though I'd never been sick before, I was pretty sure I'd finally caught the flu, or something close to it. I had all the symptoms those flu-medicine commercials listed. When I wasn't freezing, I was burning up. I couldn't stop shaking. My skin felt like I had another of my annual summer sunburns everywhere my clothes touched. And my head was pounding so loud I'd missed hearing most of Mr. Chandler's lecture. We were supposed to be working on our homework assignment now. Right, like that was going to happen. Just the idea of grabbing my book from under my desk made the bones in my arms throb. And I sucked at math even on a good day.

I shifted in my desk, and my legs bumped into Tristan's feet. Crap. I'd forgotten. As usual, the spoiled prince of Jacksonville needed more legroom and had stretched his long legs out at either side of my desk. Turning my seat into a virtual prison, unless I didn't mind our legs and feet touching every time I moved. Which I really did mind.

Honestly, I could shoot whoever had come up with the evil idea of alphabetical seating. It was alphabetical seating that had first forced Tristan and me to sit beside each other in the fourth grade. And placed him right behind me here in algebra this year.

I was tempted to slump down in my seat and rest my head on the back of my chair. But then my ponytail would land on Tristan's desk. And then he might start messing with the ends of my hair again, like Anne had caught him doing a few weeks ago. He'd probably been trying to stick gum in it. His best friend from the Clann, Dylan Williams, loved to do that to girls with long hair.

Forcing myself to stay upright, I bit back a groan, propped my spinning head between my hands and checked the clock on the wall again. If I could just make it through this last class of the day…

"Are you okay?" Anne whispered, leaning forward past Tristan. "I'm serious, Sav. You really look—"

"Anne, focus on your work," Mr. Chandler said from his desk. "Savannah, come see me please."

I almost whimpered. He wanted me to *move?*

Gritting my teeth, I pulled myself to my feet, circled around the front of my desk to avoid Tristan's legs and trudged across the room to the teacher's desk, praying I wouldn't barf all over the round little man.

"Anne's right, you do look sick," Mr. Chandler murmured. "Would you like to go visit the nurse?"

Great. So everyone thought I looked like crap today. "Um, no, thank you." I tried not to breathe on him. Wasn't the flu supposed to be highly contagious? "It's the last class of the day. I can make it a little longer. Do you mind if I lay my head down on my desk, though?"

"Sure, go ahead. Just be sure to take care of the assignment as soon as you're feeling better."

On the way back to my desk, I wrapped my arms around myself as a sudden chill swept over my skin, making me shiver. Then I made the mistake of looking up at the clock again. And missed seeing Tristan's outstretched leg.

I tripped hard over his foot. My arms wouldn't budge. No way could I catch myself in time. All I could do was close my eyes and brace for a face-plant on my desk. He'd have a real good time laughing about this later with his precious Clann friends.

Instead, strong hands stopped my fall.

I pried my eyelids open, knowing even before I did who had caught me.

Tristan had half risen from his desk and grabbed my shoulders. Too tired and sick to stop myself, I got lost in emerald-green eyes that used to be as familiar as my own. Heat from his hands seeped through my shirt, melting my bones.

"Sav, are you all right?" he whispered, his eyebrows drawn together.

The nickname distracted me. He used his old nickname for me so easily, as if we were still in the fourth grade and best friends. As if he hadn't just spent the past five years pretending he didn't know me.

His normally full lips were thin, grim lines today. He looked...furious. For having to catch me? Or because I'd had the nerve to trip over his foot?

"Sor-ry," I muttered, a hint of anger giving me the strength to regain my balance.

Once safely in my seat again, I laid down my head on the desk's cold wood surface, shivering and wishing I could just die already. As if having a monster case of the flu for the first time wasn't bad enough, now Tristan had decided to be mad at me because I'd tripped over him. Like I could help it that he was a total Sasquatch.

But I was too tired to get properly mad about it at the moment. All I wanted was to go home.

Tristan

Savannah Colbert had to be the most stubborn girl I'd ever known. I'd watched her shiver, her breathing getting faster and more out of rhythm, for over an hour now. Anyone else would've gone home early. But not Savannah.

I checked out her red cheeks, the way she never stopped frowning, how her body tried to curl into a ball.

If she were still my friend, I would've hauled her stubborn butt off to my sister's car and driven her home myself. Never mind that I wouldn't have a driver's license until next year. Or that she was off-limits to everyone in the Clann, and Jacksonville was filled with gossips who watched my every freaking move and reported back to the elders within minutes of anything happening.

I silently cursed the Clann with every swearword I knew. Bunch of controlling witches. Just because my family had led those power addicts for the past four generations didn't mean I wanted anything to do with their magic or their stupid rules. Every waking minute of the day, I had to focus on keeping my energy levels in check so I didn't accidentally set fire to stuff. It got exhausting sometimes, constantly having to keep the power under control, when all I really wanted was to be normal and play football, hopefully for the NFL someday. But even there, magic was both a help and a pain. It helped me run faster and hit guys harder. But it also meant I had to be careful not to break necks or send guys flying too far when I slammed into them. Anybody not in the Clann would be able to just relax and enjoy the game.

Unfortunately, my parents had other plans for me that had nothing to do with football at all. They expected me to follow in my dad's footsteps and become the next Clann leader. Because of that, I'd had to practically beg just to be allowed to play. Any other parents in East Texas would have sacrificed an arm and a leg for their kid to play high-school football.

Not to mention, because of the Clann, I'd had to stop being friends with Savannah. I still had nightmares about the way Savannah had looked at me when I'd had to tell her we couldn't hang out together anymore. The raw hurt in her eyes that day, and every time she'd looked at me since, was all the Clann's fault.

Someday, somehow, I would find a way to get it through my dad's head that I would never follow in his footsteps. Then I'd be free. Free to be friends with anyone I wanted. Free to date anyone I wanted…

Clenching my jaw, I stared at Savannah's back. Obviously

she was sick. She should be seeing a doctor right now, not trying to tough it out in school. She would have passed clean out if I hadn't caught her.

A foot kicked the side of my leg. What the...? I turned to my left to find Anne Albright glaring at me.

"Quit staring," she hissed.

I scowled at her, hoping she'd back off and leave me alone. The last thing I needed was somebody else telling me what to do. Especially today.

I went back to staring at Savannah. Anne kicked me again, the little wench. The sting spread up the side of my calf. I bit back another curse. That better heal before practice.

"Anne, keep your feet to yourself please," Mr. Chandler warned from his desk. "Or do I need to put you in time-out?"

Nice. I grinned.

"No, sir," Anne muttered, sounding murderous. But at least she didn't kick me anymore.

When the final bell rang, I jerked in my desk, my nerves strung as tight as if I were on the field at game time. Finally, Savannah could go home. Or even better, to a doctor.

Anne got up, circled around to Savannah's desk and shook her awake. "Hey, Sav, time to go home."

"Ungh," Savannah groaned. She tried to stand, but her legs gave out.

I jumped to my feet without thinking it through. "Need some help?"

"Not from you, no." Anne slung one of Savannah's pale arms over her shoulders so she could pull her up.

"Stop, this looks ridiculous," Savannah croaked.

"Oh, who cares, pretty princess?" Anne snapped. "Let's go. Gotta get you to your grandma's car now, and it's a long walk."

Yeah, talk about ridiculous. They would take forever to get

to the parking lot, and I could carry Savannah there in about five seconds. She probably weighed all of fifty pounds. Only problem was all the witnesses we'd have. The Clann elders—especially my parents—would hear about it through the local grapevine before I could even get home from practice.

So I stood there and did nothing, grinding my teeth and feeling like a grade A jerk for letting Anne help Savannah out of the classroom all by herself. Then I saw Savannah's backpack and books still under her desk. At least I could do *this* without attracting Clann attention.

The girls had made faster progress than I'd figured. They were near the parking lot by the time I caught up with them. Knowing Anne would bite my head off again if I took Savannah's free arm to help, I stayed a few paces back.

Anne didn't say anything to me as she guided Savannah into the passenger seat of a car waiting at the curb. "Mrs. Evans, she's really sick," Anne told the driver through the open passenger door. "I'm pretty sure she's running a fever. She wasn't feeling good at lunchtime, either, said she was tired and didn't eat anything."

"Hmm. Okay, thank you, Anne. I'll get her home and fixed right up," Savannah's grandmother promised. I snuck a peek at her. She looked like a sweet, little old lady, her cheeks round and rosy as she smiled at Anne. Then her gaze darted over to lock onto me, and I jerked upright again. The woman had eyes like a hawk. I'd be willing to bet Savannah got away with nothing at home. That woman wouldn't miss a thing, old or not.

"Here's her stuff," I told Anne, holding out Savannah's backpack and books.

Anne's eyes narrowed as she snatched them from me then set them in Savannah's lap.

Savannah's head never lifted from the seat's headrest.

I waited until the car exited the parking lot. Then I turned and started for the field house.

"Hey!" Anne's voice stopped me, but I didn't face her as she caught up with me. "Why'd you do that?"

Unsure what to say, I settled for a shrug.

"You know, if you're trying to make people think you're nice, it usually works better to have an audience to see it."

"Whatever."

She muttered something that sounded like "egomaniac."

Man, Savannah had the worst taste in friends lately. I rolled my eyes and walked away.

CHAPTER 2

Tristan

I looked for Savannah at lunch the next day, even trading seats with Dylan so I could have a better view of her friends' table. But she never showed up. Wednesday, I traded seats with Dylan again, thinking she'd have to be back by then. But she was nowhere in sight, and her seat stayed empty. She didn't show up for algebra that afternoon, either.

Algebra had never been so boring or lasted so long.

By Friday's lunch period, Savannah was still missing. Which didn't exactly put me in the mood to deal with Dylan's latest show of attitude.

"Hey, man, trade seats with me again," I told him, keeping one eye on the cafeteria doors in case Savannah walked through.

Dylan didn't move, staying slouched in his seat. "Why should I?"

"Because your spot's got the better view, and I need to watch out for...something."

Dylan smirked. "Trying to check out the chicks, huh?"

It was as good an excuse as any, and basically true. "Yeah. Now are you gonna trade or what?" I tried not to show my impatience. Otherwise he'd take twice as long to move just to mess with me.

"And what if I don't? You gonna call Daddy and have him and the other elders spank me at the next Clann meeting?"

I glared at him. Man, he could be such a pain sometimes. It was just a chair!

He snickered. "Okay, okay, don't get your panties in a wad. I'm moving." Slower than a resident at the local elderly home, he peeled himself out of the chair, then made a big show of bowing over it. "Your throne, Prince Tristan."

Letting out a long, slow breath, I sat down.

He took his time making the four short steps around the table to my old seat. Once in it, he proceeded to sit and stare at me for the rest of the lunch break, sorely tempting me to punch him.

What was with him lately? We'd been best friends growing up. But something about starting high school this year seemed to have set him off. All year long, I'd been getting more and more attitude from him. Like he resented me because my father led the Clann or something. Or maybe it was because my family wanted me to be the next Clann leader? Except that didn't make sense, either. Dylan knew better than anyone how much I just wanted to be normal and live my own life, not the one my parents wanted for me.

So why the sudden attitude from him all the time?

Whatever. Dylan's issues with the Clann and its leadership weren't my problem. Right now, my problem was figuring out what was wrong with Savannah.

No way was it normal for her to miss a whole week of school. I couldn't remember a single day when I hadn't been able to catch at least one glimpse of her in the halls between classes. She'd always been around somewhere, just waiting to suck the air out of my lungs and hit me with that ache in my chest and gut every time I saw her.

I needed information. Fast.

I waited till algebra ended, then followed Anne to the outer walkway. "Hey, Anne. Wait a minute."

She looked over her shoulder at me, huffed, then walked away faster.

Fighting back a snarl, I jogged to close the distance. She never stopped walking even after I caught up with her. Not that it was hard to keep up with her short legs.

"Listen, I...." Okay, how should I ask for updates about someone without giving the wrong impression?

With a sigh, Anne jerked to a halt. "You know, your sense of self-entitlement really knows no end, does it?"

Huh?

She glared at me. "Right. Too many big words. Moving on. I suppose you're trying to be nosy and ask about a certain sick person?"

Surprised she'd already guessed what I wanted, I nodded in silence.

She hesitated, as if thinking about what to say. "I'll tell you, but you've gotta tell me something first."

"Okay?"

"Why do *you* care?"

"Uh…" Now how was I supposed to answer *that* one?

"Let's get something straight, Coleman. Savannah is really nice."

"I know." *She'd have to be to pick you for a friend,* I added silently.

"So she deserves someone nice. Not a player who just sees her as some sort of challenge."

Was that how Savannah thought of me, too…as a player? I

shrugged off the question for now. "Aren't you kind of laying it on thick here? All I'm asking is if she's okay. Nothing more. No big deal." I tried my smoothest smile on her, the one that even won over the dragon ladies in the front office.

"Fine. In that case…"

My heart missed a beat.

"She's not dead." She turned and walked away.

Something hot and furious that had been building in my chest all week exploded. I yelled to her, "That's all you're going to tell me?"

"Yep. That's all you get, Coleman," she yelled back without stopping or turning her head. "You want more information, go buy it from somebody else."

Unbelievable.

It took a few seconds for me to calm down enough to see straight. When I could, I stomped off toward the main hallway and my locker. Too bad it was the off-season and we were mostly focusing on weight and cardio training. Otherwise I could have at least hit something during football practice.

In the main hall, I spotted one of Savannah's other friends. Michelle something. She was an office aide during first period every day and was a whole lot nicer than Evil Anne.

I took a chance, leaning against the locker beside Michelle's. I gave her a smile and hoped it worked better this time around. "Hey, Michelle, how's it going?"

She turned pink, always a good sign, and giggled. "Fine, and you?"

"Good." Switching strategies, I tried not to show any personal interest this time. "Listen, some of the girls at lunch were talking about your friend Savannah Colbert. They said she's missed a lot of school this week, and they're pretty worried about her. Sounded like they were thinking about sending her a get-well card or something. I told them I knew you and would ask how she was doing. You wouldn't happen to have any updates I could pass along, would you?"

"Oh! That's nice of them. I heard she's doing okay. I'm not sure when she's supposed to be back at school, though."

That wasn't the kind of news I wanted to hear. "Huh. Sounds like she caught something pretty serious, then. Did you get to talk to her?"

"No, just her grandma. You know, Mrs. Evans didn't actually say what was wrong with Savannah, now that I think about it." Her smile turned hesitant. "If you want, I could call them again tonight and find out more details."

Her head tilted to the side like a bird's as she inspected my expression. She was getting too curious. Not good. "Aw, it's no big deal. I'm sure the girls were just a little worried about her. I'll tell them she's okay." I straightened away from the lockers. "But hey, let me know if you hear any updates?"

I gave her another smile, waited till she nodded in agreement, then I walked off with what I hoped was a casual wave.

Why did I feel even more worried now?

Savannah

Fire and ice. They were my entire world for days. That and weird conversations I overheard between Mom and Nanna. Or maybe they were dreams.

"Sav's never been sick like this. Never," Mom whispered sometime during the first night. "Should we take her—"

"Take her where, Joan? If they do blood tests…" Nanna murmured.

"Oh, Lord, you're right. No telling what they might find. And we can't call the Clann's doctor, either. He'd tell the Clann, and that's the last kind of trouble we need. So…what do we do?"

"I don't know. Everything I try makes her fever shoot up

higher. It shouldn't do that. I've gone through all the books, read everything twice. But she's too special. There just isn't anything about her. There never has been. We've always been so lucky with her. She's never been sick in a way I couldn't fix."

"Are you giving *up?*" Mom's voice rose to a near shriek on the last word.

"Shh, no, of course not! But maybe you should call her father. Maybe his kind would know what to do."

His *kind?* Nanna must really hate Dad.

A long silence made me wonder if I'd fallen asleep. Then Mom finally replied in an odd tone that made her sound even more worried than before. "Are you sure we should involve them? If we ask for their advice, they may think things are out of control. They might want to get really involved from now on."

"We'll have to take that risk, Joan. It's ask for their help or nothing else."

Nothing else? What did that mean? Why did Nanna make those two simple words sound so scary?

I thought I heard Mom murmuring to someone, but Nanna didn't reply. Maybe Mom was talking with Dad on the phone?

"Okay, we'll try it." Mom paused, and the cordless phone beeped as she ended the call. "Mom, he says we should try removing all our influence from her."

"All of it? Even the protective…"

"Yes. He says it sounds like a conflict between the two sides within her."

"But—"

"We have to try it. It was the only solution he could think of. And…he's coming to have the talk with her."

"No. No, you said she never needed to know. He said she could have a normal life!"

"She's changing, Mom. And we can't stop it anymore. She needs to know. But that's only if...if this works."

"You mean...there won't be any need if..."

Silence.

If what?

And then my body answered me, the pain sharpening until there was nothing but the pain. Death. It felt like I was dying the worst possible death imaginable, like being burned alive then drowned in arctic water seconds later.

Hands of fire touched my throat, a horrible contrast to the block of ice my body had become. Something slipped from my neck, and the heated fingers went away. Then I threw up, my stomach emptying itself over and over into a metal bowl Mom held for me, until nothing was left, and still the heaving didn't end.

And then I slept. Hours, days, I had no idea how long. While I slept, I dreamed of Tristan.

When I woke up, three faces peered down at me. Mom, Nanna...and Dad.

Please don't let me have talked in my sleep. If I'd said Tristan's name out loud...

But then I relaxed. Crazy, to feel guilty over a dream I couldn't control. Even if I had said his name aloud in my sleep, just because I'd promised to stay away from Tristan and the other Clann kids ever since the fourth grade didn't mean I would get into trouble for dreaming about him now.

Still, I must have messed up somehow to have earned a visit from Dad. The only times he ever came to see me were for my birthday in October and once during the summer. And even then we only met for dinner at our favorite local restaurant, where we both pretended to eat in spite of the awkwardness between us, and he pretended to care about my life. He hadn't come to Nanna's house since the Christmas when I was seven, and he and Mom got into an argument that ended with her throwing plates and ice-cube trays at him.

Nanna leaned forward to touch my forehead and cheeks for signs of a lingering fever. "Hey, hon, how are you feeling?"

I tried to swallow. My throat was raw, as if someone had rubbed sandpaper down it. "Thirsty," I managed to whisper.

Mom handed me a glass of water. I moved to sit up, but my aching lower abdomen made me freeze and moan. It felt like someone had taken a baseball bat to my stomach. "Did someone beat me up?"

Mom laughed, but it sounded weak. "Not quite."

I settled for lifting only my head so I could sip some water to ease my throat. When I had finished, I said, "What happened to me?"

All three of them shared glances with one another. Talk about übercreepy. I couldn't remember the last time I'd even seen them all in the same room together, much less doing that annoying wordless-communication thing with their eyes that all adults seemed to love to do.

"Michael, you should tell her now," Mom said, moving to sit at the end of the bed by my feet.

With a curt nod, Dad clasped his hands in front of him as if he were a preacher about to speak at a funeral. He couldn't have been here long. Dressed in his usual dark blue suit, he looked like he always did…immaculate, not a wrinkle in sight, not a single strand of wavy black hair out of place. He stared down at me with the same eyes as mine. Unfortunately, his had always been better at hiding his emotions, staying an icy gray no matter what. Mine had an annoying habit of turning colors depending on my mood, making it impossible for me to hide anything.

"Savannah, there are certain things you need to know about yourself," he began.

"Because I was sick for a day or two?"

"Try five," Nanna said.

I was sick for *five days?* "That was some flu."

"You did not have the flu," he said. "You are changing."

"Changing. Meaning…?"

"I am a vampire. And your mother is a witch, along with your grandmother. This makes you a rarity in both our worlds, because my species of vampires are not supposed to be able to procreate—"

"Whoa, whoa, whoa. Did you just say you're a…a vampire? Do you mean like the role-playing kind, where you get dressed up with plastic fangs and go to weird parties?" Was this some kind of twisted, late April Fools' joke?

Nanna moved to sit on the bed at my hip. She wrapped her warm, papery hands around mine. "Savannah, honey, I know it's hard to believe, but it's true. Your father is a vampire. A special kind, called an incubus."

"A *demon?*" I gasped, finding I could still breathe, after all. I'd heard about the incubi, read something about them on the internet or in church. But my mind was way too foggy to remember the details. All my thoughts kept circling around the same thing…Dad was claiming that he was a demon vampire. A *real* demon vampire. Which didn't even exist. And my mother and grandmother were supposed to be witches. But that was impossible. They both went to church. Nanna even played the church piano every Sunday morning. Shouldn't they burst into flames as soon as they set foot on holy ground or something?

"Not quite a demon," Mom said. "At least not full-blooded. He's from a line of vampires that mixed with demons a long time ago."

Oh, *that* made it all better.

Nanna added, "This gives them the ability to get energy two ways…through the traditional methods—"

"Blood. You're saying you…you drink blood?" I gulped, looking at Dad.

He nodded. "We can also take energy through a kiss."

"Energy from a kiss." My voice came out flat.

They were all nuts.

I slid my hand free of Nanna's and flipped the comforter off my legs. "Okay. Um, I…I would really like a shower now."

Mom frowned. "Sweetie, don't you have any questions?"

"What's to ask? Dad's some funky kind of vampire that's part demon and drinks blood, and you two do magic. And now you think I will, too, right? Because I'm…what did you say? Changing?"

The carpet was cold beneath my feet as I stood up on wobbly legs. My weak body demanded I get back in bed. But no way was I staying here in the loony room. I had no idea what kind of joke they were trying to play, or if I was just hallucinating from lack of food. If this was a dream, the shower ought to wake me up pretty quick. On a whim, I pinched my forearm. "Ow!" Huh. That really hurt.

Dad grabbed my shoulders, his hands ice cold as usual.

Distracted, I frowned down at his hands. Ice-cold hands…

"Savannah, stop this right now," he said. "We are trying to have a serious conversation with you. You are not asleep. You are perfectly awake and lucid. And you need to learn what you are, and what you may become, before anyone gets hurt. There are certain…symptoms you will need to watch out for now."

The first glimmer of anger flared up in my stomach. Ordinarily I was careful about what I said to him, always trying so hard to be what he wanted, to say the right thing so he would be proud of me, love me. But I was too tired and freaked out right now to try and be perfect. And I'd had more than enough of this family prank.

"Dad, you can stop worrying. There's no way I'm gonna be jumping on anyone or sending things flying Carrie-style at school…." A sudden memory flashed through my mind of that Christmas when Mom sent plates and other objects flying at him. Weird. I couldn't remember the plates actually leaving her hands now. Goose bumps raced over my skin.

"Well, of course you won't turn into Carrie." Mom laughed. "Because we won't be teaching you magic."

"It is the bloodlust we are more concerned about," Dad said. "And if you do not learn to control it, you very well might end up jumping on people at school."

Giving in to the insanity for a second, I huffed out a short sigh. "Okay, fine. I've got a question for you. Why now? I mean, let's pretend y'all are serious, you're not messing with me here, and I'm not hallucinating. If you're truly vamps and witches, then why tell me now and not before?"

"Because we couldn't wait any longer," Mom said, rising to her feet and taking my hand. "We wanted you to have a normal life for as long as possible. But when the teas stopped working and we couldn't prevent your first monthly cycle any longer—"

"Oh, ew!" Dad was right there! Then I realized what she'd said and frowned. "Wait. Did you just say you gave me tea to…prevent…that?"

Nanna nodded. "We gave you a special tea every day that delayed your puberty."

"Until I was *fifteen?*" Horror made me shriek. All my friends had had their periods since they were twelve and thirteen. All this time I'd been feeling like a freak of nature because I was such a late bloomer. "Why would you *do* that to me?"

"Because puberty's done exactly what we feared," Nanna snapped. "It's triggered your dormant genes. Now they're all waking up, and heaven only knows what's going to happen next. And watch your tone, missy—we're still your parents."

Reaching behind me, I felt for the bed then sank onto the edge of it before my knees could give out.

"Hon, I know it's a lot to absorb all at once," Mom said. "I swear, if we could have avoided telling you, we would have. We were so hoping you wouldn't take after either side and would be...well, normal. But it's just too dangerous now for you not to know. Your being sick for a whole week is a strong sign that one or both sides might begin to kick in. Which means you could start developing any number of abilities or impulses. If and when you do, we all need to be ready so we can help you learn to control them."

Impulses. Abilities. What was I, some sort of wild animal about to go out of control?

Mom sat down beside me and wrapped an arm around my shoulders. "You could try to think of it as if you were learning you have just an ordinary hereditary illness. Your parents' genes have predisposed you toward developing certain...issues in life. But they might or might not affect your daily life. We just have to all be prepared in case they do."

"You mean, in case I start to develop a taste for blood?" I couldn't believe I was even saying this.

Dad's nod made it even more surreal. "You could begin to crave human blood. Your gaze might begin to have adverse effects on others when you look at them. Heightened reflexes, physical speed and mental processes are all possible. And then, of course, there is the possibility of fangs."

Fangs. O. M. Freakin' G. He sounded like one of those drug-commercial announcers rattling off possible side effects.

"Or strange things may start to happen when you get upset," Mom added. "Like…"

"Like flying plates," Nanna said, a hint of a snicker in her voice. As if any of this were funny.

Mom glared at her. "That wasn't an accident. Now if I'd set the kitchen on fire…"

And that's when I realized they were serious about this. This wasn't a prank, and unless I woke up soon, I wasn't dreaming, either.

Which meant…I was half vampire, half witch. And all freak. Just like the Brat Twins had been saying for years. Oh, crap. "The Clann. Do they all know…?" I remembered the way the Brat Twins called me "freak" all the time and seemed scared of me sometimes…. They definitely knew. Did Tristan know, too?

"The adults know. The kids don't," Mom said. "At least, the elders swore they wouldn't tell the younger descendants after they cast us out. Only the adult descendants were supposed to be warned."

Nanna grunted. "Now, whether the elders actually *kept* that promise…"

"Why do the adults know about me? And what do you mean, *cast out?*"

It was Nanna and Mom's turn to look confused. Mom was the one to answer. "We thought you'd figured that part out already. Our family used to be in the Clann, too. Magic is what ties all of Jacksonville's founding families together in the first place. I'm sure you must have heard at least a rumor or two about it."

Jacksonville's gossip grapevine had it right, then. "So the Clann are all witches. Like a coven."

Mom and Nanna both nodded.

"But…we go to church," I argued, trying to wrap my mind around the idea that the Brat Twins were witches in more than just a figurative way. Not to mention Tristan.

Holy heck. Tristan was a witch.

"Magic isn't a religion for us like it is for Wiccans," Nanna said. "Most of the Clann's descendants are Christians who just happen to be gifted with the ability to do magic. It's genetics, not a lifestyle choice."

Yeah, and I was sure everyone here in the Bible Belt of East Texas would really understand *that* distinction.

When I could make my brain work again, another thought hit me. "Wait. Dad, if you're a vampire, how can you go out in the daylight? And what about garlic, and holy water, and—"

"Vampires are like any other species, Savannah. We have evolved over the years. Sunlight no longer hurts us. Garlic and holy items never did—that was just religious propaganda. We all started out as humans with souls. Only our bodies have been changed by the hybrid vampire blood."

I pressed a shaking hand to my forehead, which was pounding out a rhythm I couldn't keep up with. "Okay. So you're saying I might, or might not, start turning into an even bigger freak."

"Stop saying that word," Mom grumbled. "The proper term is *dhampir.*"

"So there are others like me?"

"No," Dad answered. "Until your birth, dhampirs were a myth among our kind. We did not believe our race of vampires could procreate because of the demon mix in our origin's lineage. And no vampire in our society has ever consorted with a human long enough for a baby to be created."

"Because…?"

Mom cleared her throat. "Well, hon, because vampires don't usually have that kind of self-control. They tend to either turn their human lovers or..." The look on her face finished her sentence.

Or kill them. I snuck a peek at Dad. He appeared as emotionless as ever.

"But you didn't," I said to him. "Why?"

Nanna smiled. "Because I made a charm for your mother that dampened his bloodlust when he was around her."

"So you were actually okay with their being together?" I realized after the words were out how rude they sounded. Too late to take it back now.

Nanna shrugged. "Your mother's always been hardheaded. It was either make a charm to ensure he didn't kill her, or lock her up in a vault somewhere."

"Okay. So then you can make a charm for me, too, right? Something that'll prevent all those...those symptoms Dad listed?" Something that would keep me nice and normal and human. No blood drinking, no flying plates.

"Well, I could, but—"

"But that would be unwise," Dad cut in. "It would be similar to giving morphine to a patient who has yet to be diagnosed. Charms would mask the appearance of any symptoms. We need to see what abilities develop within you. Then we will teach you how to control them yourself. Without magic."

"So I'm supposed to...to just *deal* with it?"

"I know this is very difficult for you," Mom said. "But I promise we're all here for you, and we're going to help you through this. And hey, it might not be a big deal, after all. You could just as easily not develop any abilities at all, or take after the Evans side and have only the magical blood within you. We're going to take it one day at a time, and we'll work through it as a team."

A team. As if there was any "we" in this. There wasn't. This was me we were talking about, not them; my life, not theirs, that might go insane at any moment. My life that had been one long series of lies and crazy family secrets.

"The important thing is for you to communicate openly with us," Dad said. "If you begin to experience strange urges or abilities, you must let us know at once. I will also be calling you once a week to check in with you."

Huh, right. I should just tell them every detail about my life. Like they did for me, keeping so many secrets from me for fifteen years.

"You must also stay away from all members of the Clann," Dad warned. "Especially their leading family, the Colemans."

"Uh, not that I'm exactly friends with any of them anyways, but...why?"

"The Clann's powerful blood calls to vampires stronger than any other humans'," he said. "The more powerful they are, the more attractive they appear to a vampire. Since the Colemans have been their most powerful family for the last four generations, it is reasonable to assume that they will tempt your vampire side first and more than any others in their circle. Also, there is no way of knowing if all of the Clann parents are aware of your...situation and adequately protecting their children with charms. They have assured us that they have many of their descendants watching you on campus at all times—I believe several of them are teachers. But even still, if your vampire side does develop and one of them is not protected, you could begin to experience the bloodlust around them. Especially if one of them is injured around you. Then even a charm might not help."

Oh. Of course. So that was why I always felt so weird around Tristan. Because he was a Coleman, and I was a...

No. I refused to even *think* of myself as that word. Not yet. Not until I had to.

And then another thought hit me. Sweet Lord. No wonder the Clann kids all deserted me in the fourth grade. Their parents had probably warned them to avoid me like the plague. Because they were afraid I might try to kill their kids. Which meant Tristan must at least know I wasn't normal. But how much did he know?

I clamped my lips shut so I wouldn't say something that would give away my thoughts and get me into trouble. But inside, my stomach burned and rolled.

Mom patted my shoulder. "All right, hon, why don't you go take that shower you wanted, while your Nanna and I make you something to eat? And later when you have questions, we'll be happy to answer them."

"Joan, I must go." Something dark edged at Dad's tone.

Mom must have noticed it, too; she jumped to her feet. "I'll walk you to your car."

"What now?" I demanded, more than fed up with the secrecy. "Whatever it is, don't hide it."

"I must report to the vampire council, and your mother is probably wondering if they will send watchers to Jacksonville to mark your changes," Dad said.

Mom nodded, her hand tightening on my shoulder, though I didn't think she realized it.

"Watchers?" Council? Good Lord, it was never ending. What else didn't I know about my family, about myself, about the world I lived in?

"I do not think it is anything to worry about just yet," Dad reassured us both. "Especially if you follow the rules and stay away from the Clann's descendants."

As long as I stayed away from Tristan. Who wouldn't speak to me anyway.

Dad leaned down to kiss my forehead with icy lips I'd never thought to question before and a whisper of cold breath. Vampire lips. Breath as cold as death. And I might end up just like him. I suppressed a shudder. Then Mom walked with him out of the room while Nanna headed for the kitchen. A few seconds later, I heard the front door open and shut, followed by the revving of an engine in the front yard as my father left.

My *vampire* father.

Holy crap.

CHAPTER 3

Savannah

I took the longest shower our hot-water heater would allow, spending more time trying to wrap my mind around this strange new reality than I spent washing myself. Part of me still clung to the hope that it was all just a case of my imagination going berserk. But everything was too real…the slippery porcelain beneath my feet, the cold, wet tile wall holding me up, the hot water burning its way over my skin. And it wasn't just anyone telling wild stories here. All this stuff about demons and vampires and witches was coming from my entire family, the three people I loved and trusted more than anyone else in the world.

When the water ran cold, I got out, dried off, then studied my reflection in the mirror. Was it because I was freaked out, or did I really look…different? My eyes seemed bigger, my cheekbones more pronounced. My upper incisors might've become a little pointier than they'd already been. I was definitely paler, but who wouldn't be after being sick? And my hair seemed thicker and darker, less orange, more auburn. My imagination, too? Maybe.

I wondered if Tristan would notice, then banished that thought. He was in the Clann. Worse, he was the son of the Clann's leading family.

And I had to avoid him at all cost.

"Mom?"

A few seconds later, as if she'd been nearby listening for me, she opened the door a few inches and poked her head in. "Yes?"

"Why aren't we in the Clann anymore?"

"Well, they weren't too thrilled when I broke the rules and married your father. And when your Nanna didn't try to stop us, they kicked her out, too. It's a real no-no for vampires and witches to get involved with each other."

"Because vampires tend to kill witches." I sighed.

"They did before the truce. At one point, before even your grandmother's time, it was an all-out war between them. But now they've agreed to avoid each other as much as possible. Which is why no vampires live around here, including your father. This is Clann territory. And vampires have reason to fear descendants, too, since they can of course kill vampires much easier than normal humans can."

At my confused look, she explained, "Fire. Vampires can be killed by fire. Or decapitation or a stake through the heart, but those methods require a weapon. Witches, real ones, can produce fire in the palm of their hand." She held out her hand palm up, concentrated...and a tiny ball of orange flame burst to life in her hand. At the same time, faint prickles raced over the back of my neck and down my arms.

My brain blanked out for several seconds. Then my heart lurched back into gear. Hoooly crap, she wasn't kidding. She really could do magic! Reaching toward the flame, I opened my mouth to ask when I would get to learn *that*.

"Oh, no." She snapped her hand closed, extinguishing the fire with a sizzle. "Don't even ask, because the answer is no. Creating fire is too dangerous for you, in case your vampire genes make it hard for you to control the flame. And you're not learning any other magic, either."

"Why not?" I tried hard not to whine. But honestly, what was the point of learning all of this stuff if I couldn't even do real magic someday?

"Because both the Clann and the vampire council made your Nanna and I swear that we would never teach you how to do magic. It was the only way I could get to raise you and we could stay in Jacksonville."

"I can't *ever* learn to do magic?"

She shook her head. "Sorry, hon, not unless the Clann and the vampire council both change their minds."

"What if my magical side starts developing, like you said? Will I just start shooting out magic spells or something?"

She laughed. "Not likely, since it takes both your willpower and certain spell words for beginner witches to cast a spell. Magic is like a muscle for most descendants. If you never use it, like I haven't for a while, it atrophies and is harder to use. If you practice, you get stronger and it's easier to do. We're hoping if you never do magic, the ability will simply go away for you. Or at least be very hard to do accidentally."

Disappointed, I frowned down at the sink. This really sucked. Nanna was always telling me to focus on the good in every situation. But there seemed to be absolutely nothing positive about my life right now.

After a slight hesitation, Mom came the rest of the way into the bathroom and leaned against the edge of the sink's counter. "Look, Savannah, I know it's hard, but try to see things from everyone else's point of view, too. You are special, incredibly so. Other than in myths, you're the first dhampir in proven existence from your father's line, the first real live half vampire, half human."

"You mean half witch," I muttered, aiming for sarcasm. Which she ignored.

"Right. Until you, no one thought vampires from your father's line could even get a human pregnant. Then your father and I broke the rules, I got pregnant, and we got married."

"Wait. You got pregnant *then* got married?"

She gave a sheepish grin. "Yeah, you know, sometimes it works that way. But it was worth it. Even when our marriage meant your father lost his seat on the council—"

"Because of me?"

She winced. "Not quite. More a combination of factors... like drinking Clann blood to block his thoughts from the council so he could break their rules, marry a human and have a baby."

But they only got married *after* they found out they were going to have me. So didn't that still make it my fault that Dad was kicked off the council?

"Anyways," she continued, "when you actually made it to full term then survived the first year of life, everyone on both sides of the equation went nuts. The vampire council thinks you're going to be some sort of secret weapon for the Clann if you develop magical skills. And the Clann is afraid you'll either go fully vampire and try to eat them all or use magic against them." She laughed.

I couldn't breathe.

Her smile faded. "Oh, sorry, baby. Your father and I spent years joking about everyone's crazy fears. They're all ridiculously paranoid, on both sides of the line. Before your birth, they actually thought he and I had teamed up to rid the world of both the Clann and all the vampires! Bunch of fruitcakes. But I guess it's not that funny to you at first."

I let a glare be my answer. Inside, I was shaking again. Just when I thought I was starting to get a grip on all of this...now I was both a career ender for Dad *and* some sort of a ticking time bomb? No wonder I was such a disappointment to him.

"That's why the Brat Twins call me a freak. Why did you even keep me?" I muttered then clamped my lips shut. I so had not meant to say that out loud.

She gripped my shoulders, forcing me to meet her gaze. "Savannah, from the moment I found out I was pregnant with you, you have been nothing short of a miracle. Do you understand? *A miracle.* Not strange, not scary, not a freak and certainly not a threat to anyone. You've always been a sweet, precious miracle born out of love."

A love that had lasted all of three years. "So if I was such a miracle, and you two were so in love you just had to break all the rules to be together...why'd you get divorced?"

She bit her lower lip, hesitating for a long time before sighing. "A lot of factors, I guess. Mostly, it was my fault. I was young, far too young to handle it all. And too young to really know what love was. I thought I was in love with your father. But now I know I was more in love with the idea of being with a vampire and breaking the rules. We were like Bonnie and Clyde, modern-day rebels running from our worlds' laws, hiding out on the lam." She grinned. "It was a lot of fun. Until we had a baby who needed safety and security. Then suddenly being on the run wasn't so much fun anymore. When I realized I was responsible for your life and protecting you, it just didn't make sense anymore to be with your father. The council and the Clann both agreed you and I could live with your grandmother as long as I ended my marriage. And while I still loved your father, I wasn't in love with him anymore.

Loving your father was an adventure and a selfish fantasy, and it was great while it lasted. But having you made me realize I needed to wake up, grow up and think about others for a change."

"Let me get this straight. You broke up with Dad for me?"

"Not just for you. For peace between the Clann and the vampires, too. Both groups have members all over the world. If your father and I had stayed together, worldwide war could have broken out again between them. A lot of people would have died, and that would have been my fault. And I didn't love your father enough anymore for it to be worth that."

"But why come back to Jacksonville? Why not raise me somewhere else? Someplace where there weren't as many Clann around?"

She smiled and shrugged. "Because Jacksonville has always been my home. And besides, I needed your grandma's help to raise you. Dhampir babies don't exactly come with a handbook, you know."

I managed a smile for her, but it faded fast. "Except, now I have to go to school with kids who seem to know what I am. And call me *freak* every day."

Mom hugged me. "I know it's hard, hon. But you've got to learn how to live your own life and don't worry about what the Clann thinks, or what the vampire council thinks, or what anybody says about you. None of this changes who you are inside. That's only up to you and what you choose. And even though this is all a shock, and maybe things in your life might start to change a little here and there, I promise you're going to be okay. As long as you follow the rules, that is."

Which was to stay away from the Clann. Yeah, I got it already. Except... "Mom, you and Nanna used to be in the Clann, too. What if I—"

"Don't worry. Like you teens love to say...we've got skills."

She gave a lopsided grin. "Or at least your Nanna does. All I ever learned how to do was throw stuff and make fire. And even that was only because your Nanna absolutely insisted on it for minimal protection."

"Why didn't you want to learn how to do magic?"

"Hon, you live in the post–Harry Potter world, where you teens think magic is awesome. I lived in the pre–Harry Potter times. I was witchy when witchy wasn't cool."

Huh. "What about the Clann kids at school? Dad said to avoid them, but how can I when I've got classes with them, have to pass them in the halls, eat with them in the cafeteria?"

"You should be okay at a distance. Like your father said, they've probably got charms on them to dull their attraction to any vampire. And even if you do start to feel the bloodlust at some point, if you keep your distance and pay attention to your body, you'll know if it becomes a problem. If it does, you call me or Nanna or your father immediately and go to the nurse's station till one of us gets there. Okay?"

I thought of how close Tristan sat behind me in algebra, and the pain in my chest and stomach that hit me every time he was near. Keeping my distance might be a problem. I'd just have to try to sort out my usual confused feelings around him from anything new that might come up. Like a sudden attraction to his neck.

"Why is the Clann even letting us stay here? Wouldn't they want me as far away from them and their kids as possible?"

Her smile turned sad. "You know that saying 'keep your friends close and your enemies closer'? I think it's like that. They don't want you to get too close or spend time alone with any of their descendants. But they also want to be able to keep an eye on you. Plus there's the chance that one day you might decide to…help them out."

"Help them out?"

"You know. Be on their side if there's ever another war with the vampires."

The Clann thought I would side with them against my own father? I snorted. They must be insane. After the way the Clann kids had treated me and my family for the past five years...

Well, not all of them had bullied me *all* the time. A memory flashed through my mind of emerald eyes staring back at me. Of strong, warm hands on my shoulders, stopping me from falling in algebra class, when he could have just let me do a face-plant onto my desk.

"I guess it's a good thing I don't want to date anyone in the Clann anyways, huh?"

Laughing, Mom picked up a hairbrush and began to tug it through my tangled hair, ignoring my facial expression each time she found a new snag. "Uh, yeah. Dating someone from the Clann could start another war. Lordy, I can see it now. The Clann would think you were stalking one of their own to drain them. The vamps would think you were siding with the Clann. It'd be mass chaos in no time." She shook her head and grinned. "But we don't have to worry about that, right? You've hated the Clann's kids for years now."

I forced a weak chuckle and took the brush away from her before she could accidentally brush me bald. "Yeah. Right. They're first-class jerks."

"Any other questions?" Her tone had turned bright and cheerful, like she had simply been helping me with my homework or something.

I shook my head and tried to remember how to breathe normally past the lump in my throat. Why couldn't I just go back to my life of a week ago, back when things weren't perfect, but at least they were normal?

"Aw, honey." She patted my shoulder. "Please stop worrying. You're going to be okay."

"How do you know I'll be okay? What if—"

"Because you come from my side of the family, too. And we Evans women are strong. With or without magic, we know how to kick butt in life."

"And throw a mean plate?" I managed to joke.

She laughed. "Exactly. And speaking of which, aren't you starving by now? Your Nanna made her special fried chicken and mashed potatoes with gravy just the way you like them."

I made my lips curve into a smile. "Sure, sounds great." Why wouldn't I be hungry? After all, just because normal life as I'd known it was over, that shouldn't affect my appetite, right?

I didn't want to talk to anyone for the rest of the weekend. But Nanna said that my friends had been calling for me all week. So I made myself call Anne later that evening.

After chatting for a few minutes, I thought I'd better warn her about the changes in my appearance. But when I tried to describe how different I looked, she just laughed.

"Don't worry about it, Sav. Every year I get the flu for a few days, and afterward I swear my head looks way too big for my body. Anyways, if you want to start coming early to school next week, I could help you get caught up on all the algebra homework you missed."

"Mmm, good idea." I hesitated, curious to know if anyone else had missed me while I was gone, one boy in particular. But I couldn't find a casual way to ask and not make a big deal out of it. And why would anyone other than my friends have missed me? So I gave up and said goodbye instead.

When I called Carrie and Michelle, I didn't mention the changes in my appearance. For all I knew, I was the only one who would notice them.

But when I returned to school Monday morning, too late to meet Anne at the picnic tables for tutoring, I felt more like a freak than ever. While some of the changes in my appearance might be my imagination, the bigger chest size definitely wasn't. I'd gone up a full cup and a half. Mom and I had been forced to do emergency shirt and bra shopping yesterday so I'd have something to wear to school that didn't scream *slut*.

Still, even with the bigger shirts, I felt conspicuous in the main hall before first period. So I made sure to carry my notebook against my chest. The freshmen boys weren't exactly kind in their comments toward the curvier girls in our grade, and I so didn't need more hall harassment in my life right now.

Unfortunately, even my notebook couldn't block what happened next.

"O. M. G. Worst boob job ever!" Vanessa called out to me, laughing as she and her sister passed by, their voices somehow loud enough to carry over the noise of the hall even though they didn't sound like they were actually yelling. Magically amplified? I wouldn't doubt it. They would want everyone to be sure to hear them torture me.

And then I felt it. It was like a poisonous gas spreading over my skin, seeping past my shirt to make my skin crawl. And alien…whatever it was, the sensation definitely wasn't coming from me.

What the heck *was* it? Nobody had warned me about this.

It had to be either magic- or vampire-based. Or had the Brat Twins hit me with a spell just now? I would have to call Mom as soon as I could find a restroom where I could talk in private.

I kept walking, forcing my hands to be still when all I wanted to do was scrub the vile sensation from my skin. I tried to think about something else, anything at all.

But then I had to refocus on the weird sensation, because it was changing now. In fact, the farther away I got from the Brat Twins, the more the sinister feeling of evil intentions faded away. Now it was more a mixture of stuff I couldn't sort out. Kind of like cobwebs made of worry, happiness, sadness and fear all twisted together. Maybe I was going insane from learning too much crazy crap about my family and myself this weekend.

Unless…somehow I could sense others' emotions now?

Oh, Lord. When I concentrated, it grew worse, until I could feel each person's mood as they passed me. Experimenting, I matched up what I felt with each person's facial expression and overheard bits of conversations, and was able to piece clues together. Happiness nearly made me laugh from its tickling sensation. Worry was heavy and cold, an ice chunk sliding down my skin. Love was warmth and softness, heated cotton balls. Anger, a knife that slashed and ripped across my skin.

I managed to make it the hundred yards to my locker, then closed my eyes and tried to think about something else. Anything else to make the overwhelming mix of emotions go away. Something soothing. Something…

Tristan's eyes staring down at me. The sound of his voice, low and husky, whispering my nickname, asking me if I was okay. His hands on my shoulders, warming me through my shirt in algebra class.

After a few minutes, the sensations of others' emotions faded away. My shoulders, which had scrunched up near my ears, eased back down, and I could breathe deeply again.

Okay. So now I could sense others' emotions. It wasn't an

ideal development, and I definitely could have used a little warning. But at least I could control it if I stayed calm.

Was it magic- or vampire-based?

It had to be magic-based, some sort of natural Clann ESP ability, right? Which meant no cause for alarm, no vampire abilities developing here. It wasn't exactly *normal*. But maybe all the descendants could do this and just didn't show it. Even Tristan.

Oh, crap. Could they read my emotions around him? Could he tell—?

Face burning, I cut off that thought and headed away from my locker, debating whether to call my parents or Nanna and let them know about this new development. Then again, why should I? They'd wanted me to tell them about new developments so they could help me deal with them. But I'd handled this one on my own. All I had to do to control it and block out everyone's emotions was to stay calm. There was no need for the rescue squad. Yet.

Okay, so no phone call to the family. But maybe I should go ahead and grab my entire day's collection of books so I wouldn't have to return to the main hall later. Just to be safe.

"Go, Savannah!" Captain Kristi, leader of the Charmers dance team and the assistant teacher for my pre-drill class, whooped as she ran over to give me a high five, hundreds of tiny black braids bouncing wildly around her head with her every step.

I couldn't even feel her palm slap mine. I was too much in shock. A triple pirouette. When I couldn't even do a proper single a week ago. It was an honest-to-goodness miracle.

At the end of pre-drill class, I floated downstairs, feeling like one of those Mylar balloons, all light and shiny, while I got dressed then walked over to the cafeteria for lunch. No

CRAVE   71

doubt my cheeks would hurt tomorrow from the force of my smile. But I couldn't stop myself. Today, for the first time ever, I had been every bit as good as the experienced dancers in my class. Not only had I succeeded in performing a triple pirouette, but I'd also finally gone all the way down to the floor in my splits, and my split leaps had all landed without a single thud or shake of the room. Still better, my wimpy high kicks, once only up to chest level, had nearly hit me in the face today. And hadn't hit anyone else for a change. Even the experienced dancers in the class had seemed impressed by my improvement. And now that I wasn't such a failure at it, dancing was *fun!*

This freak had finally learned some dance skills, maybe even good enough to make the Charmers dance team next month, if I was crazy enough to audition. Ha! Let the Clann sense *these* emotions!

"Hey, girls," I greeted my friends as I dropped my backpack at our table in the cafeteria. I glanced at them, my face stuck in a broad grin. "Let me grab some food and I'll be right back to hear what I missed last week."

No one replied, but I didn't give them much time to before I hurried to join the food line. The lunchroom was packed as usual, but apparently sensing others' emotions only happened when I was upset, because I felt nothing now except my own pure joy. Which only made me happier.

Finally, I'd managed not to be a total klutz at something! Maybe I *should* try out for the Charmers. Making the dance team was pretty much an instant passport to popularity in Jacksonville, or at least a huge social upgrade. And getting to dance all the time would be a total blast.

Lost in thought, I didn't realize at first that the boy directly ahead of me in the slow-moving line was smiling at me. Surprised, I smiled back, though I didn't recognize him, then blushed and looked down.

"Hi, I'm Greg Stanwick." He grabbed a mint-green tray from the stack then offered me one, as well.

"Oh, hey. I'm Savannah." I hadn't planned on getting the lunch of the day since I usually had pizza or chili cheese fries instead. Then again, maybe I should eat something healthy for a change and reward my body for all its amazing improvements in pre-drill. "Um, thanks."

Greg seemed to take that as encouragement. "So, what grade are you in?"

"Ninth."

"Eleventh for me. Hey, do you ever go to the soccer games?"

I shook my head.

"Well, you should really think about seeing some. We've got a killer team this year. Four-time champions. I should know, I'm on the varsity team." His smile was a few watts too bright, reminding me of a game-show host. And he was only a few inches taller than me, putting him somewhere around five-nine or -ten. But overall he was kind of hot, with short black hair and soft brown eyes that reflected warmth from his smile.

I realized Greg was still talking and tried to look interested as he chatted about his soccer team and all the ways they were training hard for another winning season.

"Maybe we'll run into each other again," he said as we paid for our food.

"Um, sure. Nice meeting you."

"Nice meeting you, too, Savannah." But he didn't turn away. Instead, he stood there watching me. I could feel his gaze on me as I returned to my table.

Okay, that was weird but sort of nice. Guys never paid any attention to me. Maybe it was the bigger boob size?

I set down my tray and sat.

Suddenly, I felt someone standing next to me.

I looked up and found Greg grinning down at me.

"Hey," he said. "I forgot to mention, we've got a home game this Friday, if you want to come watch. It'll start at six at the Tomato Bowl."

Total silence, not only at our table, but at all the surrounding tables, too, made my cheeks burn. The unwanted attention had to be because of Greg, because I wasn't exactly on anyone's social radar around here.

I blinked a few times and struggled to think of a reply. Then I remembered. "Um, that sounds like fun. But I have a dance recital that night. So…maybe next time?"

Greg looked away for a moment. At the same time, goose bumps and a prickling sensation raced up my arms and across the back of my neck. Someone must have cranked up the air-conditioning or something. Shivering, I rubbed my arms.

When Greg looked back down at me, his smile wasn't quite as blinding. "Yeah, sure. Next time." Then he walked away.

I cringed, hoping I hadn't hurt his feelings. Though why he'd care if *I* came to one of his games or not was beyond me.

I glanced at my friends and grinned. Their shocked expressions matched how I felt. "Did that just happen?" I asked, a short laugh slipping out.

Silence at our table, even as the other nearby tables recovered.

In the continuing silence from my friends, I leaned forward and looked more closely at them. "Um, hello? Anyone care to comment on that?"

Yeesh. Yes, it was true that boys never talked to me, and definitely none had ever made a point to come up to me during lunch. But my friends were acting like he'd also jumped up on the table and performed a song and dance for us or something. I'd never seen them all this speechless at the same time. I had the strong urge to snap my fingers under their noses just to bring them back to planet Earth.

I met Anne's stare first, then Carrie's, then Michelle's. Without fail, each girl's eyes widened as I met their gazes. Okay, this was getting weirder by the moment.

"Look at me." Anne's command, an echo of Dad's demanding tone on Saturday, reminded me of my changed appearance. And of the crazy family secrets I wanted to forget as quickly as possible.

"Oh, yeah." My good mood faded. "I forgot, you haven't seen how weird I look." Now Anne would tell me what an imaginative idiot I was and how I looked the same as I always did.

Her eyebrows drew together. "You don't look weird. But you do look different, that's for sure. What'd you do to your hair? It looks like a flippin' Garnier commercial. Did you get it colored? It's not so orange now. And it's…poufy."

Oh. So maybe I hadn't imagined the changes in my appearance.

Feeling like a circus sideshow, I blushed. "I know, it's kind of odd. But I swear I didn't do anything new to it."

"And your eyes," Michelle whispered.

I looked at Michelle, who reminded me of a nervous rabbit today for some reason. Her gaze darted away.

Oh, crap, that's right. Dad had mentioned that my gaze might have a strange effect on others. But he hadn't said what kind of effect. He should've warned me that my friends would treat me like an alien that had crash-landed at our table.

"What do you think, Carrie?" I met her stare head-on, my hands clenching into fists under the table as fear battled with a tiny bit of curiosity. Exactly what did they see when they looked into my eyes now?

Carrie was the calmest, coolest, most levelheaded member of our group. She had a mind like a scientist, or the doctor she claimed to want to become someday. She could offer some practical, objective feedback.

I held her gaze for several seconds as something like the weekend's panic threatened to overwhelm what little curiosity I'd had. Maybe I didn't want to know, after all.

Then I saw it...that same fearful widening of the eyes just before Carrie looked away.

Ohhh, crap. And according to Dad, that *was* a vampire thing.

I tried to remember how to breathe past the growing thickness in my throat. The noise of the cafeteria ramped up, roaring in my ears like an angry ocean during a storm, even as too many different emotions from others rushed in waves over my skin. I wrapped my arms around myself in a futile effort to block them out.

Did this mean I was turning into a vampire?

"Here, let me see again." This time, Anne's voice was far from its usual command.

And suddenly, I did *not* want to make eye contact with her. I didn't want to see my best friend look at me and become afraid. Then again, maybe it was all in *how* I was looking back at them, and I just needed to relax. Maybe then they would settle down and it would be no big deal.

I slid my gaze up and over, seeing Anne's chin first, then her mouth and nose. I hesitated, took a deep breath, focused on being calm and hopefully projecting soothing thoughts with my eyes, then made direct eye contact. And heard her gasp.

Well, crap. That didn't work, either. My gaze dropped to the tray of food I no longer wanted as my head began to swim.

After a minute, Anne took a deep breath before saying, "It's okay, Sav. Your eyes aren't that different, at least not in a way I can really describe. They just seem kind of...intense for some reason."

"Yeah, exactly," Michelle said. "Reminds me of how my mom looked at me when I accidentally broke the coffee table last month. Like she wanted to kill me."

"But I'm not mad!" I blurted out. "In fact, I was pretty dang happy a minute ago. That guy who just came over, Greg Stanwick, is a junior and a varsity soccer player. He just introduced himself out of the blue while we were in the food line. It was kind of weird actually...." Weird didn't even begin to cover all the recent things I'd been going through since last week. And couldn't talk about with them. How in the world could my friends believe me, much less understand? They hated the Clann. Michelle thought witches sacrificed small animals, Carrie was too practical to ever believe in vampires and Anne's Pentecostal family would *never* let her be friends with a half vampire/half witch. They barely liked her hanging out with a bunch of Methodists and Baptists. And I still hadn't figured out how she'd convinced them to let her wear jeans every day and cut her hair. The other Pentecostals on campus had to wear skirts and couldn't cut their hair, which they wore down to their knees.

"He's a junior?" Carrie said, her stiff posture melting around the edges a little.

"Ooh, and a varsity soccer player, too?" Nothing like a new piece of gossip to make Michelle sound like her old self again. She claimed she wanted to be a nurse and help Carrie in the operating room someday, but Anne and I had a private bet that she would end up working for a gossip magazine instead.

A little of the tightness in my chest eased as all three of my friends attacked the juicy news, and gradually the tidal wave of everyone else's emotions fell away. I forced a smile as I answered their questions about Greg and ended up giving a word-for-word playback of my earlier conversation with him. But I was careful never to look higher than their noses while I spoke. I didn't want to risk freaking them out again with my eyes.

My vampire eyes.

"Oh, speaking of boys acting weird," Michelle said. "Savannah, you seem to have another fan."

As soon as Michelle said the words, I could feel it. Tristan was staring at me from the Clann kids' table across the cafeteria. I didn't know how I knew it was him, but I would have bet a lot of money on it.

"And he's staring at you right now," Michelle added with a grin, completely unsubtle in trying to bait my curiosity.

"Tristan Coleman, right?" I tried to keep my voice calm, hopefully even bored-sounding.

"How'd you know?" she gasped.

Because I can feel his gaze boring into the back of my dang head, I wanted to growl. Instead I shrugged and tried to act like it didn't bug me.

"Well, I bet you didn't know that he was asking about you last week." Pride flooded her voice. "He said he and the Clann girls at his lunch table had heard you were sick and were worried about you."

Whoa. Tristan had noticed I was gone and asked about me? Out of personal interest, or for the Clann?

Anne snorted. "Oh, please. As if any of those spoiled brats care about anyone outside their elite little circle."

Unless their parents had told them all about me, and now they were worried I would attack them in the halls.

"Well, why would he lie about it to me?" Michelle said.

"Maybe because he'd already asked me and I told him to mind his own business," Anne said.

I stared at my best friend in surprised horror.

"Well, in so many words," she added in a mumble.

"Why didn't you just tell him how I was doing?" I said.

"Because I honestly didn't know, okay? All your grandma would say was that you were sick and they weren't sure when you'd be back at school, but you weren't in the hospital. Besides, he's a mega…mega…" Anne scowled, her nose scrunching as she searched for the word she wanted.

"Megalomaniac?" I offered.

"Yeah. That!"

I sighed. "I'm sorry if I worried you. I really was…sick. In fact, I don't remember most of last week beyond Monday afternoon. I think I scared Mom and Nanna, too." There, that was the truth. Mostly.

Three faces stared at me with open shock once again. I tried not to cringe in reaction. All this unexpected attention today made me want to find a hole to hide in.

"So what was wrong with you?" Anne said.

I shrugged and braced for the necessary lie. I would have to tell them it had been the flu. But the bell rang, cutting short the conversation. Thank goodness, too, because I really sucked at lying. And there was no way they would ever believe even half the stuff my family had told me this weekend. Hopefully they would just forget that I'd been out sick and had weird eyes now.

If I was lucky, maybe I could forget, too.

Tristan

My knees bounced beneath the descendants' table as I ate my lunch and watched the clock on the cafeteria wall. Two hours left until fourth-period algebra.

I'd made the lunch-chair trade with Dylan permanent, though he wasn't happy about it. But I'd had to pull rank on him; the view was better from his old seat. Or at least it had been, until the view showed a dark-haired boy, short and wiry, stopping at Savannah's table.

Probably one of her friends' boyfriends.

Except the guy was standing inches from Savannah and talking to her, not the others.

My knees stopped bouncing.

A classmate asking for help on an assignment? No, he looked too old to be a freshman like us.

I leaned sideways toward my sister. "Who's that guy?"

"Huh?" Emily looked around then smirked. "Oh, you mean the one talking to a certain—"

"Yeah."

She got the hint and whispered, "Tell you in a minute." Then she pretended to return to her lunch. But I noticed her casually scoping out the cafeteria every few seconds.

The guy braced one hand on Savannah's table, another hand on the back of her chair, and leaned down toward her.

I sat up, my hands clenching into fists on my thighs. *Back off. Now,* I thought to the would-be Romeo, adding a little magical push to the thought. Some humans were too thick-headed to pick up on Clann mental commands. This guy wasn't, thankfully. His head shot up and he looked toward me.

I knew I should be acting more casual in case the Clann noticed. But I'd lost control. I glared back at him, willing him to take a silent hint and get lost.

After a few seconds, he straightened up and walked away.

I eased down in my chair and crossed my arms over my chest. But I still wanted to hit something.

Once the guy was several yards away from Savannah, Emily

leaned over and threw an arm around my shoulders. "That was Greg Stanwick. He's a junior. Plays on the varsity soccer team, so apparently he's good. I've heard he's pretty charming and doesn't mind dating younger girls. Like freshmen."

A growl started in my chest. Not Savannah, he wouldn't. She needed someone...taller. Someone who didn't smile like a freaking game-show host.

"Youch. Want to ease up on the energy level there, little brother?" Emily peeled her arm from my shoulders and rubbed her skin through her shirtsleeve.

"Sorry," I muttered and glanced around our table. Everyone was staring at me. "Sorry," I called out to the entire group. Several of them rolled their eyes and rubbed their arms or the back of their necks, but everyone seemed to accept the apology and looked away again. Everyone except Dylan, who kept watching me with raised eyebrows. I shrugged in answer to his silent question. He could be nosier than a girl looking for gossip sometimes.

"You know that wouldn't happen if you would focus on your training," Emily said.

"And you know I don't care about all that crap."

"Too bad. The energy doesn't go away if you ignore it. It only gets worse."

I tried ignoring her.

"Tristan, don't be moronic. If you don't learn to ground better—"

She nagged worse than our mother. "I grounded all weekend."

"Are you sure you're doing it right?"

"Yes."

"Hmm. Then you might want to try grounding at school, too."

"And how do I do that without looking crazy?"

She surprised me with a laugh. "Find a tree."

"And then what, hit it?"

"No, make like a car and gas pump but in reverse. Siphon off some of your energy through the tree to the ground."

"Good idea, sis. I'll keep that in mind for next time." I faked a grin, hoping a little charm would convince her to drop the subject and get off my back.

She shook her head, seeing through me, but at least returned to her lunch.

Relaxing in my seat, I finished eating then headed for the trash cans. On my way back, I saw Stanwick at a table with two other guys. The soccer jerk was staring in Savannah's direction with a look on his face. The kind of look that said he was thinking about asking her out.

I should hit the guy now and save time. Except Jacksonville High had a zero-tolerance policy against fighting on campus. I would get suspended if I got caught. It would go on my permanent record, and colleges weren't thrilled about accepting students who went around beating up their classmates. And no college meant no chance of playing for the NFL.

Too bad Stanwick didn't play football instead....

Scowling, I returned to my table and grabbed my books. Our entire table froze, their heads turning to stare at me.

"Tristan Glenn Coleman," Emily hissed. "Outside. Tree. Now."

"I'm going, I'm going," I grumbled and headed out the door for the nearest tree.

I found one a few yards away between the cafeteria's rear exit and the math building. Perfect. Now how to ground without looking like an idiot? I couldn't exactly hug the thing, not with all those students at the outside picnic tables for an audience. But I had to touch the tree with my hands somehow for it to work.

And then I figured it out. Leaning back against the tree like I was waiting for someone, I held my books against my thigh with one hand and let my free hand hang at my side. A turn of the wrist and my empty palm touched the rough bark. Taking a deep breath, I mentally reached inside, found the boiling flow of energy and willed it out through my hand to the tree.

The bark heated up. Aw, hell, I was going to start a fire. I slowed down the energy flow until the bark cooled. Better. I felt the resulting calm as the excess energy left me, and grinned. Yeah, that was much better.

The cafeteria doors opened, and four girls exited, one of them with red hair that seemed to glow in the sunlight. Savannah. She was laughing about something when a nearby table full of boys yelled out a greeting to Anne. Anne yelled back, and the group of girls split up as Anne and Savannah walked over to the table.

I gripped my books tighter.

Anne did all of the talking, stopping at one point to lean over and point out something in an open math book. The boys nodded and looked up at her. I recognized them from our algebra class.

I could tell the exact second when the boys noticed Savannah. Almost in a wave, one by one they froze, their easy smiles melting into blank stares. If not for Savannah's reaction and the fact that she wasn't in the Clann, I almost would've guessed that she'd just put a spell on them. But her smile faded away, too, and her chin ducked down to her chest. She hugged her notebook against her stomach and tugged on Anne's wrist. Anne studied the boys and scowled. Then the girls beat a fast exit.

Savannah looked back, maybe because she felt the boys still staring at her, and walked away faster. As the pair drew even with me, Anne glanced my way then muttered something to Savannah. I was no expert at reading lips, especially from a distance, but it looked like she'd called me a stalker.

I almost laughed out loud. Me, a stalker? Please. But a glance back at the table of boys made me frown instead. *I* might not be a stalker, but...they were still staring at Savannah, their expressions zombielike. Savannah might be earning a stalker or three, after all.

Great. As if that Stanwick guy wasn't enough of a pain. If she kept this up, Savannah would have a line of dazed idiots trailing after her soon.

The tree bark started to burn again. I ripped my hand away and gave up on grounding for now. I'd have to be dead to get rid of all this extra energy. The descendants on campus would just have to get used to my power spikes for today.

CHAPTER 4

Tristan

When I strolled along the catwalk toward algebra class an hour and a half later, I knew the descendants would all be feeling the power spikes yet again.

The creeps from lunch had cornered Savannah outside the math building.

The closer I got to the building, the better I could see her face. Any other girl who had three guys flirting with her would probably have been thrilled. But she wasn't. She looked murderous.

Yards away now, I noticed that her face was even paler than usual. Her movements were jerky, her shoulders hunched, her hands fisted around her notebook and backpack straps. Her fans seemed too dazed to notice her emotions, though, their pathetic faces eager as they continued to compete for her attention.

She glanced past them to me for a second. For help? Her cheeks turned red just before she looked past me like I was invisible.

She took a step sideways toward the building door. The creep on that side leaned against the wall, blocking her escape. She said something to him in a voice too low for me to make out. He laughed but didn't move. She tried to take a step between him and the guy in the middle. But all three closed ranks, leaving her no room to get through.

What the…?

Her eyes widened, and I was close enough now to see them turn moss-green. She stomped on the foot of the guy standing between her and the building entrance. He acted as if he were wearing steel-toed boots and couldn't feel a thing.

Time to step in, whether she wanted my help or not.

"Hey, Sav. You got a problem here?" I stopped a few feet away.

Her mouth opened like she was going to answer. But then she shut it and shook her head. Her chin rose a notch, and she looked through me again. Stubborn girl.

"Hiya, Sav, sorry I'm late," Anne called out from behind me as she jogged up to us from the catwalk. Ah, so that's who Savannah had been looking at. "Excuse me, boys." She barreled right through the creeps, grabbed Savannah's arm and kept going toward the building entrance like a bulldozer without brakes. "I got held up in English. Thanks for waiting for me."

The girls made a quick escape into the building, Anne playing bodyguard at Savannah's board-stiff back. Huh. So it was okay for Anne to come to the rescue but not me. Not a surprise, but that actually kinda stung.

I stared at the three guys. They didn't notice me, their eyes blazing now as, like magnets, they shambled after the girls into the building. Whoa, now that was extra creepy. They looked like a bunch of possessed zombies.

What would these guys do if they caught Savannah

somewhere more private on campus, like in the girls' restrooms or a locker room or something?

I slammed the building door open, wincing as the metal handle hit the brick exterior. *Gotta get it under control, Coleman.*

I took a deep breath as I entered the classroom. Mr. Chandler had just started class. Great. I'd have some time to think up a solution and make sure those guys left Savannah alone for good. Or maybe my sister would have some ideas. She was excellent at getting rid of creeps without their ever knowing it. It was one of the first things our dad had taught her once she'd started magic training.

I spent the lecture staring at the shaking strands of Savannah's ponytail and thinking about how best to convince Emily to break the rules and teach me herself. I was so busy planning that it took twenty minutes to notice the difference.

Savannah had done something to her hair.

I'd thought it was just the lighting in the cafeteria earlier. But her hair was definitely different. It used to be more of a fiery orangish-red. Now it was darker, with strands of deep red and brown running through it. And it was shinier, too.

And oh, man, did she smell good.

She still smelled like lavender. But the scent was stronger, warmer. More mysterious. And her skin looked extra good today. Especially right above the collar of her sweater...

I gulped and leaned back in my chair again as I tried to think straight. To remember all the reasons why kissing that curve where her neck and shoulder met would be a bad idea.

I had to pity the three creeps then. There was something about Savannah that went way beyond the normal attraction. I was only surprised that every male in the school hadn't gathered around her outside the building today.

A foot kicked my left leg.

My head shot up and I looked around. The lecture had

ended, everyone was working on the assignment…and Anne seemed ready to punch me. What now?

She wrote in big letters across her paper, *Quit staring!*

I wasn't, I wrote on my own paper big enough so she could read it.

Yes, you are. All you guys are such creeps, she added on her paper.

Confused, I looked at her and mouthed the words *all you guys,* raising my eyebrows. What was she talking about?

Her head jerked to the right and back before she pretended to return to her work. But I could see she was just doodling on her paper.

I waited a minute then faked a silent yawn and stretch so I could glance behind us at the rest of the class. Sure enough, three pairs of male eyes were all locked in Savannah's direction. Their dark expressions said their thoughts were anything but nice.

The guys had gone well beyond stalker level straight to "lock me up, I'm a serial killer" in just two hours.

Oh, yeah, I was definitely going to have to do something about this. The question was…what? And how much time did I have to work with?

I wrote, *I am NOT like them. But don't worry about those creeps. I'll take care of it.*

Anne's eyebrows shot up, but she didn't write anything else on her paper.

When the bell rang, I took my time gathering up my books. Then I sensed somebody coming toward our group of desks. A quick glance behind me showed it was the Creepy Three. I spun out and around my desk, positioning myself between Savannah and them.

"Hey, Ron, think we've got a shot of making the varsity team next year?" I said to the guy seated in front of Anne at

Savannah's left. I wasn't surprised by Abernathy's confused expression as he looked around at me. Though we'd both played offensive JV football this year, Ron's family had just moved to Jacksonville last year, and he hadn't made many friends yet. He seemed like the quiet type, and until today we'd never spoken to each other outside of team time.

Ron must have been raised by parents who believed in being polite, though, because he didn't blow me off. "Maybe. I heard Coach Parker's getting desperate for some solid second-string players on varsity."

I could feel three people hovering at my back, no doubt wishing I would move. Smothering a nasty grin, I spread my feet, crossed my arms over my chest and settled in. "That'd be sweet if we got moved up. Think we'd get any actual field time then?"

Ron shrugged. "Probably. You know how it is. Between grades and injuries, we might stand a good shot."

Someone had the guts to tap my shoulder. I ought to break off those fingers. Instead, I ignored them and kept talking with Ron, discussing who might be most likely to get benched next fall for injuries or failing grades.

Unfortunately, Savannah and Anne appeared to be too deep in their own whispered conversation to notice the prime opportunity I'd given them to escape. Girls. They picked the worst times to turn chatty.

When Ron leaned away to grab his books, I cleared my throat. Anne looked up. I shot her a look that hopefully told her to get her skinny rear in gear. She got the hint, grabbed Savannah, and within half a minute the girls were leaving.

Just as I started to relax, I sensed the Creepy Three shifting as if to follow the girls.

"See you at practice," I said to Ron then headed for the door, lengthening my stride so I would reach it before the creeps. At the doorway, I turned and gave them my ugliest look.

They had the nerve to glare back at me, even though all three of them were a good half a foot shorter than me. Not to mention they couldn't have weighed more than a hundred pounds combined.

"I know you're not thinking what I think you're thinking," I growled. Behind me, the math-building exit door banged shut.

They stared up at me. Man, they just had no clue what kind of danger they were in. I could beat all three of them into pulp in ten seconds flat and not even work up a sweat.

"Is there a problem, boys?" Mr. Chandler said from his desk.

"Yes, sir," I said, working not to smile. "I could've sworn I just heard these three call you a fat, bald-headed little pig."

Mr. Chandler stood up. "Well. Sounds like maybe you three should stay for a little chat with me."

Confused, they turned to the teacher and started stammering. That ought to hold them for a while, at least long enough for the girls to reach the parking lot and their rides. Satisfied, I headed outside in time to see Savannah get into her grandma's car.

What I wasn't expecting was to see Anne stalking back toward the math building.

Curiosity made me call out to her, "Hey, where are you going?"

The building door opened behind us. I glanced back. The Creepy Three slunk through, giving me pathetic excuses for scary looks before they headed down the catwalk.

Anne's glare was much more impressive as she stared after them. "I'm going toad hunting."

"Uh, I think the situation's under control now."

"They made her shake! And did you see that look they just gave you? Do you really think they're going to leave her alone now?"

Frowning, I watched the toads in question stop at the other end of the catwalk and huddle. No telling what ideas they were coming up with.

"All right, I see your point. But why don't you let me handle them?"

"Why, because you think I'll get hurt?" She sneered.

"No. I'm sure you could take them. But I think a simple man-to-man talk is a better solution." I felt my mood darken with all the things I'd like that talk to include.

Her eyes narrowed. "You really like her, don't you?"

I blinked a few times. "Why would you think that? Just because I want to help someone out..."

"Jeez, all you boys are the same. What, did you grow up on stories about Camelot or something? You know, contrary to popular Southern male opinion, not every female is a damsel in distress just sitting around waiting to be rescued by Lancelot, or whatever. We can take care of ourselves."

"Actually, I've always thought of myself more as a King Arthur type. You know, take charge, lead the troops and all that," I joked.

She snorted. "Oh, of course your ego would be king-size."

"Hey, whatever it takes to get the job done."

"Uh-huh. Okay, Arthur, we'll see how you do with the toads."

"That's *King* Arthur to you."

"Don't hold your breath for that one." She headed for the parking lot, then stopped after a few yards and turned back. "You really think I could've taken them?"

I laughed. "Oh, yeah. Easily."

"Good answer, Coleman! You *might* actually be good enough for her someday," she yelled back.

I cringed and glanced around, but thankfully no one seemed to be paying attention.

I checked my watch, cursed and broke into a jog toward the field house, bracing myself for the punishment I'd get for being late. Laps, probably, at least five of them. Maybe more depending on Coach Parker's mood today. Oh, well. It'd be worth it. Along the way, I tried to figure out what I would do about the Creepy Three. Or the toads, as Anne had called them.

I had to focus during weight training. Part of my punishment for my lateness was being paired up with some wimpy kid who needed a spotter to save him from the evil bench press every few seconds. But as soon as practice ended and I finished all ten laps around the outdoor track that ringed the practice field, my brain went right back to the problem at hand.

All joking aside, Anne's claim that she could take care of the boys herself was overconfident. Sure, maybe she and Savannah could handle one boy. Maybe two. But three at a time? No way. And what about when Savannah wasn't with Anne?

I had options, though none of them were great. Beating up the toads would make my fists happy and ensure the jerks got the point. But there was that whole problem with Jacksonville High's no-violence policy again.

I could settle for threatening them instead, but I doubted they'd be smart enough to listen and stay away from Savannah.

That left me with only one solution that couldn't be traced back to me, at least by normal methods, and would take the choice away from the creeps. For that, I'd need my sister's help.

I got to the car before Emily. Kicking back, I propped my feet on the dashboard and waited. I must have drifted off.

"Hey, sleepyhead." Emily tossed her poms onto my face as she got in. "Get those grubby feet off my dash, please." Using her index finger like a wand, she magically lifted my feet in the air for a few seconds. Man, I hated it when she used telekinesis on me! It made me feel like a puppet. Seriously creepy. Not to mention the small pinpricks that raced over my skin whenever she used magic around me. And that was just from a tiny use of power.

Swatting away the annoying piles of plastic, I sat up. The sun was already setting. "What took you so long?"

"Cheerleading practice. Remember? Cheerleaders have to train hard, too."

"Uh-huh." I frowned at the fast-sinking sun then glanced at my watch and swore. I was running out of time, and no way could I risk waiting another day to get rid of Savannah's stalker club. "Listen, sis. I really need your help. And I know what you're going to say, but hear me out first, okay?"

Her eyebrows rose, but she nodded and started the car.

As we drove, I gave her a quick rundown about Savannah's newest fans and how scared she'd looked. I might have played it up a little, but they had acted half crazed over her, and she'd seemed pretty upset at the end of class. "So, I need your help."

"You want me to use my power to make them leave her alone?"

"No. I want to do it." With Savannah's looks, this could become a weekly problem. And I didn't want to have to go to my sister for help every time.

Emily didn't even hesitate. "No."

"You won't teach me?"

"No. You know the rules. Not just Mom and Dad, but *all*

the elders would kill me or worse if I teach you anything I know. You can only learn from an elder, no one else."

I groaned and ran both hands through my hair.

"Oh, calm down, you spoiled brat. You're a Coleman. You know you'll get your way in the end. You're just making this way too hard." Emily pushed a button on the remote clipped to her visor. The wrought-iron gates swung open ahead of us at our driveway's entrance and we pulled through, the gravel crunching like potato chips under the car's tires.

"Oh, so you think I should just beat them up, lose any chance of going to college and break our mother's heart? Okay, but remember, it was your idea."

"Of course not, you idiot. I meant that you need to learn from an elder how to protect her." She pulled into the garage and let me think over her suggestion while the door slid shut behind us.

"Yeah, I guess I could ask Dad. But you know their rules about her. They would kill me just for saying her name, let alone for trying to help her."

"Who says they need to know how the information will be used? You know Dad's been waiting for you to start taking your training seriously. So why not make our dear old dad happy for a change?"

I stared ahead into the gloom of the dim garage, thinking over everything Emily was and wasn't saying.

She was right. Dad did want me to "buckle down and train harder"—harped on it, in fact. And self-defense was the first thing he'd taught Emily after she'd learned to ground her energy. So the odds were pretty good that I could get him to start on the same type of stuff with me. A hint or two from me about being ready to focus and needing help in the self-defense area should do it. But would I learn what I needed to fast enough to help Savannah? The Creepy Three might come to their senses with a little distance, time and sleep tonight. Or they might not. What if they were making plans right now to catch her alone somewhere?

"What time did Dad say he'd be home tonight?"

Emily glanced at her watch with a smile. "In half an hour."

I jumped out of the car, leaving my books on the seat. "I'd better go change."

"Don't you need your books?"

I shook my head and gave her a grim smile. "I'll be too busy. Got a different kind of homework tonight."

"Okay. Just be sure to ask Dad how to do a targeted memory confusion spell. Every time those creeps try to get near Savannah, they'll become confused and go away again. Put it in something small to hide in her backpack, and you're all set."

"Thanks." I shot her a grin then ran inside and up to my room.

Savannah

I thought about telling my family about today's algebra class. But they all seemed stressed about me already. I knew if I told them, Dad would have to tell the vampire council. Both the Clann and the council already thought I was a ticking time bomb. If they knew I was changing already, what would they do? Would they take me out of school? Would they take me away from Nanna and Mom and my friends?

So on the way home from dance class, I decided to give it another day and see what happened. Then if I felt like I really couldn't handle things, I would ask for help.

"Hey, hon, how was your day?" Mom called from her couch office as Nanna and I entered the house. Mom seemed tense, her elbows braced on her knees, her cell phone strangely quiet for once. Had she been waiting for me to come home and report?

"It was fine. But I really need a shower now. Ballet and jazz class were…" Great. Fabulous. Amazing. "Brutal." I made a beeline for the bathroom so neither of them could see my face while I lied. "What's for dinner?"

I should have known avoiding them wouldn't be so easy.

Mom came into the bathroom just as I was pouring on the shampoo. Great, now I was trapped for at least the next few minutes. Knowing my mother, she'd probably timed it that way, too.

"Did you have any…issues today?" she asked, obviously trying and failing to sound casual.

My throat choked up. Part of me was desperate to wimp out and tell her everything.

I slid open the frosted-glass door an inch and peeked at her. Worry lines creased her forehead. I shut the door again and scrubbed my hair faster. "It was fine. Though dancing today was…different. My dancing is a lot better now."

Silence.

Finally, she said, "Define 'a lot.'"

"Um, like I was able to get my splits down to the floor finally. And I learned how to do high kicks and turns and leaps without taking out any of the other students for a change."

She laughed. "Well, that sounds good, then. Anything else?"

Besides the fact that I seemed to have created a scary new fan club and my friends couldn't stand it when I looked them in the eye? "Nope."

"Okay. Well, I'd better go help your grandma get dinner ready. I'm glad you had a good day."

"Thanks, Mom. I'll be out in a minute." My stomach, already knotted and rolling with acid, cramped at the idea of eating. Lying could make a really good diet plan for me, if it didn't kill me first.

She left the room, shutting the door behind her, and I found I could suddenly breathe again.

Now all I had to do was pray that tomorrow would prove none of us had anything to worry about in the first place.

Tristan

I took a deep breath at his study door then knocked.

"Come in," Dad's voice boomed out.

Inside, I was surprised to find Emily already there. She gave him a hug.

"Thanks for listening, Daddy," she said as she walked toward me and the door.

"Anytime, Princess," he replied, a big smile barely visible beneath his bushy silver beard.

Huh? I searched Emily's face, trying to figure out why she was here. She never came to Dad's study, preferring to chat with him either at the dinner table or while they played golf together.

She gave me a sneaky two thumbs-up before she passed me and left the room. She was up to something. I'd have to trust that it was helpful somehow.

"Hello, son. Come and have a seat." He sounded stern, his smile gone now.

Trying to act relaxed, I sat in one of the two leather chairs before his massive oak desk.

"Dressed for sports?" He loosened his tie and sat back down in his desk chair.

I glanced down at the hoodie and sweatpants I'd changed into. "Yeah, training practice."

"Hmm. Yes. Well, that reminds me. I'm glad you came in here. I heard you had a bit of trouble today at school?"

My hands nearly clenched up before I could stop them. What had Emily told him? "Yeah, a little."

"She also said you needed her help?"

Emily wouldn't have ratted on me about our conversation in the car. Would she?

"I see." He must have misunderstood my silence for an answer. "So the grounding training hasn't helped?"

Oh. So Emily had told him about my power spikes instead. "Well, sort of. She told me how to ground by using a tree at school. And it helped."

"Mmm-hmm. But it sounds like you still have a lot of excess energy?" He took another sip of his drink, picked up a letter on his desk and began to read it in silence.

I was losing his attention already. "That's actually what I wanted to talk to you about, sir. I've still got a lot of energy sometimes, even with the grounding. And I was thinking today that maybe it keeps building up because I'm not putting it to good use."

His sharp green eyes bored into me. He dropped the letter and set down his drink on his desk blotter, the dull thud loud in the too-quiet room. "Go on."

Had I already messed up? "So I was thinking…maybe it's time for me to really focus on my training. Emily said the powers won't go away by ignoring them. But if I could learn how to use them—"

"Stop right there."

Crap, I'd already screwed up somehow. I held my breath.

He rose from his chair and came around the desk toward me. "You're saying that, after months of refusing to work on your training, *now* you're ready to buckle down and learn?"

I cleared my throat, waited a beat, then nodded.

A slow smile spread across his face before he clapped a huge paw of a hand on my shoulder. "Well, all right, then, let's get started! You're already dressed for training. That's good. Have you eaten? If you grounded at school today, you're gonna need to fortify the body and fuel the energy, you know."

I grinned with relief and rose to my feet. "Yeah, Dad. I just had a couple of sandwiches and some milk."

"Good, good, good. Then let's head to the backyard and get going. We've got a lot to cover."

I glanced down at the slacks and dress shirt he still wore. "Uh, don't you need to change?"

"Why waste time? I've got a million suits."

As we stepped out the patio door to the backyard barely visible in the dusk, I took another chance. "Hey, Dad, do you think we could start with some self-defense training?"

"Problems at school?"

I forced a laugh. "Oh, you know, nothing a good right hook wouldn't take care of. But you know Mom and how much she wants me to go to college."

He chuckled. "I understand completely. Gotta go the subtle route this time, right?"

"Right."

"Well, sure, we can start with some defensive training. Although if you ever get ready for a real fight..."

"You'll be the first to know, Dad, I promise."

"All right. Have a seat there on the grass while I pull up a chair." He grabbed a wicker chair from the back patio, brought it onto the lawn and sat down, muttering, "Getting too old to sit on the ground."

I sat in front of him, legs crossed kid-style as he'd taught me for grounding training even though it seemed stupid. I felt like a kindergartner getting ready for story time.

"Okay, so here's the basics of casting a spell. Every witch starts off at the beginner level of spellcasting by saying a word and using a small hand gesture. This helps you focus and control when the spell is actually cast, until you learn how to discipline your mind. Someday, when you're ready, I'll teach you how to cast a spell even if you're tied up with your mouth taped shut, just by thinking the word and using your willpower. Eventually you'll learn to cast a spell even without a word at all, just by thinking about the results you want to create. Like you do when you create fire or ground your energy."

As much as I hated magic, I had to admit, throwing a spell with just my mind would be kind of cool.

He continued. "The first thing you need to know is, when someone is coming at you, you've gotta react fast. So we'll start with the word and hand gesture to cast a blocking spell. Just remember, though, no spell's going to work until you really want it to.

"Now, are you feeling confident?"

"Yes, sir."

"Good. Then stand up."

I obeyed.

"And come at me."

"Sir?"

"Go on. Try to come at me like you're gonna tackle me."

I took two slow steps toward him. And found myself ten yards away, walking in the opposite direction, and a million tiny stabs of pain racing over my neck and arms.

I muttered a curse and shook my head, rubbing the sensation from my skin. Was this how all the descendants felt when a Coleman used magic near them? No wonder the descendants hated it when I had power spikes at school.

"See how it works?" he said as I walked back. "It just moves you away and turns you around. Really good for fighting in hard-to-see situations, because it can confuse your attacker and give you time to get away."

I nodded and paid close attention as he taught me the word and wrist flick. But when I tried it for myself, nothing happened.

"Ah, but you've really got to want it to happen, son. Your will is the key to it all. Now try again. This time, I'll come at you."

He walked toward me. I said the word and performed the hand gesture. And…nothing.

He glared at me. "Tristan Glenn Coleman. You can do better than that. Boy, I'm gonna tan your backside if you don't get it in gear!" He came at me, his long legs eating up the distance between us despite his huge gut. I'd never realized he could move that fast.

Fear rammed through me, making me feel like a little kid about to get a serious butt whipping. I whispered the spell. Then he was at the end of the backyard and facing the opposite direction.

"All right! You did it!" He walked toward me, beaming. "I thought I might have to give you some motivation there."

He was faking it? "Well, it worked." My laugh sounded shaky even to my own ears.

The garden lights kicked on, flooding the yard and reminding me that time was running out fast.

"Okay, what's next?" I said.

"Whoa, slow down, Tristan. Don't you think you ought to practice that one a few more times?"

I reached for the energy within. Closing my eyes, I mentally whispered the word to that energy. When I opened my eyes, I focused on Dad and visualized myself performing the wrist flick at him. He reappeared at the other end of the yard.

He strolled back, shaking his head. His eyes, green copies of mine but wrinkled at the corners, were wide beneath his thick eyebrows. "Wow, son. You didn't even use the word or hand gesture!"

"I did, just in my mind instead."

"Impressive. That's not usually something we teach until the fourth or fifth year of training. Remember, though, you can use the silent casting method, but you've gotta be extra careful if you're only considering casting the spell. You have to keep your will out of it. Otherwise as soon as you think of the spell, you'll end up casting it. That's why we usually start off with the verbal method first. It gives you better control."

"I understand."

He shook his head one more time then grinned at me. "Should've known my son would be more advanced at this stuff than normal."

"Of course. I'm a Coleman, right?"

"Right!"

I smiled back at him, but guilt made it tough to pull off. He looked so proud of me, so happy that I'd decided to focus on my training. But the truth was I still wasn't the slightest bit interested in leading the Clann someday like he wanted me to. I just needed a spell or two so I could help Savannah. Then I could go back to trying to be normal.

"Uh, Dad? Can we…"

"Right, right. Back to work. Okay, so what other defensive spells might be useful?"

I remembered Emily's advice. "How about a memory confusion spell? You know, so I could block someone from messing with something."

"Ah, yes. Emily likes to use that spell to get rid of punks who bug her too much."

"How long would a spell like that last?"

"If your sister cast it, a couple days at best. She's too soft-hearted to will anyone to stay away longer than that. If I made it…" His face darkened. "A few months. Maybe years."

"And if I made one?"

"Thinking of Christmas presents for your sister already?"

I laughed with him. "Yeah, something like that."

"Well, like I said, it would depend on how often the boy tried to go near her. And how much you wanted him to stay away. But for one of Emily's normal punks, I'd say at least a month if you cast it."

The Creepy Three seemed pretty obsessed today. They might wear out a spell quicker than one of Emily's usual fans. Then again…I thought of how much I wanted them to leave Savannah alone. I bet I could make my spells last at least a couple months bare minimum. Maybe by then they would move on to someone else to obsess over.

"Okay, what do I do?"

He grinned at me. "Well, you know your sister. She hates to feel like she can't handle her own problems. So it's best if she doesn't know what you're doing."

"So I'd need to know who the creeps are without asking her, then find objects to charm that she'd carry around without suspecting?"

"Exactly!"

That last part might be tough. What could I give Savannah that she would keep with her at all times and not suspect? She'd question anything I gave her.

Unless she didn't know about it. Emily said I should put a small charm in Savannah's backpack. Maybe I could manage to sneak something small in there without her noticing.

"Okay, what else do I have to do?"

He taught me what to say and how to tap a finger on the object to load it with the memory confusion spell. "Every time you tap it, you've got to sort of push your will into the object. Every push should equal one memory block."

"Should?"

He shrugged, looking a little embarrassed. "Well, I've never been able to ask your sister or mother how many times certain people we know have started to approach them then ended up walking away confused."

Ah. So he had been doing a little secret protection work of his own. Mom and Emily would go nuts if they ever learned what he had been up to. I grinned. "I see your point."

"All right, let's try it. I'll turn my back, and you charm one of the lawn chairs. Then I'll try to approach each one. That way when I get confused, you'll know it really worked."

"Sounds good."

We practiced for a while to make sure I had the spell down. Then he had to call it a night. "Sorry, son, but I'm worn-out and have a board meeting early in the morning."

"No problem, Dad. Mind if I stay out here and keep practicing awhile?" I held my breath, expecting him to say that I couldn't keep casting without his supervision according to Clann rules.

Instead, he nodded and headed for the patio door. Then he hesitated and looked back. "You know, I really am proud of you today. Feels like I'm seeing my little boy becoming a man right in front of me."

My throat suddenly tightened. I managed a nod.

"Let's train again tomorrow night," he suggested with a grin.

Before I could think it through, I found myself nodding in agreement. He was still grinning as he entered the house.

Great. Now he probably thought I'd changed my mind

about following in his footsteps for the Clann leadership. If so, I'd have to figure out a way to let him down gently. Later. Right now, I had some serious memory confusion to create.

CHAPTER 5

Tristan

I ran up to my room and looked around. What could I put the spells in? Pens? Pencils? Paper clips? Nah, Savannah was always loaning out stuff like that in algebra. Maybe Emily had something I could use.

I had a sudden image of my sister handing me tampons just to torture me, and shuddered. No, I'd better not ask Emily. I glanced at my bedside clock. Eight fifty-six. Not too late to call for some insider advice. I grabbed a telephone book and my cordless phone.

"Hello, may I speak with Anne, please?" I said when a woman answered.

"Who is calling?" It was probably Anne's mother, who worked in the accounting department at Coleman BioMed, Dad's company. Not good. If she mentioned to any coworkers that I was calling Savannah's best friend at home…

Thinking fast, I replied, "Arthur."

"Arthur, it's a little late for phone calls."

At eight fifty-seven? Now I knew where Anne got her

personality from. "Yes, ma'am. Sorry for the late phone call, but it's a math emergency." That wasn't too much of a stretch on the truth.

"One moment."

I heard murmuring in the background. Then Anne picked up the phone. "Why, hello, *Arthur.* Having trouble with that warty little problem we ran into today?" Her voice dripped with smug satisfaction.

I rolled my eyes. "Yeah, I am. I need to know what types of things S—I mean, your friend usually carries around in her backpack." I barely stopped myself from saying Savannah's name out loud. Knowing my parents, they'd probably put a spell on my room to warn them if I ever said her name again.

"What doesn't she have in there? The girl never cleans anything. Not her backpack, not her locker, not even her bedroom. Every time I sleep over at her house, I end up spending half the time cleaning her room just so I have some space to breathe. Drives me crazy!"

I pictured lacy scraps of underwear and bras lying around a sleeping Savannah, and fought to exhale. "Uh, not to interrupt the venting here, but I could use your help now."

"Ha! I knew you couldn't handle it on your own." She sighed. "All right, what do you want?"

"I need access to her backpack at lunch tomorrow. Or better yet, maybe you can make the delivery."

"And what would *that* be exactly?"

"Don't worry. I wouldn't give you anything that would get her or you in trouble. It's just something that needs to stay in her backpack for as long as possible, say a couple months, at least."

Silence filled the phone.

"Anne? You still there?"

After another few seconds' hesitation, I heard a door click

shut on her end of the line before she whispered, "These things for her backpack...are they a...a Clann thing?"

Surprise made it my turn to hesitate. What had Anne heard about the descendants? "Define what you think 'Clann things' are."

"You know, *witchy* stuff. Stuff that would make my parents go nuts. They're Pentecostal."

She said "they," not "we." It sounded like she was about as on board with her family's religious choices as I was with my parents' plans for my future.

I couldn't decide if it was a good thing or simply disturbing that Anne and I had anything in common.

"No offense, but I'm really not allowed to talk about the Clann." There, that was honest and still playing by the rules. Descendants weren't allowed to discuss their abilities with outsiders other than their husbands and wives. And even those outsiders had spells cast on them to bind them from ever mentioning the Clann to anyone else. The elders didn't mess around when protecting Clann secrets.

Anne's sigh gusted into the phone. "Fine. Just tell me this... will it really help Savannah?"

"Yeah. It will."

"Then I'll do it. Just don't use anything made out of chocolate, or she'll eat it. It's like her kryptonite."

I laughed before I could stop myself. "I'll have to remember that." I scanned my room, wondering what I could use and starting to get frustrated again.

Then I saw it...a box of those little conversation heart candies. Savannah had given them to me on Valentine's Day in the fourth grade. The same day we'd pretended to get married and kissed. She hadn't signed her name on the box, so Mom never made me throw them out.

"How does she feel about really old conversation heart candies?"

"Oh, she hates those. Apparently they make her think of a certain backstabbing traitor, or something like that."

I glared at the ceiling, unsure whether to be happy that Savannah had talked about me, or bugged that she still seemed to be ticked off at me.

"So don't put them in a box, or she'll throw them away," Anne added in a softer tone. "She'll probably ignore them if they're just loose in the bottom of her backpack, though."

"Okay. When should I bring them to you?"

"Before school would be best. She's always running late, so she won't be there."

"Right. See you then. And, Anne?"

"Yeah?"

"Thanks."

"Don't let it affect your ego there, Arthur. I'm doing it for Savannah." I could practically hear the eye roll in her voice. Man, she was a pain. But I was also starting to get why Savannah was friends with her. Some people would think twice before doing something that went against their family's religious beliefs, even to help out a friend.

I grinned. "Yeah, yeah, as if I could forget."

She hung up without saying goodbye. I hit the phone's off button with a shake of my head, then jumped up and grabbed the box of hearts, feeling good for the first time in days. This just might work.

Back outside, I sat down in the wet grass at the edge of the patio then shook three hearts out of their box. As an afterthought, I added a fourth to the lineup for that Romeo-wannabe soccer player.

While touching the first candy, I pictured one of the creeps, mentally whispered the spell word and tapped the candy while visualizing a surge of energy entering it. How many times might these guys want to talk to Savannah? Twenty times? Fifty? I thought about how many times a day I was tempted to say something to her. Better make that at least a hundred times per candy. I could always create more charms later if it looked like any of them were wearing out too soon.

I went down the row of hearts, saving the soccer jerk for last. With every tap of my fingertip, more of the constant edginess seeped out of me. I finished charming all four candies, then decided to go back over them again just in case Savannah's weird pull on these guys proved to be even half as strong as the effect she had on me. But the first pass had really relaxed me. Stretching out on the grass seemed a good idea. The yard was wet and cold, but I could deal with it. This was more important.

The dream began just as I started the second pass on Stanwick's memory confuser.

Savannah looked like some sort of goddess, her hair down and blowing behind her in the wind along with the folds of her long white nightgown. She stood facing a setting sun, dark asphalt sparkling beneath her bare feet. We were on the flat rooftop of a building overlooking Jacksonville.

Behind her, a crowd of guys I recognized from school stood together in a tight group. They were edgy, staring at Savannah with wild expressions on their faces, ready to lunge at any second. Like a pack of jackals snapping at her heels. What held them back?

I would.

I was outnumbered, but I had to try anyway. Maybe if I stood close to her when they attacked, I could cast a blocking spell strong enough to protect both of us at once. If that didn't work, I'd have to risk taking the brunt of the attack myself and focus the spell only on her for as long as I could make it hold.

A voice whispered through the dream, hers but huskier, more sultry. The voice of Savannah as a dark seductress. And yet her lips didn't move. "Look at them, Savannah. Give them what they crave, and they will end your thirst."

The words made no sense.

Savannah seemed to understand though. Tears slid down her cheeks as she shook her head and whispered, "No. I won't look at them. It's not right."

"Look at them!" the voice shrieked, and Savannah's hands darted up to fidget with the gold locket she always wore at her neck.

"No, don't, Sav," I said, trying to walk toward her. But something invisible and hot, like heated glass, held me back. I pushed my hands against that barrier, willing it to give and let me through. "Savannah, listen to me. Do not look at them."

The boys snapped and growled, their patience wearing out. They bumped into each other, and the group inched forward almost as a single, seething mass.

"Savannah!" I yelled. But she couldn't hear me.

Cursing, I hit the barrier between us. The heat burned my knuckles.

She stepped toward the edge of the roof and looked down.

Cold terror poured over me. "Savannah, don't! Wait for me." I hit the invisible wall again and again with my fists, my will and power, even ramming my shoulders against it. A monstrous growl rumbled in my chest.

"You *will* give in to the temptation," the evil voice whispered, already sure of its triumph. "You need them. You need the power."

"No. Never," Savannah promised, her voice choked and hollow.

And then she dived over the edge.

"No!" My roar swallowed me up until I thought it would never stop. I could feel myself losing it, right there on the edge of crazy, but it didn't matter. Nothing mattered but the pain slamming into me in waves that brought me to my knees.

I needed her, needed her to be alive even if we couldn't be together anymore.

I was still yelling out the pain as I woke up the next morning, my body cold and aching in the wet grass of my backyard.

The minutes passed as I sat there, teeth clenched against the need to keep shouting, my breaths coming out fast and harsh through my nose. My chest burned. My fists were on fire. The dew on the grass became a sweet relief to my hands, cooling the flames on my skin.

Just a dream. But the dream had felt way too real. It had the same sharp-edged quality to it as the dreams I used to have of her in the fourth grade.

I stared at my hands, holding them up in the light of the sunrise. They weren't even red. But the pain had seemed so real.

Sighing, I dried them off on my sweats then scooped up the charmed candy. Time to face reality and get ready for school.

I couldn't shake the memory of that dream, though. Its gut-twisting terror and pain stuck with me all day. I barely said more than "Here" and "Thanks" to Anne when I shoved the protective charms at her outside the main building before school. I wasn't in the mood to even fake a smile for anyone in the hallways or my morning classes, much less talk.

At lunch, I couldn't eat, especially after seeing Savannah enter the cafeteria and join her friends. She'd worn her hair down today for a change. The ends looked wet, maybe from taking a shower after her pre-drill class. Seeing those red strands down and flowing with her every little move reminded me too much of the dream. And the way her hair had streamed out like blood as she'd flown over the side of the roof...

"See you later," I muttered to my sister before ducking out. I was tired for the first time in months, definitely in no need to do any grounding. Still, my feet led me to the same tree as yesterday for some reason.

I leaned against its trunk. The rough bark scraped at my skin through my clothes, reminding me that I was awake, that this was reality. I tilted back my head and stared up at the branches, watching the play of light and shadow above me as the leaves rustled in the wind, making a sound like someone whispering. Whispering like that evil voice in last night's dream as it drove Savannah to jump off the roof.

I closed my eyes and swallowed the knot in my throat. I saw her again in that dream, giving up, stepping over the edge. Again and again I saw her fall. The repetition should have numbed me to the images. But the pain only grew worse, until I wanted to yell from it.

I couldn't stand it anymore. I had to fix this.

There was only one solution, only one way to keep myself from going insane here. I would stay away from her. Stop looking for her at lunch. No more staring at her in algebra or reacting to her laughter in the hallways. These crazy feelings she created in me were just too much. I'd have to check on her every now and then to make sure the charms continued to protect her. But I couldn't keep feeling like this.

"She's just a girl," I muttered to the leaves, the clouds, to no one at all. "A girl. Nothing more."

Savannah

I was tense throughout the morning, bracing myself for an-other encounter with the boys from algebra. Though I didn't have math class today, it seemed inevitable that I would run into them at some point during the day. I thought I saw one of them in the main hallway before first period. He looked at me, took a couple steps in my direction, then frowned and headed the other way.

Lunchtime was even worse.

"Are you okay?" Anne leaned over and whispered while Michelle and Carrie worked together on homework.

"Sure! Why?" I pasted on a smile.

One of her eyebrows arched. "You haven't eaten anything. And you're paler than usual. Which means you're white as a sheet today."

I gave up trying to fake a smile. "Just a little...nervous."

"Worried about running into the Warty Boys again?"

Warty Boys? I looked at her, letting my confusion show on my face.

"You know, the toads from algebra. The creeps that were bugging you before class."

"Oh. Yeah. Think they'll be as...weird today?"

"Only one way to find out. We'll walk past them after lunch and see how they react."

My stomach cramped. "Maybe being around them again so soon isn't such a good idea."

"Why?"

I hesitated. I couldn't tell her the truth, at least not all of it. But not telling her anything made me feel so alone here on campus. Couldn't I tell her just a little without breaking any rules?

I decided to take a risk. "Promise you won't laugh too loudly."

She nodded.

"I think it's because...because I made eye contact with them after lunch."

"You think, just because they looked into your eyes, you did something to them? Like you hypnotized them, or something?"

"Um...yeah."

She snickered. "Oh, sure. Because I do that all the time, too. All us girls do. One look in any girl's eyes, and poof! All the boys are gaze dazed."

Irritated, I forgot and glared at her, making eye contact in the process.

Within seconds, she shivered and looked away. "Huh. Okay, maybe you have a point."

I didn't know whether to feel smug about winning the argument or sick to my stomach. Part of me had really hoped I was wrong about yesterday and that my friends would prove it by acting normal after I made eye contact with them today. But they didn't. They just kept getting weirded out.

Anne cleared her throat. "Have you made eye contact with anyone else and had strange reactions?"

"You mean other than you guys?" I gestured at everyone at our table. Carrie glanced up from the biology book she was using to tutor Michelle, then went back to their studying.

Anne nodded.

I tried to remember, but there was no telling how often I'd made eye contact with people since getting sick last week. "I don't know. Maybe Greg Stanwick? I can't remember now."

The bell rang, signaling the end of lunch. I shuffled after the others to the trash cans, taking my time dumping my tray and adding it to the stack at the dishwasher's window.

"Maybe we should go out the other exit," I suggested, my chest growing tighter by the second.

"Come on. We'll go together." Anne linked her arm through mine. The contrast between her tan and my milky-white skin was awful, but at least the contact was reassuring, a reminder that I wasn't totally alone.

We stepped out into the spring sunlight and its blast of warmth, which actually felt good. I'd been a little chilled indoors all morning, so stepping outside was like thawing at first.

But even being wrapped in bright sunshine and warmth couldn't make my muscles loosen up. The picnic tables were only yards away from the cafeteria building.

Too soon, I saw the three algebra guys from yesterday.

"Hello, boys," Anne called out, making several heads pop up.

"Anne, shut *up!*" I muttered, trying to steer us closer to the cafeteria wall and away from the tables. If Anne would only cooperate a little, we could sneak by without being seen. But she was hardheaded as ever and literally dug in her heels.

"Oh, hey, Anne," one of the algebra boys replied. Then he frowned and rubbed his forehead. "Huh. I could've sworn I wanted to ask you something. I guess I'll remember it later."

I carefully avoided direct eye contact with any of the Warty Boys, as Anne had called them. But looking at their noses still let me indirectly search their expressions for the dark, crazed obsession from yesterday.

And what I found was…only confused frowns, as if nothing out of the ordinary had happened. They didn't even look at me, ignoring me just like they used to.

Had the gaze daze, as Anne had called it, worn off overnight?

I stopped shielding and allowed myself to sense their emotions, bracing myself for that churning, black turmoil from yesterday. And instead found only more confusion from them.

Maybe the gaze daze was just a temporary effect.

As Anne continued to chat with them about our latest

algebra homework assignment, something dangerously close to hope filled me, and I took a deep breath. If the gaze daze-effect on guys was temporary, then maybe everything would be okay, after all. I just had to be sure I never, *ever* made eye contact with a boy again. Simple, right?

Yeah, sure.

The algebra boys didn't bother me anymore, so I could actually focus on prepping for my studio's dance recital at the end of the week. Not that I needed as much practice as before, now that my dancing was quickly improving. Still, I wanted to be sure I did the best I could at the recital. If I could blow away my family with my dancing, maybe they'd quit watching me all the time when they thought I didn't notice. If I could be good at something for a change, then maybe it would show them that I was normal, after all. Not a freak. Just a regular teen doing something she really had fun doing.

The only thing that continued to bug me was Greg. I couldn't tell if I'd gaze dazed him, too, or not. He hadn't spoken to me again since Monday. And the few times I saw him in the cafeteria later in the week, he always looked away with a frown.

Boys were just plain weird.

Including Tristan, because he'd started acting differently all week, too. It was like the wall that separated us in my frequent dreams about him had stretched out to divide us in my waking life, as well. Even with my senses wide-open, I couldn't feel his magnetic tug anymore when we were in algebra class together. And while I'd never thought it possible before, I missed having his legs and feet at either side of me now that he'd started to keep them folded under his desk. I also missed the way he used to whistle *Nutcracker* music to annoy me. And the way he used to stare at me in the cafeteria. Lately, he'd started skipping lunch, choosing to stand outside against a tree near the picnic tables instead. I caught myself searching for him in his new spot as my friends and I left the cafeteria each day. Some crazy part of me yearned to make eye contact with him, to see if he could be gaze dazed, too. But he always kept his eyes closed. My head said that was a good thing. My heart said something else.

And then there were all the other little things that added up to make the hours at school long and lonely. I still had my friends, but not being able to make eye contact with anyone made me feel like I was cut off from the world around me. Even weirder was the Red Sea effect that happened every time I walked through the halls. It was subtle, but people moved away from me as if I had something contagious they didn't want to catch. Worse, they didn't even seem aware that they were doing it.

But why? I didn't feel *that* different from before I got sick.

The one good thing that came out of it all was my continued progress in dance. Because of those improvements, dancing had become my one relief. When the music played, I got lost in it. For a few precious minutes, I could forget the craziness, the family secrets, all the weirdness that set me apart from everyone around me. When I danced, not only was I no longer a freak or an embarrassment, but I was actually *good* at something. And getting better at it every day.

So deciding to try out for the Charmers Dance/Drill Team was sort of natural. Where else would I ever fit in at this school, unless it was among other dancers? If I became a Charmer, I wouldn't be a freak anymore. The Charmers were like mini celebrities, not just at our school but in Jacksonville, too, because of all the awards they won every winter at dance competitions. Every time they brought home another trophy, they were featured on the front page of the *Jacksonville Daily News,* earning our school's and entire town's approval.

If I made the team, I would get to be a part of all that, *and* I'd be doing something I loved while I was at it.

But first, I had another approval to earn…Dad's. If being a great dancer didn't do it, I didn't know what would.

So when he called on Wednesday to check up on me, I took the biggest risk of my life so far.

Suddenly nervous, I played with the laces on my sneakers and tried to be patient as we went through our usual list of questions about school. A long pause filled the conversation after a while, and I spotted my opening.

"Um, Dad? You know how I've been taking dance lessons this year?"

"Yes?" His voice had turned cautious, like he was bracing for bad news.

Even more nervous now, I hesitated, forced my tight chest to expand and take a deep breath, then pushed the words out fast. "Well, the studio is having its annual dance recital this weekend and I'd really love it if you could come." *Please say yes, please,* I chanted in my head, holding my breath in the dead silence that followed.

Why didn't he say something?

"Dad?" I whispered, my voice tiny. Oh, crap. He was going to say no, that he couldn't make it, just like when I played volleyball, and basketball, and ran at the junior-high track meets….

More silence.

Finally he spoke. "I suppose it is time that I come see how you have progressed. Give me the details and I will be there."

Yes! Grinning, I told him the recital's date, time and location, then gave him quick directions to the local junior college's theater where the show would be held.

"Hey, you might even be surprised by how good I've gotten," I joked, excitement making me relax and be myself more than I usually was around him.

Silence.

Okaaay. Did he doubt my judgment about my own dancing? Or was he simply not looking forward to sitting through a recital in general?

I'd just have to make sure my performance impressed him enough to make attending worth the effort.

Two days later, I joined my ballet class in the dark wings of Lon Morris College's theater. Finally, the night I had been working so hard for all year long was here. Now was my chance to prove that having me wasn't the biggest mistake my parents had ever made.

The three-year-olds were wrapping up their cute version of the Sugar Plum Fairy dance from *The Nutcracker*. A sudden memory of Tristan whistling the tune made me smile and my eyes burn a bit. I blinked away the unexpected sensation. Better to think about something else. Like the people who were in the audience waiting for me to dance.

My friends couldn't come to the show. They had volleyball tryouts tomorrow morning and needed to practice this evening. Plus, their parents wanted them to go to bed early so they would be rested for their early start. Though I was sort of irritated, I also tried to understand their point of view. Volleyball was everything to them, just like dancing was for me now. So I'd faked yet another smile for their sakes and wished them good-luck.

But there were three people somewhere in those dark rows of seats who had been able to come and cheer for me. I just hoped I didn't screw up and disappoint them yet again.

The spotlights dimmed, and polite clapping sounded from

the audience while mothers volunteering as stage crew herded
the giggling girls offstage and into the wings.

This was it.

Determined yet also breathless with wound-up nerves, I
walked with my classmates onto the dark stage as the audience
grew quiet again. My heart pounded against my ribs. I found
my opening position and posed. I could hear the audience a
few yards away, shifting in their creaky seats, the occasional
cough or murmur.

The recorded piano notes began, so much louder than at
the studio. I would have jumped in surprise, but last night's
dress rehearsal had braced me for the difference in volume.

The spotlights brightened in tiny increments, bathing me
and my classmates in soft blue light as we began to dance in
fluid movements. Though I knew I was dancing, a rush of
adrenaline made the moment surreal. It seemed just a dream,
and I was separate from it all, feeling myself turn and leap as
the music built faster and faster toward that peak note.

Then the music slowed toward its quiet ending. I reached
for the light above, everything inside me held captive by the
music and the moment. And then I blinked, and it was over.
I was in my final pose, smiling so hard my cheeks hurt, as
the audience clapped and cheered far louder than politeness
required. The harder they clapped, the faster my blood rushed
through my veins, until it seemed I could jump out onto that
sound and fly on it like a strong wind.

Ohhh. So *this* was what the Charmers felt when they performed. And they got to experience this all the time.

I could definitely get addicted to this.

Forming a horizontal line with my classmates, we walked
to the front edge of the stage to take our bows. In midcurtsy,
I looked out into the audience, squinting to see Nanna and

Mom beyond the spotlights. And Dad's back as he walked up the aisle toward the exit.

He was leaving already? I still had a jazz routine to perform!

My throat choked up. Breathing was nearly impossible as I finished the curtsy and followed the other dancers offstage on legs that had suddenly turned awkward and stiff. As soon as I reached the wing's darkness, I started running, weaving down the hall past props and mothers and dancers. Didn't Dad know I had two routines to perform tonight, not just one? I had to reach him, had to stop him before he left.

Rain poured down outside. I could hear the water pounding the building's front cement steps as I reached the foyer. The glass doors thudded closed after his retreating figure.

I slapped the door open again. "Dad! Wait!" Could he hear me over the rain? Oh, wait, of course he could. He was a vampire with that same supersonic hearing I had.

Despite the weather, he carried no umbrella to protect the dark suit he always wore, now soaked and clinging to his trim figure. The water didn't seem to faze him as he stopped halfway down the sidewalk and turned to face me with those emotionless eyes so like my own.

"I—I'm glad you came." I couldn't close the distance between us. I was still in my ballet slippers, and rain had splashed under the entrance's metal awning. My slippers' leather soles would be ruined if I got them wet. I edged out as far as I dared so the door could shut behind me and block my voice from carrying back into the theater.

"Um, did Mom mention that I'm doing two routines tonight?"

I thought he would be surprised. Instead, he nodded.

He knew I had another routine to perform...and was still leaving?

I forgot about the wet cement and took a step forward.

"Well, the second routine is a jazz number. So if you don't like ballet, you don't have to worry about it because all the ballet routines are done now."

"I enjoy ballet, Savannah. But I must leave now."

"You've got somewhere else you have to be? Right now?"

"No. But I watched your ballet routine and have seen enough. Probably too much, in fact."

"I…" What could I say to that? I played with the stiff, scratchy folds of my romantic-style tutu. "Was my dancing that bad?"

"No. Your dancing was beautiful."

My head popped up in confusion.

He sighed. "That is the problem. Your performance was too good. You should not be able to dance even half so well for a beginner. How long do you think you will be able to outshine the others in your classes before someone begins to ask questions?"

"So…you're saying you'd rather I danced like crap instead?"

"No, I am saying you need to stop performing. Completely. As you continue to change physically, you are sure to improve at everything you do. Eventually, you will dance better than even the professionals. And then the inevitable questions will begin. People will want to know how you can leap so high, turn so fast, balance so well. They will see you for what you are…as something different. Something not quite human."

A freak.

My heart hammered faster, and I found myself shaking my head without even deciding to. "No." He had to be wrong. No way could my one happiness in life make me an even bigger freak. "I…I can control it. You know, not push myself so hard. I mean, I only did so well tonight because I wanted to impress you and Mom and Nanna. To make you proud of me and show how much I've improved."

"If you really want to make me proud, you will stop dancing. Immediately."

He might as well have slapped me. I struggled to breathe
for a second as I tried to imagine never dancing again. And
couldn't. "But dancing is a really big deal to me, Dad. It's the
only thing I've ever been good at."

"I am sorry. But if you do not stop dancing, your actions
could risk the exposure of our world." He glanced around as
if to point out the potential for eavesdroppers. Like anyone
else would be dumb enough to hang out in a downpour in
East Texas during tornado season just to listen to us. "And if
you risk exposing our world, the council will have no choice
but to step in and stop you."

I bit my lip. Everything seemed to be about the big bad
vampire council. What the council wanted. What the council
demanded. What about what *I* wanted for a change? Whose
side was he on anyways? "Can't you just tell them that I'll be
careful? I can learn to blend in, honest. Just give me time to
practice at it."

"It is too high a risk. You have no idea what the council
is capable of. The only safe course is for you to never dance
again. Ever."

"Mom wasn't worried about my dancing. Aren't you just
being...overly cautious?"

"I am doing what your mother should have done...protect
you. You should never have begun dance lessons in the first
place. I warned your mother that this would happen, but she
was as headstrong as ever." He took a step closer to me and
held out his hands palms up. "Please, Savannah. Do as I ask
and do not persist in this."

Or what, his oh-so-important council might be even more
unhappy with him? What was with him and this stupid coun-

cil? Couldn't he care about his own daughter's needs for a change?

And yet…he was practically begging me. And despite it all…the fact that he hadn't bothered to come to a single game of mine last year, despite every Father's Day event he'd missed when I was a kid and how little I saw him every year…despite how much I loved to dance and the chance it gave me to finally fit in at school, I was tempted. Out of sheer habit from years of trying to make him happy, I was tempted to give up on my dreams, to throw away everything I wanted, just because he wanted me to. He was my father, vampire or not, and I loved him. Even though it made no sense to. It seemed like the perfect opportunity to finally make him proud of me. All I had to do was give up the only thing I'd ever been good at. The only thing I'd ever wanted to do.

But if I stopped dancing, what would I be? What would I have? It was my one chance to fit in somewhere. He had no idea what my life at school was really like, or how becoming a Charmer could change it. He didn't understand what he was asking me to turn away from.

No. I couldn't do it. Not even for him.

"Dancing is all I have, Dad. I'm sorry if that doesn't matter to you or your council. But Mom and Nanna know the risks, and they were still okay with my dancing this year. So as long as they stay okay with it…I'm going to keep dancing."

His face hardened, making him look like a cold statue in the rain. "I am very sorry to hear that."

And there it was, all that I had worked so hard for years to end. His disappointment in me.

Almost too tired to reply, I turned to go inside. "I'm sorry, too." Sorry I couldn't be the kind of daughter he wanted me to be. Sorry I'd cost him so much. Maybe he and Mom shouldn't have decided to have me, after all.

I opened the theater door, but something made me stop and look back at him over my shoulder. Finally I could see a hint of emotion in his eyes. But it was nothing I wanted to see. He looked…worried. And that made my chest ache even worse.

"You don't have to worry, Dad. I promise I'll work hard to blend in. I won't expose your world."

"I believe you will try. Let us hope the council has equal faith that you will succeed." Then he turned and walked away.

My ballet shoes were ruined. I stared at them in the backseat of Nanna's car on the way home.

Dad's words kept echoing inside my head. With every echo, I heard his stinging emphasis on the word *try*. He knew I would try to blend in…but he obviously didn't think I could succeed.

I gritted my teeth and took out my anger on my soaked shoes, my hands crushing them around their middles.

Why should I care what Dad thought? I hardly saw him; we were practically strangers to each other. It was just like with Tristan, this stupid need to care about someone who barely even knew I existed. Both of them had hurt me countless times. Why couldn't I just cut them out of my mind and heart so they couldn't hurt me anymore? Was I some sort of masochist who needed to make myself miserable?

"Hon, what exactly did your father say?" Mom asked from the front passenger seat, her voice gentle even as her words poked at me. I wanted to forget everything he'd said.

"Well, according to him I have a new problem. I used to be terrible at everything. Now he says I'm too good. He wants me to stop dancing, and says if I keep dancing I'll end up exposing the entire vampire world. Or something stupid like that."

Mom's face creased with worry under the flickering light of the streetlamps we passed. She turned to look at Nanna behind the wheel.

"Savannah, maybe…" Nanna began as she guided the car around a corner.

"Yes, maybe you should listen to your father this time," Mom finished.

I stared at Mom. "You've got to be kidding."

"Well, how often has he asked you to do anything?" Mom said.

"Because he knows he has no right to!" The words exploded out of me. But I wouldn't take them back, because it was the truth. Just because my father had helped create me didn't make him a real dad. He had never been there for me when I needed him. What gave him the right to tell me what to do now? And not even for *my* own good. He was only worried his precious council would get mad at him.

"He's just worried about you," Mom insisted.

"Oh, come on! You know that's a load of bull. He's just trying to make his council happy. Bunch of paranoid dictators. Did *you* think that my dancing was too good tonight? That people would look at my dancing and know I was a freak?"

"Stop using that word!" Mom snapped.

I was too mad and desperate to care. I just stared at her and waited for her to answer me.

She sighed. "No, I don't think your dancing is a problem. At least, not yet."

"And that's with me trying to impress everyone," I added. "I know I can learn to blend in with a little practice. Until tonight, I didn't even know I needed to worry about that."

"Hon, you really don't want to upset the vampire council. They aren't the nicest of vampires." Mom's hands twisted together in her lap.

I rolled my eyes. "But they don't rule the world, do they? I mean, who are they to say whether I can dance or not? If you two say it's all right, shouldn't that be what matters? You could watch me practice at home and tell me when to…to tone it down, or whatever."

Mom looked at Nanna.

Nanna gave a sharp nod. "Savannah's right. They shouldn't get to tell us what to do."

"Mother…" Mom whispered, her eyes widening. My heart-beat sped up with hope.

"It'll be all right, Joan." Nanna's eyes narrowed as she stared at the road. Her gnarled hands gripped the steering wheel harder. "Remember who we are, the strong line of women you've both descended from. If Savannah wants to dance, I say she ought to do just that. We've gotta give her a chance to learn how to control herself through all these changes. And have faith in her that she can. Michael's people can just butt out of things and mind their own darn business."

Smiling through fresh tears of a different kind now, I took one last risk. "So, if I wanted to try out for the high-school dance team in three weeks…?"

I stared at them and waited, my heart hammering at the base of my throat.

Mom sighed. "Then I guess you'd better bring me the permission form to sign. And start practicing in the backyard for your Nanna and me."

Letting out a short whoop of victory, I reached through the front seats and hugged Mom, then squeezed Nanna's shoul-der in thanks. So what if my crappy excuse for a father and his council didn't approve? The two women who had raised me, my *real* family, who had always been there for me, sup-ported me now. And that was all I needed. Once I became a

Charmer, I would show him, all the rest of those controlling vamps and everyone else in Jacksonville that I could fit in just fine.

CHAPTER 6

Savannah

Seventy girls all spraying their hair at once made one heck of a smell.

All of the freshmen dancers had been packed into the third floor of Jacksonville High's sports and art building. The twenty-seven Charmer veterans had been given much more room to spread out downstairs in the theater. They also had less distance to walk, since the theater shared a large foyer with the main gym.

Where a panel of judges awaited to determine all our fates.

I was in the second-to-last group, made up of myself and three dancers from various other pre-drill classes. Just my luck to audition during the year they'd decided to order everyone alphabetically in reverse, which they claimed they did every other year to make things more fair. I would have to wait for hours before I'd get to perform before the judges.

The auditions began at 8:00 a.m. The Charmers Head Manager, a junior named Amber, took turns with Captain Kristi in leading the audition groups to and from the gym.

Each time one of them reappeared at the hallway entrance, everyone else jumped. One look at the expressions of excitement and worry around me, and I knew all the freshmen must be wondering the same things: *Is it my group's turn this time? How did the others do? Will I be good enough to make the team?*

Except me. I was only worried about two things...not forgetting the routines, and not looking like some sort of gravity-defying alien.

Finally Head Manager Amber came for my group. I added a quick smear of petroleum jelly over my front teeth as Captain Kristi had recommended in class last week. The hideous, chemical-flavored stuff was supposed to help us smile easier even if our mouths went dry from nerves. Then I followed the head manager and my group down the stairs.

My legs were shaking so much I stumbled and had to use the metal handrail to keep from falling. Until that point, the chant in my head had been, *Please don't let me forget the routine or look like a freak.* After the stumble, the chant changed to, *Please don't let me fall down during my audition.* I knew it could happen. One of the other candidates had slipped during her audition and, upon her return upstairs, had disappeared straight into the bathroom. It had taken a small battalion of the girl's friends to coax the crying dancer to leave an hour later.

Could have been worse for her, though. She could've brought a ceiling tile down on everyone's heads instead. With an audience.

My audition group was allowed two minutes to stretch and warm up in the foyer. But I'd been stretching and practicing for hours now. At this point, all I wanted was to get in there and get the audition over with.

I felt the hairs at the back of my neck prickle, as if someone was watching me. Maybe one of the veterans was peeking out the theater doors? Everyone else in the foyer was visible in front of me and looking elsewhere. I ignored the sensation. No way would I let some curious veteran psyche me out today.

The gym doors squeaked open, and Captain Kristi poked in her head with a bright smile. "Ready, girls?"

We all nodded and lined up, hands on our hips like we'd been taught for our entrance walk. My heart pounded even harder than it had three weeks ago at the dance recital.

We took our positions in the center of the cavernous gym and waited for Captain Kristi to start the music on the sound system. While we waited, I had a chance to study the judges seated several yards away at a folding table. There were five of them…two women, two men and Mrs. Daniels, the Charmers director. I recognized the director from all the times I'd seen her at her desk in the Charmers office outside the dance room this year. None of the judges smiled as they held their pens ready over their papers. Probably too tired by now to smile back. I avoided direct eye contact with them out of habit.

The music began. We started with the jazz routine, and just like at the recital, the adrenaline rush made it all feel like a dream. I was outside myself, watching my body fly and twist. I was pretty sure I wasn't doing freakishly well, but it was hard to tell. I'd been practicing modifying all my moves according to the veteran Charmers standards, not the awkward freshmen I'd been grouped with for today.

The song ended, and we dancers hit our basic standing pose while the judges scratched out notes on our score sheets. In the silence, I could hear the others in my group panting for air. That's when temptation kicked in.

Two of the judges were male. I could try to gaze daze them and affect how they scored my performance.

But it wouldn't really be my dancing they would be scoring then, would it?

Then again, hadn't Captain Kristi told us in pre-drill class to be sure to make eye contact with our audience?

"Left splits, please," Captain Kristi ordered.

My body followed her directions even while my mind continued its quiet debate.

I couldn't look them in the eye. It would be wrong. It was wrong to even consider it. My changed gaze was not some tool to use to get ahead of the other dancers. It was a curse, something weird and wrong that had to be controlled and hidden.

"And your right splits, please."

I stood up then slid down into my right splits, landing flush with the floor and pointing my toes as Captain Kristi had taught us.

I hadn't been nearly this flexible before the change, either. Wasn't I already sort of cheating? And what would one quick little glance into their eyes really hurt? No one would find out about it.

I gritted my teeth against the temptation. No. I would either make the team fairly like a normal dancer, or not at all.

I saw movement at my left. I'd almost missed the cue to perform my center splits. Oh, crud. I had to focus.

Maybe I didn't want to be a Charmer badly enough, after all. If I did, wouldn't I be willing to do anything it took to make the team?

I stood up with my group and waited for the kick routine's music to begin, my heart pounding for a new reason now.

I did want to be a Charmer. More than anything else in the world. I'd practiced countless hours twice a day every day for this moment, for this chance to prove I belonged on the team. I'd even argued with my father for the right to keep dancing, something I never would have done before this year. I *had* to make the team. Otherwise I would forever be the school freak, an outcast who would never fit in anywhere. Heck, I didn't even fit in with my volleyball-obsessed friends!

But if making the dance team meant I had to cheat...

Too soon, before I could decide what to do, the last routine ended. We hit our basic standing pose once more, and I knew this was it. Last chance to sway two of the judges. Just one quick meeting of the eyes with two guys I'd never see again. The effects would only last a day, just like with the algebra boys, just long enough to convince them to give me a better score and help me make the team.

At least, I hoped so.

My gaze slid over the table toward the male judges. They were even sitting beside each other. It was too perfect, too easy. My gaze found their hands, the space separating their bodies, flicked over to the one on the left, slid up his shoulder to his chin...

And then over their heads to the bleachers behind them.

I couldn't do it. What if the gaze daze wouldn't be temporary this time? Both wore wedding rings. If the effect lasted longer than a few hours, could it mess with their families? Their marriages? I hadn't dared meet any male's gaze since that one disastrous mistake last month. Even when I'd wanted to look Tristan in the eye, wrong as that had been. I had no idea if it had gotten stronger with time. All I knew was that my gaze still made my friends look away after a few seconds. And I didn't want to have to cheat in order to be a Charmer.

I'd just have to hope my dancing had been good enough without it.

"Okay, ladies, thank you," Captain Kristi said. "You may exit through the doors now."

It was over.

The line turned, and now I was the one leading the way out of the gym. My chance to sway the judges was gone. Dazed,

I left the gym, heard the metal door slam shut after the last group member exited, and then silence.

Wrapped in invisible cotton, I shuffled back upstairs, deaf to all sound.

I slumped down beside my duffel bag. I'd had the perfect opportunity, a real advantage today. Had I thrown it away in some naive attempt to do the right thing?

An hour later, Head Manager Amber dismissed everyone, reminding us to be back at the gym that evening for the new team announcement, and to wear blue jeans and a plain white T-shirt with our audition numbers pinned to our chests.

Lost in thoughts and doubts on my way out, I wasn't paying attention in the foyer and stumbled into someone. Ice-cold hands on my bare arms both shocked and steadied me as I mumbled an apology and looked up at the man I'd run into. He was a stranger, dressed in a tailored, dark-blue suit. His face was expressionless as he stepped away from me toward the gym doors where the judges were inside tabulating scores. I blinked in surprise as he strode right into the gym like he owned the place.

A woman's voice called out from within, "I'm sorry, but no parents are allowed in here right now."

The door swung shut behind him as he continued in, cutting off any further sound.

Amazing. Apparently being a Charmer was an honor big enough to make a father try to sway the judges for his daughter's sake.

Sway the judges unfairly, just like I should have done. I was so stupid. I shoved open the foyer doors, the moist heat blasting my face and then the rest of my body as I shuffled down the cement ramp to the parking lot and Nanna's waiting car.

"Well, how'd you do?" Nanna asked as I threw myself into

the air-conditioned car, the sweat on my skin turning clammy as I put on my seat belt.

"No clue. I didn't forget any of the steps, at least." I should have used my gaze on those two judges. Even just swaying two of the five judges would've given me an advantage over the other freshmen dancers.

"Then you made the team, hon." She steered the car toward home, her smile confident.

I couldn't help it; I rolled my eyes. "Aren't you a little biased?"

"Of course I am." She laughed. "But I've also got eyes, don't I?"

Which only reminded me of my dumb decision. "Well, I guess we'll find out in a few hours."

"What time do we need to be back here?"

"At six. But you don't have to come inside with me. It probably won't take long."

Her sharp gaze flicked my way, and her smile disappeared. "And miss hearing my grandbaby's name being called out? I don't think so."

Warmth spread in my chest, and a smile tugged at the corners of my mouth. "I think they'll be calling out numbers, not names."

She sniffed. "Same thing. I plan to be there taking lots of pictures for your mother."

My mother, who was, as usual, away selling safety products.

I didn't know what thought was worse to dwell on for the next four hours…whether I'd made the team, made the wrong choice during my audition or performed too well and made the judges question whether I was even human.

I showered, ate a late lunch and listened to my iPod in an effort not to think. It didn't work too well.

At five-thirty, wearing the required outfit, I led Nanna into the gym. We'd arrived half an hour early in the hopes of getting there before everyone else so Nanna could sit on the front row. Her knees were too bad to let her climb up the bleachers.

We should have gotten there even earlier.

It seemed everyone else had the same thought. The entire right side of the gym was packed. It looked like every girl had brought at least one of her parents. Some had brought their entire families plus their grandparents. And the expandable bleachers on the left side of the gym were still folded into the wall. At least none of them were Clann families. Maybe the Clann preferred cheerleading instead?

"Looks like we'll be standing," Nanna muttered.

We stood against the entrance wall near the doors with other similarly unlucky families.

And waited.

Thank goodness Nanna was naturally quiet. Mom would have embarrassed us both by chattering nonstop, most likely about things better left unsaid when standing six inches away from strangers.

But the silence also gave me too much time to think. And wonder. And doubt. And regret.

Just when I thought I couldn't stand the inside of my head anymore and would have to find something to talk about with Nanna, the Charmers director entered the gym.

Funny how fast everyone stopped talking without even being asked.

"Hello, everyone. My name is Elizabeth Daniels, and I'm the director of the JHS Cherokee Charmers Dance/Drill Team." She waited for the polite applause to die away then continued. "Since we're all here for one reason, I'll just skip right to it, okay?"

Someone gave an overly excited cheer, making Mrs. Daniels smile as she pulled a folded sheet of paper from the pocket of her linen slacks.

She unfolded the paper and read the numbers, having to pause after each one while families and friends shrieked and cheered in response. Candidate after candidate climbed down from the stands to form a group under the basketball hoop near the entrance. The members gave each other tearful hugs and whispered among themselves, bonding before the new team had even finished being formed.

Number 101, I thought with rising desperation. *Call my number. 101. Please.* I belonged with that group. Dancing was everything to me. Where else would I ever fit in except on the dance team? I would keep practicing every day, twice a day, morning and night. I'd work to be the best dancer they'd ever had. *Just give me a chance. Call my number.*

"And finally, the last number is…" Mrs. Daniels glanced down at her list. "Number 101."

My heart leaped into my throat, cutting off all airflow.

Mrs. Daniels frowned down at her list. "I'm terribly sorry, that number should have been ninety-one. Number nine-one."

I froze, staring at Mrs. Daniels, willing her to take it back even as someone else screamed with joy and ran forward to take the last spot on the team.

My spot.

In total, stunned horror, I stared at number ninety-one as the bouncy, tearful blonde joined the team. I knew that girl; we were in the same pre-drill class together. Bethany Brookes.

I turned to Nanna. "Tell me she didn't call my number first, then change her mind."

"Yes, she did. I'm going to go make her double-check that list." Nanna marched over to speak with Mrs. Daniels, but I couldn't bear to watch. I couldn't take my gaze off the happy group of girls. Next year's Charmers. A team I wasn't good enough to be on.

Nanna returned, her furious expression all the answer I needed.

I had to get out of here. I rushed out of the gym, pushing through the crowd already trickling into the foyer. I could feel those prickles of awareness once again telling me someone was watching me. Probably Nanna. Or maybe a stranger. Had the tears already started before I could get to our car? Were people in the crowd pitying the sad loser as I made my way through? I couldn't tell. I couldn't feel any part of my body now beyond the burning of my lungs.

I reached the car, lurching into the oven of a backseat for some reason. Only when I'd laid down on the warm charcoal-colored upholstery and covered my face with a folded arm did I let go.

Someone else was in my dream with me later that night. As soon as I saw him, the dream changed, the colors and edges around things sharpening, becoming more like a waking memory instead of a fuzzy dream.

Oh, no. Not *him*. I could not take another of these too-realistic dreams about invisible barriers between myself and Tristan Coleman.

But it *was* him. This time, he was stretched out on a patch of short grass in the bright moonlight. A yard somewhere. Trees, maybe some kind of forest, formed a dark and peaceful backdrop behind him. But definitely a dream location, because even at night, East Texas in May was muggy and stifling. Yet here the air was cool and light against my skin.

Tristan looked incredibly good, though he wore just a gray T-shirt and black sweats, nothing special or dressy. It had never been his looks that drew me, though. That was the problem with him. If Tristan had been just another pretty boy, I could've ignored his entire existence. Our school had plenty of those to crush on. But I'd never cared much about how a guy looked.

Except this one.

I liked to think I wasn't stupid. It had to be some inner rebellion thing on a subconscious level that I had going on. I just wanted him because he was off-limits. Right? That had to be why my heart insisted on racing every time someone mentioned his name, why I continued to look forward to algebra class. And why my dumb subconscious insisted on torturing me with these dreams about him.

Well, I wasn't that stupid. No matter how realistic and vivid it seemed, I knew this was a dream. A very unwelcome dream, especially after the day I'd just had. But still a dream.

Usually in these dreams, I wound up kicking and scream-ing at the invisible barrier between us, and he ignored my existence. This time, I wasn't in the mood to play along.

So I sat down, drew up my knees to my chest, tugged my oversize T-shirt over my bare legs, then rested my cheek on them. Maybe if I accepted in my dreams that Tristan wasn't meant for me, I'd finally stop dreaming about him.

That would be nice. Seeing him at school always hurt more after nights like these. It would be a huge relief not to feel this yearning in the pit of my stomach and chest anymore.

I closed my eyes, intending to ignore him. But after a min-ute, my eyelids crept open again. Maybe just one last peek at him. After all, it was only here in my dreams that I could safely stare at him without his knowing it.

Except this time…he stared back at me.

Maybe he was just looking in my general direction.

I met his gaze, and his eyes widened. Holy crap. Nope,

he was looking right at me. He'd never looked at me in my dreams before, not even once. But he was now, and…

And I was wearing nothing but a T-shirt and underwear.

Maybe trying to confront my dreams about him had forced my subconscious mind to react with more drastic measures. Like morphing my dreams into a new take on the "in my underwear at school" nightmare.

I pulled my T-shirt down farther. I should look away from him, too. But I couldn't, because he was staring back at me, his green gaze unblinking as he rolled to sit up.

Of course he'd be graceful even in that one small movement. Everything Jacksonville's golden prince did was perfect. Oh, well, at least my imagination had gotten the details right.

Like the way his honey-blond hair curled over his ears and at the nape of his neck, stopping just short of brushing the collar of his shirt. And the way his sleeves stretched around his biceps. I sighed and laid my cheek on top of my knees again, giving in to the temptation to stare at him. Maybe my subconscious knew just what I'd needed today, after all.

He stood up in one fluid movement, making my heart trip at the base of my throat. He approached me, his steps cautious. But no barrier stopped him. Ah, a good dream.

And so detailed. As he stood before me, towering above me, our bare toes almost touching in the grass, I noticed for the first time the veins running along the backs of his hands. He held out one of those hands as if to help me up.

I laughed and shook my head. Even if it was a dream, no way was I going to stand up until my subconscious gave me some pants to wear.

"Then I guess I'll have to come to you." He sat down beside me, facing me as he mimicked my pose and wrapped his arms around his bent knees.

Amazing. He even sounded right. I had a better memory

than I'd given myself credit for. His voice held exactly the right amount of rumbling deepness. And just like in real life, he sounded as if he was trying not to laugh at me.

Well, I *was* the one in my underwear here.

"Why do you keep staring at me? Aren't you going to say something?" I blurted out. This dream was getting a little ridiculous. Who fantasized about a boy sitting there staring at them? Shouldn't that be more in the first-date nightmare category? Not that I'd know about first dates from personal experience, seeing as how I'd never been on any.

His thick eyebrows shot up. "What should I say?"

"Oh, I don't know. But if this is a dream, it could at least be interesting." Where were my pants already?

He chuckled, tempting me to smile. "You're a lot more talkative than usual."

I shrugged. "It's my dream. Shouldn't I be allowed to say what I think and feel?"

"I thought this was my dream."

"Great. So even in my dream, you have to be cocky."

"Cocky? Look who's talking, Miss Nothing-but-a-T-shirt-and-Attitude."

"Yeah, you'd think since I know it's a dream, I could fix that."

He grinned. "Oh, I don't know, it's not a bad look on you."

"Mmm, a compliment. Finally. I thought players gave those out a lot more often." I returned his grin. "Quick, say something else nice." My toes scrunched down in the grass. I could get used to having this kind of dream.

"Bossy."

I had to laugh. "I said say something *nice.*"

It was his turn to laugh now. "You didn't want the truth?"

Hmm, good point. "No, actually, a large dose of truth

would be lovely right now. But maybe with a touch less rudeness."

"Had a bad day?" His smile faded.

"You can say that again." I sighed and yanked up a piece of grass. "My life would've been a lot easier to handle lately if everyone had just told me the truth all my life. At least then I could have grown up knowing…things, and be better prepared for them, you know?"

"Okay, so we'll stick with the truth, then, if that'll make your day better."

"Yes, please," I breathed out on a sigh.

"Why don't you make eye contact with anyone at school?"

My head popped up, and I instinctively turned my face away. "I didn't mean I wanted to play Truth or Dare."

"Chicken?"

"No." I met his gaze and discovered I couldn't breathe. When he grinned at me like that, with the laughter shining in his eyes…it was almost too much, the feelings too intense to handle. Like he could see my every thought and emotion.

"That's better," he murmured. "So tell me about your day."

"I'd rather not think about it, to be honest. Tell me about yours instead. You looked like yours was much better." I waved a hand at the spot where he'd been lying and looking so peaceful a few minutes before.

"Yeah, it was pretty good. Which is a surprise, since it was training with my dad."

"Training…for football?"

The smile melted out of his eyes first, then from his mouth. He gave a short, stiff nod.

"So tell me why it made you happy." I didn't want my subconscious to turn this into an uncomfortable dream.

It was his turn to pluck a blade of grass and play with it. "Oh, I don't know. I guess it was just cool that I could have fun hanging out with my dad. He always used to sort of scare me. But lately we've become almost like friends."

"I've seen pictures of your dad in the newspaper. He does look a little scary with that beard. Kind of like a big polar bear."

Tristan laughed with me. "Yeah, exactly. But it turns out he's pretty funny. Like how protective he is of my mom and sister and does all this stuff to keep them safe, and they don't even know it. So he's playing the big bad undercover body-guard because he thinks they're so fragile, and yet he has to be sneaky while he's doing it because he's afraid they'll find out and get mad."

That really made me laugh. "You men always think women are weak and need to be protected."

"Aren't you?" Smirking, he reached out and brushed my toes with a piece of grass.

I sucked in a breath and jerked my feet in closer. Oh, no, he remembered how ticklish I was. Though saying I was ticklish was a major understatement.

"Hmm, still ticklish? There you go, a sure sign you're a fragile female in need of protection. Can't even stand a little piece of grass on your toes."

He tickled me again, forcing sharp laughter out of me. I swatted at his hands. Laughing, he captured both my hands with one of his and continued tickling my toes with the other. I wanted to focus on the warmth of his hand on mine, the thrilling strength in those fingers, but that blade of grass couldn't be ignored.

Out of reflex, my feet pulled in then shot out to try and avoid his merciless attack. My heels thwacked against his right shin.

"Oh, sorry!" I yanked my feet back in as I reached out

to pull up the elastic cuff of his sweats. "Ouch. It's already turning blue."

He grinned and rubbed his shin. "No worries, it's just a dream, right? Besides, it was worth it."

"Why?"

"It got you to bare your legs for a few seconds."

I gasped, and heat flooded my cheeks.

Tristan

I was still laughing at her when I woke up in the backyard.

I lay there for a few seconds, grinning like an idiot. I'd done it. I'd dream connected with Savannah. And all I'd had to do to avoid Mom's spell was fall asleep in the backyard again.

My parents would kill me if they found out.

That wiped the grin off my face. With a sigh, I rolled to sit up. Okay, so I'd pushed the rules a bit. But couldn't a guy have a little bit of fun every now and then? I'd been good for weeks. I'd kept my distance from Savannnah. I'd even tried dating some other girls. But none of them were quite like her.

Savannah would think last night had been just a dream, so what would it hurt? She'd wake up clueless that we'd actually connected in our dreams. And I'd woken up feeling better than I had in years…

…with a monster-size bruise growing on my shin.

Savannah

I woke up Sunday morning with a smile. One that faded too soon, along with last night's dream about Tristan, to be replaced by the memory of my failure to make the Charmers team yesterday.

Too bad I couldn't bottle up the peace and contentment I'd felt with Tristan in my dream and carry it around with me in real life. I felt anything but peaceful or content all day long. By the time Dad called that evening for his weekly check-in, I had to fight to keep my tone polite. He was the absolute last person I wanted to speak to right now.

"Savannah, you sound…upset."

I glared at the popcorn ceiling over my bed. "I tried out for my high school's dance team yesterday."

"And?" He drew the word out like a man attempting to verbally defuse a bomb. Which was perfect, considering how I wanted to explode with fury right now.

"And I wasn't good enough. So I guess your council will be thrilled." Part of me was shocked at myself. I'd never spoken so rudely to him in my life.

"While I realize it is not what you want to hear right now, that really is for the best."

My jaw dropped, and my eyes burned for a few seconds while I tried to find a response. But I couldn't. Why couldn't he be a loving father, normal, caring about my feelings instead of what his council wanted all the time? Like that father at the auditions. Again I saw that man walk into the gym, intent on doing battle to make his daughter happy. And then the image froze in my mind. Something about that man…something was off.

Wait. That was it.

May in East Texas averaged in the low nineties with eighty percent humidity. No man would've been able to wear a full suit like that without sweating at least a little. That guy hadn't, though. His hands had been ice-cold, just like Dad's always were. Even if he'd just come from an air-conditioned car, the parking lot was too far from the foyer doors. That man would have already warmed up by the time I ran into him.

"Trust me, Savannah. What I said about the council is the

truth. It is better that you do not dance, or play any sports, either. One day you will thank me."

Distracted, I frowned at the ceiling, seeing the man's face again. His eyes…hadn't they been that same weird shade of silver like both Dad's and my eyes turned? "You make the council sound all-powerful or something."

"They are powerful. Extremely so."

A horrible, crazy idea formed, and the words slipped out before I could reconsider asking. "Powerful enough to send someone to talk to a few judges at a dance audition?" I expected him to laugh and tell me how ridiculous that was.

Instead, the silence stretched on and on.

I sat up with a jerk, nauseous, my head swimming. Oh, no. No way was I *that* important to a bunch of immortal vampires I'd never even met, no matter what I might or might not be turning into. I'd assumed the man was there to convince the judges to let someone on the team. Not to keep someone off it.

"You told me once that you'd never lie to me, Dad. So tell me the truth now. Your council wouldn't do something like that, would they?"

He didn't reply.

"Dad?" I gripped the phone tighter, making the plastic creak in protest. "Did they?"

"I did warn you that they would step in if you forced them to."

Fury raced through me, quick and hot. "I can't believe this! You didn't even *try* to tell them that I could control myself, did you? Why didn't you tell them that I would be careful, that I could learn to blend in?"

"The council are very cautious, Savannah. They do not like any threats to the secrecy of our world, and they are not tolerant of risk. There was nothing I could say to convince them that you might learn to control your abilities well enough to blend in with the humans on a dance team."

I took a deep breath and tried to rein in my anger. But I couldn't remove the edge from my voice. "Did you even try to convince them?"

"You must understand, my reports are not in verbal form. They simply read my mind. Sometimes they allow me to verbally add information to help interpret those images and memories. But they feel that what they read from others' minds is the purest, most objective and truthful form of reporting possible. They saw how your dancing stood out from your classmates' at the recital, and the risk was high enough that they made their decision. You are not to dance either with your school dance team, on any other dance team or at any dance studio."

I gritted my teeth. "And if I keep taking dance classes at Miss Catherine's anyways?"

Silence filled the phone for a minute that seemed to stretch into thirty before he replied. "That would be very unwise. Both for your own safety, as well as your family's."

My mouth fell open. "Are you saying..."

"I am saying that they are determined. That nothing is allowed to risk the exposure of our world. And that they will do anything—and I do mean anything—that is necessary to protect the secrecy of that world."

Holy crap. They would actually threaten my entire family. Just to keep me from dancing. This went way beyond paranoia.

"So may I please have your promise that you will abstain from any further extracurricular physical activities?"

"Uhh..." Shock made my thoughts fuzzy. "I have to finish out the year in pre-drill class. It counts for my P.E. credit."

"And school ends in two weeks?"

I managed a grunt of agreement.

"Does this pre-drill class require any additional public performances?"

I shook my head then realized he couldn't see it. "No."

"That should be permissible, then. They only want to avoid public displays of your growing abilities. However, you must try very hard to hide your talents even in class before your peers. We do not want them to begin to question you, either."

Unbelievable. This was ridiculous.

Another silence filled the phone before Dad sighed. "Savannah...I still have not heard you promise me that you will stop dancing after school ends."

Shock gave way to fury again. This man on the phone with me wasn't my father; he was just a spy for the council sent to do their bidding, calling for updates on how I was changing. He didn't care about me. Why should I care about him or help him do his job?

And yet, I couldn't endanger my real family, either.

Grinding my back teeth, I took a deep breath then let it out. "Fine. Yes, Michael, I promise, no more dancing. Or anything else that involves public displays of my *abilities*. Will that make your council happy?"

"Yes. I believe it will. But since when did you start calling me by my first name?"

"When you stopped being my dad. Then again, you never really were, were you? So tell your council that I'll obey their rules. But if they want reports on how I'm doing, they'll have to settle for getting them from Nanna or Mom. Because I don't want to talk to you anymore."

I hung up the phone, my whole body shaking. And then I burst into tears.

A few minutes later, Mom called on her way home from a

meeting with a customer. "Did you just tell your father that you refuse to speak to him ever again?"

"Yes."

"Hon, I know you're upset about giving up dancing for the council, but—"

"No, not for the council, Mom. For you and Nanna. They threatened you guys, and he passed on the message for them! A real dad would never do that. He's not my father anymore. He's just some guy who helped create me, then spent the last fifteen years spying on me."

"That's not true. We don't know exactly what's going on with the council. We have to trust that your father is trying to do what's best for you and our family."

I seriously doubted that. "Fine, whatever. But that doesn't mean I have to talk to him."

She sighed. "You can't just cut your father out of your life—"

"Watch me."

"The council—"

"I'm giving up everything I wanted because of that council! And from now on, that's *all* they're getting from me."

Silence filled the phone. "Fine. I'll start passing on the updates to him while you cool off."

But I didn't think I would be getting over this anytime soon. He'd hurt me way too many times, and I just couldn't take it anymore. Cutting him out of my life today hurt. But it was also freeing, like throwing off a heavy backpack I'd carried around for way too long.

I went out to the backyard to dance in the dark where no one but the moon and stars could see me. It might have been childish, but it was either dance or sit in my bedroom and scream. At least the council couldn't stop me from doing *this*.

Slowly, I spun in a circle and stared up at the stars. But even that couldn't distract me from the two thoughts that kept echoing through my mind…

I'd just agreed to no more dancing. Ever.

How would I ever fit in at JHS now?

CHAPTER 7

Savannah

The following Tuesday, I found the answer. Mrs. Daniels had posted a notice on the dance-room doors inviting all pre-drill girls who hadn't made the dance team to apply for Charmers team manager. The applications were due Friday, and the new managers would be announced the following Monday. A quick glance through her open office door showed a stack of applications on the corner of her desk, just waiting for anyone to pick one up.

I was actually tempted.

On the one hand, becoming a Charmers manager would be totally masochistic. I'd have to watch the dancers practice every day while I stood around on the sidelines fetching stuff.

But on the other hand...what else did I have to do? I couldn't dance anymore. I'd promised not to do any other sports, either. I wasn't into art, chess, debate or the school yearbook. At least if I became a Charmers manager, I could be around dancing on a daily basis, if not directly participating in it. Which should keep the vamp council off my back, too, since I would technically be keeping my promise to them.

And at least I'd have something to do with all my extra time next year.

Before I could change my mind, I grabbed an application packet.

That afternoon, I rode home with Nanna in silence, the Charmers manager application burning a hole in my backpack. After supper while Nanna was gardening in the backyard, I found myself wandering through the house lost in thought about it.

Tiny prickles of sensation spread over my arms, as if I were at school and Tristan was around. Weird. Frowning, I went to the patio door to tell Nanna about it, then stopped.

She'd turned the gardening tools into a magically automated army of helpers.

It was past sunset out there, but moonlight flooded the huge garden that took up most of the backyard, giving me plenty of light, enough to see a small basket and a pair of garden clippers floating just above the plants nearest the house, the clippers darting here and there to snip off herbs that then drifted into the basket. Even in the moonlight, the clippers's neon-orange handles contrasted sharply with the surrounding greenery. Nanna had painted them herself so she wouldn't lose them in the yard. A Martha Stewart tip. Nanna was crazy about Martha.

Somehow, I doubted Martha had ever considered using magic to automate *her* tools while gathering herbs under the full moon, though.

Nanna was several yards away, kneeling on a cushion while she took more clippings. To her right, a shovel stabbed at some weeds near the fence that had turned into small bushes.

And she didn't even seem to need to look at her tools in order to magically tell them what to do. I'd always wondered how she had managed such a huge garden all year long by herself.

I slid open the patio door. Nanna glanced over her shoulder at me. "Oh! Hi, sweetie." She waved a hand, and all the tools fell to the ground lifeless.

"Aw, you don't have to stop them for me. That was really cool, Nanna! I didn't know you could do all that! How do you keep them going without even looking?"

Smiling, she resumed cutting some herbs in front of her. "Trade secrets, dear. I wish I could tell you, but..."

I sighed. "Clann rules."

She nodded.

"Well, you could at least keep going. I mean, you don't have to tell me how or anything. Just watching them was fun." And it was. For a minute there, I'd felt just like a little kid again, wanting to giggle and clap.

Her smile turned apologetic. "No, I'd better not. Wouldn't want any descendants to get suspicious and wonder whether I'm keeping my promise. Besides, it just seems rude to do magic in front of you when you're not allowed to use it, too."

Stupid rules.

"You've been awfully quiet today," she said as she continued to work.

"Mmm." Which reminded me about the Charmers manager application. And the promises I'd made to my father and the vampire council. Should I even bother asking Nanna for permission to apply? Or would she tell me it was against the vampire council rules just because it was related to dancing?

"Why don't you grab those clippers and help me gather herbs?"

I picked up the now lifeless clippers and basket and brought them closer to Nanna so we could still talk easily. I took a few cuttings, but kept getting distracted by the view around me. I should come out here at night more often. It was really nice. The air was clean with a hint of dew in it. It felt good to breathe it in, like it was cleaning out my lungs. And hopefully my head.

"Taking cuttings always clears my mind," she murmured. "Quick, name the plants you see."

It was an old game she'd taught me ages ago, and it still made me smile. "Lemon verbena. Chamomile. Basil. Wolfsbane." I slowly spun in a circle, pointing out every plant I could see in the moonlight around us.

Smiling, she nodded her head in approval, every bit as regal as a queen. "Now…back to what's eating you today. Want to talk about it?"

"Um, yeah, I guess. But don't get mad or anything, okay?"

She gave me a sharp look. "Okay, spit it out."

"Well, the Charmers are taking applications this week for managers. They're going to pick them this weekend then announce their picks next week."

"And you want to apply."

This was where it got tricky. "I…don't know."

She laughed quietly. "What don't you know about it? Are you unsure you want to do the job, or are you unsure you'd be allowed to do the job?"

"Uh, both?"

Smiling, she sat back on her heels. "Do the managers dance?"

"No. Well, I think sometimes they might get the chance to fill in as alternate dancers. But obviously I'd have to tell the director no if she asked me to."

Nanna nodded. "And the rest of the job…what would you be doing?"

"Helping the team at fundraisers, practices and performances. Probably a lot of fetching stuff, cleaning up the costume and prop closets. Putting out good-luck notes for the football and basketball players' lockers on game days. Stuff like that."

"And every day you'd watch them dancing?"

I nodded.

"Would that make you happy?"

I chewed my lower lip for a few seconds, then sighed. "Yes and no. It's as close as I could get to it, at least. And I wouldn't be breaking any rules, right?"

She nodded, tying a clump of plants together before tossing them into the basket.

"And...I guess I'd sort of be a part of the Charmers team."

Nanna didn't say anything for a long time as she gathered more herbs. Finally she sighed. "This situation your parents put you in...I always knew it would come to something like this, that it would be hard on you, and unfair."

Her words made my throat tighten. I swallowed hard to try and loosen it.

"I think if you can be okay with the not-dancing-yourself part, then you might like being a manager for the dance team. It'd give you something to do, like a hobby. Maybe it would open up other options for you, too."

"Like what?" I scowled down at the clippers in my hand, testing their spring-loaded squeeze action.

"Like becoming a dance-team director or choreographer someday. If dancing is still your thing then, of course. There are ways to be a part of the dancing world without personally dancing. There are always ways to deal with the rules life gives you. Just because you can't have one thing in life doesn't mean you have to give it all up."

I looked at her with one eyebrow raised.

She raised her hands. "I'm just saying, is all."

"So you think I should do it?"

Slowly she rose to her feet, her knees cracking and popping. I knew from repeated experience that she'd only get annoyed if I offered to help her up. Stubborn Evans women. "I'm saying you've got my permission if you want to apply. It's up to you as to whether you go for it or not."

"Gee, thanks for the help in deciding." I shot her a wry grin as we headed for the house.

"And thank you for all the help with the herbs back there." With an equally wry grin of her own, she nodded at the still mostly empty basket hanging from my forearm.

I laughed. "Sorry. I was too busy thinking."

At the door, she patted my shoulder. "If you do decide to apply and need help with the application, let me know."

"Thanks, Nanna."

She opened the patio door, and we went inside. After we put away the cutting tools on a shelf near the door, she took the baskets of clippings and set to work hanging them to dry over the kitchen sink. I helped her tie my loose clippings into bunches with bits of green and blue yarn she had left over from old crochet projects. Then we got to the last bunch.

With a naughty grin that gave glimpses of the mischievous young girl she probably was once upon a time, Nanna waved a finger as if it were a magic wand, and the cuttings drifted to the window and tied themselves into place.

Who knew my grandma was so *cool?*

Grinning, I went to my room, flopped on my bed and pictured again the seemingly effortless way she had used magic right there in front of me, like it was as easy as breathing for her. There was no telling what else she could do, too. Did she use magic to make tea or cook or crochet when I wasn't around? She could definitely get a lot more done and faster that way. It had to be frustrating, or at the very least boring, for her to resist using it even when I could see.

If I could do magic, I'd do it all the time...to finish my homework, to help untangle and style my hair.

Maybe on the Brat Twins and Dylan, too.

Which of course was why I wasn't allowed to do magic.

Stupid rules.

But Nanna said the rules didn't have to stop me from doing everything. Like being a Charmers manager. The Clann and the vamps never said I couldn't do that. And the Clann kids seemed to prefer to rule the cheerleading squads instead of dancing, because not a single descendant was a Charmer. Maybe it was easier for them to get away with using magic in cheerleading without being so obvious?

Then again, from what little I'd seen and heard about the Charmers director, Mrs. Daniels, maybe the real reason no descendants ever made the team was because she wouldn't let them. She seemed like the type of person who wanted total control over her team. And everyone knew how the descendants' parents had a habit of taking over everything their kids were involved in.

Whatever the reason, the Charmers was a Clann-free zone. And that was reason enough for me to want to be a part of it in any way I could. *If* I could handle watching others dance without feeling miserable all the time.

After a few minutes of lying on the bed feeling restless, I gave in to the urge, dug the application out of my backpack and read over it. And felt my jaw drop.

I'd expected one of those simple forms that asked the usual boring questions about me...name, address, phone number, my hobbies and interests, maybe job skills or a short essay or two.

What I found was something way different. And challenging in an intriguing kind of way.

The packet was six pages long and filled with things like, "Suggest a good-luck game-day note for the volleyball teams," "Create a costume design using a long-sleeve unitard for the base, and only adding costume parts that can be quickly taken off or put on in between dance routines" and "Suggest a Charmers Spring Show theme, then design coordinating stage decoration."

I had plenty of ideas for the application. But I had only four days to get it all on paper in some kind of way that wouldn't look like a kindergartner did it.

I came back to the kitchen, where Nanna was busy prepping some of the freshly cut herbs for use in her various teas. I held up the application and winced. "Uh, you know how you offered to help?"

Nanna was true to her word. With her help, I managed to finish my application notebook just in time for Friday's deadline. But it was close, with a few late nights thrown in at the end to make sure I got it done in time. And I was pretty sure I'd never get out the glue and glitter from under my fingernails.

Mrs. Daniels had said in the packet's directions that she was looking for creativity. Well, she'd gotten it. I'd done everything possible to demonstrate my creativity in that notebook, from shaping it like the Charmers knee-high white boots to using glitter paint and including paper dolls complete with changeable costume designs. The paper dolls were Mom's idea; hopefully the director would think they were creative instead of childish or crazy.

My name and pre-drill class number were on the cover, so

I felt safe leaving the completed notebook on the director's desk after school on Friday.

Then all I could do was wait until Monday's pre-drill class.

Where I found a list of three names posted on the dance-room door under the heading Next Year's Charmers Managers. Two girls' names I didn't recognize topped the list.

And my name was at the bottom.

I should have been excited. After all, Nanna's and my hard work on the application notebook had won me a spot on the Charmers team, one that the vampire council shouldn't have a problem with. And being a Charmers manager might even turn out to be fun.

But in that moment, I didn't feel much of anything. I'd become a Charmers manager. Right now, all that meant was that I'd have something to do with my free time next year.

The weekend after school ended, I met the other two Charmers managers for the first time at the sophomore Charmers summer kick-off party. All thirteen new Charmers plus the managers had crowded into a small, two-story lake house owned by Bethany Brookes's parents on Lake Jacksonville.

I had only been to parties with my best friends and had no clue how to make small talk with strangers. But after introducing themselves, the other two managers, Keisha and Vicki, seemed as uncomfortable to be there as I was. Somehow, that made me feel a little less out of place.

When everyone trooped outside to the private pier, I was worried that I'd be the only one to sit in the shady area where the shoreline trees overhung the pier and lake house. All the dancers chose to strip down to their bikinis and roast themselves on towels by the water. But Vicki and Keisha sat beside me in the shade, too. And like me, they also opted to keep on

their T-shirts and shorts over their swimsuits. Thank goodness. What with my natural paleness and tendency to burn
at least once every summer, no way would I be baring any
more skin here. Besides, I wouldn't want to accidentally blind
anyone today. Everyone else looked like they spent their lives
in a tanning bed.

While Keisha and Vicki chatted about their families, I overheard bits of conversations from the others on the pier. I'd
expected everyone to be chatting about the upcoming sophomore year and what being a Charmer would be like. Instead,
all they talked about was boys, who was dating whom, which
couples had broken up and which girls in school slept around.
At first, it made me tense. How would I ever manage to fit in
on this team when I wasn't one of the dancers and I'd never
even been on a date, much less had a boyfriend?

But after a few minutes, I realized listening to the Charmers was like listening to thirteen Michelles all vying to share
the best tidbit of gossip. That made me smile and relax a
little. After all, I didn't usually know half the people Michelle
gossiped about every day at lunch, either, but she was pretty
entertaining to listen to.

I learned more in that hour about my fellow classmates than
I'd ever wanted to know. Just wait till I could relay it all to
Michelle; she'd be thrilled for weeks.

A low buzzing in the distance on the lake changed the
group's general topic of conversation as five boys approached
on Jet Skis.

I had to fight hard not to laugh as the girls changed their
poses to ones they seemed to think were sexier, their hands
darting up to readjust their bikinis and smooth their hairstyles.
As if they'd actually had a single strand out of place.

When the Jet Skis were a few yards away, several of the
girls suddenly found their conversation partners terribly funny.

But their natural giggles had changed to high-pitched, fake laughter.

Did I act that way around Tristan?

The boys pulled up to the pier. But no way could I keep watching the scene unfold and not laugh out loud. So I focused on Keisha and Vicki again instead, who had somehow gotten into a hot debate about whether wearing pink helped support sexist stereotypes. Judging by the conversation and the fact that Vicki was wearing a hot-pink bikini, it seemed Vicki loved the color and Keisha hated it.

"Hey, Savannah," a male voice called out.

I looked up. Greg Stanwick floated three feet away from me on a now-silent Jet Ski that rocked with the waves against the pier. His black hair was slicked back from his grinning face.

He hadn't spoken to me in months, not since the day we'd met last spring. Why would he be speaking to me now? Especially when he had thirteen other girls, most in revealing bikinis, whom he could talk to instead.

"Um, hi," I replied.

"Do you remember me? We met in the cafeteria a while back." He flashed me a huge grin that begged to be returned.

"Sure. Greg, right?"

"Yeah, Greg Stanwick. So how've you been?"

"Good, and you?"

"Doing great. Getting ready to graduate next year. Still playing soccer."

I nodded politely, wondering where in the world he was going with all of this.

"Is this party for something special?" His gaze flicked over the group then returned to me.

"Just the new Charmers and managers having a summer get-together." I could feel several pairs of eyes staring at me.

"Nice. You're a Charmer now?"

The muscles in my shoulders tightened. "Nope, just a manager."

He studied me for half a minute then grinned. "Want a ride?"

That made me blink. His grin stretched wider. I glanced over at our audience in time to see two other girls climbing onto Jet Skis with his friends. Apparently temporarily leaving the party was no big deal.

I'd never been on a Jet Ski before, but it looked like fun. "Uh, sure."

I gave Keisha and Vicki a quick wave, then got to my feet and walked over to the edge of the pier beside Greg.

He eyed my clothing. "You got a swimsuit on?"

"Yeah, why?"

"Might want to leave your shirt and shorts here or they'll get wet."

Uh-huh, still not happening. Blinding the guy by showing more of my pale skin before letting him drive us around on a fast-moving machine with no brakes was so not a good idea. "That's okay, I won't mind."

He shrugged, put a foot on the pier, and dragged the end of his Jet Ski around until it was parallel with the wooden platform. "Your chariot, my lady."

A laugh escaped me. "Um, how do I…"

He reached out, took my hand and placed it on his nearest shoulder. His hard muscle flexed beneath my touch. "Hold on and swing a leg over the seat."

Once I was seated behind him, he shot me a grin over his shoulder. "Might want to hang on."

As he started the engine, I had a sudden vision of myself flying off the end and doing a back flop into the water. The Charmers would laugh at me for months about it.

Wrapping my arms around his warm waist, I held on as the Jet Ski lurched forward with a loud gurgle.

I'd braced myself for a wave-jumping, crazy ride, but it was actually nice. Greg took me around the lake, pointing out houses whose owners he could name, plus his own family's house set back several yards from the shoreline. He stopped the Jet Ski about twenty yards from the shore so I could look at it.

"Is that your vacation home?" I didn't know much about Jacksonville High's senior class.

He had a great laugh, warm and genuine. "No, that's our permanent home."

"Must be nice living near the lake all the time."

"It's mostly nice. Though the water moccasins sometimes make our backyard parties a little too exciting."

"I can see why. And is that when you impress everyone with your manly snake-killing skills?"

"Uh, no." He twisted halfway toward me, his smile lopsided. "That's when my dog Jake impresses everyone with *his* snake-killing skills, while I run off screaming like a girl and grab a shovel."

I laughed. Waves from a passing boat bobbed the Jet Ski, making my thighs bump his hips. Hello. We were sitting a little too close. Self-conscious now, I loosened my hold on his waist, dropping my hands to my knees instead.

"So...are you seeing anyone?"

His question startled me so much I nearly forgot and met his gaze full-on. At the last second, my gaze stopped at his nose out of sheer habit. "No. Why?"

"So I'll know if I can ask you out on a date."

Suddenly I wished I hadn't answered him so quickly. Talk about uncharted waters here. If he asked, what would I—

"Would you like to?"

"To…?" I needed more time to think. Was I even interested in dating him? My friends all considered him gorgeous, and obviously the sophomore Charmers thought so, too. But he wasn't six feet tall with curly blond hair and green eyes I dreamed about on a regular basis. His voice was deep enough, but not that exact low rumble that made me shaky inside. Hanging out with him was nice, but he didn't make me yearn to be around him or know what he was thinking about.

He wasn't Tristan Coleman.

But he also wasn't in the Clann and off-limits. The council never said I couldn't date regular humans. And because he didn't make my body go all wonky when I was around him like Tristan did, being with Greg was easier, more comfortable. Like being a Charmers manager, I could take him or leave him. Which made him a much safer bet in case things didn't work out.

"Would you like to go out with me?" He had a nice smile. It made his brown eyes softer. But did I really want to go on a date with him?

"Maybe." I was answering my question more than his. But once I said it, it seemed a good enough answer for both of us. If I waited for the impossible, I would never have a life. Greg was here. He was interested. He was funny at times and good-looking. Why not go out with him and see what happened? "Okay, sure. Sounds like fun. Now are you going to take me back to the party or what? They're going to think you kidnapped me. Besides, I think I'm starting to burn a little here."

Eyebrows raised, he glanced at my arms. "Ouch, you're right. Next time, wear more sunscreen, okay? Then I can show you more of the lake."

Hmm. Next time, huh?

Smiling, I wrapped my arms around his waist again and

hung on. And surprisingly, I didn't stop smiling until he dropped me off at Bethany's pier. Hanging out with Greg was a lot of fun. Maybe going on a date with him would be just as nice.

My smile disappeared when I realized how many pairs of eyes watched us. "Thank you for the ride."

"Anytime. See you around, Savannah Colbert."

I returned his smile, waiting for him to leave before I went to sit by Keisha again.

"Well," Keisha said, as if that was all she needed to say.

It was enough to push me into explaining in a whisper, "I met him a couple months ago. I think he just took me around on the Jet Ski to be nice."

"Uh-huh," she replied, her eyes more than a little curious.

Vicki leaned forward to stare at me past Keisha. "Ha, I saw his face. He wasn't just being polite. Did he ask you out?"

"Um…" I really didn't want to answer that with an audience of gossipy girls eavesdropping. I glanced at my watch then the circle driveway, visible past Vicki, and spotted Nanna pulling up right on time for the end of the party. "Oh, there's my grandmother. I'd better run. See you two next week at boot camp."

I jumped to my feet and said a general goodbye to everyone before making a quick escape.

The following week, Greg didn't call, of course. But I knew he wouldn't for one simple reason…I hadn't given him my home phone number, which was listed under Nanna's name. And none of my friends would give out my number.

I should have been upset about our date's delay. But running around in the sweltering hundred-plus-degree heat all week at the high school for the Charmers boot camp left me too tired to care about anything but cold showers and sleep each evening. And when I could think straight long enough to wonder about Greg, I kept picturing him calling every Colbert in the phone book and asking for me. No doubt that mammoth ego of his was getting frustrated. The idea made me grin.

I wondered if it would take him until the start of school in two months to find a way to get my phone number, or if he'd just give up. How fragile was Greg's ego? And how badly did he really want to go out with me?

I got my answer that Saturday at the annual Charmers team slumber party to celebrate the end of boot camp and the start of regular summer practices. We gathered at the main gym in the high school's sports and art building, the same place where we had all auditioned for the right to be Charmers. I kept my gaze away from the side of the gym where the judges had sat. I still wasn't sure I'd made the best decision that day. Who knew if the effect from my gaze could have overridden the council representative's vampire persuasion?

But it didn't matter anymore. I couldn't change the past and was tired of even thinking about it. Better to think about the future and how to fit in on this team.

Surprisingly, it turned out not to be hard at all to fit in with the Charmers. The team traditions definitely helped, because the managers were included in all of them just as if we were actual dancers on the team. We received the same sterling-silver team charm bracelets as the rest of the team, with the same team logo, boot and star charms symbolizing our team goals. Our names were included in the bowl when everyone drew for Secret Sis game-day gift giving. We learned about the team's rule to call each girl "Miss" and whatever her first name was, and that rule applied to us managers, too. And when Mrs. Daniels played our team's theme song for the year, Luther Vandross's version of "The Impossible Dream," I wasn't the only one who got a little teared up by the emotional music.

Suddenly, tenth grade didn't look so bad.

After the ceremonies and gift giving, the team played a long game of pillow fighting while balancing on one foot. It turned into a tournament, and I nearly won until Keisha yelled out my name and distracted me. One surprise wallop to the head from this year's new captain, Paula, and I put my foot down and lost.

"Miss Keisha!" I whined, making everyone laugh.

"Maybe next year," Captain Paula sang out with a smirk.

A loud pounding on the locked building's foyer doors made everyone jump and squeal.

Captain Paula ran to the gym doors, peeked out then yelled, "Pizza's here."

"That's us," Head Manager Amber said to the managers while climbing to her feet. Keisha, Vicki and I followed her out to the foyer, its linoleum freezing cold under my hot feet.

Wonder what we do if there's a fire? I thought as Amber unlocked the foyer's glass doors in a blast of heat to let in the delivery guy.

"Hello again, Savannah, ladies," Greg Stanwick greeted us from behind a stack of pizza boxes.

Stunned, my lips curved into a smile before I could think about it. "Hi, Greg."

We each took two boxes from him. He stared at me throughout the process, making me feel a little self-conscious as the summer heat made my T-shirt stick to my back.

I should probably say something to him other than hello. Then again, Amber was there and I was on official Charmers time, so maybe I shouldn't.

"Okay, we'll be right back with the receipt," Amber told him.

I gave him a sheepish smile goodbye and followed the head manager into the gym. While Amber had Mrs. Daniels sign the credit-card receipt, the rest of us set out the pizza boxes on the food table.

"Miss Savannah…" Amber joined us at the table. "Why don't you take this for me." She handed me the receipt and a pen.

Her expression was innocent-looking, but her eyes gleamed with mischief. Apparently she'd picked up something from Greg's greeting and approved of him.

I took the paper and pen back to him.

"So…" he said as he pocketed the receipt. "Do you have any idea how many Colberts there are in this area?"

I laughed. "I don't know. How many?"

"Four. Strange thing is, no Savannahs seem to live with any of them."

"Mmm. That's interesting to know. Of course, if you had simply asked for the correct number in the first place…"

"Yeah, yeah, yeah," he said, but one corner of his mouth stayed up in a half smile. "Now may I please have your phone number?"

"Okay." Giving in, I reached for his wrist, turned his palm up and wrote my number on it. "I didn't know you worked at Pizza Shack."

"I don't. I talked one of my friends into letting me ride with him while he makes his deliveries tonight. Everybody knows about this little shindig y'all have every year."

I peered around him and saw the delivery car idling at the end of the cement ramp that led to the front foyer doors. The driver stuck out an arm through his open window and waved at me.

I laughed and waved back. "Nice friend. Though you

itcould've just waited until school started and asked me for my number then."

"Wait two months to take you out? No way. Besides, you'd probably have a boyfriend by then. So do you mind if I beat out the competition and ask you for that date now?"

He thought he had competition for a date with me? My pulse sped up. "Um, sure, now's fine."

"Okay, how about next Saturday? I could pick you up at six for dinner and a movie?"

"Sounds great." I struggled to keep my smile casual. But inside I was leaping around shouting, *My first date!*

He smiled at me, and it was the nice smile I preferred. "Okay, I'll call you later and get directions to your house then."

Nodding, I stepped back, eased the door shut and watched him jog down the cement ramp to the waiting car. Then I returned to the gym, grinning so hard I must have looked like an idiot. But I didn't care. Greg was no Tristan Coleman, but he was funny, charming, easy to be around and pretty good-looking. And he'd just asked me out on my first date.

Amber laughed and gave me two thumbs-up, then promptly turned and told Captain Paula that I was dating Greg Stanwick.

The rest of the evening passed in a blur of pizza, snacks, giggles and gossip as the team broke up into small groups to eat and lounge around on our sleeping bags and blankets. Thankfully, just like with Michelle, all my new teammates seemed to require from me was an interested listener who laughed or looked shocked, depending on what gossip they had to share. I fell asleep half worried that I would wake up with toothpaste in my hair and shaving cream on my face. But Mrs. Daniels must have forbidden pranking in order to preserve the team-bonding atmosphere. The party ended at nine the next morning when our parents came to pick us up. In the already muggy, way-too-early morning heat, the girls left in a flurry of laughter, sleepy chatter, hugs and the tinkling music our bracelets made when we moved. Music that I, too, carried everywhere I went now.

Nanna immediately noticed my smile. "Must have been some party."

The light feeling inside me bubbled out as laughter. "It was." I replayed the evening for her, hesitantly including the part where Greg asked me for a date.

"You just met this boy last night?"

"No. I met him a couple months ago in the cafeteria. Then I ran into him again at the lake party last week." I opted not to mention that I'd gone with Greg for a ride on his Jet Ski. No way would Nanna like that. "So can I go out with him? He's not in the Clann."

She glanced at me with a frown. "Do you think that's wise? What with the changing, and all?"

My mood deflated a bit. Jeez, why couldn't they just let me forget and pretend for a while that I was normal? "Nanna, everything's totally under control." Or at least it had been for the past month.

She sighed. "Well, you are turning sixteen in a few months. I guess we can't keep you locked up forever."

"So is that a yes?"

"That's a very reluctant yes," she replied with a small smile. "But you have to promise to keep your phone with you at all times. And don't hesitate to call me or your parents if anything happens or you start to feel weird—"

"I know, I know." I shook my head. After weeks of no new developments, I seriously doubted I would suddenly get a mad craving for Greg's blood. And as for everything else weird about me, well, that really was under control.

All I had to do was remember not to make direct eye contact with Greg. Piece of cake.

What I wasn't so confident about was what I would wear for my first date.

CHAPTER 8

Savannah

I shouldn't have worried about my first date with Greg. Not only was he a total sweetie with the best manners I'd ever seen in a guy—opening doors for me, asking what movie I wanted to watch and where I wanted to eat afterward—but he didn't even get grabby at the end of the date, and only kissed me on the cheek at the door when he took me home.

The best part of the date was how much he made me laugh. I'd never realized before how little I laughed.

So when he asked if he could see me again, I said yes. And this time, I didn't hesitate.

And then somehow the summer just flew by. I didn't get to see my friends much, what with the church and science camps and family vacations that went on all summer, and the Charmers practices and fundraisers filling up my own schedule. Not to mention seeing Greg at least twice a week. In a lot of ways, he was even easier to talk to than they were. He had nothing against the Charmers, so he didn't mind that I was a manager for the dance team.

A detail I hadn't quite told my friends about yet.

I knew eventually I'd have to tell them. But I was waiting for the right time, or the right setting, or…something. Okay, the truth was I just didn't want to have to deal with their negative reactions about it until I absolutely had to. Just because they didn't like the dance team didn't mean I had to share their view.

I did tell them about Greg, though. They seemed mildly curious about him and wanted to meet him officially when school started back up.

By the time school began in mid-August, Greg and I had been dating for two and a half months. And I still hadn't told them I was a Charmers manager. Which was exactly what I was deep in thought about when I reached our usual table in the cafeteria for lunch only to find Greg already there waiting for me.

We hadn't really talked about who would sit where each day, so I was a little surprised and worried as he kissed my cheek. None of my friends had ever had a boyfriend sit with us. Probably because none of them had ever had a boyfriend, at least that I knew about. Would they be okay with Greg joining us today, or should he just say hi then go eat with his own friends?

"Oh, hi, Greg." I held my smile in place even as three pairs of curious eyes stared at us.

"Hey." He gave me a sweet grin, then turned toward my friends.

"Oh, right." Quickly I introduced everyone, appreciating how he made a point to say hi or hey to each girl. Michelle giggled her hello. Carrie gave a cool nod in response. Anne just stared at him with one eyebrow raised.

"So, listen, do you ladies mind if I sit with y'all today?" At their blank looks of shock, he held up both hands as if in surrender and added, "I swear I won't butt in every day of the week. Maybe just every other day, if that's all right with you?"

I expected Michelle to answer first. She liked everyone but the Brat Twins.

Instead, Anne was the one who said, "Sure, pull up a chair. I'm sure we jocks can all find something to talk about together. Right?"

Carrie laughed in agreement, and half the tension melted from my shoulders.

We all dropped our stuff at the table.

Then Greg turned to me. "Ready to grab some lunch?"

I nodded and walked beside Greg toward the lunch line in silence, feeling as if the whole cafeteria was staring at us the entire way. Even as a Charmers manager, I was still pretty much a nobody for the gossip mill, so it must be because of Greg.

We didn't say anything as we waited in line then chose our lunches. The great thing about hanging out with Greg was that, not only was he really easy to talk to, but he also didn't mind the occasional silence.

As we neared the cashier, he said, "I keep thinking it's because you're nervous around me, but I just realized...you're not like most girls, are you?"

My shoulders stiffened, my heartbeat instantly kicking into overdrive. "What do you mean?"

He shrugged. "Most girls would be talking nonstop by now."

The air eased out of my lungs. I forced a smile. "My grandmother says you learn more by listening."

"Uh-huh. And yet we've been dating for nearly three months now. So what's left to learn about me?"

It was my turn to shrug. "Does anyone ever fully know anyone else?"

His eyebrows shot up, but he didn't say anything. We paid for our lunches. Greg went first then waited for me to pay for mine. Once I had and we moved a few steps away, he smiled at me and said, "Well, when you figure out what else you want to know about me, just ask, okay?"

Too bad I couldn't be so open with him in return.

"Want me to grab you a soda?" he offered, jerking his head at the soda machines twenty yards away. "Orange, right?"

"Sure. Want me to take your lunch for you?"

"Good idea. Thanks." He handed me his tray, leaning in to kiss my cheek in the process. My cheeks burned as we headed in opposite directions.

"He is cuuute!" Michelle squealed as soon as I reached our table.

I had to laugh and nod in agreement as I sank into my seat.

"And polite." Carrie sounded surprised.

"He's a former Boy Scout," I added, then had to pause. Was that…pride I was feeling? Good grief. I was turning into a total Neanderthal, thrilled to show off my "catch." And we girls always griped about boys and their trophy girlfriends.

Shaking my head at myself, I joined my friends in digging in to our lunch. It was necessity, not lack of manners. With only a twenty-minute lunch break, we didn't have time to wait for Greg's return before eating.

A few minutes later, Greg jogged back to the table with our drinks. "Sorry, stopped to tell my friends where I'd be today. I promised them I'd try to talk you into meeting them tomorrow."

Was meeting his friends a big deal? It felt like it, but then again, Greg was my first boyfriend, and I was completely clueless as to how it all worked.

"Um, sure, I'd like that." Working not to grin like an idiot, I focused on popping the tab on my soda. Something clinked against the side of the can. Oh, crap, my Charmers bracelet.

Anne glanced toward the noise, did a double take then grabbed my wrist. "Hello. Anything you want to *mention?*" She held up the team-logo charm with her other hand like it was dirty underwear.

"Um, yeah. I...I'm a manager for the Charmers this year."

The air heated up over our table in a matter of seconds. I could practically see it turn red and start to boil, fueled by Anne and Carrie's combined fury. A matching sensation of heat flowed over my skin, despite my usual efforts at shielding all the emotions around me. Ouch.

Maybe Greg's presence would at least make them bite their tongues until they had a chance to calm down and get over the news.

"Oh, congrats!" Michelle's smile faded as she glanced at Anne then Carrie. "Or...not?"

"The Charmers?" Anne spat.

Or maybe they could care less what Greg thought of them.

"A *manager?*" Carrie added, her voice even louder. Several people at neighboring tables turned to stare in our direction.

"Shh, keep your voices down," I muttered, my cheeks warming up. "You two are acting like I committed a crime or something."

"Committing. Present tense," Anne corrected. "You've lost your mind, Sav. Why in the world would you want to have anything to do with that bunch of spoiled brats?"

"And as a manager, too. That's just another name for 'gofer girl,'" Carrie said.

I sighed. This was exactly why I'd held off telling them about it all summer. "It's not like that. And they're not like that, either. Even you guys have to admit you never found out for sure who started that rumor last year."

The JV and varsity JHS Maidens volleyball teams were convinced the Charmers had spread a rumor last year that all the volleyball players were lesbians.

"Oh, please." Anne dropped my wrist as if it had morphed into weeks-old garbage. "Who else would have started it?" She flopped back in her chair hard enough to make her ponytail bounce. "I can't believe my best friend just signed on to be a fetcher for the pampered-princess club."

Enough already. "That's not fair, Anne. The Charmers actually work really hard. You should have seen them practicing this summer. And did you know they're about to start twice-a-day practices, both at six-thirty in the morning *and* every afternoon after school? Even varsity volleyball doesn't practice that much."

Mrs. Daniels had given the team this morning off since it was the first day of school. But tomorrow we all started the two-a-days. I was so not looking forward to having to be here at six-fifteen every weekday. Making it here by eight last year had been tough enough. At least I wouldn't be expected to run and dance and leap around at that hour of the morning.

"Varsity soccer doesn't practice that much, either," Greg said in between bites of pizza.

"Maybe the Charmers have to practice more because their dancing sucks more," Anne said, shooting him a dark look.

Miraculously, he smiled and shrugged it off.

Rolling my eyes, I flopped back in my chair in silence. I wasn't going to argue anymore about this. They didn't have to like it, but they would have to get over it. I did not live my life to please my friends, much as I cared about and appreciated them. I was already doing way too much bending over backward for my family and the vampire council.

"I'm done. See you later," Carrie announced a few minutes later to no one in particular as she grabbed her things and left.

"Don't worry, she'll calm down," Michelle whispered as she jumped up and grabbed her things. "Nice to finally meet you, Greg." She gave a hasty smile and wave before she took off after Carrie.

"Carrie will get over it," Anne said on a sigh. "But *I* might not." Which meant, of course, she would. Eventually. Sighing, she picked up her books and tray. "See you later, Stanwick." He raised his cola in reply, his mouth too full to speak.

She gave me one last glare. "See you tomorrow, gofer girl."

"Bye," I muttered.

I watched Anne stomp off. Should I go after her and apologize? For what, though? For not checking with my friends before picking an extracurricular activity? Give me a break. I did not need their approval.

Though it would have been nice to have it.

Awkward silence filled the table for several minutes as we watched my friends leave the cafeteria. Hopefully they would chill out by tomorrow.

"Guess we'll be finishing up here alone today?" Greg broke the silence first as the chaos of the lunchtime crowd flowed around us.

"Yeah. Sorry about that. I guess I should have told them before now." I prayed the blush would fade from my cheeks soon. Preferably immediately.

He leaned over and bumped shoulders with me. "Well, you sure know how to clear a table."

I laughed. "Blunt much?"

He shrugged with an apologetic smile. "I'm told it's curable, but the pills aren't working lately."

Shaking my head, I finished eating then wiped my mouth and sighed. "They'll get over it. Eventually."

"Why don't they like the Charmers?"

I explained the rumor to him. "But no one ever found out for sure who started it. Now they just hate all the Charmers automatically." I caught Greg's confused look and laughed. "Ridiculous, I know. I think it's really just a team thing. Like how the cheerleaders hate the Charmers and girls' volleyball teams, and vice versa. A few of them are brave enough to cross the lines and have friends on the other teams, but mostly they all seem to think their own team is the only good team to be on."

"And you're one of those girls who cross the line, huh?"

Holding back a laugh, I shook my head. "You know, I could take that the wrong way."

It took him a few seconds to get it. When he did, his cheeks turned ruddy and a cute, embarrassed smile tilted his lips. "I meant…"

Laughing, I grabbed my lunch tray. "Yeah, I know what you meant. But you should know…they're not usually like this. When the Clann kids decided to start ganging up on me in athletics in junior high, Anne and Carrie and Michelle nearly got into a fistfight with them."

His eyebrows shot up.

"They'd just really rather I kept playing volleyball with them instead of doing the Charmer thing."

"You used to play volleyball? Why'd you quit?"

I stood up, grateful the bell was about to ring. "That's kind of a long story." One involving a series of events where I managed to accidentally take out part of a tiled gym ceiling, bloody Carrie's nose and get tangled in the net…all at the same tournament. "I'll tell you about it…later." As in never. No way did I want him to know what a klutz he was dating.

We headed for the trash cans. While I dumped my tray, he

asked, "So why don't the Clann girls like you? Is that some sort of a team thing, too?"

"Uh, no, that's a Clann thing," I muttered, just as the bell rang.

"Hey, where's your next class? Maybe I can walk with you there."

I checked my class schedule. "History with Mr. Smythe."

"My bad luck. That's in the portable buildings on the east side. My next one's over in the computer building on the north side. Guess I'll have to settle for walking you to the catwalk."

I had to admit it was a little thrilling when Greg held my hand and led me out the doors and up the steps to the catwalk. No actual tingles from his touch, but the contact was still nice. So was his smile as he said "See you tomorrow" before he kissed my cheek then walked away.

Okay, the boy was *yum*. I would never faint over him, but he was definitely sigh-worthy. And allll mine.

My first real boyfriend!

A small sigh slipped out of me as I turned and headed the other direction toward history class.

And then I felt it...prickles racing down the back of my neck and over my arms. Ouch. That was all I needed to know who was behind me without even looking. After not seeing Tristan Coleman for two-and-a-half months, and no new vampire/witchy developments, I'd hoped my awareness of Tristan's presence would have gone away. But if anything, I could swear it had increased ten times over. I used to feel only a warm ache tugging at my gut and chest whenever he was within twenty yards of me. This time, it felt more like the back of my neck and arms had somehow fallen asleep and the blood was finally rushing back through all the veins. I had to fight against the urge to rub my skin.

Once again, someone just *had* to remind me that I wasn't quite normal.

Oh, boy, this better wear off soon. Maybe he was headed for a different class and the feeling would go away.

But when I heard his heavy footsteps follow me down the sidewalk then up the short cement steps and into history class, I knew I was doomed. And then I looked around at the other students in the class and realized just how doomed I was. Not only would I be sharing this class with the prince of Jacksonville, but I'd also be in here every A day with the Brat Twins and Dylan Williams.

And then Mr. Smythe made my year complete by saying, "Okay, kiddies, let's get you all alphabetically seated, shall we?"

I couldn't decide whether to laugh or cry as I took my assigned seat of torture on the front row beside Tristan, the Brat Twins seated directly behind him.

Yes, it was going to be yet another *very* long year.

Tristan

Talk about a crappy start to the year.

Obviously my protection spell against Stanwick had worn off. Why couldn't the guy just forget about Savannah already? I saw her out of the corner of my eye for the thousandth time in an hour and mentally cursed as my heart slammed into my throat like a caged bear trying to break free. On second thought, I knew exactly why Stanwick couldn't forget about her.

My knees bounced harder under my desk as I considered my options. The solution should be simple. I'd just have to make another protection spell for her. Maybe a couple of them. And I'd drink some coffee or something before doing the spells so I wouldn't fall asleep this time. Although now that Dad had taught me how to draw energy from nature to use instead of my own, I doubted that would be a problem.

At the moment, I had too much energy. I should have grounded at lunch when Emily asked me to after I'd seen the soccer jerk walk with Savannah to the lunch line. But then they had exited with their food, and Stanwick had kissed her cheek. And I'd lost all ability to think as my gut dropped somewhere down to my toes. The sick feeling had only grown stronger as the two of them, apparently a couple now, had sat together at Savannah's table with her friends.

How long had they been seeing each other?

I knew then that I should leave, go outside and ground as much energy as I could. But I couldn't tear myself away from the sight of the two of them laughing together, talking with her friends, the casual way the soccer jerk touched her hand or shoulder or put his arm around her. And she let him.

She liked him. Maybe even loved—

Acid rose up in my throat, and I had to look away, pretend I was listening to the other descendants talking at our table, to think about anything but the nightmare that was taking place just yards away from me.

But when the bell rang, no matter how much my gut was twisted into knots, I still found myself following them out of the cafeteria. I exited the doors and started up the walkway just in time to see Stanwick kiss her goodbye on the catwalk. She hesitated for a minute, her shoulders hunching up near her ears. Could she feel me watching her? She didn't turn to look, instead heading down the sidewalk toward the portable buildings. It was only as she walked up the steps to Mr. Smythe's class that I realized we had history together this year.

And now we were seated by each other, and it should have been great, but it wasn't. Because not only could I see her from head to toe out of the corner of my eye without even looking at her, but I also couldn't help but see how pink her cheeks were. And her constant smile.

The soccer jerk made her happy.

And that just made me want to punch something.

Savannah frowned and rubbed her arm, and I noticed for the first time that the skin below her short sleeves was covered in goose bumps. Huh, that was weird. It didn't feel that cold in here. But maybe I should ask Mr. Smythe to turn off the AC for a while.

I had to stop looking at her.

Jerking my wandering gaze to the dry-erase board ahead of us, I tried to copy down the notes as the class had been instructed to do. But my peripheral vision was a real curse, letting me see her long legs uncross then recross the opposite way.

Oh, man, I was so screwed. I'd be able to see her from head to toe all year, every other weekday, without even turning my head. For an entire hour and a half.

I'd have to beg my sister to help me with my homework again, this time in history.

Giving up on the note taking, I tilted back my head and stared at the ceiling. Ah, better. At least this way I could only see Savannah from the waist up. Too bad I couldn't shut out the sound of the Charmers bracelet she wrote. Apparently she'd joined the dance team over the summer, too. The tinkling was going to drive me crazy. Every movement of her wrist seemed to sing, "Tristan, look at me."

"Mr. Coleman, come see me, please," Mr. Smythe barked from his desk at the back of the room.

Surprised, I got up and walked over to him.

He held out a piece of paper. "Take this note for me."

Confused, I accepted the sheet of unlined paper. "You want me to deliver a note, sir?"

"Yes. Now."

Okay, this was a new one. I took the note and headed outside, shutting the door behind me.

The note wasn't sealed, which was also weird. Didn't teachers always seal their notes with tape or something so students couldn't read them? I glanced at the handwritten lettering on the note then saw it was addressed to me.

Tristan,
Get your emotions under control. Now. You're killing me and probably every other descendant on this campus. Take however long you need, but get it done and make sure it doesn't happen again. And burn this note.
Smythe

And then I remembered. Mr. Smythe was Dylan's uncle and a descendant. Cursing under my breath, I headed for the nearest trash can, did a quick flash burn on the note until it crumbled into ashes in the container, then headed for my usual grounding tree.

Only to realize halfway there that I'd have to find another method. Now that it was no longer lunchtime, anyone who saw me at my grounding tree would grow suspicious and maybe even report me to the office for ditching class. I needed some element of nature other than air that would directly connect me to the earth. Fire, wood, earth, water...

And then I had it. Changing course, I headed for the nearby restroom. Once inside, I checked to be sure no one else was there. I turned on a faucet, put both hands under the cold stream and willed the excess energy out into the flow of water. The heat from my energy immediately combined with the cold water to make steam that fogged up the lower half of the mirror. Cool. I hadn't expected that.

The bathroom door opened behind me, and a zit-faced freshman walked in, signaling the end of this grounding session. Hopefully it had been enough.

The kid hesitated, his eyebrows raised. Probably at the steam.

I turned off the water, dried my hands under a blower. The boy was still frozen near the door, his eyes squinting in suspicion.

"Watch that hot-water knob. They must have cranked up the settings on the water heater," I joked.

That did it. The boy chuckled, nodded in understanding, and headed for a urinal.

I took my time strolling back to class. The water grounding was a good idea. But I'd better find a way to get over Savannah quick or people were going to notice my grounding efforts and think me a freak. At the very least, the descendants on campus would tell Dad that I was getting out of control again.

I needed to find a way not to care about Savannah. I'd thought dream connecting with her that one time last year would be okay, that it would take off the edge. But she was like a drug for me. Every little contact with her made me want to spend even more time with her just to see her smile or hear what she'd say next. I'd wanted to dream connect with her again. But I'd been unable to. Not for lack of trying, though. I'd slept outside so much, Mom had complained that she should buy me a doghouse. I'd tried training harder with Dad, flying through the last of the beginner-level lessons plus several intermediate ones in no time. Then I'd taken a month off, thinking a break from using my power would make it increase and give me the oomph I needed to dream connect again with Savannah. Recently, I'd even talked Dad into teaching me how to draw power from nature to supplement my own.

But nothing worked. All I'd gotten for months of effort was the nightly return of those frustrating beat-the-barrier dreams. Just like in my dreams, Savannah was once again so close in history class, and still as unreachable as ever. Even worse, now she was some other guy's girl. And that made her about as untouchable as a girl could get in my opinion, short of being related to me. I'd dated a lot of girls, but I made it a personal rule never to go after someone else's girlfriend. I'd always figured if a girl was interested in me, she'd break up with her boyfriend before I ever had to make a move in her direction.

Of course, none of those girls had been Savannah, either.

I headed back to class, taking my time. Was there a spell to make a guy act enough like an idiot to make his girlfriend break up with him, but not so bad that he broke her heart in the process?

I'd have to ask Emily.

Savannah

Over the next two weeks, my friends gradually quit grumbling about the Charmers, and Greg became a steady part of my school schedule. For our daily lunch break, we compromised. Mondays and Thursdays we sat with his friends, Tuesdays and Fridays we sat with mine, and Wednesdays we didn't sit together at all. This kept both sets of friends happy. Surprisingly, Anne didn't hate Greg like she did most guys, and she didn't even tease us when he rested his arm across the back of my chair sometimes. I had no idea what his friends really thought about our dating, but Mark and Peter didn't seem bothered by it. Usually they either talked about soccer or asked me endless questions about why some girl they liked had done something they didn't understand. At least I knew I had a possible career as a therapist someday. If I didn't turn into a vampire first.

Somehow, we slipped into a new routine, until gradually Greg became a regular part of my life. I saw him five out of seven days of the week, sometimes six when he took me out for a quick dinner after the Friday-night home football games. We wrote goofy notes to each other a couple times a week just for fun, and sometimes he called me on the weekends so we could talk without an audience of friends.

He was easy to talk to, as well, both on the phone and on our dates. By the time he finally kissed me on the lips, he knew almost everything about me, and I was more than ready for my first kiss. It was nice, no tongues or slobber involved, and I kind of liked the gentle press of his lips over mine and the way his arms cradled me as if I were breakable.

By our three-month anniversary, I was surprised to find my life mostly calm and, if not perfect, at least reasonably happy for the first time in too long to remember. Now that I'd given up trying to please my father, I wasn't so stressed-out all the time. And I loved being on the Charmers team, even if just as a manager. The team made me feel needed, an important part of something special. I had my first boyfriend, whom everyone seemed to like, including my friends. And his ex-girlfriends. And every weekend was filled with stuff to do and people to see. If not for history class with four of the worst descendants every other day, plus the fact that I still didn't dare look anyone in the eyes, I could almost forget that I wasn't quite normal.

At least I could pretend that I was.

But I should have known the happiness wouldn't last forever.

At the beginning of September, Greg was my date for the

homecoming dance after the game. The homecoming dance
was a fundraiser jointly held by the Charmers and the cheerleaders, our team directors' annual futile attempt at forcing
the two squads to bond. Greg's mother had made me a custom
mum that had to weigh at least twenty pounds, and I couldn't
stop grinning with pride at how good my boyfriend looked
in his matching mini mum attached to a garter around his left
bicep. Even if I didn't get to actually dance with him much
because I was too busy working the concession stand with
other Charmers most of the night.

When I did get a break, dancing with Greg proved to be…
interesting. At five-eleven, he wasn't too much taller than
my own height of five-five. This would have been great for
soul-deep eye gazing. Except obviously I couldn't do that. So
I had to be careful while dancing with him. Every time we'd
danced together that evening, I'd nearly slipped and looked
directly into his eyes instead of at his nose.

By the final slow dance of the night, I was more than a little
frustrated. That's when the doubt started to creep in. And the
questions.

It had been five months since I'd made direct eye contact with any male. The weird incident with the three boys
in freshman algebra seemed like a dream now, or a nightmare faintly remembered. What if I was remembering it as
much worse than the situation actually had been? After five
months, anyone's memory could blow something small out
of proportion.

Not to mention, those algebra boys had been virtual strangers. I knew Greg. The entire time we'd been dating, he'd
never been anything but sweet. He was nice to others, too,
holding doors for strangers even when he thought I wasn't
around or looking. He was a preacher's kid, the oldest of five,
and regularly babysat his younger siblings so his parents could

go out on dates or hold religious events. He even cleaned up other people's trash on the sidewalk outside the movie theater sometimes. Greg was a total Boy Scout through and through. I'd never known a nicer guy.

And after five long months, I was sick and tired of having to avoid eye contact with people. Especially Greg, who knew so much about me, yet I still couldn't seem to really connect with him. Compared to Greg, I felt closer to Tristan, whom I still hadn't had a conversation with in years outside of that one dream. And I knew why. It was because of my stupid eyes. I'd made eye contact with Tristan lots of times before I'd gotten sick last year. I couldn't remember ever meeting Greg's. I wanted to be truly normal again. Surely it was safe to stop staring at people's noses and try making eye contact with Greg to start with. Then if nothing bad happened…who knew? Maybe it would be proof that I was taking after the Clann side of the family instead.

Better to be a witch than a vampire.

My gaze inched up to Greg's mouth. Then his nose. Could I really do this? My hands shook, so I gripped the folds of his shirt at the small of his back.

And then I looked at him. *Really* looked at him, making direct eye contact with soft brown eyes I'd grown to care about but only dared to sneak indirect peeks at till now. I felt the zing from the connection our gazes made, and held my breath.

Greg stumbled and stopped dancing. But he didn't let go of me.

"What?" I whispered. Should I look away now? No, I'd wait a few seconds longer. It was so nice, maybe too nice, to make eye contact with someone again. And yet incredibly intimate, as if I were baring my soul to him. As if he'd be able to see everything I felt. And didn't feel.

"You've never looked at me like this before. Not since we first met," he murmured, his voice husky. His eyebrows drew together into a frown.

"I can stop if you like."

He gave a slow shake of his head, never breaking our stare. His arms held me tighter. "No, don't. I like it. You should do it more often."

He wasn't freaked out. Relief escaped me in a shaky laugh. "Okay."

"Wow, you're beautiful. I feel like the luckiest guy here."

"And you're sweet."

He sighed without smiling, a rarity for him. "I'd rather you said something else."

"Such as?" I teased.

"Oh, like whether you think I'm good-looking or insanely hot. Things like that." And still he didn't smile.

"Okay. You're the hottest guy here. Better?"

"Much. Savannah, have I told you lately that I love you?"

I grinned. "Isn't that a song from the nineties or something?" I expected him to laugh. He was rarely serious. At the moment, he was working on a record for the longest I'd seen him go without smiling. On second thought, he'd already broken that record.

He frowned at me. "I'm being serious."

"Uh, yeah. And it's a little strange for you."

"So you don't like me unless I'm smiling and joking around all the time?"

"Umm...I like you to be yourself, remember?"

"Okay, then. Right now I feel like being serious. And I'm telling you that I love you."

Whoa. That sure sounded serious. Was I supposed to say it back, or could I have some time to think about this leap in our relationship?

"Will you wear my senior ring?" He took it off and held it out.

"Wow." Hesitating for a moment, I finally nodded and let him slide the heavy ring onto my right ring finger. But the cold chunk of metal felt all wrong. Maybe because I'd imagined this happening with someone else.

His hand cupped the back of my head as he ducked his head to kiss me. But Mrs. Daniels had a strict team policy against public displays of affection at any team or school function. Kissing at this dance was definitely PDA. I leaned away from him.

"Savannah, it's traditional for a couple to kiss after they say I love you." Greg almost sounded angry. I must have bruised his ego. Probably not a good time to point out that I had, in fact, not yet repeated those three little words back to him.

"I know. But Charmers can't have public displays of affection at team or school events," I explained, nervous for the first time in months with him. "I'll get into trouble. It makes the team look bad."

He scowled, his eyes darkening to the color of bittersweet chocolate. "That's a stupid rule."

Actually, I'd always thought it was a good one. But Greg's expression was angry enough as it was; I didn't want to add fuel to the fire by arguing with him. So I didn't reply.

"Maybe you should quit."

My mouth dropped open. Had he really just said that? He knew more than anyone how much I loved being a Charmers manager. I glanced around to see if anyone had overheard him, but everyone seemed lost in their own worlds.

Thankfully the song ended, and so did the dance itself. Time for me to help the other Charmers and cheerleaders clean up. "I have to go. See you in a little while?" He'd driven me to the dance. But if he was too mad, I could grab a ride home with one of the Charmers instead.

He gave a terse nod and stalked off.

Wow. Were all boys this weird when they gave a girl their senior ring? I watched him go for a minute, then shook my head and waded through the exiting crowd toward the concession stand.

By the time the team finished cleaning up the building an hour later, Greg's strange mood still hadn't changed. We drove to my house in silence. I was too tired to think of anything to talk about, and apparently he was still mad about the PDA rule. At my house, he walked me to my front porch.

"Hey, you're not wearing my ring," he said.

Blushing, I searched the pockets of my denim jacket. Wait, this jacket didn't have any pockets. Then I remembered. "Oh, yeah, I put it on my necklace while I was cleaning. It's kind of big for my fingers and I was scared I would lose it." I lifted the chain out of my shirt.

He touched his ring where it lay along with my gold locket on my chest at the top of my cleavage, his knuckles grazing my skin. The intimacy of his touch made me uncomfortable, but I held still for now, waiting to see what he would do. After a long moment, he nodded. "I like it there. Lets everyone see that you're my girl."

I lifted my face for our usual light kiss goodbye, more than ready to end the night, only to find myself trapped within the coil of his arms. His tongue stroked across my lips, making me gasp. We'd never kissed like that. He seemed to take my gasp as an invitation; his tongue slipped inside my mouth then aimed for my throat. He moaned as his hands rubbed my back.

This was supposed to cause all those fireworks and stars I'd read about?

"Savannah," Greg whispered against my lips before he trailed kisses over my cheek and down the side of my neck.

Whoa, too much. I leaned back and tried to ease out of his arms. "Uh, okay, down, boy." I forced a laugh.

He stared at me with intense eyes, his breaths coming out fast and harsh. "I love you, Savannah. When you look at me like that, you make me feel things I've never felt before."

"Uh…" Realizing I was making direct eye contact with him again, I jerked my gaze away. Too much of a good thing there apparently. I'd have to limit his exposure to my gaze again. Thankfully today was a Saturday. He'd recover overnight like those algebra boys had, and be back to normal by Monday. Maybe I should try smaller doses of the direct gaze on him in the future, let him build up a tolerance to it.

"See you Monday." I pasted on a smile as I slipped out of his arms.

But he held on to my hand, stopping me from escaping into the house. "Hey, let's go out tomorrow."

"On a Sunday?" Sundays were strictly for church and family at his house.

But he didn't even hesitate. "Sure. We could go on a picnic."

No way would the gaze-daze effect wear off if he saw me again tomorrow. He needed space and time away from me so he could recover. "Um, I'm sorry, Greg, but I've got stuff to do with my grandma tomorrow." I'd find something to do with Nanna so it wouldn't be a lie. "But I'll see you on Monday, okay?"

"Okay. See you then, Savannah." He stood there staring at me.

Okaaay. I went inside the house with a sigh. Apparently it still wasn't a great idea to make eye contact with a male. Even a really nice one.

CHAPTER 9

Savannah

Unfortunately, Greg was anything but back to normal by lunchtime on Monday when I joined him and his friends at their table.

"You ready to go grab some lunch?" Greg said, already getting up from his chair, not a smile in sight on his face.

Feeling nauseous, I shook my head. I was anything but hungry today.

He frowned, his eyes growing even darker and more intense. "You really need to eat, Savannah. I'll get you something." He took off at a jog for the food line.

"Hey, guys, does Greg seem different today?" I asked his friends.

"Now that you mention it, yeah," Mark said before taking a large bite of his nachos. "I think it's cuz he's in *l-o-v-e*."

"Dude," Peter punched his arm. "You're not supposed to reveal a dude's secrets like that, man."

I gave a half smile. "It's okay, he already said the big three words at the homecoming dance this weekend."

Peter looked relieved. "Figures. The guy's been talking about you nonstop ever since."

"Is that...normal for him?"

"No. Not that he hasn't talked about you before. But this is something else. The dude woke me up at two in the morning after the dance, calling me to rave on and on about your eyes."

My eyes. Cringing, I stared down at my hands in my lap. *What have I done?*

"Ah, don't worry about it, Sav," Mark said. "He'll come to his senses. All us guys do."

"Here you go." Greg returned and set an overloaded tray in front of me. "I didn't know what you'd want, so I got one of everything."

He wasn't kidding. He'd bought enough food to create a mini mountain on the table. A short laugh of disbelief burst out of me. This could not be happening. "Uh, thanks, Greg. But I'm really not hungry."

"Are the Charmers teaching you not to eat or something?" He held up a piece of pizza and shoved it against my lips. "Here, just eat a little. You're too skinny anyways."

A glance around the table showed two male reflections of what I was feeling.

"Greg, I'm not hungry," I insisted, leaning away from the pizza. "Drop it please, or I'll have to go sit with the girls today."

"Yeah, man, lay off her already," Peter said.

"Back off," Greg growled at his best friend. "I know how to look out for my own girlfriend."

Judging from Peter's stunned expression, Greg had never spoken to either of his friends like that. He had to be acting this way because of me. I had to do something before this situation got any worse.

I stood up. "Sorry, guys. But this is getting out of hand."

"See ya, Sav," Mark said. Peter just looked embarrassed.

"Don't call her that," Greg muttered. "Only her friends and I call her Sav."

I gasped. "Greg, I can't believe you're being so rude. Peter and Mark are my friends, too, now. I don't know what your problem is with them today, but if it's because of me, you need to stop it." I nodded at Peter and Mark. "See you guys later." I turned to walk away.

But Greg grabbed my wrist. "Where are you going?"

I gazed down at his nose, studying his eyes with my peripheral vision. What I found there made me want to dig a hole to hide in. He looked...possessed, just like those boys outside the math building five months ago. As if he'd like to drag me down a very dark and private alley, whether I wanted to go with him or not.

"Uh-uh, not cool, man," Peter muttered.

I made my voice as steady as I could. "Until you can cool off and apologize to your friends, I'll be sitting with the girls." I looked down at his hand clamped on my wrist and tried not to think about the pain radiating out from his grip. "Let go of me, Greg."

He hesitated, and my fingers started to go numb from the lack of blood flow past his grip. What would I do if he refused? If I made a scene today, and then he went back to being his normally sweet self tomorrow...

Finally he let go.

The blood rushed back to my fingers. But I couldn't manage to breathe yet. He might change his mind. I tried to keep my pace slow and steady as I walked away on shaking legs, my sense of hearing in overdrive, my shoulders hunched with worry that he'd try to follow me across the cafeteria. The forty yards between his table and mine had never seemed so long before. I think I managed a normal pace. Yet all I wanted to do was run, to get out of that cafeteria with all those people watching and keep going until I was off the campus and safe. Safe from Greg, my own boyfriend.

Just three days ago, Greg and I had walked over to my table together, laughing and looking forward to the homecoming dance. Tears burned my eyes and threatened to spill over by the time I reached my friends.

"Sav? What's up?" Michelle asked. "I thought today was Monday."

"It is." Carrie's gaze was too observant for comfort today. I avoided looking in her direction.

"What'd he do?" Anne snapped, half rising from her seat while tightening her ponytail as if in preparation for a battle.

I sank down into my chair. "Don't—don't worry about it. He's just being…weird today. He and his buddies started to argue with each other, and I didn't want to listen to it." I was shaking all over. My voice didn't sound right even to my own ears. Taking a deep breath, I held it before slowly letting it out. Forcing a smile, I glanced around the table without actually seeing anything. "So, Michelle, fill me in. What gossip did I miss this weekend?"

Michelle launched into a story long enough to take up the rest of the lunch period. Carrie and Anne let her talk uninterrupted, a feat unheard of in the history of our group friendship. But I didn't hear a word of it.

I kept listening for Greg's approach, dreading the familiar squeak of his sneakers. *What am I going to do?* My wrist continued to throb where he'd grabbed it. I snuck a peek at it beneath the table then wished I hadn't. The skin was already starting to turn blue with bruises in the distinct shapes of his fingers. I pulled my sleeve down to hide my wrist. Somehow, seeing the physical proof of the change in him made it worse, made it too real to pretend away. I could feel myself shuddering, like a rickety old car barely staying together. But I *had* to hold it together. I still had two more classes plus Charmers practice to get through.

And then, as the bell rang, signaling the end of lunch period, I remembered. Even on days when we didn't sit together, Greg always walked me out of the cafeteria and up to the catwalk. Oh, Lord.

"Anne, can you walk with me a little today? At least to the catwalk?" The words tumbled out so fast I wondered how she even understood me.

She scowled but nodded. After Carrie and Michelle left with raised eyebrows, Anne and I followed. I refused to look over at Greg's table. I did not want to give my possessed boyfriend any encouragement to join us.

As soon as we exited the cafeteria, Anne stopped me. "All right, what really happened?"

"I... Nothing. It's fine, don't worry about it. Things will settle down soon." I chewed the inner corner of my lips, using the physical twinge of pain to distract me from my fears.

"Uh-huh. I see you're wearing his ring now."

My hand darted up to my necklace. Oh, yeah. I tucked the ring and chain inside my shirt. I couldn't look at her as we walked up the steps to the catwalk. I peeked behind me, but he was nowhere in sight. "Okay, thanks for walking with me. See you tomorrow."

"Promise you'll call if you need me?"

I nodded, the lump in my throat keeping me from speaking as I hurried off to class.

But I might as well have skipped history today for all that I heard in there. The only thing I could focus on was Greg's ring. I couldn't stand the feel of it against my skin, so I took it out of my shirt. And remembered how easily he'd held me captive outside my house after the homecoming dance.

He'll snap out of it, I tried to reassure myself. *This is Greg, after all.*

Not anymore. Only one direct look from my eyes, and I'd turned him into someone else. Something else.

A little more time, more space, it'll be fine, I thought again, needing to believe it, to believe that I still had it all under control. That this would turn out to be just a bad memory soon. Because this could not be a permanent change I'd created. If it was...

If this was a permanent change, it would be all my fault.

Deep down, though, I knew this was already my fault. Even if the effect eventually wore off and Greg went back to his normal, sweet self, I wasn't sure I could ever forget feeling like this. Even those boys from algebra last year hadn't actually touched me, and they'd been scary enough without the physical contact. I had the proof on my wrist today to show just how far Greg had been willing to go in a crowded cafeteria. What might he have done if we'd been somewhere alone together?

Would I ever be able to go on a date with him again without some part of me being afraid?

At the end of the day, I found a note from Greg in my locker, full of rambling apologies and promises that he wouldn't be rude to me or his friends like that again. I read the letter then folded it up and put it back in my locker. I wasn't sure what I should do yet. But I knew I wasn't ready to talk to him.

He called that night, but I pretended to be asleep when Nanna checked so I wouldn't have to speak to him. When I was sure she had ended the call, I snuck out, grabbed the cordless extension and began to dial my father's phone number. Then stopped.

What would my father do if he found out I'd gaze dazed my boyfriend? What would the vampire council do? They'd already threatened my entire family just to get me to stop dancing. If they found out I had vampire eyes and could sense others' emotions around me…

I remembered Mom's words from last year, about how both sides feared I would become a secret weapon for their enemies to use against them. If I told my father that I'd gaze dazed some-one, would the council demand that I side with them against the Clann? Would they take me away from Nanna and Mom?

No, that could not happen. I couldn't risk anyone knowing about this. I would just have to find a way to deal with it on my own, like I had before.

Besides, it would all be fine soon. Greg would recover and go back to his ordinary, sweet self. He *had* to. Because if he didn't, I honestly didn't know what I was going to do.

The next day, I stopped by the girls' bathroom before lunch. Greg would be waiting for me in the cafeteria. What if he wasn't recovered yet, or was in the process of recovering, and seeing me again set him back somehow?

The only safe option was to stay away from him and hope that a little more time and distance would help the effects wear off faster.

I didn't look in my locker that day, not wanting to find any more borderline-insane letters from Greg. When I got home after Charmers practice, the first words out of my mouth to Nanna were to tell anyone who called for me that I was sleep-ing. Thankfully she didn't press for an explanation, though the look in her eyes promised she would soon if the problem continued. The sound of the phone ringing an hour later made me want to throw up.

On Wednesday at lunch, I peeked through the narrow windows of the cafeteria doors, took one look at Greg's wild hand gestures and wide eyes at my friends' table, and my feet steered me right back to the nearest girls' bathroom.

I leaned against the long counter and stared at my reflection in the mirror. How could such ordinary, boring-looking eyes like mine cause so much trouble? This was ridiculous. I couldn't keep spending my lunch breaks in the bathroom. If Greg didn't recover soon, I would have to figure out something else, and fast. Though what could I do except break up with him? Even if the effects wore off in the next day or two, I would still continue risking this same situation every time I saw him. Better to break things off with him now, for both our sakes. After all, this wasn't just about him and me anymore. The gaze daze was obviously affecting other areas of his life, too, like his friendships with Mark and Peter.

Then again, how fair would it be to dump him? He hadn't asked to be changed, and probably didn't even know what he was doing under the gaze daze's influence. Should he really be held responsible for a change my freaky eyes had caused?

Never mind how much I would miss talking to him every day. Who else would I be able to laugh with about the Charmers latest drama? I already missed looking forward to his phone calls and notes in my locker. They used to be the highlight of my day.

"There you are," Anne said, scowling as she entered the bathroom. "Hiding out from Greg again?"

"No, just…debating. I don't know what's the right thing to do here. And until I can figure it out, I don't think I should see him."

"Yeah, well, you don't have to figure it out all alone in the bathroom. Come on, what good are your friends if we can't protect you from one measly boy?"

Protection. From Greg, Mr. Boy Scout himself. I didn't know whether to laugh or cry. "Anne—"

"I promise, Sav, you'll be okay. Although it would help if you told me what was going on."

Staring at the grubby linoleum floor, I sighed and nodded.

She was right. But I would have to be careful about what I revealed. "Remember the three boys from algebra last year?"

She sucked in a breath, the sound echoing off the tiled walls. "Same problem?"

I nodded, my eyes burning.

She swore. "Savannah, what made you think—"

"It's *Greg!* It's been five months since the last time. I thought maybe it would be okay."

"You know I love you like a sister. But that was pretty dang stupid."

"I know. I don't suppose he seemed better today? I saw him at our table, but I couldn't hear him."

"Nope. He asked about you, and the boy looked straight-up possessed. Asked me to give you this letter, too." She fished in her pocket then handed me a folded note.

His letters always used to make me smile before I even read them. Now all I felt was dread. Slowly I forced my fingers to unfold it. The entire sheet of paper was filled with two words repeated over and over...*I'm sorry.*

A laugh that felt more like a sob burst out of me. I gave her the note so she could read it for herself, knowing she wouldn't have already without my permission.

"He's gone off the deep end," she whispered, her voice bordering on awe. "What did you *do?*"

"I made eye contact with him. Apparently that's all it takes." And suddenly, I couldn't take it anymore. "Anne...I think I'm turning into a monster."

Tristan

The same old ache sucked the air from my lungs as I turned the corner from the walkway and the sunlight hit a too-familiar head of red hair up ahead. Savannah was wearing it down today for a change. Nice. Too freaking nice.

Man, how I wished I could get her out of my system.

I hadn't put a spell on Stanwick to make him hurry and screw up his shot with Savannah, but only because I didn't want to see her upset. Otherwise, Emily said I easily could have magically convinced him to cheat on her or drive her to break up with him for hundreds of different reasons.

For now, Stanwick had won. He made her happy. A blind person could see he was all wrong for her. But as long as he made her smile, how could I get in the way of that?

In the meantime, I couldn't decide if sharing history class with her made it the best or worst period in my schedule.

Several yards ahead, Savannah disappeared into the history class's building. Anne turned, saw me and frowned. She was looking extra ticked off today. I expected her to walk past me. Instead, she walked right up to me and planted herself in my way.

"Tristan, I need to talk to you."

"Whatever it is, I didn't do it," I said with a half smile. It was the best I could do, and a lot more than anyone else had gotten from me in months.

"Funny. No, I mean a certain person we both know needs your help again."

Everything went cold inside me as the blood rushed down to my gut. Savannah was in trouble again? I opened my mouth to reply then heard footsteps approaching from behind me. I glanced back over my shoulder and nearly cursed out loud. It was Mr. Smythe, Dylan's uncle and a descendant. He was within hearing distance.

"Don't know what you mean." I faced Anne again. I tried to tell her with my eyes that I got it, though.

Apparently I wasn't obvious enough. "Oh, come on. Remember the Warty Boys last year, Arthur? Time to draw out the ole Excalibur again, take care of some toads and all that."

"Nope, sorry, you lost me." I gave her a huge, slow wink this time. *Come on, don't be thickheaded* and *blind*.

Her eyes widened then narrowed. "I should have known all you football jocks are just selfish jerks. See you later, snob." She stomped off so believably angry-looking that I actually wondered for a few seconds if she'd understood. Once she was past Mr. Smythe on the sidewalk, though, she turned back and mouthed, "Thank you."

"Planning on being late for my class, Mr. Coleman?" Mr. Smythe said as he drew closer.

"No, sir. Headed there now."

"And are you going to have to deliver any notes for me again?"

Translation: Would he have to send me off to do more emergency grounding? Sitting beside Savannah every other day wasn't always the easiest thing in the world. Every now and then, I lost control in class and my power spiked. When it did, Mr. Smythe had to pretend to send me to the office to deliver a note, so I could actually release the excess energy.

"Going to try not to, sir."

"Good."

I took the three cement steps in one bound up into the building and hurried to my desk. While I shoved my books under my desk, I snuck a peek at Savannah. And nearly flash burned my books.

Despite the makeup, she looked like someone had back-handed both her cheeks. No wonder she'd left her hair down today. She was obviously trying to hide the fact that she'd been crying recently, and hard from the looks of it. Even her nose was swollen and pink. Someone had done this to her. From what Anne had said, the someone was a guy. Another stalker maybe, but who?

I'd have to call Anne tonight and find out who the new

stalker was. *Wonder what time she gets home?* Hopefully not too late. I'd need as much time as possible to load up the protective charms. Anyone who made Savannah cry didn't deserve to speak to her again. Ever.

Her Charmers bracelet jingled, distracting me. She was playing with her necklace. No, wait. She was doing something else with it.

She took off Stanwick's senior ring.

I froze. I wasn't sure if even my blood moved right then. There was only one meaning behind a girl taking off her boyfriend's senior ring. She was going to break up with him.

Pure joy rushed my blood straight to my head, making me want to whoop out loud. Yes! I knew Stanwick wasn't good enough for her, knew he couldn't make her happy for long.

Then I saw her face. She looked ready to cry again. Aw, man, I was a jerk. Here I was ready to do a touchdown dance, and she looked like someone had just killed her dog.

I would break Greg's face for hurting her like this.

Then her sleeve fell away from her wrist. Were those… bruises? In the shape of fingers, too.

Blinding rage filled me, and it was all I could do to keep my energy level contained and not burn the building down around us all. Stanwick's face would more than pay for those bruises on her. If he'd done it, that is.

Confirmation on my hunch came sooner than I'd hoped for. Anne and I got out of volleyball and football practice after school at the same time.

As we walked parallel with each other toward the front parking lot, separated by a few feet so we wouldn't appear to be walking together, I asked, "Stanwick?"

Like me, she kept her gaze straight ahead. "Yep."

"Just him?"

"Yep. He scared the crap out of her at lunch on Monday. She's been hiding in the bathroom during breaks ever since."

He must have given Savannah those bruises on Monday.

"She took off his ring in history." I was almost to my truck now.

"That's my girl. Still…"

"Yeah. Don't worry, I'm on it." Judging by her smile, Anne didn't know about the bruises. Was Savannah keeping secrets from her best friend now?

Had Stanwick hurt her before?

"Keep it low-key and don't embarrass her. Try not to go all Neanderthal," Anne said.

"Who, me?" At my truck, I shot her an innocent look I was sure quickly turned ugly as I unlocked my door. "Meet you at the cafeteria picnic tables in the morning."

"Yep, see you there."

Grinding my teeth, I jumped into my truck and pulled out of the parking lot, squealing the tires by accident. Luckily the cop posted at the corner was a descendant and just shook a warning finger at me. I had too much work to do to wait for a ticket this evening.

The next day, I stayed in the cafeteria long enough to see Anne slip something into Savannah's bags at their table while Savannah stood in the food line. Then I headed outside to get rid of some serious energy overload. Even making all those charms last night hadn't put a dent in my energy level. The descendants had looked ready to kill me at our table today. Emily had just pointed at the doors in silence, her eyes murderous.

But there was just no way to stop feeling like this. All I could think about was the need to hit Stanwick. Over and over. And how, as far as everyone else knew, I had no right to feel this way, much less act on it.

Leaning back against my grounding tree, I'd just started siphoning off the energy when I felt it—a too-familiar ache in my chest and gut that only one girl caused. But Savannah should be inside with her friends and protected by four of my memory confusion charms.

Still, the sensation was too strong to ignore. So I opened my eyes. And cursed.

Stanwick and Savannah were at the cafeteria's rear exit near the Dumpster station. The curve of the building blocked them from the view of the outside picnic tables. But not from me.

Her eyes were wide, the hurt in them like a punch to my stomach as she handed Stanwick his ring. He pushed back her hand without taking the ring. She tried again, and he ignored her hand, instead pressing his body into hers against the cafeteria's brick exterior.

I was stalking over to them without ever deciding to move. As I got closer, I could hear them.

"No, Greg. Stop. This isn't really you. It's my fault. I did this, I know. But you have to stop."

He tried to kiss her lips. She turned her head and shoved at his shoulders, but he only leaned harder against her and kissed her neck. She stomped on his toes, but he didn't even flinch.

I saw the fear and frustration in Savannah's eyes a second before she recognized me. That look in those eyes fueled my own fury, pushing it to a point I'd thought impossible for my anger to reach. The rage ate me up from the inside out, burning away all logic and reason.

I grabbed Stanwick's shoulder and spun him off her, then threw the dazed senior behind the nearest Dumpster.

It felt too good, landing that first surprise blow to Stanwick's chin and sending him sprawling. I went after him again. But I should have remembered to avoid the soccer jerk's feet; he kicked me in the thigh. The pain had me on a knee in the gravel before I even realized it.

Then we were on each other, Stanwick on top long enough to get in a couple of good hits to my jaw and splitting my lip before I could use the advantage of my bigger size to flip him. Once on top, I landed three good blows to his nose, mouth and right cheek.

Then two soft hands grabbed my upper arms, and her warm, lavender scent drifted around me. At the same time, a red curtain of hair covered my face, blinding me.

"Tristan, stop! It's not his fault," Savannah demanded right against my ear.

"Like it's your fault instead?" I snapped back, trying to hold on to the anger. But the feel of her lips against my ear and the light scent of her was drowning me with a different need.

I leaned down to mutter in Stanwick's ear, "You know if we're caught fighting on campus, we're both screwed. Still want that soccer scholarship?"

He glared at me for a long minute then gave a quick nod. Satisfied we understood each other, I stood up. I stared at Stanwick as he picked up his ring from the grass and stomped off.

"Tristan. Your face," she whispered, reaching up to touch my stinging lip.

"It's nothing."

"That is *not* nothing. How are you going to hide that?"

I froze so I wouldn't scare her away. She didn't seem to be aware of how she was pressed against my side and arm in her effort to reach my face. "I don't have to hide it. I play football. It's a rough sport."

"That regularly messes up your face?"

She was so close, her face just inches from mine. It would be too easy to kiss her....

"It's a *really* rough sport."

She smiled up at me, and my gut clenched. The way she looked at me...I could see every tiny fleck in her irises, which were dark blue at the moment. Her pupils dilated as she pulled in a sharp breath through her nose and froze. As I watched, her eyes turned to pale silver.

And then, with our gazes locked together...something just clicked inside me. And I knew.

Knew she was the only one for me.

Knew she always had been ever since that kiss in the fourth grade.

"Savannah..." I had to tell her. Who cared about my parents and the Clann and all their stupid rules? Savannah and I were meant to be. All I needed was for her see it, too, and everything would be okay.

"Oh, no," she whispered, her eyes widening. "First Greg, now you."

Huh? I blinked a few times in confusion.

"Twice in one week. It's almost a record," she said, though the words sounded more like a sob. She stepped away from me and pressed her fingertips to her temples.

"Sav..."

"I'm so sorry. I'm so stupid!" A sob burst out of her, and the sound ripped across my skin. She moved away from my outstretched hand. "No, don't. Tristan, I...I can't believe I did it again. I'm an idiot. Whatever you're thinking or feeling right now, please try to forget it."

Forget *this* feeling? No way.

"It's not real," she continued. "The feelings will go away in time. I think. I hope. Oh, Lord. Just...I'm truly sorry I looked at you. What a way to say thank-you."

Okay, maybe the stress of the moment had made her snap, because she wasn't making much sense. She turned away.

I grabbed her arms to stop her from leaving. "What are you talking about? You didn't do anything to me."

"Of course I did. I looked at you. Really looked at you. That's how...what...Greg and those boys last April..." She couldn't find the right words apparently. But she believed what she was saying.

"Savannah, look at me."

She did but not fully, her gaze stopping somewhere around my mouth.

"No, really look at me."

She shook her head.

"Okay, listen to me, then. I feel perfectly normal. I'm not going to turn into one of your stalkers just because you looked at me."

"All the others did. Ever since I got sick last year."

"But not me."

"Why would you be different?"

I started to tell her the truth about the Clann, my family's power and how it probably made me immune to whatever she was talking about. But I couldn't; revealing Clann secrets was an unforgivable offense that would jeopardize every single descendant. "Just trust me."

"Do you want to kiss me right now?"

I sucked in a long breath through my nose. If that was an invitation... Except Savannah didn't look like a girl who wanted to be kissed. She must be trying to build an argument. "What's your point?"

"That's what happens when I screw up and make direct eye contact with a guy. They want to kiss me, grab me, trap me. Own me."

I opened my mouth to tell her that was nuts, then looked

down at my hands where they gripped her arms, probably hard enough to bruise.

Muttering a curse under my breath, I let her go. "I won't become another of your stalkers. I've felt this way about you for a long time now. I just didn't get it until today. But it's not because of your eyes."

Tears glittered in those eyes, which were begging me now. "Prove it."

She wanted me to leave her alone. Now, when I finally understood the connection between us. A connection I'd fought for years.

"For how long?"

"Until I know for sure you're not obsessed, that you're acting of your own free will."

"And then?" I stepped closer, not touching her, and dipped my head.

Her eyes widened, her lips parting in surprise. Her short, quick breaths puffed against my lips. "That won't happen. When you come to your senses, you won't still feel like this."

"And when I do still—"

"*If* you do," she corrected in a whisper.

"Then?"

"Then…maybe…"

Maybe. She didn't want to commit to future possibilities between us. But I could see the longing in her eyes. She wanted to believe this was real. All she needed was proof.

"Fine." I pushed the word out between gritted teeth. I might die trying, but I would stay away from her. For a while. But only long enough for her to see that I wasn't like the others. "But in the meantime, you have to do something for me."

"What?"

"Keep your backpack and dance-team bag with you at all times." Her raised eyebrows demanded a reason. I thought fast. "I don't want Stanwick to try to hurt you by putting something bad in them or stealing them. And if you've absolutely got to date someone else, at least try to pick a better guy."

Her laugh sounded empty. "Don't worry, I won't be picking any new boyfriends for a long time. If ever."

Even better, I thought with a smile. I followed her to the cafeteria door.

She jerked to a halt. "Are you following me?"

Because that was exactly what I'd been doing, I took a moment to reply. "No. Just going inside for a cold soda to put on my jaw." Actually, now that I'd thought of it, that sounded like a great idea.

With a face full of glaring doubt, Savannah continued into the cafeteria.

I let her go, stopping to duck behind my still-seated sister for cover as well as to steal Emily's half-full soda.

"Ah," I sighed as the cold can both hurt and began to numb my aching jaw.

"What *happened?*" Emily demanded when she saw my face.

"Got a mirror?"

She took a makeup compact from her purse and pretended to check her lipstick so I could sneak a peek at my reflection over her shoulder.

"Huh. It actually looks like it feels." I stuck the can back on it, gritting my teeth against the pain.

She snapped the compact shut. "Well? Are you going to 'fess up?"

"The official story is…football. Really rough practice today."

"Except you don't have football until *after* school and yet somehow got this way at lunch, genius."

Hmm, good point. "Okay. Suggestions?"

"Only if you promise to fill me in on the truth later."

"Deal."

"Okay." She sighed. "It was football, all right. But the amateur kind with a bunch of freshmen, you don't know who, outside during lunch. You were running for the ball and hit a tree face-first instead."

Of course her story would have me looking like a complete idiot. But it would do. Grinning, I gave her shoulders a quick squeeze. "Genius. And our parents worry how *I'll* turn out."

"Get to class, heathen. And I want a full report after dinner tonight."

"Uh-huh, sure thing." I returned her soda then ducked out the nearest exit and took the shortest route possible to my third-period class. Along the way, I braced myself for the torturous wait ahead.

Sometimes, not knowing really was better. Because now that I knew exactly what Savannah Colbert meant to me, I suddenly had no clue how I would hide it. And not just from the Clann, but from her, too, for as long as it took for her to see that I wasn't one of her stalkers.

Knowing how hardheaded she was…this might take a while.

CHAPTER 10

Tristan, four weeks later...

I was obeying her wishes. The wait really might kill me, though.

I'd played like crap today, and my body ached from the punishing tackles I'd endured because of my lack of focus. Because of her—the only reason that could make this kind of pain worth it. I didn't usually hurt this much even after a game against our toughest rivals. Thankfully the wait would be over soon. Her stalkers hadn't made it two hours after making eye contact with her. Four weeks of ignoring her was more than enough time to prove I wasn't one of Savannah's stalkers.

No more secrets soon. No more hiding how I felt about her. No more following stupid, unexplained rules from the Clann.

I was just stepping out of the locker-room shower when I felt that unmistakable ache tugging at my gut and chest. But what was Savannah doing here at the field house? Usually one of the other Charmers managers came to the field house for ice for the injured dancers.

"Female in the house," I roared out the warning a little louder than usual. After all, this time it was Savannah coming in. Good thing you could only see into the locker room if you looked through the hall doorway a few yards past the ice machine. As long as we guys either covered up or stayed out of sight from the door, she wouldn't get flashed while she filled ice bags.

I sat on a bench out of view from the hallway, dried off with a few quick towel swipes, then pulled on my boxer briefs.

"Well, hellooo, baby," Dylan called out.

I looked up. Dylan was standing nude and minus a towel in front of the door.

"Dylan!" I barked, half rising from the bench as quick anger rushed through me.

Laughing, Dylan jerked his blond bangs out of his eyes then sauntered over to the bench.

"Man, the ladies don't want to see your two puny inches," someone joked from the other side of the lockers.

"You're a jackass," I muttered to Dylan. Why did I still call him my best friend? Right now, I was seriously considering hitting him upside the head.

Hmm. I couldn't hit him, but I *could*…

The twisted wet towel hit Dylan's bare butt with a loud crack, followed by his even louder howl.

Yeah, that would do for now.

Savannah

I ignored Dylan's leer as I entered the tiny portable building for yet another fun-filled history class. Talk about a grade A jerk. Dylan probably thought he was a real stud, flashing me this morning. Usually Head Manager Amber sent

Vicki or Keisha out to the field house for bags of ice at the end of Charmers practice. But this weekend, Mrs. Daniels had dropped a bomb on us. Head Manager Amber was moving away; her mother had gotten a new job in Dallas. Vicki and Keisha were filling in as alternate dancers for two Charmers who had gotten hurt last week in a stunt that had gone wrong. Since I was still reluctantly keeping my promise to the vampire council about not dancing anymore, that left me as the new head manager who had to lead around two silly freshmen office aides temporarily on loan from the front office.

I hadn't trusted the new managers not to get lost or distracted at the field house, so they had been given the job of stowing the music system while I fetched ice bags and wrapped injuries at the end of the morning practices. After this morning, though, I might have to change that job assignment around.

Not because of Dylan. Dylan's immature display this morning had made me blush, but he was just an annoying moron, like most of the Clann kids who tried to bully me. I could ignore him.

The football player and descendant whom I couldn't manage to ignore, despite my every effort to, was Tristan. Four weeks had only made me see more clearly how dangerously strong my feelings were for him. Unfortunately, or maybe fortunately, those same four weeks had totally killed his sudden feelings for me. If he'd ever really felt anything in the first place.

Like now. Here I was, unable to stop thinking about the guy stretched out in his desk just inches away from me. And he obviously couldn't care less in return. Not an eye flicker my way. No reaction if I moved or dropped a pen. Nothing. Four weeks ago, it was all hearts and roses and promises of undying love outside the cafeteria after beating up my ex-boyfriend. Now I didn't exist at all. Exactly as I should have expected all along from him, given our history together.

Part of me—the logical part—said I was extremely lucky that my gaze daze had worn off both him and Greg right after their fight. And yet my heart still stupidly ached over the fact that they were both avoiding me now. Tristan was a player; of course he would blow hot and cold, and I was just an idiot for hoping otherwise. But Greg had never seemed the type of guy to act like that. His other ex-girlfriends were still friends with him. Why couldn't we stay friends, too?

I found myself missing Greg at the weirdest times now. Like last Saturday on my sixteenth birthday when I should have been nothing but happy, I ended up spending most of the slumber party with my friends wondering whether Greg might remember my birthday and call or text or something. If we had still been together, he probably would have taken me out somewhere to celebrate.

And then last Wednesday when I passed my driver's exam and got my license, one of the Charmers teased me about how the blue backdrop in my photo made my hair look the exact same color as carrots. I couldn't tell my friends about that; they would have seen it as proof that all Charmers were evil, when in fact the girl had only been joking around with me. But I could have told Greg. If we were still friends. If he wasn't avoiding me like the plague.

Maybe it was better that both boys were ignoring me now. That way, there was no danger of Greg getting accidentally gaze dazed again. And I wouldn't have to argue with Tristan about why we shouldn't break the rules and date each other.

I just wished I could forget as easily as they did. Then I wouldn't be constantly tormented with the memories.

Memories of dancing with Greg at the homecoming dance…

Tristan whispering my name, looking down at me as we stood so close together...

Greg hissing my name over and over as his mouth pressed bruising kisses along my cheeks and neck...

The look in Tristan's eyes as he'd thrown Greg to the ground...

Sighing, I rested my forehead in my hand, using my forearm to block my peripheral view of Tristan. Lord, how I hated this class. Everywhere else, I could stay busy, find ways to think about something else. But in here, with Tristan just inches away, it was impossible to think about anything but the past.

A past I wanted to forget. Needed to forget, if I ever hoped to like myself again.

Because in that moment when I'd found myself pressed against Tristan outside the cafeteria, my fingertips touching the blood on his lip, when I'd realized I was staring right into his eyes...

I'd *wanted* my gaze to affect him.

Worse yet, while part of me was happy to see him clear eyed now and able to focus on Mr. Smythe's lecture, a darker part of me wished he hadn't recovered at all.

I should be locked up. I was a menace to the male half of society. And a scary freak to the other half.

Since no one had locked me up yet, the next best thing I could do was aim for nunhood. Which wasn't a hardship, since the only guy I wanted was a notorious player who was off-limits anyway. Mom might have been exaggerating when she said my dating someone in the Clann could start a war between them and the vampires. But just in case she wasn't, I planned to avoid Tristan as much as possible from now on.

If only I could stop myself from craving him every waking minute of the day!

One of my many mistakes with him was ever allowing him to see that I still cared about him. But I wouldn't be repeating that mistake again. I would just have to get better at hiding my emotions around him.

Starting now.

With a sigh, I rested my chin in my hand and tried to ignore Tristan's long, muscled body stretched out in the desk beside me. And his soft, curly hair as he bent over to gather up his stuff from under his desk...

"What, the view this morning wasn't enough for you, princess?" Dylan's too-close drawl yanked me from my thoughts.

He was standing in front of me, planting his crotch in my direct line of sight. I'd been too lost in thought to notice the bell had rung and everyone was getting up to leave. Great.

Don't react, I told myself. *That's what he wants, to see you look embarrassed.*

Freezing my facial muscles into the coldest expression I could manage, I looked up at his nose. "I'm sorry, was there something to actually see?"

Tristan snickered at my right, threatening my self-control.

Dylan's sneer tightened in anger. His eyes squinted. "You know, I was wrong. You're not just a princess. You're an ice princess. Must be why Greg Stanwick dumped you. You were too frigid for his taste."

If he only knew the truth. That thought curved my lips into a smile. "Ice Princess. Hmm, I kind of like that one." It was better than some other possible names. Like *monster.*

Scowling, Dylan shook his head and walked away, muttering something that sounded like "freak."

Like I hadn't heard that one before. I didn't even blink.

The Brat Twins giggled at Dylan's remark before they got up from their desks behind Tristan.

Two more reasons to play the Ice Princess in here.

I smiled to myself as I gathered my things and joined the traffic exiting the classroom. Dylan didn't realize it, but he'd just given me the perfect strategy for the rest of the year. I could still be myself everywhere else. But in history, I would play the Ice Princess—cold, emotionless, untouchable. Dylan would get no reactions from me to feed his sadistic-bully side. The Brat Twins would be deprived of their entertainment.

And Tristan wouldn't see how I really felt about him.

Tristan

My new plan was backfiring, and I had Dylan to thank for it.

I'd thought that playing things extra cool around Savannah for a month would make her realize I wasn't going to stalk her, so she could relax around me. And she'd almost seemed to at the beginning of this week. But then that idiot Dylan just had to mess with her and call her an ice princess. Ever since, she'd seemed to take the jerk's teasing to heart. Her face was like a mask, her body moving so little during class that I sometimes wondered if she were miming a statue. She blinked, breathed, took notes and read. But there was zero visibility into her real personality.

If possible, she'd become even more untouchable.

Having four fellow descendants in class with us didn't help, either. With Dylan one row to my left and back, the Brat Twins directly behind me, and Mr. Smythe running the class, my every move was under watch in history. I might as well have not even had a class with Savannah this year, for all the opportunity I'd had to talk with her. I couldn't even look at her for two seconds without the Clann knowing.

By Friday, all the hope I'd started the week with was morphing straight into frustration. I'd have to come up with a new plan.

Mr. Smythe was late getting to history class today for some reason. The bell had rung, but with no teacher in sight, everyone was talking. A few people stood around, adding to the low-key party atmosphere. Dylan was one of the few walking around. His movements were casual as he flirted with some of the girls two rows over. But something about the look in his eyes set me on edge.

"Hey, Tristan." Vanessa laid a hand on my shoulder.

I turned in my desk to look at her. "Yeah?"

"I was wondering, do you have a date for the Fall Ball yet?"

As if I'd ever be stupid enough to date *her* again. "Not interested, Vanessa."

Something slammed to the floor hard enough to shake the entire building. All conversation stopped.

I jerked my head to the right in time to catch Dylan's smirk.

"Oops." He laughed and strolled away from Savannah's books and papers, which now covered a three-foot span of floor in front of her feet.

What the...

"Did you want to help me pick up all the stuff you just knocked off my desk?" Savannah muttered. In the dead silence of the room, her every word was as loud as if she'd shouted.

There you go, Sav, don't take any of his crap.

I gripped the edge of my desk, too aware of the giggles the Brat Twins didn't bother to hide. Evil witches; they must have been in on Dylan's plans and distracted me on purpose. They knew I'd never let Dylan bully anyone. Though I'd thought he'd outgrown this crap back in junior high. Unless he'd just been hiding it from me for the past few years.

He stood by his chair with an arrogant grin. "Who says I knocked your books off, sweetheart? They probably just fell off on their own."

"I have eyes. I saw you, Williams," Savannah replied in a calm voice.

His grin turned nasty as he slid into his desk sideways, stretching his legs across the aisle. "Yeah, I've been hearing some strange stories lately about those freaky eyes of yours, Colbert."

I started to lunge out of my chair, but Savannah was faster. She seemed to glide down the aisle, reaching Dylan's desk in three long-legged strides.

Planting a hand on his desk and another on the back of his chair, she leaned over one slow inch at a time until her nose almost touched Dylan's. "Better to have freaky eyes than an entire face that looks like you were dropped on it as a baby," she murmured.

Someone giggled on the other side of the room.

Fury filled Dylan's eyes, and I felt light prickles race over my forearms. Son of a… Dylan was going to use power on her.

I let my own energy level shoot up, knowing Dylan would feel it as even sharper prickles on his skin. My ancestors hadn't led the Clann for four generations based on their good looks. Just because I had no intention of following in my father's footsteps for Clann leadership didn't mean I didn't have the strength for it. And it was time Dylan remembered that.

He glanced at the twins with raised eyebrows. They answered with tiny shakes of their heads. Then his angry gaze shot over to me.

That's right. Now you're getting a clue, I thought.

He sighed, and his energy level backed down. But he still didn't look sorry.

Then Savannah leaned over and whispered something in his ear.

He jerked away, scowling again. "Pick up your own crap, Ice Princess."

Smiling, she straightened up and strolled to the front of the room to gather her things. I wanted to help her, but I could feel three pairs of spying eyes watching me.

So I stayed stretched out in my chair, staring at the dry-erase board that ran the length of the front wall. But to punish and warn the other descendants, I kept my energy level high. Vanessa hissed my name, wiggling in her chair, and I grinned. Maybe this would teach her and her sister not to help Dylan mess with innocents anymore.

Strangely, Savannah's forearms broke out in goose bumps. Frowning, she paused to rub them for a few seconds, then finished gathering her papers and books and returned to her desk.

She'd done that before when I was ticked off. Could she somehow be sensitive to the Clann's powers?

As soon as Mr. Smythe opened the classroom door, I pulled the energy level down to normal, showing them a little of what my dad had taught me over the past month. I'd worked hard for weeks to develop control over my energy levels. No more emergency grounding for me.

I wasn't surprised when Mr. Smythe glanced at all four of us descendants with obvious suspicion. Every descendant on campus had to have felt the energy spikes Dylan and I had just released. But instead of trying to send me out for yet another emergency grounding session, Mr. Smythe dived into his daily lecture.

Not that I listened much. History was easier to remember when I read about it at home. Besides, I was too busy reconsidering my friendship with Dylan.

He was waiting for me outside the building after class. "What was that crap in there?"

I waited for the last students to get outside of hearing range before I replied, "A reminder. You seemed about to lose your control."

"Unlike some people, I don't lose control."

I ignored the insult. My issues with energy control were old news. "Then you were about to use power against an innocent on purpose."

"She's no innocent. Not with those freaky eyes of hers."

Because my energy wanted to spike out of control, I lashed out in a different way. "What did she say that scared you so badly?"

"She didn't scare me, she threatened me! She said if I wasn't careful, she'd use those eyes on me. Have you heard what some of the guys are saying about her, about what she can do?"

"Then maybe you should leave her alone."

"Are you siding with her?"

"I'm saying leave her alone. She's done nothing to you, so just back off."

"Or what?" His energy level jumped. "You going to fight your best friend over her?"

I studied the ugly look on his face. We had been best friends once. But in the past year or two, Dylan had changed. I didn't even know the guy anymore. Now all I saw when I looked at him was a power-hungry bully who preyed on others. Had he always been this way and I just didn't see it?

"I will if I have to." Because no true friend of mine would attack an innocent. My energy flared out to match his then shot up a level higher. His hands flexed then fisted, the muscles in his arms cording as the greater energy stabbed at his skin.

He held my stare a few seconds longer then hissed, "See you at the game."

I dipped my chin in acknowledgment, then watched my former best friend turn and walk away. Something inside my chest tightened. Why did I get the feeling this conversation wasn't over?

Tonight's game against Herndon High, Jacksonville's biggest rival, had been a tough one so far. Apparently their defensive line didn't like Dylan any more than I did right now, because they'd been after the quarterback especially hard all night. Unfortunately as an offensive tackle, it was my job to protect Dylan's sorry butt. As a result, I'd been taking hits intended for him all night, when what I really wanted was for one of their defensive line to take Dylan's head off and save me the trouble.

Seeing Savannah running herself ragged helping the Charmers in the bleachers didn't improve my mood any. Why she was helping them was beyond me.

Body aching, I stood on the sidelines while our defense took over for a while. I should be focused on my team's efforts out on the field right now. Focusing on the field had been easier last year on JV, because they didn't have the Charmers or pre-drill classes at their games. The varsity team, on the other hand, got all the school-spirit groups at our games. As a result, my gaze kept straying sideways and up to the home bleachers. Third quarter now, time for the Charmers to take their break. Which meant Savannah would be in the concession-stand area instead of with her duffel bag and the protective charms I'd created for her. If they were even still in there. I'd have to get Anne to sneak a peek into Savannah's bag at lunch next week and make sure.

In the meantime, I'd just have to hope that none of her stalkers tried to mess with her right now.

After a few minutes, Savannah returned to the Charmers

bleacher section. My heart rammed into my throat as a breeze grabbed her long ponytail and toyed with the red strands, spreading it out like dark fire around her head.

"Playing with fire?" Dylan removed his helmet as he walked over.

I jerked my gaze back to the field. "No clue what you're talking about."

"I'm talking about Freaky Eyes up there."

I turned to face him. "Man, what is your *problem* with her?"

"My problem is with *you*. I just can't get it out of my head how you're willing to side with her over your best friend."

"I'm not siding with her. I'm just saying we don't attack innocents. You know the rules."

He closed the foot of space between us. "Screw the Clann's rules." He waved an arm around us. "These people are sheep, and you and I both know it. We should be ruling this town, not hiding in it."

"Keep your voice down," I warned, glancing around us. But everyone was focused on the game.

Dylan sneered. "You're pathetic. Look at you, afraid someone might hear us talking about the Clann. But everyone already knows! That's the real joke. Everyone knows about us, and the elders are still holding on to their stupid, outdated rules. What we need is new rules. Maybe new leadership, too."

It was my turn to sneer. "Like who? Your dad? You?" The Williamses had always been nothing but a bunch of butt-kissing weasels. I'd thought Dylan was different. Today he'd showed me I was wrong.

"Why not? The Colemans aren't the only ones who can lead. Why not give somebody else a chance for a change?"

What a crybaby. "If the Clann thought your dad could lead better, they would have voted for him. They didn't. So get over it. And get over the rules, too, while you're at it. I don't always like the rules, either, but you don't hear me whining about it all the time. If you've got a problem with the Clann's rules, take it up with the elders who made them."

He stepped so close our face guards almost hit. "You might not make the rules, but your dear old dad does. And for someone who says he doesn't like the rules, you sure don't seem to mind enforcing them."

"Whatever." I was getting tired of this argument fast.

He cocked his head. "Or maybe you're not supporting Daddy."

I scowled. "Now what do you mean by that?"

"You've never wanted to fight me before. Maybe this whole 'protect the innocents' crap isn't about the rules at all. Maybe it's just about *her*."

I clenched my teeth together. "You need to go away now, Williams."

He smiled. "That's it, isn't it? Even after all these years, you've still got a thing for the redheaded freak! Wow, what a freakin' hypocrite. All that talk about following the rules, but really you want to break the biggest one of all."

"I said drop it."

"Ooo woo, your mommy and daddy would *love* that, wouldn't they? Their precious baby boy dirtying himself with the one girl who is off-limits. And a freak at that."

Fury flash boiled my skin. "I told you, leave her alone!"

"What's wrong, Coleman? Don't like me calling her a freak?"

"Dylan…" I was on the edge, could feel the anger crowding out rational thought.

"Just remember, if the leader's son can get it on with the freak, so can I," he murmured, his smile turning into a leer.

I snapped.

My hands shot out at Dylan's chest. To everyone else, it must have looked like a hard shove. But while my hands were still inches away from contact, my energy and will burst out, an invisible force that slammed into him. It knocked him off his feet and sent him sliding five yards away on his back.

For five short seconds, seeing the shock on his face was worth it. Until I remembered where we were.

Aw, hell, I was in for it now. No way had any descendants here missed that. Including my parents up in the bleachers.

Mom hadn't stopped shrieking for the past forty-five minutes. It was all along the same lines.

"What were you thinking, using power in public like that? You've jeopardized everything we have here. And not just our family, but everyone else in the Clann, as well! I can't believe I raised such an irresponsible idiot for a son." Her heels were wearing a path in the rug. If she kept this up, she'd have to buy a new one for Dad's study soon. "How many times do we have to tell you? Our power here is fragile. If any of these farm-loving bigots ever found out what we can do, every one of us would be run out of town faster than you could say *witch hunt.*"

Up to that point, Dad had sat in a glaring silence propped up on the corner of his desk. But now he jumped in. "Well, now, I wouldn't go that far, Nancy—"

"And you! You're responsible for his training," she snapped at him. "What were you thinking, teaching him to use power like that? We haven't taught combat training since the vampire wars ended, Samuel. And even then, they're to be used against that undead filth, not on our own kind."

"But—" I began.

Dad flashed me a look of warning, and I shut up again, slouching in the leather chair in front of his desk.

"Nancy, why don't you head on up to bed and let me handle this?" he said.

"I want him off that team."

No way. Mom couldn't do this to me. She knew I wanted to play for the NFL someday. I always had. If she yanked me out of football my sophomore year, it would look bad to the coaches and college recruiters. Not to mention hurting my stats.

"Nancy—" Dad tried again.

"No, Sam." Her eyes blazed with determination as she stared down at me. "I never wanted him to play a contact sport, and you know it. It isn't safe for any descendant. Dylan shouldn't be playing sports, either. But at least he's not the future leader of the Clann. Tristan is. And tonight just proves my point. Tristan could lose control again, but worse. What if he really hurts someone? Or gets hurt by someone else? Where would the Clann be then?"

"Mom, I—"

"You screwed up, Tristan Glenn Coleman," she shrieked. "You know the rules as well as everyone else. If we don't punish you, the Clann will. So no more football. Or basketball. Or any other sports. Maybe then you'll finally focus on your magic training instead of wasting your time."

And that's when I knew the truth. I could see the victory in her eyes. Tonight, my stupidity had given her the perfect opportunity to make sure I never did anything other than school and magic training again. Exactly what she had always wanted.

Rage burned in my chest, but I held on to my energy with everything I had, keeping the power level down by sheer will alone.

"Your mother is right." Dad sighed. "You have to be punished, at least for the rest of the year, and it's got to be a public one. Otherwise the Clann will start making demands. At least if we're proactive with your punishment, we'll retain control over what that punishment is."

"So, what, you want me to join the chess club now?" This wasn't really happening, was it? It was a bad dream. I'd wake up soon, right?

"Chess club, Spanish club, I don't care as long as it's not sports," Mom replied. Then she left the room.

"Sorry, son." Dad walked over to clap a heavy paw of a hand on my shoulder. "At least there was only a month left in the season."

"But we're in the playoffs."

"Well, there's always next year. If you keep your nose clean. And I better not hear about any revenge taken against Dylan, either. It's not his fault you couldn't control your temper."

I glared at him.

"What do you want me to say? You really screwed up tonight. The only reason the Clann's not ringing my phone off the hook already is because from the bleachers it looked like just a regular shove. What did you do to Dylan anyway? You and I both know I didn't teach you anything like that."

I lifted one shoulder in a half shrug. "I hit him with my energy."

"Impressive. Did you think any spell words or…?"

I shook my head. I hadn't even meant to use magic on him.

"Wow, son." He stared at me for a minute, his thoughtful frown nearly lost within his silver-white beard. "Well, guess we'd better add to your training time, then. Teach you how to control it better mentally."

I managed a nod. "Can I go? I've got to figure out the least socially dead activity I can do now instead of football." I choked on the last word.

"Sure. Just one more thing. What did Dylan say to tick you off so bad?"

I rose from the chair. "Oh, you know all those Williamses. They like to push people's buttons. Dylan just finally found mine." And then some.

My stomach in knots, I started to go up to my room then changed my mind. The grass was already wet with dew, the fall air sharp like knives inside my burning lungs as I flopped down in the backyard and stared up at the stars. And wondered what Savannah was doing right now.

Savannah

Exhausted, I took my time showering at home after the game. Tonight was my first game as the new head manager, and it was an epic failure. Between supervising the freshmen pre-drill girls in the bleachers next to the Charmers, trying to remember Amber's instructions on how to wrap injuries and which girls needed ice after halftime, and fetching stuff all night long, the night had been nothing but chaos. Seeing Tristan and Dylan's fight on the sidelines at the start of the third quarter definitely hadn't helped. Lost in thought about it, I'd messed up everyone's wraps, requiring the football team's trainer to redo them. I didn't bring enough bags of ice, forcing me on an extra trip up and down the bleachers for more. And I screwed up not one but three orders for snacks for the Charmers who had to stay seated in the bleachers during the team's third-quarter break while they iced down their knees or ankles. It was a wonder Mrs. Daniels hadn't fired me as head manager already.

Still drying my hair, I headed for my bedroom and pulled on a nightgown. But my body was on autopilot as my thoughts once again shifted to tonight's fight.

What had Tristan been *thinking?*

I doubted anyone at the game hadn't either seen or heard about how Tristan had shoved Dylan to the ground. But why had he done it? True, Tristan's fight with Greg had been much worse. But he had just been trying to save me from Greg at the time. Otherwise, I'd never seen or even heard about him losing his temper.

Not that Dylan hadn't deserved a good shove or two long before tonight.

"Hey, hon." Nanna knocked on my door before coming in. "You forgot this in the bathroom." She held out the gold locket she'd given me in the fourth grade.

"Oh, thanks, Nanna." I smiled and set it on my nightstand so I could finish drying my hair.

"You seem distracted tonight."

"Mmm, just tired." I yawned and climbed into bed.

"Well, get some rest. Don't forget, you've got that carhop fundraiser to do tomorrow."

I *had* forgotten. Good thing Nanna never forgot anything. Nodding, I turned off my lamp and settled in under the covers as she left the room and shut the door behind her. But in the darkness, my mind returned to thoughts of Tristan.

I'd seen him stalk off to the locker room after shoving Dylan. Probably sent there by his coach. I could only imagine how upset he'd been to miss playing in the last two quarters of the game. Especially during the playoffs. Watching Tristan play football always reminded me of how I felt when I danced. Like watching pure joy in action.

I was still thinking about Tristan as I fell asleep. So I wasn't surprised when I dreamed about him.

After all, I dreamed about him a lot. But except for during that one memorable dream, the invisible barrier always stood between us like unbreakable glass that held me back and prevented him from seeing me.

Not tonight, though.

Tristan looked heartbreakingly sad as he lay on his back in the moonlit grass, his hands laced behind his head. His eyes were open, but he didn't move or look at me as I approached.

Maybe he wanted me to go away.

No, that was ridiculous. This was a dream, and he was just a product of my masochistic subconscious.

I sat down beside him, tucking my legs to one side. At least this time I was wearing a long nightgown instead of just a T-shirt.

After an awkward minute of silence, I murmured, "Hard day?"

He nodded.

"I don't usually get to talk to you in these dreams. This is sort of special. So…want to talk about it?"

Sighing, he rolled toward me onto his side and propped up his head in his hand. "I lost my best friend today."

"Dylan Williams?"

"Yeah. Though maybe we really haven't been friends for a long time, and I just didn't know it until today."

"You're not friends anymore because you shoved him at the game?"

"No, we got into an argument earlier today. You could say tonight was just our way of ending the argument."

"What was the argument about?"

"He was talking crap about…someone. Someone who didn't deserve it."

I hesitated, but curiosity pushed me to go ahead and ask, "Someone I know?"

He stared up at me, the answer in his eyes.

"Me? You got into a fight with your best friend over me?" Yep, this was definitely a dream. I knew it for sure now. Even still, guilt swamped me as if this were a real conversation we were having and not just a fantasy. "You shouldn't have. It wasn't worth the fight." I wasn't his girlfriend. He hadn't even spoken to me for years. Why fight his best friend over me?

"Don't say that," he ground out, his eyes darkening a little. "Fighting for you is always worth it."

His words made tears prick my eyes and my breath catch in my chest. Oh, how I wished this weren't just a dream.

"Will Dylan…want to get even?" Maybe I shouldn't have asked that. After all, we were talking about his former best friend.

"No." He gave a wry smile. "He already got his revenge. My parents are yanking me off the team for the rest of the year."

I forgot to breathe. How many times had I overheard Tristan talking about wanting to play in the NFL? Football was everything to him. Just like dancing had been for me.

And now he'd lost his dream…because of me. "Oh, Tristan. I'm so sorry."

My eyes burned, and I blinked tears away. I had to remember this was just a dream. It wasn't reality.

So why did I have this urgent need to hug him?

"It wasn't your fault," Tristan said. "If he hadn't picked a fight with me about you, he would have eventually found some other way to tick me off. My dad's right. I shouldn't have lost control like that during the game."

And yet he still sounded upset, his voice tight, every word short and clipped.

The idea of him hurting caused my chest to ache. I had to do something.

And so, because it was just a dream where I could do anything I wanted with no consequences, I laid a shaky hand over his where it rested in the grass.

He drew in a quick breath and looked down at our hands.

Okay, maybe I shouldn't touch him, even in a dream.

I started to pull my hand back, but he spread his fingers then squeezed them together again, capturing mine in between.

I couldn't help it; I sighed.

He smiled but didn't look up from our intertwined fingers.

"Why does that feel so right?" I murmured past the tightness in my throat.

His smile faded as he looked up at me with green eyes that were darkening like emeralds turned away from the light. "Why do you keep fighting this feeling?"

"Because I'm not supposed to want this."

His smile returned, slowly curving his lips up. "But you do anyway."

I nodded, staring right into his eyes instead of at his nose. Only in my sleep could this ever be safe. It was a luxury I would take advantage of as long as I could.

"So do you still think I'm another of your stalkers?"

"I don't know. You seem fairly recovered in history, judging by how you've ignored me for weeks now."

His chuckle was a deep, warm rumble that made my pulse race. "I'm not ignoring you. Just trying not to scare you away again. You know, I'm not supposed to want this, either."

My heart stopped for a second.

He huffed out a short sigh. "Savannah, can't we at least be friends?"

"I would love that." It came out on a sigh without any hesitation. I wasn't breaking my family's rules by being friends and holding hands with someone in a dream, right?

"Good. I'll remember you said that." He slowly raised our hands to press a too-warm, too-real-feeling kiss to the back of my hand.

CHAPTER 11

Savannah

When I woke up, I could swear I still felt the press of Tristan's lips against my skin, and I wanted to cry. Why did the good dreams never seem to last long enough?

Then again, maybe I should be glad it was only a dream. Otherwise I would be responsible for Tristan's missing out on playing football for the rest of the year.

I rolled over, looked at my alarm clock then sighed. No time for bawling like a baby over a dream. I needed to get up and ready for the fundraiser. The Charmers were working as carhops at the local Sonic today. All tips would go toward paying for things like our team charm bracelets, duffel bags and game-day team shirts. I and some of the other Charmers were working the early lunch hour, so the tips should be good for our shift.

The job was easy, just delivering food and taking money, and made even easier by the Sonic manager's counting out change for us. Or at least the job *had* been easy until a certain black, chromed-out, single-cab Dodge Ram rumbled into a parking spot near the glass doors of the Sonic building. Instantly, that familiar ache filled my chest and stomach.

The driver-side window rolled down, revealing the driver. I barely held back a sigh. Tristan should *not* be allowed to wear sunshades. It ought to be illegal to look that good.

My muscles tensed as he placed his order, the speakers near the grill filling the kitchen with his deep voice.

I willed the regular employees to slow down, to take a little longer at putting together Tristan's order. We were swamped with customers now, and all the other Charmers were still out delivering orders. Which left only me to deliver Tristan's.

Just as his order was ready to go, Bethany Brookes returned, granting me a reprieve.

"Here you go." I thrust the tray of food at the stunned blonde. "Car five."

"Uh, okay," she muttered, no doubt wondering why I didn't take it myself. Oh, well, let her think I was being lazy. Anything not to have to take that particular order myself.

With a sigh of relief, I watched her go. No way could I have faced Tristan today. Not after last night's dream. My hand tingled again with the memory of his kiss. I rubbed the spot and turned away from his truck.

I could swear I felt someone staring at me.

I tried to ignore the urge to rub my tingling neck. When someone else's order came in, I was only too grateful to take it to a car parked on the row opposite from Tristan's.

When I returned, the relief was short-lived.

"Milk shake for car five," the manager said, sliding a red plastic tray with a foam cup toward me. I searched for someone else to take it, but I was the only Charmer there. Lovely.

Clenching my teeth, I grabbed the tray, headed toward Tristan's truck and braced myself for emotional impact.

"Hey, Savannah," he murmured when I reached his

Melissa Darnell

window. He'd removed his sunshades, and I felt the full effect of that watchful gaze on me. Maybe his wearing sunglasses shouldn't be illegal, after all. At least they would have given me some protection against those soft green eyes and long, gold-tipped eyelashes. Why, oh, why, did the boys always get the long eyelashes?

I couldn't speak; my throat was too dry. So I forced a small smile instead.

"I guess you heard the news by now."

That got me to look up, at least as high as his nose. "Hmm?" He was wearing an electric-blue polo today. A white T-shirt peeked out from beneath its opening. My fingertips itched to trace that ribbed collar.

"About last night's game?" he prompted.

"Oh. Yeah, I saw it."

"Seems like everyone did." His chuckle sounded just like it did in my dreams. "So, I suddenly have a lot of extra time on my hands. And a free first period every day."

Wait. What? "You're not playing football anymore?" Why wouldn't the coaches have just temporarily benched him or something? Getting kicked off the team for shoving a team-mate seemed a bit overkill.

"Yeah. My parents yanked me from the team for the rest of the year."

Holy crap. Just like in my dream. My heartbeat took off. How the heck had I dreamed about *this*? Was this some kind of witchy thing, like clairvoyance or ESP?

And in my dream, he said that Dylan and he had been fighting because of me.

Was it true?

"Tristan, did you shove Dylan because of—" Wait. I couldn't say that without sounding like an egomaniac. But I had to know. "Um, why were you and Dylan fighting? If you don't mind my asking, that is."

He froze, then lifted one shoulder in a half shrug. "Don't worry about that. So listen, Bethany had an interesting suggestion."

I fought the urge to frown. Of course he would think anything Bethany said was brilliant. Everything the perky blonde said captivated the boys. Good thing she was actually nice or more girls would fantasize about murdering her on a daily basis.

Tristan continued. "She said your team has an opening left for an escort."

A Charmers escort? Him? He'd be bored out of his mind. All they did was sit beside the managers at the football games. That and escort the officers around the field during the second quarter when the officers went over to meet and greet the other dance teams. Not to mention Mrs. Daniels and the new Charmers captain usually handpicked each year's escorts. The job was invitation only.

Then again, no Charmer would ever turn down the opportunity to hang on Tristan's arm if given the chance. If he asked, they'd let him be a Charmers escort in a heartbeat.

But why in the world would he want to?

"Um, that's an…interesting idea," I finally managed to stammer out.

"Yeah. So what do you think? Should I give it a shot? Am I Charmers escort material?" He put on his best grin and waggled his eyebrows like a goofy comedian while he gave me money for his order.

I tried to put on my Ice Princess mask but wasn't quick enough. A small laugh escaped me. "Well, it would be convenient for flirting with the Charmers." In fact, the escorts were notorious for dating the Charmers. Since his player notoriety was already firmly established in our school, he'd fit right in.

"Good point. It would make it easier to actually see a Charmer, since your team seems to have nonstop practices and performances."

I nodded, though the idea of his dating a Charmer made my stomach churn.

"So you think I should do it?" He stopped smiling, solemnly waiting as if my answer actually mattered to him.

"I…" Because I yearned to gaze into his eyes, I stared down at the five-dollar bill he'd given me instead. "I'll go get your change."

I tried not to run for the safety of the kitchen. What refuge could it really offer anyway? The building was mostly glass on the upper half of its front three walls. And I knew with absolute certainty that Tristan was staring at me now. Probably wondering if I was nuts.

I lingered inside until the manager frowned at me, then I slowly walked back to his truck. "Here's your change." I counted it out, careful not to touch him in the process.

"Aren't you going to give me something?"

Pulse racing, my gaze slid up to his mouth. "What?"

"A straw?"

"Oh!" With a relieved laugh, I got him a straw from my half apron's pocket.

And gasped as his fingers wrapped around both the straw and my hand. "And your answer to my question?" he murmured, his hold a gentle torment to my skin.

A breeze kicked up around us, bringing with it the slightest hint of his cologne, a little bit spicy, a little bit cool and crisp. I wanted to drink it in.

What was the question?

Oh, yeah. Should he be a Charmers escort?

Oh, Lord, what a question to ask me of all people, and while holding my hand, too. He must know or at least suspect that I had a crush on him. Okay, a bit more than a crush now, but that was beside the point.

He stared at me, still waiting for my answer, his strong fingers gentle and warm on my skin. Oh, crud.

"Um, Tristan, I think you should do whatever will make you happy." There, that was a good reply. "I'd better go. Thanks for helping out the Charmers. Have a great…" Whatever else I had meant to say was forgotten as he lifted my hand to press a kiss to the back of it.

He paused then murmured, "Thanks for helping me decide."

After he released my hand, I stumbled away a few steps, completely speechless. We both froze for what seemed a long time. When I could think again, I turned and slowly walked to the safety of the kitchen, rubbing my still-tingling hand as I went.

Tristan

I sat in my truck, unable to move or do anything but watch Savannah walk away from what she probably thought was another crazy stalker.

Was it too much too soon, kissing her hand like that? I'd hoped it would remind her of our shared dream last night. But what if it scared her off instead?

I'd hoped that after last night we could make more progress today. I'd had it all scripted out, though I'd had to order a milk shake I didn't want just to get her to come to my truck. But the conversation hadn't followed the plan at all. Why couldn't I get her to relax and be herself with me in real life like I could in our dreams?

Somehow I had to get her to let her guard down around me

in real life, too. One or two shared dreams a year wasn't going to cut it. We needed to spend more waking time together.

Hmm. Well, she did say I should do whatever would make me happy. Mom had said "any activity but sports." And seeing Savannah every day up close and outside the Clann's spying eyes would definitely make me happy as well as give her time to learn to relax around me.

Grinning, I grabbed my cell phone, pulled up the internet and searched Google for a certain woman's number.

Savannah

I clutched my thermos cup of tea in one hand and the ring of team keys in the other as I got out of my truck in the JHS front parking lot. The truck was an old, single-cab Chevy S10, primer gray and in desperate need of a few layers of paint. My father had had it delivered last week for my sixteenth birthday, an obvious and unsuccessful bribe to try and get me to talk to him again. Apparently speaking with his daughter didn't even rate a truck with an actual paint job. Not that a brand-new sports car would have been enough to make me forgive him for threatening Mom's and Nanna's lives, either.

Even my friends had teased me a little at my slumber party, suggesting I buy some Rust-Oleum spray paint to keep it from rusting any further. Still, it got me where I needed to go and was free, so I'd asked Mom to pass on my thanks to him. But I also didn't feel too bad about pushing the door shut with one foot. It wasn't like I could damage the finish.

In the early-morning, late-October hush, the campus was cooler now that autumn had finally arrived. It was also empty and peaceful, just the way I liked it best. No one around watching me, judging me. No one to have to try to hide all my secrets from. Until the Charmers began to show up in the next fifteen minutes, the campus was all mine. And maybe the janitors', though I never saw them around this early before school. At this time of the day, the normally confining pines surrounding the school felt cozier, like a giant green blanket to hide in.

I adjusted the headphones over my hair and ears, pushed Play on my iPod, then walked fast past the cafeteria and math building. I needed to get moving or I'd be late with the sound system for practice. I'd switched out this duty with the freshmen managers today so they could start fetching ice bags and deliver roll-call charts to the front office instead. This new system should work out perfectly since I had to unlock the dance rooms anyway.

Sighing, I passed the math building, started up the cement ramp that led to the sports and art building's foyer doors... and nearly dropped my thermos and keys.

Tristan was leaning against the doors, his hands tucked into the pockets of his faded jeans. In the early-morning light, made gray by the shadow of the building, he looked surreal against the royal-blue painted doors. Maybe I was still half-asleep and imagining him. I yanked off my headphones.

"Good morning, Savannah."

I stumbled but quickly recovered. Nope, he was definitely here. "Um, good morning, Tristan."

"You use the old-style headphones. Interesting choice." He nodded at the hot-pink and black headphones still dangling from my hand.

Blinking fast, I jerked open the zipper on my duffel bag and shoved my iPod inside. "Uh, yeah. My ears are too small for those earbud things to stay in." Plus the old-style headphones stayed on better when I danced. "What are you doing here?" I winced. That came out ruder than I'd intended, but it was better than showing how I really felt about him. "I mean, if you're here about the escort thing—"

"Yes and no."

Okay. That cleared it all up. "Are you here to talk to Mrs. Daniels?"

"No, I already talked to her on Saturday. I gave her a call and explained my situation."

Even walking as slowly as I could, I still wound up at the doors. And much too close to him. I fumbled through the team keys one-handed, trying to hurry up and get the doors unlocked so I could move away from the temptation as quickly as possible.

"Here, let me." He eased the thermos from my hand, his fingers sliding over mine in the process. A tiny shiver rippled up my spine. I froze for a few seconds then recovered and focused on unlocking the doors. He held open the door for me and offered me the thermos.

"And what did Mrs. Daniels say?" I took the thermos back, careful not to touch his fingers, then darted under his arm and through the doorway. But not fast enough to miss catching the tiniest hint of his cologne.

"She and I came up with a better idea." He followed me inside, the heavy door slamming shut behind him. The sound echoed, emphasizing how empty the building was. How alone we were together.

Why, oh, why, did he have to be a descendant?

I had work to do. I should remember that and stay focused on my duties. I headed down the length of the shadowed foyer, pausing at the base of the stairs. Was he going to follow me around?

Oh, good Lord. I could not handle being this close to him much longer. He needed to leave so I could breathe right again. "So are you going to tell me why you're here?"

"You're looking at the newest Charmers manager." He gave a wry smile.

I couldn't help it; I snorted. Like the dancers, the Charmers managers had always been females since the team's founding in 1984. "Yeah, right. You? A manager for the dance team? What happened to being an escort?"

"I'll be doing that, too. But I needed something to replace football first period and cover my P.E. credit this year. The Charmers team class will do both. And Mrs. Daniels mentioned you were short on managers. So I figured, why not?"

Why not? I could think of a million reasons why not. "Uh, hate to break it to you, but I don't think we have a manager's suit in your size."

Laughter burst out of him, and I felt a ridiculous thrill in response. "Not a problem. I'll be in escort clothing at the games. I'll only be helping out as a manager at the practices."

He'd be with us at *every practice and game?*

Oh, no no no no no. This was *so* not good. Ignoring him in history class was hard enough. How in the world would I manage to hide how I felt about him if I had to spend hours with him, alone, every morning and afternoon?

To cover my dismay, I started up the stairs but had to stop halfway as another thought hit me. My family. They would make me quit the Charmers for sure. No way would they be okay with my spending time alone with any descendant. Especially not with the leader's son. Not to mention what the vampire council might assume if they found out about it, too.

I already wasn't allowed to dance. Now I would lose even the right to be the head manager.

"Uh, Savannah?" he asked, making me realize I was still frozen on the stairs.

Twisting slowly, I frowned down at him. "Why are you really joining the Charmers? I mean, is this because of...you know, what you said after that fight with Greg?"

"After five weeks?"

Huh. He had a point. Even as bad as Greg had been affected by the gaze daze, it had still taken him less than a week to recover.

"So you're really doing this for the P.E. credit?" I searched his face.

He shrugged. "It seemed like a good solution, since my parents banned all sports as part of my punishment."

I cringed as the question I hadn't been able to stop thinking about all weekend returned to me now. Why had he and Dylan fought? Logic said it couldn't possibly have been because of me. But logic also couldn't explain my dreaming about his being pulled from the football team before I should have known about it.

Chewing the inside corner of my lips, I continued up the stairs, my mind and heartbeat racing. Okay, I needed to chill out and think clearly here. So what if my subconscious or imagination or whatever had gotten one thing right in a dream? That didn't mean the rest of it was true. And Tristan showing up here to become a Charmers manager...well, that didn't have to be about me, either. He just needed something that would fill first period every day. Only the sports and spirit teams took up first period on both A and B days. And if his parents banned him from all sports for the rest of the year, that would only leave cheerleading or Charmers.

He could have asked his sister to let him be a male cheerleader for a while, my mind whispered.

I tried to picture Tristan in a male cheer uniform yelling on the sidelines. Hot, but unlikely. He'd never be happy having to take orders from his older sister all the time. Not to mention having to cheer for the football team he used to play for.

So that left Charmers as the last option available. Nothing to do with me, no reason to think I was the cause behind his fight with Dylan or his volunteering to help the Charmers. Right?

Unfortunately, Mom and Nanna were still going to have a fit and make me quit the team, no matter what his reasons were for joining. Unless…they never found out. And why would they? Neither of them came to any of the games or team performances since I wasn't an actual performer.

Besides, I might get lucky. Maybe he'd quit soon. Mrs. Daniels was tough to please, and flirting with a bunch of giggling dancers could only be fun for so long. One, two weeks tops and he'd be so bored he'd be begging Mrs. Daniels to let him quit.

Funny how that thought didn't make me feel relieved as I reached the third-floor landing and pushed open the hallway door. But at least the panic stopped clawing at my throat. Maybe this would turn out to be no big deal, after all. It was just another shared class with Tristan. Right? Nothing romantic. No major rules broken, really. Surely I could hide my feelings for him for a couple weeks.

The upstairs floor was dark, with just enough light coming in from the windows to prevent me from running into anything. Tristan dogged my every step, so closely that, when I stopped at the hallway light switch, he bumped into me. He grabbed my waist, I was pretty sure from reflex.

"Oomph." His chest felt like a solid wall as it thumped against the back of my head.

"Sorry," he muttered and stepped away, his fingers sliding from my sides.

I worked not to sigh and tried to think straight again. "Um, why don't you stay here? I'll be done in a minute."

My hands shook as I unlocked the dance-room and director's office doors, turning on lights in both areas as I went. I grabbed the MegaVox portable PA system, jam box and trainer bag from the office closet then rejoined him in the hallway. I was surprised to find a dark scowl on his face.

"What, afraid of the dark?" My feeble attempt at a joke.

"This is part of your daily routine?"

"Yep." I headed out of the hallway, but he stopped me to take the sound system. "And I do it all in reverse each evening. Except the foyer doors—those the janitors lock up at night."

We headed down the stairs, the heavy trainer bag thudding against my thigh suddenly making me feel about as attractive as a pack mule.

He waited until we were out of the building before speaking again. "Do the other managers usually go with you for safety?"

"You sound like me on my first day as a manager. I asked my head manager almost the same thing when she used to do this. There used to be three full-time managers plus the head manager. But then Head Manager Amber moved away, and the other two sophomore managers were needed as alternate dancers for the rest of the football season after two of our dancers got hurt. So now it's just me filling in as the head manager, and two freshmen office aides temporarily on loan."

"So you're doing it all? The unlocking in the mornings, the setup, the locking up at night?"

We headed down the cement ramp toward the road that cut through the campus, connecting the front and back parking lots.

I shrugged. "Somebody's gotta do it, and the team director's already working her butt off creating choreography, putting together music, working with the school band on music and dance routines for halftime performances, running practices…"

He grumbled something under his breath, making me wonder if maybe he had the same problem I did with being awake this early in the morning.

At the end of the cement ramp, we turned to the left, heading down the road past the back of the math building toward the practice field. In the growing morning light, dew sparkled like thousands of diamonds on the grass that bordered the woods at our right, reminding me of my dreams. Of fantasies spent sitting in the grass at night with the very boy who walked beside me now. I ducked my head to hide the rising heat in my cheeks.

At the practice field, we entered through the chain-link gate and crossed the spongy black track that circled the grass.

The Charmers were already gathering at the center of the field, though practice wouldn't officially start for another ten minutes. As they waited, they stretched individually. But even at this hour, they were anything but quiet. Someone's laugh rang out, startling birds in the thin woods that ran along the outside of the field's fence.

Ugh. Morning people. Needing fortification, I sipped my tea then used the thermos cup to hide a smile as the Charmers visibly reacted to Tristan's presence.

I watched the change among the dancers with a strange sort of fascination. Honestly, I didn't know whether to laugh or roll my eyes. Even the seniors sat up straighter and pushed out their chests.

Bethany came running over with a perky smile. "Hey, Tristan! What are you doing here?"

Tristan shot me a smile for some reason. "Everyone seems to be asking that this morning."

Why was he smiling at *me?* I took the sound system from Tristan then tuned them out as best I could, moving away a few yards to drop my duffel and trainer bag so I could start setting up. Unlike the dancers, my duties started as soon as I hit campus and didn't usually end until practice was over. I didn't have time to stand around and chat.

"Hey, Miss Savannah." Keisha crouched down beside me and the MegaVox at the fifty yard line. Her knees popped from the action, making me cringe. She'd need wraps for those soon. "What's he doing here?"

"It seems we have both a new escort and a new manager."

"Him?"

I nodded, keeping my gaze down on the jam box I was checking the batteries on.

He must have heard us talking about him, because he came over and squatted beside me so close our knees bumped.

"Have fun," Keisha murmured. I tried to ignore the now familiar pain at seeing her join the dancers instead of working with me.

"*Miss* Savannah?" he asked after she left.

"We all call each other 'Miss,' then the person's first name, except for the director. It's a team rule to help us remember to always show each other respect."

"And you have to do that all the time, or…?"

"No, just during team time. Though sometimes we forget and do it in the halls and stuff, too." I dug through my bag for the clipboard and legal pad I used to take team notes on each day. "You'll need to follow it, too, if you stick around."

He gave me a wolfish grin. "Oh, I definitely plan to stick around."

Yep, he was already checking out the Charmer buffet.

"You close with a lot of the team?" He jerked his head in Keisha's direction where she stood talking with Vicki now. They didn't try to hide the fact that they were talking about Tristan. I just hoped they weren't including me in the conversation, because I so had nothing to do with this.

I shrugged. "Most treat me like a stand-in mom or

something. They know they can come to me if they need something or someone to talk to. But Keisha and I are closer than most. She's a manager, or she was till she became an alternate dancer for the season."

I felt him staring at me, though I tried to ignore that sensation, as well.

"Is that hard, seeing her dancing with the team while you do all the work behind the scenes?"

I looked at him now, wondering if he was trying to be mean. But his eyes were wide with innocence and something else…like he actually wanted to know the answer.

"A little. But I'm really proud of her, too." I was lying, of course. It was more than a little tough. But I was keeping my promise to the vampire council. No more dancing. And Keisha was a good dancer and worked hard as an alternate. She and Vicki both deserved to get to dance with the Charmers.

After a long, uncomfortable minute, he said, "So, what are we doing here?"

Grateful for the change in subject, I explained how to work the sound system, showing him the MegaVox's two headsets with microphones, one for the jam box and one for Mrs. Daniels to wear so she could call out directions to the team from the bleachers.

Meanwhile, Mrs. Daniels and the rest of the Charmers arrived. The director chatted with her dancers for a couple minutes then climbed into her usual spot at the top row of the metal bleachers.

As soon as Mrs. Daniels was seated, I stood up. The director liked me to hurry and get to her for our pre-practice meetings. "I'll be back in a few minutes. Try to save the flirting for after practice, or you'll tick off Mrs. Daniels."

He grinned up at me. "Good to know. I'll try to contain myself."

He'd probably make a beeline for the nearest Charmer as soon as I walked away. No telling how many of them were his exs. And how many more were soon to be.

The week passed smoother than I'd hoped for, though everything Tristan did seemed to have both advantages and disadvantages. He asked to be in charge of fetching the ice bags toward the end of each practice. Probably so he could play knight in shining armor for the injured dancers. But at least neither I nor my loaner managers had to deal with Dylan in the field house for a few days.

Tristan also liked to stand close to me and watch my every move while I wrapped strained knees, ankles and shin splints at the end of each practice. Either he enjoyed how the girls blushed from his nearness, me included, or he was gunning for my job. At least he was helpful, handing me things from my trainer bag when I requested them, though his fingers managed to brush mine every single time. I was starting to get used to wearing goose bumps from head to toe now.

Unfortunately, the temporary managers still hadn't completely settled down around him, which was becoming a problem. The two freshmen giggled and whispered a lot more now, which grated on my nerves. So I had to keep finding more things for them to do. The charming smiles he occasionally sent their way didn't help, either.

By Thursday afternoon, I had to pull him aside. "Could you please stop smiling at my loaners?"

"Uh, your who?"

I jerked my head in the freshmen girls' direction. "You know, the girls from the front office? The ones you've kept giggling for days now?"

He looked sincere in his confusion. But how could he possibly have missed the effect his smiles had on them? "I was just being nice to them."

"Well, would you quit it already? It makes them…" I waved a hand at the two giggling girls a few yards away on the track. "It's getting beyond annoying."

"So you want me to be rude instead?"

"No. Just try to be more, I don't know, big brotherly."

"Yes, ma'am, Miss Savannah," he said, his fake salute making me fight the urge to giggle myself.

Tristan

I hadn't expected to feel much while watching the Jacksonville Indians football team play without me that Friday night at the Tomato Bowl in downtown Jacksonville.

But it stung. A lot.

As I sat beside Savannah in the bleachers in my new escort uniform of a long-sleeve button-up denim shirt and khaki slacks, I remembered how it felt at the start of a game. The adrenaline rushing through my veins. Suiting up in my protective gear and uniform like a warrior readying for battle. The excited roar of the crowd, and knowing they were all yelling for me and my team.

Second quarter was worse. I'd been assigned to escort one of the Charmers officers. As we followed the line of escorts and officers to the visitor bleachers on the other side of the field, I could feel my shoulders and neck steadily knotting up. The tiny blond senior clinging to my arm was cute and sweet. But she wasn't who I wanted at my side. I gritted my teeth and glanced across the field toward the home bleachers.

Just in time to see Savannah returning to the Charmers section with what looked like a box lid full of foam cups.

Heat raced over my skin, and I had to work not to growl.

She shouldn't be fetching for the dancers. She was too nice for her own good.

Most girls wouldn't be so helpful all the time, or put up with half the crap she did. All night tonight, I'd had to listen to Charmers whispering, "Miss Savannah, do you have some hairpins?", "Miss Savannah, do you have any boot polish?", "I have a run in my tights, Miss Savannah. Do you have any fingernail polish?" And on and on and on. How could she take the constant neediness? Why didn't these girls bring their own emergency supplies?

I kept expecting Savannah to get onto them for forgetting so much stuff, or at least tell them she didn't have whatever they were requesting. Yet she never once frowned or hesitated to help them. One girl had even forgotten her hat and lived too far outside of town to get it, so Savannah had to leave the Tomato Bowl, drive two miles over to the high school and then walk around alone on a dark campus to find a spare.

Which didn't exactly help my mood. She should have told me where she was going. I could have fetched the stupid hat for them, or at least gone with her and made sure she was okay.

Either she was a doormat, or she was too brave for her own good. I couldn't decide which. One thing I did know…she'd rather be out on that field at halftime in the limelight with the rest of the dancers. She'd tried to hide it, acting busy with prepping wraps and ice bags for the dancers who needed them after performing. But I'd caught the pure longing in her eyes when she'd thought no one was looking.

So why wasn't she a dancer? Was it because she couldn't dance well enough to make the team? It couldn't be for religious reasons. Bethany Brookes had told me earlier this week that everyone had to try out for the Charmers before they could apply to be managers. Including Savannah.

Even if she was the world's worst dancer, she still didn't have to be the Charmers head manager. She could do something else with her life, something that took far less time, energy and patience. Was she aiming for sainthood? Didn't she ever get tired of helping others? Didn't she ever want something for herself for a change, instead of always doing what others wanted her to do?

And why did she put up with the twins calling her a freak in history class when they thought I couldn't hear them?

By the end of halftime, it had all combined into a heated ball in my stomach…. Anger at myself for taking Dylan's bait and getting pulled off the football team during the playoffs. Rage at the Clann for brainwashing all the descendants' kids into thinking a nice, innocent girl like Savannah was somehow a freak who should be avoided at all costs. And fury at Savannah herself for putting up with it and settling for being just a head manager.

So much stupidity and unfairness. And for what? *Why?*

I didn't get up when everyone else did for the third-quarter break. I was so mad I couldn't pry my hands from my bouncing knees. I didn't care that staying in the empty Charmers section practically guaranteed that my parents would see me here since they came to every JHS Indians football game to see Emily lead the cheerleading squad on the sidelines near the bleachers. Let them see that I was a Charmers escort. They'd pushed me into this.

I'd had enough of their controlling ways. Because I understood now. I was just like Savannah, wasn't I? I always did what my parents wanted, never stood up for anything I wanted for myself. My parents ran every part of my life. And I let them.

I hated to admit it, but maybe Dylan did have one thing right…some of the Clann's rules were just flat-out wrong.

At some point toward the end of the third quarter, everyone returned to the bleachers. Savannah came back to her seat beside me but didn't sit down. I could feel her looking at me, though I didn't look at her. I couldn't. If I did, I might yell or go hit a brick wall or something. I was already having a tough time controlling my energy level without seeing that sweet, patient expression I knew I'd find on her face.

"Tristan, did you want to go grab something to eat or drink? There's still enough time left in the quarter."

Once again, Savannah was thinking of someone other than herself. Bitter acid rose up in my throat. "No, thanks."

"Would you like me to bring you something instead?"

As if my legs were broken? Did she fetch for the dancers so much that she'd become everyone's servant? Gritting my teeth, I pushed out the words, "I don't need a slave, Savannah. If I want something, I'll get it myself."

"What?" she said, so quietly it was almost a whisper.

"You heard me. I said I can get it myself."

I never looked at her directly, but out of the corner of my eye I saw her body tense up. A few seconds later, she sat down, her back stiff.

Regret shot through me. I pushed it away. I wasn't going to apologize. Maybe I could have said it better, but I was still right. She did need to stop slaving for others all the time. Apparently I was the only person in her life who cared enough to tell her the truth.

She didn't speak to me for the rest of the game. Which was probably a good thing, because unlike her, I wasn't that nice. I couldn't just swallow my real thoughts and not spit out something that would show how ticked off I was by it all.

My foul mood carried me home, where Mom and Dad waited in the dimly lit kitchen. Dad was already in his favorite green house robe and matching slippers. Mom hadn't changed out of her designer jeans and Cheer Mom shirt yet.

Mom began, her arms tightly crossed. "So just when were you going to tell us about becoming a Charmers escort?"

I shrugged. They knew now. "What else was there? I'm barely passing Spanish and I suck at chess. You took away football. This is all I've got left."

"But, son, you know the Clann rules about staying clear of that Colbert girl," Dad said.

"She's not in charge of the escorts. And helping the Charmers is no different than having the same history class with her," I said, working to keep my returning fury in check.

Mom threw her hands in the air with a loud huff. "Why must you be so difficult? Why can't you just go to school, come home and do your magic training? You're already so far behind. How do you ever expect to lead the Clann if you keep wasting your time like this? And what is the Clann going to think about you working with that Colbert girl?"

"It's always about what the Clann thinks. What the Clann wants. What about what I want? You already took football away from me. What else are you going to take?" Blowing out a long breath, I turned and braced my hands against the cold granite surface of the island. "Maybe I should just leave the Clann."

Mom gasped.

"I get how important it is to you that I follow in your footsteps and become the next Clann leader," I said. "But that's what *you* guys want. It's not what I want."

Dad stepped closer to me. I turned my head to look at him. His face was twisted with hurt and confusion. "I thought you were enjoying the training. Do you really hate magic that much? Do you hate the Clann? Do you hate what I stand for as the Clann leader?"

My anger deflated a little. "No, Dad. Training with you has been fun. I love the time that we spend together working on spells and charms and stuff. But it's not what I want to do with my life. Magic is cool, but it's like a hobby."

"I thought football was your hobby," Dad muttered. "Something you would eventually grow out of. Just a passing phase."

"Yeah, well, it's not." I dropped my head and stared at the chaos of the mottled black-and-tan granite. "Look, I get it. I know I screwed up, and maybe I deserved to be taken off the football team for a while. I was stupid and I lost control. But my life can't be just about school and magic for the rest of the year. I need something else to do, or I'm gonna go crazy here."

Silence filled the kitchen for a long moment.

Finally Dad sighed and said, "All right, son. Let your mother and I talk this over tonight, and we'll all discuss it over breakfast. In the meantime, why don't you go do a little grounding and then get some rest."

They wanted me out of the house so they could talk. Fine, whatever. I nodded and headed out the patio door, sitting on the grass for a couple minutes. But for a change, I was already drained. I'd never spoken to my parents like that. All I wanted to do now was sleep. So I went back inside, up the stairs and down the hall toward my room.

At my doorway, I heard my parents' voices coming through their closed bedroom door. I hesitated, then eased closer until I could make out their words.

"Now, Nancy, you can't keep pushing him so hard," Dad said. "He's going to rebel, just like I did. Then he'll end up taking off, and we won't see him for years."

"Oh, please. Like he'd really run away from home. He wouldn't last a day on the streets."

Dad chuckled, the sound muffled through the wood. "Oh, you'd be surprised. I made it for two years before I met you and you talked me into coming back home. Plus, I didn't have that big ole trust fund to rely on like Tristan will when he turns eighteen."

Mom sighed. "I'm just so sick of all this football nonsense. How are we ever going to convince the Clann to make him the next leader if he won't buckle down and focus on his training?"

"He'll come around. If you stop pushing him. Let him be on this whole helping-the-Charmers thing. It won't hurt anything, and besides, he probably just wants to be around all those dancers. If I was his age, I'd want to be a Charmers escort, too."

"Are you sure it's not the Colbert girl he wants to be around?"

"Nah. That was over years ago. If he wanted to rebel, he would've done it back when we first separated them."

"I don't know, Samuel. I still think it's a bad idea."

"You think too much. Come to bed."

Time to leave. I eased along the hall, paused at my doorway, then continued on down the stairs and outside, flopping onto the grass on my back so I could stare up at the stars.

So Dad hadn't wanted to be the Clann leader, either, at first. Huh.

I spread my hands palms down on the grass, not to ground, but just to connect. To sense once again where I fit in this world. If I cleared my mind, I could actually feel it, that subtle pulsing of nature's energy beneath me. I was lying on one big battery, every blade of grass an outlet I could plug in to and take from or give back to as I wished.

I didn't reach for that energy, though. It was enough tonight to simply feel it, to know that I could tap into that power if I needed to.

I wasn't powerless against my parents, after all.

Until tonight, all my life I'd been drifting, unsure of who I was or what I wanted other than to play for the NFL. I'd let my parents make every decision for me, and I'd never complained much.

Now I still didn't know who I was. But I knew with absolute certainty what I wanted. Who I wanted. What I would give and do for her.

I'd finally found something worth fighting for. And somehow, I'd found my own freedom while I was at it.

I had a new kind of dream that night.

In the dream, I seemed to be connected with Savannah. No barrier separated us. I was able to sit down right beside her in the moonlit grass.

But she wouldn't speak to me or even look at me. And for the first time in any dream I'd ever had of her, she wore what I thought of as her Ice Princess mask. She was right there, just a few inches away from me. I could reach out and touch her if I dared. But I didn't, because no matter how near our imaginary bodies were to each other, she was still every bit as untouchable as in history class.

I woke up the next morning on edge and spent the rest of the weekend worrying about Monday.

CHAPTER 12

Tristan

I knew things were off track as soon as I saw Savannah headed my way Monday morning. She wasn't carrying her thermos cup of tea. And she was wearing the Ice Princess mask, her face cold and remote.

I tried to reassure myself that she was just having a rough morning. "Good morning, Savannah."

"Good morning."

No tea today meant no chance to hold her mug for her and touch her fingers in the process.

She opened the doors and headed upstairs, her steps brisker than usual. She didn't glance back at me on the way up, didn't pause once she reached the hallway.

She was silent as always during her morning routine of unlocking doors and grabbing equipment. But her silence was somehow different today, cooler, as if she were all business and the real Savannah wasn't even here.

"Rough morning?" I asked as we exited the building and the silence became too heavy.

"No, not really." Her lips formed a smile that looked suspiciously like the same one she'd given Dylan in history after he'd knocked her books to the floor.

Okay, obviously I'd screwed up at the game Friday night.

We entered the practice field and drew closer to the gathering dancers. But I didn't care that we'd run out of time for private talk. If I didn't apologize now, she might not give me a chance to later.

"Listen, Sav, about what I said—"

"Mister Tristan, while we are on team time, I'll have to ask you to please call me Miss Savannah. As I clearly stated before, it's the team rules, and how we show *respect* for one another." She didn't look at me as she spoke, her brisk stride never hesitating until she reached the edge of the fifty yard line where we always set up the sound system.

"Okay, *Miss* Savannah." The formal address felt all wrong coming out of my mouth now. Another barrier between us. "I'm—"

She held up a hand. "We need to get to work. Let's discuss this later please."

And then she walked away to do her early-morning meeting with the team director.

Oh, yeah. I'd screwed up big-time.

I thought I'd at least get to apologize at the end of practice. But she was sneakier than I'd expected. She had one of the freshmen managers walk with me to put up the trainer bag and sound system instead. The next morning, she got to the school before me and already had the sound system set up on the field by the time I arrived. Even that wouldn't have been an obstacle, except she had the sophomore managers there with her, too.

Tuesday through Thursday's practices were more of the same, with her constantly hiding behind her managers or sending me on office errands so she could avoid being alone with me. But then Keisha told me what time Savannah had been getting there at the school each morning.

So Friday morning, I made sure to get there even earlier.

Savannah

As soon as I saw him waiting outside the foyer doors, my shoulders stiffened. I pressed my lips together. If I opened my mouth right now, this could turn ugly. I might start talking and be unable to stop. There were too many things I wanted to say to him, questions I yearned to ask. Like why couldn't he just leave me alone? Why did he have to keep on breaking my heart?

Did he feel even the slightest bit sorry for all the years he'd refused to speak to me and pretended I didn't exist?

I unlocked the doors in silence, the clicking of the lock's release echoing in the foyer. He held the door open for me, and I tried my best to squeeze past without touching him. Even as my entire body begged for the exact opposite to happen.

Anne had tried to warn me and everyone else that he was a heartless, spoiled player. I should have listened to her instead of thinking he'd changed.

My eyes burned as we crossed the shiny linoleum floor and entered the staircase, my hands shaking as I gripped the metal rail and climbed the winding stairs.

Was it some kind of game to him, messing with my heart and my mind? Was it a big joke, getting me to open up and talk to him so he could turn around and treat me like crap again? And in front of others, too. At the end of the game, no less than five Charmers had asked me what I'd said to make Tristan act like that.

What *I'd* said! When all I had done was try to be nice to him.

He waited until we were halfway up the stairs before speaking. "Now can we talk?"

I swallowed hard as tears filled my vision. Praying my voice wouldn't shake and give me away, I mumbled, "What about?"

"I want to apologize to you."

I froze at the third-floor landing, sure I'd heard him wrong. After a few seconds, I found the strength to push the hallway door open. Maybe this was a new part of his game.

I unlocked Mrs. Daniels's office.

He followed me inside. "Sav, I'm sorry I was rude to you. It was…hard to see my team playing without me."

Part of me melted a little at that and wanted nothing more than to turn and hug him.

But then I really thought about his words, and fury replaced the ache in my chest. Even if he'd been upset, he shouldn't have taken it out on me. He acted like he was the only person in the entire world who had ever lost something that mattered to them. Like I wasn't in his exact same position at every Charmers practice and performance, watching others do what I would give anything to be able to do, too.

Not to mention the lovely experience he'd given me twice now of making me think we were friends only to toss me aside yet again like the worthless trash he apparently thought I was.

The anger gave me the courage to swallow back the tears, turn and face him.

"You say it was hard to see your team play without you." Just talking hurt my throat, it was so tight. Still, I somehow pushed out the rest of the words. "But what do you know about what's hard? All your life you've had it so easy. Jacksonville's golden prince, the rich boy all the girls want to date. The Clann's future high Pooh-Bah witch leader." I waggled my fingers in the air, the years' worth of hurt and anger all boiling up to push me close to the edge. It was all I could do not to yell at him right now.

He froze, those achingly gorgeous eyes of his widening. "What are you talking—"

A laugh escaped me, sounding hollow and empty even to my ears. He truly thought I was clueless, didn't he? "I know all about the Clann and your magic. My family are descendants, too—they were Clann until they weren't perfect enough, pure enough, for your kind anymore." I closed the distance between us until only inches separated us. He wanted to talk? Maybe it was time we really talked. About everything. "You want to know what's hard? Try having your best friend suddenly refuse to speak to you. Try not knowing what you did wrong, and begging your former friends to forgive you, and them just pretending you don't even exist anymore. For *seven years*. I must have been out of my mind to think you and I could be friends again. All you're going to do is treat me like crap, just like you did Friday night. And all I was trying to do was be nice to you!"

He dragged a hand through his hair, making a mess of it. "Look, you're right. I was a jerk all those years, and an even bigger jerk last week at the game. I mean, yeah, my parents told me to stay away from you, and I was trying to be a good kid and follow the rules. But I shouldn't have. And I'm not anymore." He cupped my shoulders, his hands burning me right through my sweater. "Please believe me, I never wanted to hurt you like that. And I'm more sorry about it than I can ever tell you."

His voice poured over me like ice on a burn, his words everything I'd wanted to hear for years.

But it still didn't quite explain his acting like an ass at the game. "I get why you were upset Friday night. But why take it out on me? Are you sure this isn't a Clann thing? They didn't put you up to this, did they?"

"What? Hell, no! I had to fight with my parents just to get to stay on as a manager."

That stunned me into silence for a few seconds. "What? Why would you do that?"

His entire body froze, and I wondered if he was even still breathing. After a long hesitation, the muscles in his neck worked as he swallowed hard. His hands, shaky now, slid down to cup my elbows, bringing my hands up to rest on his forearms. "Because I miss hanging out with you. We were best friends once. I miss that. I miss *you*."

All my anger drained out of me, leaving this strange sense of lightness and returning warmth inside. Tears of a different kind burned my eyes now. "Really?"

He grinned. "Yeah, really."

I couldn't stop an answering smile from forming. "Okay. But no more acting like an ass. I'm the head manager. I've got a rep to maintain here. How am I supposed to boss those Charmers around when I can't even keep my own managers in line?"

He laughed and faked a salute. "Aye, aye, captain."

"And you get to carry the sound system *and* the trainer bag. For at least a week, for your rudeness to the team head manager." My lips twitched with the effort not to laugh.

"Yes, ma'am, Miss Savannah." He grabbed the bag's strap and slung it over his shoulder.

As I followed him down the stairs, he looked back at me and grinned.

And that's when I realized how hard just being friends with him was going to be.

Tristan

At the end of practice, I hung around Mrs. Daniels's office with Savannah.

"Hey, I was thinking…you should keep an extra hat or

two in your truck," I said. "You know, in case anyone forgets theirs at the game tonight."

"Hmm, good idea. I'll have to remember to grab a couple this afternoon."

"Why not grab them now while you're here?"

She shut and locked the closet door. "Because I have to come back up here this afternoon anyways."

"I thought we didn't have practice the afternoon before a game?"

"We don't. But I do have to load all the Secret Sis gifts into my truck for the game." She waved a hand at the dance room.

I peeked through the doorway. A cabinet ran down the length of the back wall opposite the mirrors. Its counter was covered with blue-and-gold gifts of all shapes and styles. I gave a low whistle. That was one heck of a gift pile. With forty girls on the team, even if she put the presents into big boxes, she'd still have to make several trips.

"Do the other managers usually help you?"

"No. But they're not heavy, and I like the exercise."

"Yeah, as if you need that. Okay, I'll see you this afternoon, then."

"No!" Sheer panic erupted in her voice and across her face. I looked at her, eyebrows raised.

"I mean, it's fine," she added. "I really don't need your help. I'll see you at the game, okay?"

Her cheeks were pink, and she was looking everywhere but at me. Oh, yeah, she was definitely hiding something.

I'd just have to swing by the dance room after school and see what she was up to.

Savannah

I kept thinking the more time I spent around Tristan at Charmers practice, the easier it would become to ignore him in history class. But the only people I could successfully ignore in there were Dylan and the Brat Twins. In fact, I'd gotten so good at tuning them out in class that the twins actually seemed to think I was deaf now. Which was pretty amusing, considering my already batlike hearing seemed to be growing *more* sensitive every month. Thankfully Dylan had decided to leave all the bullying attempts to the girls for a while.

Unfortunately, even my supposed deafness didn't stop the twins from trying to bait me before the start of every history class in increasingly louder voices.

Today, the conversation was about who in the school was worth taking a bullet for. A stupid question, in my opinion, but the twins seemed to consider it a deep, debate-worthy topic.

"Hey, Tristan," Vanessa said. "Who would you take a bullet for?"

"Uh, anybody in the school, I guess," he muttered without turning to face them.

That's my Tristan. Smiling to myself, I pretended to focus on reading a book for an English assignment and prayed Mr. Smythe would hurry up and get to class.

"Oh, surely not just anybody," Vanessa whined. "I mean, you wouldn't take a bullet for the freaks, would you?"

"Such as?" Tristan sounded like he was warning the blondes about something, his voice dropping to a near growl.

"Well, like Freaky Eyes there," Vanessa stage-whispered.

Three guesses who *that* was. It took everything I had not to snort with laughter. The Brat Twins were so transparent they were pathetic. They were just trying to make me mad. But they kept using old material in their attempts. And then they were dumb enough to wonder why being called a freak no longer bothered me much. I turned the page in my book and continued reading, confident that my Ice Princess mask was in no danger of cracking today.

"Sure," Tristan replied. "Why wouldn't I take a bullet for her?"

"Because she goes around putting these horrible love spells on the guys," Hope answered, not even bothering to fake a whisper. Half the class had to have heard her. "Probably because she's so ugly. It's the only way she could ever get a guy to like her!"

The twins erupted in high-pitched giggles.

Now that was going too far, even for them. Fury tried to warm up my stomach, and my eyes stung. Oh, no, *no way* was I going to cry. I quickly imagined my anger turning into ice water running through my veins. *Ice Princess,* I reminded myself. *You are surrounded by ice and untouchable.* My heart rate slowed down, and I felt that coldness within spread to my face.

Sometimes, like now, my ability to embrace the emotionless cold within me was almost frightening. It had to be from the vampire side of my genes. It even made me *feel* like a vampire. But it was a heck of a lot better than breaking down into pathetic tears in class.

I was so lost in thought, I almost didn't notice how my skin broke out in prickly goose bumps. Probably another sign warning me not to slip too deep into Ice Princess mode.

"Girls, should you really be talking about this sort of stuff?" Tristan was definitely growling at them now.

"Oh, you're right," Hope whispered. "I didn't think..."

"You never do," he muttered.

Nice comeback. It almost made me feel better. But not quite. The coldness inside me wasn't appeased much. It wanted revenge. The chilling fury grew, spreading like poison, settling in my chest and stomach and making the muscles stiffen then cramp. Oh ow. Okay, that actually *hurt.*

Out of the corner of my eye, I saw Tristan glance my direction with a frown.

As soon as I thought about him, a new sensation took over, a pure and seemingly endless need that crowded out all other thoughts from my mind. Need for him. This was worse than simply wanting something, worse even than the usual yearning I felt around him. This was like being trapped in the desert for days and stumbling across a jug of ice-cold water. I craved him. My body screamed at me that I would feel so much better if I just leaned across the aisle toward him and...

Oh, no. Was this the bloodlust my family had warned me about?

I had to get out of here. Now!

I managed to stand up then stagger down the aisle to the teacher's desk. But Mr. Smythe wasn't there yet.

I kept going, changing direction toward the door. I was outside and a few yards from the building when I met the teacher.

I gasped out the first thing that came to mind. "Going to be sick."

"Do you need to see the nurse or—"

"No. Bathroom. I'll be right back." I kept going until I reached the nearest girls' restroom at the top of the hill and around the corner to the left.

But I wasn't really nauseous. Just...thirsty, or hungry, or something. It was as if my body had become this foreign thing I was trapped inside, and my mind didn't know how to communicate with it anymore. I didn't know what it needed. But at least I was pretty sure it wasn't blood. Hopefully.

I leaned against the edge of the sink, which felt warmer than me at the moment. I focused on my breathing, willing the pace to slow and deepen. Okay, that was one area I was still in control of, at least.

Then I looked up at my reflection. My eyes…they were nearly white. I'd never seen them that color before. They didn't even look like my own eyes anymore.

Closing them, I made myself calm down. Then I noticed my hands were freezing. I turned the hot water on and stuck my hands under the stream until I could feel my fingers again. The heat felt so nice, I pushed up my sleeves and scooped the water over my forearms, too. Gradually, the coldness inside faded away, leaving me exhausted. But normal again, thankfully.

I really had to get a grip on my temper. This was ridiculous.

When I returned to the classroom, the Brat Twins started giggling again just as the usual ache from being near Tristan spread through my chest and stomach like another muscle cramp.

"Quiet, girls," Mr. Smythe said.

The twins fell silent.

I ignored them as I returned to my seat and tried to listen to the day's lecture.

But deep inside me, I could feel that alien coldness waiting for the next time I lost control.

Tristan

Maybe Savannah was hiding the fact that she was seriously sick.

She'd shot out of history class today like a rocket and stayed gone for half an hour. When she'd returned, she had been white as a sheet and shaking, and she hadn't taken any notes during Mr. Smythe's lecture like she normally did.

And I never had heard a good explanation for why she had been so sick last spring. Maybe she hadn't made the Charmers team as a dancer because she had a medical condition. Though that still wouldn't explain why she didn't want me near the dance room this afternoon.

The rest of the day took too long to get through, but finally the last bell rang. I waited a few minutes at my locker to give Savannah time to get to the dance room. Then I headed that way, walking up the sports and art building's second-floor stairs as quietly as I could.

I could hear music, something sad and moody. Easing the door open at the third-floor landing, I entered the hallway and jerked to a stop.

I'd always known that Savannah was beautiful. But this... this was something else. I'd had no idea she could even move like that.

She'd turned off the dance-room lights and shut the room's double doors. But I could still see her through the long, narrow windows at either side of the entrance. In the faint sunlight slanting in through the exterior windows, with her red hair down and flowing around her pale skin...

She didn't look real. She looked like something I'd dreamed up.

Suddenly, she froze, her back to me, her body tense. When she turned toward the doors, she had one hand pressed to the center of her chest, her fingers spread wide just below her collarbone. Her other hand spread over her stomach below her rib cage.

I knew it. She *was* sick. I yanked the doors open. "Sav, what's wrong?"

"What are you doing here? I told you I didn't need your help."

"Just tell me what's going on. Are you okay?"

"Of course I'm okay. Why?"

"You look like you're in pain." I nodded at her hands.

She dropped them to her sides, where they clenched into fists. "No, I'm fine. I was just—"

"Then why aren't you a dancer with the Charmers?" The question blurted out before I could reconsider asking it. But if she was sick, I had to know.

She flinched as if I'd hit her and took too long to reply. "I wasn't good enough apparently."

"That's bull. You just danced better than their current captain does." Not that I was an expert, but it didn't take a rocket scientist to see how she'd been practically defying gravity in there.

One small shoulder rose and fell as she stomped over to the stereo and snapped it off. "That's how things work sometimes. I'd better get going."

I knew when someone was lying to my face. But why would she lie about this? I followed her into the uniform closet. "Why aren't you at least filling in as an alternate dancer this year with Keisha and Vicki?"

She stopped before a step stool, keeping her back to me. "That's a long story."

"I've got all night."

She hesitated, then sighed and reached for the stool, her movements suddenly jerky. "My father's...family didn't like me dancing last year. So I promised them I wouldn't anymore."

Must be some religious thing.

She dragged the stool a few feet to the left.

"What are you doing?" I asked.

"Hats." She pointed at a long row of square white boxes on the shelf above the uniforms, then stepped onto the stool. She was taking my advice, after all. Good. Except I was tall enough to get the boxes for her without needing a stool.

I stepped up beside her and reached over her head for a box.

She froze and drew in a long breath, then suddenly gasped and wobbled on the stool. Forgetting the hats, I grabbed her waist before she could fall.

Her entire body tensed like a string stretched to the breaking point. Gripping my shoulders with surprising strength, she met my gaze head-on.

Her irises were a gray so light they looked almost silver as she stared at me, the stool making her nearly my height now. The only other time I'd seen her eyes this color was after my fight with Greg. The last time we'd stood this close together.

"Tristan…" she whispered.

"Are you okay?"

She nodded, leaning closer to me. Then there was only one thought. Forget the plan. I lowered my head and kissed her.

I'd kissed other girls. Lots of them. Nothing had ever felt like *this,* though.

She kissed me back, her arms wrapped around my neck so our whole bodies lined up. My head swam, and my knees shook.

Too quickly, the burn in my lungs forced me to lift my head and take a long gulp of air. I kept holding her in case she felt as light-headed and weak as I did.

"I… We…" she gasped.

"Yeah," I agreed, still breathless. "Wow."

The dazed look left her face, replaced by horror. She pushed away from me and stepped down from the stool as all the color drained from her cheeks. "You *kissed* me!"

"You kissed me back." How had she recovered so fast? She had to have felt the world slam to a halt during that kiss, too.

"I did not. I got a little…light-headed. And you took advantage of my confusion."

"I can tell when a girl is kissing me back."

She pressed a hand to her stomach and another to her chest like before.

"Why do you keep doing that? And why are you feeling light-headed? Are you sick? Tell me the truth."

"No, I'm not sick. I just…" Frowning, she pressed a hand to her forehead. "I didn't eat much at lunch. And don't change the subject. This is not okay. You and I can't—"

"Have dinner with me." I cringed at my total, sudden lack of self-control. Good job, Tristan. So much for being her friend first.

"Okay."

"Okay?" My pulse shot up through my skull. Yes!

"No! Wait. No. I can't. *We* can't."

"Is that your final answer?" I joked even as my heart dropped down somewhere near my gut. I should have known getting her to date me wouldn't be so easy.

"I—I'm the head manager. You're one of my managers. I can't date you."

It sounded like she was reaching for excuses on the fly. "Did Mrs. Daniels say that?"

"No. But—"

"Then I'm allowed to date anyone I want to on the team?"

She frowned. "Yes. But it's—"

"Okay, then. I want to date you, Savannah." I crossed my arms over my chest, bracing myself for the argument I knew she'd need to convince her. "Obviously you feel something between us, too. Why not have dinner together?"

"Because I can't." She ducked out of the closet faster than I could move to block her.

I followed her to the hallway, hoping the shakiness in my knees didn't show. "Can't? Or don't want to?"

She froze just inside the dance room, her back to me as she gripped the doorjamb hard enough to make her knuckles turn white. I thought she wouldn't answer, or maybe she'd lie. "I wish I could. But I can't. I'm sorry."

"Can you at least tell me why?"

"You know why. Clann rules." Moving to the back of the room, she grabbed a box from inside the cabinet and started filling it up with gifts from the countertop, her movements jerky with not a single hint of that ghostlike grace she'd shown while dancing just a few minutes ago. "Will you grab two hatboxes, please? That is, if you're still insisting on helping."

Frustrated, I stayed where I was for the moment. "So you won't date me because the Clann forbids it."

She sighed loudly. "That's right. We're not even supposed to be friends, much less date. You know that."

"But their rules don't make any sense. They're stupid. Just because you're not in the Clann anymore shouldn't stop us from dating. Descendants can date regular humans. What's the difference?"

Her frown deepened. "They have their reasons. Hats?"

I stood there, rubbing the stubble starting to form on my chin. I'd need to shave again before the game tonight. "What reasons? It doesn't make any sense."

"It makes sense to them, and that's all that matters. A promise is a promise."

"You promised not to be friends with me, or not to date me?"

"Uh, both. It was sort of an all-inclusive kind of promise."

"You actually said the words 'I promise'?" When we were kids, she used to get so hung up on making me say those words and pinky swearing when I promised her something. Otherwise, she seemed to think I might wriggle out of the deal, whatever it was at the time.

And she remembered that, judging by how she had to duck her head to hide a grin now. "Well, not in so many words.

It was more like an understood thing. They said to stay away from you."

"Ah, but you never actually promised, did you?" I said, stepping closer to her.

She quickly grabbed the now-full box of gifts. "They made sure I understood the rules, and that's all it should take." Closing her eyes, she took a deep breath, letting it out slowly. "Look, maybe you don't care about following the rules. But I do. I made a promise to my family, and they trust me to keep it. So that's what I'm going to do. Okay? It doesn't matter what I want, or what you want." She started out the door.

"Hang on," I growled, ducking into the uniform closet to grab two hatboxes before joining her in the hallway.

She looked tired as we walked down the stairs and out the building, her shoulders slumping as we made our way down the cement ramp then cut across the grassy hill between the math building and cafeteria.

"Is that too heavy?" I tucked the hatboxes under one arm, reaching out for her box with the other. "I can carry—"

"No, it's fine." She jerked the box out of my reach and walked faster toward the front parking lot.

It was my turn to sigh in frustration. Man, she was hardheaded.

We filled up the seat of her truck. On the way back, as we passed my grounding tree outside the cafeteria, I said, "Go ahead, I'll catch up."

I pretended to tie my shoe until she was out of sight inside the sports and art building again. Then I pressed a hand to the dirt and pulled up some energy from the earth. The boost of energy helped clear me of the lingering weakness and light-headed effects from our kiss. Feeling better, I stood and jogged to catch up with her inside the foyer.

We made one more trip, both of us loaded down with the

last of the gifts. The entire time, her cheeks and ears stayed a bright pink. Then she opened her truck's driver-side door and slid in. But I couldn't let her go yet. Not till I knew where we stood now that we'd crossed the line beyond friendship.

I held on to the open door. And noticed her hands were shaking on the steering wheel. "You know this thing between us isn't gonna go away, even if you ignore it. Clann rules or not. It's not about them. It's about us."

Staring at the dashboard of her truck, she whispered, "It doesn't matter. We can be friends, but that's all. I can't date you."

"And if I keep asking?"

One corner of her mouth tightened. "Anne's right. You are spoiled."

"No, just determined." I shut her door for her. Then she started the engine and pulled out of her parking space.

At least look back at me, I thought. *Come on, just one little sign.*

As she left, I caught her looking at me in her rearview mirror. *Yes!*

Maybe I hadn't totally blown my chances with her. I just needed to find some way to get past this whole family-rules hang-up of hers. After all, some rules really were made to be broken.

Savannah

The glow singing through my body faded as soon as Tristan was no longer visible in my rearview mirror. I couldn't believe I'd kissed him. I hadn't even been that stupid in my dreams about him. What had I been *thinking?*

Oh, that's right, I hadn't. I'd gotten caught up in my emotions. Again.

I always got emotional during the few stolen minutes each week when I could safely have the dance room all to myself.

Maybe it was the fact that I had to keep my dancing ability a secret that made it that much more of a pure pleasure.

Whatever the reason, I'd been lost in the moment and the flood of emotions as I moved. And then I'd felt him there. But the usual ache from his nearness had been intensified to the point of pain, as if magnified through the lens of my other emotions.

The pain might have gone away eventually, if he hadn't kept poking at my feelings about things. I'd tried to push on, to ignore the pain and focus on getting back to work.

But then Tristan had moved to stand so close to me, his warmth at my side, his crisp cologne like a pile of autumn leaves I just had to dive into. The ache in my chest and stomach had exploded, and I'd lost all common sense. Something had driven me to stare into his eyes, to put my hands on his shoulders. Only one thought, one need had pounded through my veins. I'd wanted him to kiss me.

I'd used my gaze on him again.

I groaned and slapped the steering wheel. "Idiot, idiot, *idiot!* Sav, how could you? Twice on the same guy?"

I really should be locked up.

How long would it take for the gaze-daze effects to wear off him this time? Would repeated exposure make it take longer, or less time? Probably more. I hadn't been brave enough today to check his eyes for that possessed-stalker look afterward. I would have to find the courage and check tonight at the game.

Crap. This time I'd used my gaze on a guy I worked with almost every day. And was frequently alone with. How could I do that to Tristan? And just when things seemed to be clicking between us again.

If he—no, *when* he did, because they always did—when

Tristan went into stalker mode, I might have to ask Mrs. Daniels to take him off the team.

No. I couldn't do that. It wouldn't be fair to him, especially since I was the one who had messed up and used the freaky vampire gaze on him.

I'd have to be the one to leave the team. It was only right. My throat closed up at the idea.

That night at the game, I got to lead the pre-drill girls in their first bleacher routine. It was fun, it took my mind off the afternoon's disastrous events...

And it got me away from Tristan.

I couldn't understand why he affected me the way he did. Even last week, before everything had gone haywire between us again, sitting beside him in the bleachers had been excruciating. Tonight was way worse. Though frequent glances at his profile showed that he didn't seem bothered at all. At least my standing at the head of the pre-drill section put several yards and people between us so I could breathe easier.

And the ache in my chest and stomach wasn't as bad as it had been this afternoon.

Though if he kept staring at me while I danced in place with the pre-drill girls, it would be. I didn't even have to look his way; I could feel his stare. And because of it, tonight's game was very long and tense.

As the fourth quarter began, my phone beeped to let me know I'd received a text message. But who in the world would text me? Team rules forbade cell-phone usage of any kind during a game, except when we took our third-quarter break. Feeling conspicuous, I nudged my already unzipped bag open farther so I could see my phone's lit display inside.

Want 2 grab some pizza after the game?

It was from Tristan.

I nearly squeaked. Without lifting my head, I peeked at him through my eyelashes. He was staring at the field as if watching the game. But I noticed a cell phone barely visible in his hands.

While pretending to search for something in my bag, I quickly text messaged back, Sorry, we can't. Then I turned off my phone and zipped up the bag so I wouldn't give in to the urge to check it again.

Sitting beside him now was excruciating. I only stayed in my seat a couple minutes longer, my cheeks burning the entire time, before I retreated to the pre-drill section and worked on teaching the freshmen a new bleacher routine. Mrs. Daniels's idea to give them something to do. When the game ended, I tried not to notice how his denim "escort" shirt accentuated his wide shoulders and narrow waist.

When I got home, I was surprised to find Mom in the kitchen, just removing a pizza from the oven. "Hey, hon! How was the game?"

"Oh, you're home! And to what do we owe this honor?" I joked as I gave her a quick hug.

"I know, I haven't been home much lately. What can I say? I've got demanding customers." She slid the pizza onto a plate then took it to the table.

I grabbed us two sodas from the fridge and sat down with her. "Where's Nanna?"

"She already ate, and since she's got an early get-together with her crochet club in the morning, she went to bed already. It's just you and me, kiddo."

We chewed in silence for a while. Nanna's snoring traveled through her closed bedroom door and echoed faintly up the hall to us, making my lips twitch with the urge to laugh.

Then I looked at Mom and saw she was trying not to laugh, too. We both burst out in laughter at the same time.

"Lord, that woman snores like a freight train," she gasped when the giggles died down.

"Definitely."

She sighed, still smiling. "You know, I really miss hanging out with you."

My throat tightened. "I miss you, too." I took a careful sip of my drink then found myself asking her, "Mom, why did you ever start to date my dad? I mean, weren't you scared to, since he was a vampire and all that?"

She surprised me by laughing. "Why does anyone ever break the rules? I thought they were stupid. Growing up, I heard so many stories about how terrible vampires were. Then I met your dad, and he was the complete opposite of everything I'd expected. He was kind, and funny, and charming. He made me laugh. And of course there was that whole mystery element to it, since I couldn't read his mind. Being with him was peaceful, a break from the constant chatter of the rest of the world. I thought the Clann was just unfairly prejudiced against vampires, especially after I fell in love with him."

"You couldn't read his mind at all?"

"Nope. And it was such an unbelievable blessing! See, we witches can read the minds of fellow witches and humans. And vampires can read the minds of vampires and humans. But witches and vampires can't read each others' minds. It's probably a safety mechanism that developed over the years after warring with each other for centuries."

Then another thought made it even harder to swallow or breathe. "Does that mean…you and Nanna can read my thoughts?" Just saying the words made my heartbeat race like crazy. I clenched my hands into fists under the table so she wouldn't see them start to shake.

"No, we can't. Trying to read your thoughts is like trying to read your father's. It's like hitting a wall, even for a fairly powerful witch like your nanna."

"So if you can't read my mind, does that mean I'm turning into a vampire for sure?"

"Not necessarily. It could just be that you have some vampire genes. Your father wasn't able to read your mind, either, last time you saw him. Who knows? Maybe the mix of genes will make you permanently immune to both sides' abilities."

I could sure hope so. Otherwise, they would find out about Tristan, and my feelings for him, in no time. "So if being around Dad was so peaceful and all, and you were in love, why did you ever break up?"

She sighed, relaxing back in her chair. That made me relax and my hands were again reaching for pizza. "Because I grew up, and breaking the rules got old. Especially after you were born. The idea of constantly being on the run from not one but two international societies of witches and vampires with a baby on board was just too much. We started fighting all the time, over little things at first, then bigger issues, until it got to the point where I couldn't remember why being on the run with him was even worth it anymore. That's when we both realized it was over. Going against the flow might seem adventurous at first, but eventually you get worn-out. The river always wins."

Something in her words, or maybe the softness in her voice, made my chest ache, like a heavy weight had just been dropped onto me. My eyes burned, and I had to blink sudden tears away.

"Oh, hon, don't be sad." She leaned forward and covered my hands on the table with one of hers. "I had some good times with your dad, too. And, hey, I got you out of the deal. What more could I ask for?" She grinned.

But I wasn't really feeling sad for her, so much as for myself and Tristan. Because Tristan was asking me to do the exact same thing my father had once asked of my mother...to go against the flow. To break the rules. To be adventurous.

Except I had a feeling Mom might be right. How could we ever win against both the vampire council and the Clann, if they found out about us?

The river always wins....

But even that didn't change how much I wanted him.

"Have dinner with me?"

Tristan had added something new to our morning and afternoon routine. Telling him no should have gotten easier, considering he was now asking me twice a day. But nothing about fighting the attraction between us was getting any easier.

Probably because deep down I didn't *want* to fight it.

By the end of a solid week of his new routine, I thought I really might go nuts. Five days of telling him no, I could not go out with him, twice a day, and every time he asked, all I wanted to do was shout *yes*. By Friday morning, I couldn't take it anymore. I needed a break from him. He was trying to wear me down with temptation. But he didn't understand; this wasn't about what I wanted. Mom and Nanna trusted me to follow the rules. I absolutely could not go out with him.

Still, I couldn't get the memory of our kiss out of my mind, and he seemed to find a thousand different reasons to be close to me or accidentally touch me. Every time I looked at him after yet another casual brush or bump, he seemed unaware of the contact. But no way did he not know what he was doing.

I wanted to scream.

The situation had started to affect my memory, too.

Tristan stunned both me and Mrs. Daniels at the start of Friday morning's practice by interrupting our pre-practice chat for the first time.

"You forgot this," he said to me, handing me the director's headset for the MegaVox.

Oh, crap. I'd *never* forgotten her headset before. But why didn't he just hand it directly to Mrs. Daniels? I accepted the headset from him, my cheeks burning with embarrassment. His fingers brushed mine. Oh, of course. If he'd given the headset directly to Mrs. Daniels, then he couldn't touch my fingers and drive me even more crazy.

My temper shooting up, I snapped, "Thanks."

I finished the conversation with the amused director, then stomped down the metal bleachers, my footsteps ringing clear as bells despite the fact that the captain was yelling out instructions for the team.

"Miss Savannah," one of the freshmen managers said as I returned to the sound system. "Are you ready for us to go put out the game-day locker notes?"

"Yes," I replied out of habit without looking up. We switched out this duty every other week with the cheerleaders and had it down to a science. Then I had an idea. "On second thought, wait. Let's change things up. Tristan needs to know how to do that, too. So one of you stay with me, and one of you go with him to put up the notes." It was pure genius. Why hadn't I thought of this before?

"Which one—"

"Either, I don't care." I was snapping at the poor freshmen now. Great. I took a deep breath, made myself smile a little and said in a softer tone, "You two decide."

My forced smile turned into a real one when the girls had

to resort to a quick game of rock-paper-scissors to decide who would go. The victor gave a short squeal of delight.

Tristan scowled at me before walking off with the winner toward the school buildings.

Once he was gone from sight, I sighed and rolled the tension out of my shoulders. Carrying the sound system back to the office this morning wouldn't be fun, but I'd done it most of last summer without his help. I'd carry the heavier MegaVox so my manager could have the much lighter jam box. It would be worth it just to have a break from the relentless need I felt when around him. Plus, he wouldn't have a chance this morning to ask me out, since he always asked right after we locked up the sound system at the end of every practice.

Once we reached Mrs. Daniels's office, I had another brilliant idea. I also had my manager help me load all the Secret Sis gifts into my truck so Tristan wouldn't need to help me later.

Unfortunately, a quick stop by my locker before lunch proved I hadn't totally thwarted him. He hadn't just put out good-luck notes on the football players' lockers. He'd also left me a little note, handwritten across the back of a blue Charmers' game-day note and stuffed between the slats of my locker. Usually the game-day notes said something like "Good luck at tonight's game!" This note said something different.

Please have dinner with me.

That night, I went through the first half of the game on autopilot, too lost in thought to see any of the action on the field.

I wished I could ask someone what to do about Tristan.

Then again, I knew all my friends and family well enough to guess what each one would say if asked.

Michelle kept an eye on social status like some people memorized sports stats. For her, my dating Tristan would be an easy and ecstatic *yes!* After all, Tristan was rock-star hot in every way. And as Michelle and many other girls at JHS would see it, dating Tristan would mean an instant rise in social status, making a girl immediately worthy of notice. The longer a girl could hold his attention, the more noteworthy she became.

How many girls used Tristan for status points alone, and not because they cared about him as a person?

I sighed.

Then there was Anne's take. She would be quick to point out how notoriously short Tristan's attention span was when it came to girls. No girl had lasted longer than two months on Tristan's arm before he moved to the next.

Did I really want to fall for someone who would break my heart in a matter of weeks?

Carrie also wouldn't hesitate with her answer. Boys were a waste of time. Focus on getting into a good college.

"Miss Savannah?" someone whispered. "Do you have an extra bobby pin?"

Without even looking, I grabbed a few from my bag and handed them over.

Nanna would scowl and threaten to throttle me for even asking. *You know the rules!* she would say while shaking a gnarled finger at me.

And my mother—

The referee blew his whistle, signaling the end of the second quarter and the start of halftime. And time for me to get back to work.

For a while, I was too busy to think about anything other

than helping the dancers get warmed up and stretched out before their performance on the field. Afterward, when we were all back in the bleachers and I had finished rewrapping dancers' strained knees, shins and ankles, I returned to my seat beside Tristan. He looked worried about something tonight, his eyebrows drawn into a constant frown as he stared out across the field. I yearned to ask him what was wrong, if he was upset about having to watch his former football team playing without him again. He looked so frustrated and miserable; I wanted to hug him, to tell him it would be okay.

What would Mom say, if I asked her for advice?

If I could go back in time and ask her when she was a teen, her answer would obviously be to go for it. *What would one date hurt?* her teenage self might say. *Live a little.* Or as Tristan would say, *Some rules were meant to be broken.*

One date. One glimpse of what it would be like to be with Tristan. Just for a few hours, I could pretend that we were someone else. He wouldn't be in the Clann. I wouldn't be a half-blood outcast. We could just be Tristan and Savannah, two people on a date together.

All I had to do was say yes. One word. Three little letters.

Out of the corner of my eye, I could see Tristan's hands gripping his knees. I visually traced those fingers, imagined them reaching out to hold mine. To be able to hold his hand for a while...

My gaze slowly slid up to his mouth. I remembered how those lips had felt against mine, the warmth and light that had flooded me, filling me up from the inside out. To be able to kiss him again...

The world around us grew fuzzy and out of focus. But that was okay, because inside my mind everything was crystal clear now, every thought zipping like lightning.

The Clann and the council were only worried that I would

try to bite and drain him, right? But I wouldn't do that. I would never, ever hurt Tristan. And, yeah, my body was acting a little weird lately. But only when I lost control over my emotions. I could work harder to keep them under control. I could control myself around him.

I looked down at my duffel bag, still open. Lying right on top was his note, which I had been unable to throw away. And beside it…my phone.

One date couldn't hurt.

Before I could change my mind, I reached down and grabbed my phone. Breathing fast, my heart racing, my thumbs leaped across the keys with a will of their own as if possessed, sending just one text message to Tristan.

Yes.

Then I dropped the phone back into my bag.

I didn't look directly at him, didn't need to. I could still see him out of the corner of my eye as his cell phone buzzed in the left pocket of his slacks. He pulled the phone out, looked at it, and his entire body tensed up.

His thumbs practically flew over the keys as he text messaged me back.

I peeked through the opening of my bag at my phone's lit display. It read, Tonight?

Feeling his gaze on me I gave the tiniest of nods. It had to be tonight. I might come to my senses if we waited any longer than that.

He sent me another message. Meet me back at the school after the game?

I dipped my head half an inch in agreement, my heart pounding against my chest wall.

He put away his phone with a grin. Then his knees began to jiggle, just like they used to do in the fourth grade when he'd been nervous. They didn't stop for the rest of the game.

When the third-quarter buzzer sounded, he got up and disappeared into the crowd at the concession-stand area. I swear it felt like a rope had been tied around the both of us and was trying to drag me after him. The rest of the team soon followed, but I ignored the urge to go and stayed behind instead. After a few minutes, I received a text message from him.

Do you like pizza?

I smiled and typed, Doesn't everyone?

Favorite kind?

Cheese.

He took a while to reply. Someone must have interrupted him. Favorite drink?

Playing 20 questions?

I'm thinking picnic.

Another thrill raced through me, making me shiver. A picnic. At night. Just the two of us. Orange soda, I replied.

OK. Meet you at the school.

I couldn't help it. I sighed. Maybe tonight would be our one and only date. Maybe tomorrow I'd wake up and find that this had only been a crazy dream.

But I would definitely enjoy it while it lasted.

CHAPTER 13

Savannah

Nope, this was no dream. Because in a dream, my date wouldn't be late. Though he would be in a nightmare. And this was starting to feel like one.

I'd spent the past ten minutes waiting in my truck in the school's main parking lot. The longer I waited, the more I wanted to slap myself.

What had I been *thinking,* agreeing to this date? No way could this be a good idea! I must have gone temporarily insane at the game tonight. Did I have some secret wish to start a war between the Clann and the vampires? At the very least, I must have a death wish. Because if my family ever found out I'd even agreed to go out with Tristan…

Panicking now, I reached for my duffel bag and dug for my phone, determined to send Tristan a text message calling the whole thing off. It was easier to think when he wasn't around; text messaging was definitely the way to go.

But a familiar black truck pulled up beside mine just as my

hand closed around the phone. Crap. I'd have to tell him in person instead.

He jumped out of his truck, carrying a pizza box and a plastic bag. My heart shot up into my throat. I got out of my truck on wobbly legs.

"Hey," he said with a broad grin. "Sorry it took so long. They got the order wrong, and I had to wait for them to make another pizza for us. Did you get my text message?"

Us. The word sent a warm glow through my chest, replacing some of the panic and making it easier to breathe. "Um, no, it was in my duffel bag." I glanced down at the phone in my hand. I'd grabbed it for…some reason. Oh, yeah, because I'd been planning to…

He stepped closer to me, a foot away now, and I could smell the tiniest hint of his cologne. It slipped up my nose and down my throat. Oh, crap, I was losing it here. Maybe he'd put some sort of spell on me.

Okay. One date with him. Then I would absolutely have to put a stop to this. As long as the Clann and the vampire council didn't find out, one date would be no big deal, right?

"Still got your keys?" he murmured, his grin making him look like a little kid about to do something naughty.

Oh. The dance room. Perfect! No one would even know we'd been there.

Stuffing the phone in my pocket, I grabbed the keys from my truck's ignition then followed him across the dark campus up to the sports and art building's foyer doors.

"Déjà vu," I murmured, unlocking the doors while he stood beside me, the warmth from his breath reaching out to caress my cheek in the cool night air.

He chuckled then followed me inside. The moon lit the way across the foyer. The stairwell was another matter though. It was on the side of the building opposite the moon. Lighted by the sun through the windows during the day, the stairs usually had no need for artificial lights to guide the way. Halfway up, the moonlight from the foyer faded away.

Strangely, I could still see. Weird.

On the third floor, I unlocked the dance-room doors and reached inside for the light switch. But a warm hand over mine stopped me.

"Maybe just the closet light?" he murmured.

I left the overhead lights off, found the closet light switch around the corner, then pushed open the door so the smaller room's light could shine into the dance room. He was right; the costume-closet light was equal to a lamp in the larger space beyond. And it shouldn't light up the dance room enough to be visible from outside the building.

"Sorry, I should have brought a blanket or something to sit on," he said with a sheepish grin.

"It's fine." Feeling suddenly shy, I sat down with him on the floor in the center of the dim room and tried to remember that this was the boy I'd spent countless hours with as a kid.

"I brought music if you want to put some on." He pulled out a stack of CDs from the plastic bag.

I took them over to the stereo then picked one out with shaking hands. The CD's label read *Stressed Out #1*. Smiling, I turned the volume all the way down before putting it in, then gradually turned the music up until it was at a good background level.

I returned to sit near him. "*Stressed Out #1?* Should I even ask how many volumes there are in that series?"

He laughed. "A few. The Clann are control freaks. All their rules make life a little...stressful."

"I know what you mean. I've got a lot of people setting the rules for me, too."

"You live with your grandma, right?" He opened the pizza

box, picked up a slice of cheese pizza and set it on a paper napkin for me. Thank goodness he'd gotten a medium; I was so hungry I could eat the whole thing by myself. "I saw your grandma once. Last year. She looked like one tough lady."

I smiled. "She is. I live with my mom, too, though she's gone a lot of the time." He raised his eyebrows in silent question. I added, "She's a sales rep for a safety-products company."

He nodded, and we ate for a few minutes. I tried to chew slowly, but it felt like my stomach was eating itself with impatience. The pizza wasn't even making a dent in the hunger yet.

He'd gotten us both bottles of orange soda. He opened one and handed it to me, as if he'd assumed I wouldn't be able to get the lid open. The gesture was both sweet and amusing. Then he opened the other bottle for himself.

"So...will you finally tell me why you wouldn't go on a date with me before?"

Embarrassed, I looked down at the bubbles floating up in my soda. "Well, don't be mad, but you're sort of off-limits to me. You and everyone else in the Clann, actually."

"It figures. You've been off-limits to us ever since you and I got married in the fourth grade."

Heat flooded my cheeks, tempting me to press my drink against them. "You remember that?"

He grinned. "Hey, it's not every day a guy gets hitched."

I played with my bottle lid for a moment before getting the courage to ask, "Did your parents ever tell you why we couldn't be friends anymore?"

"Nope. Did yours?"

I shrugged, considering how to answer without lying or revealing too much. "My mom broke some Clann rule before I was born. So they kicked out my family and banned me from ever learning how to do magic."

"Huh. Must have been a major rule. I've never heard of any descendant being kicked out of the Clann before. Your grandma break the same rule, too?"

"Um, no. I think they just held her responsible for not stopping her daughter in the first place."

"I'd love to know what that rule was." He sounded grim.

"Uh…why?"

"I might have to try breaking it myself."

"What? Why? Don't you want to be the Clann leader someday?"

"No, I don't."

"Why not? I would think being able to do magic would be amazing." I almost confessed that I'd tried to do magic a few times with no luck. But something inside me held back.

He gave a short, humorless laugh. "Magic isn't always amazing. Sometimes it's a real pain in the butt." Something about the surprise on my face pushed him onward. "No, really. Magic is the reason I'm not playing football now. You know when I shoved Dylan out on the field during that game?"

I nodded.

"I didn't exactly hit him with my hands."

My mouth dropped open. I'd seen magic being used right in front of me and didn't even know it. Wow. "What does it feel like? Doing magic, I mean?"

"Like relaxing."

"Is it like that for everyone in the Clann?"

"No, I don't think so. At least no one else seems to have the problems I do in controlling it."

Because he was the leading family's son? "Well, I'm sure it's like anything else in life. You probably just need more practice, right?"

"That's what Emily says. But that's the problem. All I do is control it. Otherwise I would be blowing up crap and setting fires right and left by accident. It's like keeping your hand clenched up in a fist every second you're awake. I can never relax, never forget about it. I get tired of it. And then there's the whole issue of the Clann elders trying to run my life. They don't care what I want, only what they have planned for me."

"My parents told me descendants can read each others' minds. Can you? Read minds, I mean?"

"Sometimes, if I try really hard and the other person is focused. Mostly all I pick up are random thoughts, though, and it's too confusing to understand."

"Aren't you worried your parents will read your mind and learn about tonight?"

One corner of his mouth kicked up. "My sister's got me covered." He lifted his left wrist and pointed at his watch. "She gave me this a couple years ago. She told my parents it was to help me get to class on time. What she didn't tell them was that she'd also charmed it to block my thoughts from them. They just think it's some kind of new ability I naturally developed with puberty, and a sign that I should be the future Clann leader."

Nice to know even the all-powerful Clann elders could get it wrong sometimes.

"You know, you're really lucky to have such a good sister." I'd always wanted a big sister to look out for me, tell me what to do, what to wear, how to act to fit in at school.

"Yeah, she's cool. Though most of the time I'm pretty sure she only helps me because she likes getting away with things."

I laughed, trying to fit Tristan's description of his sister with the sweet, outgoing cheerleader image I had of Emily.

After a few seconds of surprisingly comfortable silence, I asked, "So if magic is such a pain for you to control all the time, why stay in the Clann?"

He stared down at the pizza box for a long moment before

shrugging. "I guess part of me isn't ready to destroy my parents like that. My dad still thinks he'll convince me to follow in his footsteps. I told them I'm not interested, but..."

I studied the unhappiness in his eyes. He really loved his family; that much was obvious. But I didn't understand one thing. "If you don't want to hurt your family, then why..." I waved a hand at us, the pizza, the sodas.

"Because asking me to stay away from you is asking too much. They have no right to tell me who I can and can't see." He stared at me, tempting me to make eye contact. I barely managed to keep my gaze at his nose.

"Maybe they're just trying to protect you," I murmured.

"Protect me from *you?* Yeah, right."

Oh, crap. I had to tell him the truth about me, about my father. About what I could be turning into right now, right here with him. I opened my mouth—

Tristan rolled up to his feet then held out a hand. "Dance with me?"

I gulped. Here was one of my fantasies just handed to me on a silver platter. Okay, dance with him first, then confess. At least then I'd have the memory to hold on to.

I took a deep breath and placed my hand in his, then had to draw in another deep breath at the contact as tingling arced down my arm. Uh, maybe this wasn't such a good idea, after all. But he was already pulling me to my feet and into his arms.

It was like coming home. A sigh slipped out of me as he wrapped one arm around my waist, his hand pressed against my lower back. He held my other hand in his and led me into a two-step. My hand fit perfectly in the curve of his.

The music changed to a slow song. He never hesitated as he led me into the new rhythm, his steps confident, his hands guiding me with the subtlest of nudges and pulls.

"A guy who can actually dance. I'm impressed," I murmured, unable to hold in the surprise. Greg hadn't been anywhere near this smooth.

His chuckle sent a whisper of warm air over my forehead. I glanced up through my eyelashes to find he'd bent his head down close to mine. "My mother drags me to a couple charity balls every year. She insisted I learn how to dance right so I wouldn't embarrass her."

"She teach you herself?"

"Yeah, much to *my* embarrassment." He spun us around in a series of turns that made me grin. "At least every now and then the skill comes in handy."

I laughed as he twirled me out then in against his side. "I see what you mean."

He made me laugh twice more as he dipped me then waltzed me around the room, narrowly missing stepping on the pizza. Then another slow song came on. His steps changed to half count so that we barely moved. The top of my head just reached his shoulder, making it seem natural to rest my cheek against his chest and wrap an arm around his waist. It was like we were made for dancing together.

I could both hear and feel his sigh. He lifted our joined hands to his chest, as if he wanted me to feel how hard his heart was pounding. Moving this close together, our thighs brushed, our knees and feet nudging each other at times. I wished I could melt into him. He was holding me closer than I'd ever dreamed possible for us. I should be afraid of all the people who might find out about this. But all I felt was peace and total contentment. I wanted to stay here, in this exact moment, for the rest of my life.

My phone buzzed.

Oh, no. Nanna. She'd be worried. "Oh, crap. I forgot to

call my grandma and let her know I'd be late coming home."
I started to pull away, but his arms stopped me.

"Savannah, wait."

I looked up at him in confusion, having to tilt my head way
back so I could see his expression. And was surprised to find
a hint of…was that *worry* in his eyes?

"Can I see you again?" His voice was impossibly deep and
a little hoarse, its rough edges delicious on my nerve endings.
I tried not to shiver.

A second date?

Needing time to think, I grabbed my still-buzzing phone
from my pocket and answered it. "Hey, Nanna. I'm sorry,
I went out for pizza after the game and forgot to call you."
Good, no lies there. Technically.

"Mmm-hmm. Well, next time be sure to call. I was getting
worried. You coming home now?"

"Yes. See you in a few minutes." I ended the call, put the
phone back in my pocket and turned around.

And nearly collided with Tristan's chest.

"I would really like a second date with you." He gave a
crooked half smile, but his eyebrows were still drawn together.

He wanted to see me again.

Part of me was leaping around inside, whooping with joy.
He wanted to see me again!

But the other part of me didn't know what to do. Obviously
I wanted to go on another date with him. Desperately. But…

He slid his hands up my arms to my shoulders and ducked
his head until his mouth was an inch above mine. "May I?"
His breath whispered over my lips, making me shiver.

Oh, Lord. Should I? No, I really shouldn't.

I nodded anyway.

He touched his lips to mine, a small brush, then again,
lingering. The need rose up, making me want to fall through

the floor and fly at the same time. Someone whispered, it couldn't be me, I'd never sounded like that before. I grabbed his shirt at his lower back, hanging on to the soft folds for dear life as the kiss deepened. *This* was what I had needed so badly in history today. I knew how to define that craving now. His mouth on mine, his arms around me, was food and water enough to survive on for the rest of my life.

He moaned, the sound filling my mouth like a dessert to savor. Something told me I should stop kissing him now, that continuing this kiss could be bad in a way I didn't understand. There was something I was supposed to remember. But that nagging thought was gone, lost beneath the swamping need. He tasted so good, his warmth filling up that cold cavern inside that had tried to drown me in icy waves in class.

Then he staggered, breaking off the kiss, and rested his cheek against the top of my head.

I listened to his ragged breathing with a dazed smile of my own, and had to bite my still-tingling lower lip. Wow. I could swear I'd just swallowed the sun. I was filled with light and heat. Kissing Greg had never felt like this. Not even close.

When I eased back, I was surprised to feel Tristan shaking a little. Wait. Boring, plain-Jane me had made the most gorgeous guy in school shake? Impossible. I stepped away, and he leaned back against the wall with a grin.

"Um, are you okay?" I asked with a laugh. Now he was just being goofy.

He gave me that little-boy grin and laughed, too. "Yeah. Your kisses are...a whole new ball game for me."

Hmm. "Um, is that good or bad?" Biting my lower lip, I moved over to our picnic area and began to gather up our drinks and trash. I let my hair fall forward to hide my face. Could he tell I'd only kissed one other boy besides him?

"Definitely good. Maybe too good. I'll probably need some

practice to get used to them." He startled me when he was suddenly there beside me and pulling me to my feet again.

I laughed, my hands grabbing on to his shirt for balance. "Tristan, we have to go! I don't want to go, either, but I told Nanna I would be home in a few minutes and—"

"I know."

"Then…" I waved at our things still left to be cleaned up.

"I'll do it. I don't want you cleaning up for me. I meant it when I said I don't need a slave." His hand coasted over my hair in the lightest of caresses, making me glad I'd left it down tonight.

"Helping others isn't being a slave, Tristan. It's called team-work and getting things done."

He grunted in response, apparently unwilling to argue any more about it tonight, and helped me gather up every-thing. I waited for him to reach the hall door. Then I shut off the closet light, which I made the mistake of looking up at first. Temporarily blinded, I had to find my way over to him by following the soft sounds of his breathing. For once, my supersensitive hearing was actually helpful.

I knew I'd found him when my hands touched the hard curves of his upper arms.

His hands were full of the pizza box and plastic bag. The darkness hid me, made me bolder, and the temptation was too much to resist. Grinning, I slid my hands up to his cheeks, stood on tiptoe, leaned in and whispered, "May I?" before I kissed him.

I understood then why humans have noses. So we can find each other to kiss in the dark.

I held the kiss long enough to make us both breathless. Then I pulled away while I still could and led him down the stairs, my entire body buzzing.

Once the building was locked up again, we headed down

the cement ramp to our trucks. He shoved the pizza box under one arm so he could reach out and hold my hand. During the slow walk together across the campus in the dark, the silence broken only by the occasional cricket and our feet rustling over the grass, a sudden thought hit me.

Mom had been a senior here at JHS when she'd met my father. Had my parents done this? Walked side by side across this same campus, defying the rules so they could be together, risking starting a war, too, just because they loved each other?

They'd ended up getting married, yet even that hadn't started a war between the vamps and the witches. But it had ended up getting my family kicked out of the Clann.

Then again, what could the Clann do to us now? They couldn't exactly kick us out again. I was already banned from learning magic. And Mom could've been exaggerating about our starting a war anyways. Not to mention...talk about her being a hypocrite! How could she have the nerve to tell me to stay away from all descendants when she'd *married* a vampire?

He followed me to the driver side of my truck, waiting while I got in, snapped on my seat belt and rolled down the window.

"Can I see you again next week?" he asked.

I frowned. All arguments aside, we were still breaking the rules. "Tristan, let me think about—"

He leaned forward and kissed me. By the time he stopped, I couldn't think straight again. "Ohhh, no fair using kisses...."

I felt his lips curve into a grin against mine, teasing me as he whispered, "Please, Sav? We can keep it a secret if you want. The Clann and our families wouldn't find out."

Could we really manage to date each other without anyone finding out?

He kissed me again, slowly this time, the tip of his nose nuzzling mine, robbing me of breath and reason.

Before I knew what I was doing, I found myself nodding in agreement.

And then praying during the entire drive home that we weren't making the biggest mistake of both our lives.

Nanna met me at the door, already dressed for bed in her favorite long, old-fashioned cotton and lace-trimmed night-gown. She held the cordless phone in one hand and a slip of paper in the other. "Your father wants to speak with you."

"Right now?" I froze. I hadn't spoken to my father in months, not since that phone call last spring when he'd made me promise never to dance again and passed on the council's threat to hurt Mom and Nanna if I refused.

"No, he left a message. But he wants you to call him back as soon as possible."

She took a message for him. I growled under my breath.

"You know I don't want to talk to him," I said as I quickly circled around her, moving fast down the hallway toward my bedroom in the hopes of avoiding an argument.

She followed me, her bare feet silent on the worn linoleum floor in the hall then whisper soft on my bedroom's brown shag carpeting.

"I know you don't want to talk to him," she said. "And I'm sure he knows it, too. But he said this time it's important, and if you don't call him back, he'll just keep on calling till you talk to him."

I kept my back to her to hide my burning face as my heart pounded in my ears. Had the vampire council somehow found out about my date with Tristan tonight? "Did he say why?"

"Nope. I wrote down the number for you."

Okay, then my father hadn't called about anything too life

threatening or he would've told Nanna. Maybe he was just in an extra-demanding mood or something tonight.

Reluctantly, I accepted the phone and slip of paper from her. After one last stern look, she left the room, shutting the door behind her.

I took off my socks and shoes. But that didn't take long enough. So I went ahead and got ready for bed, brushing my teeth and washing my face in the bathroom. Then I pulled on my favorite long white nightgown, the one with the spaghetti straps that made it almost like a dress. As I brushed my hair, it tangled with my necklace. The only way to free the strands was to take off my necklace and slowly unthread it from my hair. I tried to put the necklace back on, but my hands were shaking too hard to work the clasp. After several frustrating attempts that only wound my nerves tighter, I gave up and dropped the locket on my bedside table.

With nothing else to do to delay the inevitable, I took a deep breath and forced myself to dial the number.

"Do you always stay out this late?" were my father's first words.

Unbelievable. "This is the first time I speak to you in months, and *that's* how you want to start this conversation?" I was shaking from head to toe. I had to sit down on the edge of my bed and take a deep breath before I totally lost it. "And in answer to the question you really have no right to ask… on Fridays, yes, I'm usually this late coming home. Especially when our school has out-of-town games during football and basketball seasons. But shouldn't you and your council already know that from spying on me through Nanna and Mom?"

Silence filled the phone before he sighed. "I understand why you are angry, Savannah. I do not like the situation any more than you do. But I am just doing my j—"

Oh, spare me. "What did you need to talk to me about?"

More silence filled the phone, and I could practically hear him gritting his teeth. Good, maybe I'd finally made a dent in that infamous icy-cold vampire self-control of his. Of course, for him to truly get mad, he'd have to actually care in the first place. Which he didn't.

"I am calling officially on behalf of the council tonight."

Oh, *crap.* They knew! I held my breath and waited for him to continue.

The silence lengthened for a full minute before he finally spoke up again. "Savannah, is there anything you would like me to tell the council?"

They did know! How had they found out so fast? I slid off the bed to the floor and struggled to breathe as my mind raced. "Umm, no, why?"

"The council has requested my presence at their headquarters overseas, and I am leaving tomorrow. I needed to check for any last-minute updates regarding your changes before I leave. And to be able to truthfully tell them I have received those updates directly from you."

I tried not to sigh with relief. They didn't know.

He continued. "While I am away, however…"

My heart started racing again.

"I would like you to seriously consider coming to live with me instead."

Now *that* was random. "Why?"

"The council has expressed concern that you have been raised your entire life by former Clann members, and that this may have biased you. They would like you to consider living with me instead so that you will have a more balanced upbringing during your formative years."

Of course it would be the council's wish and not his. "I don't mean to hurt your nonexistent feelings. But like you said, I've spent my whole life here. With my *real* family. This is my home. All my friends are here. And I only have two years till graduation." Not to mention I'd rather die than live with a heartless council spy like him.

He sighed. "I will suggest to them that such a change in your living situation be delayed at least until you begin college. Perhaps that will appease them for a while."

"Tell them whatever you like." He would anyways. The council always came first for him. My needs probably didn't even make it onto his list.

"You should know, while I am there I may not be able to call your mother and grandmother for updates as frequently. So please tell them I will be in contact with them as often as I am able to."

Well, that sounded mysterious. Was he trying to bait me into asking him questions? Because that would require me to actually care about him.

After another long silence, he gave one last sigh. "Goodbye, Savannah."

"Bye." I ended the call then stared at the phone. That's when I realized just how badly my hands were shaking. If the vampire council had found out about me and Tristan...

Unpleasant as talking with my father had been, at least it had revealed one thing. The vampire council didn't know about my date with Tristan tonight. At least, not yet. Because if they had, my father would have asked me about it, or at least sounded disappointed with me.

I'd broken one of their stupid rules. Yet as all-powerful as they claimed to be, they still didn't know about it.

I closed my eyes and instantly remembered how it had felt to kiss Tristan. A slow smile spread across my mouth. If anyone found out about us, we would both be sooo dead. But... it had been totally worth it. Tristan's kisses were beyond addictive. And I was one hooked girl.

I thought of never seeing him again. If the council made me go live with my father now, I'd have to move to another state. I wasn't even sure which state my father was in at the moment; he moved around so much, living for months and occasionally years at a time wherever his latest historical-home restoration project took him. But I could guarantee that he would never live anywhere near Jacksonville, not with so many descendants concentrated here. Which meant living with my father would definitely force me to switch schools.

No more history or Charmers with Tristan. No more glimpses of him in the halls…

I shuddered.

I fell asleep remembering how it had felt to dance with Tristan. So I wasn't surprised when I immediately began to dream about him.

"Hi, Savannah." Tristan stood at the edge of a forest turned gray with moonlight. "Want to take a walk with me?"

"Okay." I walked over to him, my bare feet making a whispering sound with every step across the cool grass. When he held my hand, the warmth and strength I felt from his touch seemed every bit as real as if I'd been awake.

He smiled down at me, his eyes like mysterious emeralds in the silver light. He led me deeper into the forest, and I realized neither of us seemed to feel any pain, despite the fact that we were both barefoot. Shouldn't we have stepped on sticker burrs or pinecones by now? I looked down. A thick bed of soft moss covered the entire forest floor and halfway up the trees like a green snowbank. It felt spongy beneath my feet, like walking on a cool, thick towel.

We continued in silence for a while until we came to a clearing with a waterfall and a stream. On the bank, someone had spread a blanket and left a picnic basket. The moonlight shone in slanting rays through the trees here, making me yearn to dance and spin among them like a little kid. It all felt so familiar, too, as if I'd been here before.

"Come sit with me," he said, and I was only too happy to follow him to the blanket.

"This is where I wish I could have taken you for our first date. Somewhere as beautiful as you."

"Me, beautiful? Now I know this is a dream."

"What if I told you this wasn't a normal dream? That our minds really are connected right now?"

"Uh-huh. So you're saying you're not just a figment of my imagination?"

"Basically, yeah." He traced a finger over the back of my hand, then he looked at me, and I loved the fact that I could safely stare directly into his eyes.

"So then you've done this a lot before? Connected with other people's minds while they're asleep?"

"No, just yours. You're the only descendant I've ever wanted to dream connect with. It takes two descendants to dream connect. Otherwise I could see you but you wouldn't be able to see or hear me."

"Weird."

He grinned. "But fun, too. We used to dream connect all the time when we were kids. Do you remember?"

And in a rush, all those dreams came back to me. I *had* been here before...in our dreams. This was our place, our clearing where I'd dreamed that we'd played together countless times. "You ate all my pretend cupcakes when I asked you to, and you helped me decorate our tree house. Oh, and you also showed me how to dig really good tunnels for toy cars! Though I preferred Barbie cars and scooters instead." I laughed. "My mom used to ask me why I kept chewing off my nails. I told her it was to keep the mud from getting under them. She never understood, since I didn't play in the dirt in real life."

He chuckled.

"But why did we stop?"

He frowned, thinking about it for a moment. "Well, it hasn't been for my lack of trying lately. I thought at first that it was because my parents stuck some charms or a spell on my room. But I managed to get around that. Connecting has still been hit or miss, though." He tilted his head, studying me. "Something's different about you tonight." He kept staring at me for a long moment, then snapped his fingers. "That's it. Your necklace. You always wear that gold locket."

I instinctively reached for my necklace, then remembered. "Oh, yeah, I had to take it off tonight. It was tangled in my hair. And then I couldn't get it back on, so I just left it off."

"When did you get it? Did someone in your family give it to you?"

I nodded. "My grandmother gave it to me...in the fourth grade."

We stared at each other in understanding.

"That's gotta be it," he said. "The locket must have a charm on it that keeps you from connecting to me. Otherwise we'd have no problem. Everyone's parents in the Clann can dream connect. My parents joke about it all the time."

And obviously my vampire genes hadn't prevented it before.

"Okay. But how do I know what you're saying is true, that we're really connecting and my subconscious isn't just making all this up?"

"Easy. Tell me something now that I wouldn't know in real life, and I'll repeat it to you Monday morning."

"Okay." I had to think for a minute, then it came to me. "Tonight, my father tried to talk me into moving in with him and switching schools."

Tristan stared at me, his smile fading. "Are you making that up?"

I shook my head.

"What was your answer?"

"I told him no way. I barely know him. And he's..." I almost said he was a vampire and a council spy. "He definitely cares more about his job than me." I told him how my father had left my dance recital early last spring without seeing my jazz routine.

"Ouch, that must've hurt. Did he say why?"

I pulled up a section of moss at the edge of the blanket, choosing my answer carefully. "His family doesn't approve of my dancing. That was the night he asked me to totally quit dancing."

"But you tried out for the Charmers anyways, right?"

I nodded. "His family pulled some strings and made sure I didn't make the team, though."

He muttered a curse almost too quiet for me to hear. "I'm sorry your dad and his family suck. But at least you tried to fight for what you wanted."

My eyes stung. I shrugged and stared down at the hunk of moss in my hands, tearing off the little fuzzy pieces from its surface. After a while, I swallowed. "Maybe we could talk about something else."

"Okay." He reached out and tucked my hair behind my ear so I couldn't hide behind it anymore. "Have I told you how brave I think you are?"

That made my cheeks burn. "Yeah, right." I wasn't brave at all. Just one secret date with Tristan had made me shake in my shoes with guilt and fear that we'd end up getting caught.

"No, you really are," he murmured, his voice dropping even lower. "It's one of the things I kind of admire about you."

"Tristan, if I was so brave, I would be dancing with the Charmers now anyways."

"What about all the stuff you do for the Charmers?"

I frowned in confusion. "Like what?"

"Like how you're not afraid to be alone on campus early in the mornings and late at night after practice. Or when you go to the school alone during a home game just to get another hat for one of the dancers."

Part of me wanted to hold on to those words like they were treasured bits of gold. He seemed almost proud of me, or at the very least impressed. But I had to shrug off his words. He just didn't know what I really was. Why would I be afraid of being on campus alone? I was the scariest thing that would ever walk those grounds, what with my monstrous mixed blood. Not that I could ever hope to explain any of that without totally repulsing him.

"Well, what about you?" I said to change the focus back to him. "I mean, you're not supposed to even be friends with me. Yet you asked me out on a date. And kept asking for a week."

"Because you're irresistible." Grinning, he leaned closer to me.

I had to smile back. "Oh, yeah, so irresistible you just had to break fifty years of tradition and become the Charmers first male manager?"

I was joking, but he became serious. "Well, yeah. How else would I get to be around you enough to convince you to date me?"

I made a face and threw the clump of moss at him. "Ugh, I knew it! You sneaky—"

Laughing, he pulled me over to him, swallowing my annoyed groans and grumbles in a kiss. It was like plugging myself into a low-voltage battery minus the unpleasant shock…

I could feel the electric energy, so warm, so bright and good, flowing from him to me, filling me up. The energy rushed to my head, pulsed against the top of my skull, pounded through my heart...

I woke up with a jolt, already grinning. That had to have been the best dream *ever.* I wished I could go back to sleep and pick up where it had ended. But I'd promised to spend some much-needed girl time with my friends today. I only saw them at lunch lately since I'd been so busy with team stuff. Anne would be picking me up in an hour for a group trip to the nearest mall, about thirty minutes away in the small city of Tyler. We were all going to do last-minute costume shopping for the Fall Ball, which the Charmers would be hosting next weekend.

Not that it really mattered what I wore, since I'd be working the concession stand all night. I just missed getting to hang out with my friends beyond lunch at school every day. I jumped out of bed and got ready. I hesitated, then put on my locket. Was it really charmed?

When Anne pulled up an hour later in her forest-green Ford F150, I yelled goodbye to Nanna and ran to the truck. It must have rained last night after I got home. The thick bed of damp pine needles beneath my shoes was soft and spongy, reminding me of the moss in my dream last night and making me grin.

Since Anne had picked me up first, I got to ride shotgun. I hopped onto the front seat in one step.

"Whoa, you're energetic this morning." Anne gave me a startled scowl as she backed out of the driveway.

"Yeah, I guess I am."

"Since when did you become a morning person?"

"This morning, I guess." I shrugged. Actually, now that

I thought about it, I really did feel amazing. "Hmm, that's weird. I don't know, I just had this great dream and woke up with all this energy."

"What'd you do, drink a ton of energy drinks in that dream?"

"No. But I did kiss a really hot guy in it."

She rolled her eyes, but a smile tugged at the edges of her lips. "All right, all right. Tell me all about it."

"Okay. But I won't tell you who, so don't bother asking."

"What? Why not?"

"Because. So listen…he's standing there at the edge of a forest, and he holds out a hand and says, 'Come walk with me.'" I did my best to imitate Tristan's deep voice. "Then we go into this forest, and the floor is all covered in really soft moss—"

"Oh, brother," she muttered. "Do you realize it is all of nine o'clock in the morning and you sound more hyper than Michelle usually is? Honestly, try to remember you're talking to the unconverted night owl here, and sound less like a squirrel high on drugs."

"But, Anne, I have to tell you about this dream before we pick up Carrie and Michelle, and we're almost to Carrie's house already. If I tell them about it, they'll just tease me and ruin a perfectly fabulous dream."

She sighed. "Fine, by all means, continue where you left off. But just so you know, you are officially banned from caffeine for the rest of this trip."

I hurried through the dream so I could tell her how the kiss at the end had seemed to fill me with energy. "And kissing Tristan in the dream was *just* like kissing him in real life—"

She slammed on the brakes and yanked the truck over to the side of the road.

CHAPTER 14

Savannah

I gasped, "Anne, what are you—"

"You kissed *Tristan?* Is this the Tristan I think it is, as in Tristan Coleman, the guy who dated you then *dumped* you in the fourth grade?"

What had I said? Biting my lower lip, I replayed my own words then cringed. Yep, I'd slipped and said his name despite being so careful not to. Oh, crap. I shouldn't have even told Anne about the dream. But it had been such an amazing dream, and I hated not having a single person to share it with.

So I told her almost everything. I told her about how Tristan had stepped in and fought Greg for me in September, and then I'd accidentally gaze dazed him, too. I told her about his joining the Charmers as a manager and escort after his parents made him quit all sports as punishment for fighting Dylan during a game. And how he and I had ended up on our secret first date last night.

Being able to talk to someone about Tristan was such a huge relief, even if Anne wasn't exactly his biggest fan. But either she was mellowing out or she'd given up on hating him as much as she used to, because even though I was braced for it, she didn't give me even one warning about his being a player who would only break my heart. And out of all the people in my life to accidentally slip and confess to, there was no one better than Anne, Jacksonville's very own human vault of secrets. She had never once spilled anyone's secret, not even in anger or revenge. So I knew I could trust her with the details about Tristan and me.

And yet…I still couldn't tell her everything. I couldn't tell her about my father, or anything about the existence of vampires. What might the vampire council do if she learned about their existence and they found out about it? I also couldn't tell her that my family used to be in the Clann.

She already knew about the Clann's abilities, though. Or at least strongly suspected.

"They're all a bunch of witches, aren't they?" she said. "I *knew* it. Everyone says they are, and I believe it. You know why? Because it explains everything. I mean, how else would he have saved you all those times? It had to have been either magic or some crazy high-tech CIA-mind-control type gear he gave me. They just worked way too well and way too fast."

Huh? "Anne, what are you talking about?"

She pressed her lips together, considered then nodded. "He never made me promise not to tell, so… Do you remember how all your gaze-daze victims just suddenly left you alone?"

"Yeah, but that was because the effects wore off."

"Sorry, my friend, but no. Tristan gave me these little heart candies every time you got a new stalker. He asked me to put them in your backpack and duffel bag. And immediately your stalkers stayed away. I always wondered how he did it, though."

"And now you're thinking it was some kind of magic spell?"

She nodded.

So it wasn't just the gaze-daze effects eventually wearing off. I'd had help all along.

At first, I absolutely melted at the idea of Tristan secretly playing knight in shining armor for me. He was so incredibly sweet and good to me, looking out for me like that months before we'd even started talking again. Not to mention the fact that his working with Anne could not have been fun for either of them.

But then the blood drained from my head and seemed to pool in my toes, taking my smile right along with it. Oh, no. If this was true, then...

"What?" she demanded.

"I've made eye contact with Tristan twice now. Once right after he fought with Greg in September, and then again last week. Though I could swear he wasn't affected." I cringed in anticipation of Anne's reaction. She hadn't thought me too brilliant when I'd messed up with Greg. I could guess how she'd react this time.

She leaned back against her door with a thump. "And you said ever since he's been asking you out?"

I nodded, saw the direction of her thoughts and felt sick to my stomach.

"No wonder. He's gaze dazed." She sounded like a doctor announcing I had cancer.

Suddenly it was hard to breathe. My fingers twisted together. "But he didn't *look* possessed like the others. And besides, why would he want to help with the algebra boys? That was way before he and I ever made eye contact."

"That was just guilt from dumping you so badly in the fourth grade."

I cringed. "You really think so?"

"The pattern behind his actions seems pretty clear to me. He protected you from the Warty Boys in algebra and then later from Greg because he was feeling guilty for being such a jerk for years. And then you popped him with the gaze daze, so he joined the Charmers so he could be around you, then was driven by a second hit of the gaze daze to ask you out until you finally gave in." She stared at me like it was all too obvious and I was an idiot for even doubting it. "Why else would Mr. Macho go from not talking to you at all to joining your dance team and begging you twice a day to date him?"

So much for the knight-in-shining-armor image.

My stomach cramped so hard I had to wrap my arms around myself.

I remembered how Tristan had smiled at me last night, how he'd held me while we danced, how he'd touched my face as if I were something delicate and precious while he kissed me. How he'd staggered and seemed ready to fall over after our kiss, and was worried that I might not want to see him again. And how I'd wondered why in the world he would be so into someone like me. Oh, crap. Anne was right. I *knew* it had all been way too good to be true.

"Fine, he's gaze dazed." Anger at myself and the whole situation, along with a sinking sensation I didn't want to think about just yet, made me snap. I took a deep breath, blinked away the burning sensation in my eyes and tried not to take it out on her. "Okay, so now what? If he's the only reason those other guys left me alone...who's going to save *him?*"

"His sister?"

"I can't ask her for help! Can you see that conversation? 'Hi, Emily, I'm the reason your brother has gone all goofy and obsessed lately. Listen, could you do a spell to keep him away from me? I know it's my fault, but it would be such a big help. Thanks so much!'" I shook my head. "Yeah, that would go over so well."

She sighed and put the truck back into gear. "Well, you can always go with plan B. See how long it really takes for the effects to wear off without help."

The only problem was…that evil side deep within me didn't want the effects to wear off Tristan. Ever. "Or there's plan C."

"Which is?"

"Do what my father wants, switch schools and move in with him."

"Oh, you will *not* move in with your dad! Coleman can just get over it naturally. I'm not losing my best friend just because some player finally got hit with a dose of karma."

I sighed, my shoulders slumping in defeat. No matter what I did, someone was going to be hurt. And it would be all my fault. Again.

That night as I climbed into bed, I wondered…what if I really had dream connected with Tristan last night? Would he try to connect with me again tonight? And if he did, should I try to end the dream? If he didn't see me anymore, at least romantically, maybe the effects would wear off faster. It seemed almost cruel to encourage his feelings for me when, as Anne had clearly pointed out, they obviously were just a product of the gaze daze.

Which meant nothing about our date had been real, either. The dancing, the kisses, his asking to see me again… He was just acting from a vampire effect I'd put on him.

And I was a horrible, selfish person for even partly wanting him to stay under that spell.

Reluctantly, I took off my gold locket. If we dream con-

nected again tonight, I would do the right thing and tell him
I couldn't date him anymore.

The next morning, I didn't know whether to be grateful
or depressed that I hadn't dreamed about him at all.

What I did know was that it was time to learn how to control this awful gaze of mine. Unfortunately, the only person
who knew how to control vampire abilities without magic
wasn't answering his stupid cell phone, because apparently my
father was still too busy with his precious council. I thought
about leaving him a message then decided against it. A pan-
icked plea for help would only make this into a huge deal the
council would want to get involved in, and who knew what
would happen then. Better just to wait until he called me
again. Then I could casually ask about the gaze daze's cure in
general as a hypothetical situation.

He'd said he would be out of contact for a while. Hopefully
it wouldn't be too long, though. Because in the meantime, it
looked like I would be on my own to clean up the mess I'd
made.

And what a gorgeous mess he was as he leaned against the
foyer doors of the sports and art building Monday morning.

I gulped and steeled myself even as the familiar ache
slammed into me. The pain wasn't too bad today. Maybe my
body had gotten its fill of his kisses for a while.

I also felt something else, though…a strange tingling at the
back of my neck, as if I were being watched. I shook it off.
Of course I was being watched. Tristan was staring straight
at me.

How in the world would I work beside him today without
everyone knowing how I felt?

"Good morning, Savannah," he said, taking my tea from
me just like always while I unlocked the doors.

"Good morning, Tristan."

He didn't say anything as we crossed the entrance hall. When we started up the stairs, I dared to breathe a sigh of relief. Maybe Anne was wrong and he wasn't gaze dazed, after all. It was going to be okay. I would just have to be sure to see him only at school and nowhere else.

So why did I still feel so miserable?

Sighing again, I led the way into the dim hall.

And shrieked when he grabbed me from behind, spun me around and kissed me. My blood began to sing through my veins, humming in my ears like the dull roar of a far-off ocean.

"Now that's the proper way to say good-morning," he mumbled against my lips. I had to cling to his shoulders so I could stay standing.

Oh, crap. I couldn't think straight. He stepped away from me and leaned back against the wall. There was something I'd wanted to talk to him about. Some reason kissing him was a really bad idea. But with my blood whooshing through my head so loudly, I couldn't remember why feeling this pumped with energy would ever be a bad thing.

He definitely knew how to kiss.

I stumbled over to the dance room to begin my usual un-locking routine. And yet, I had a feeling nothing would be normal about our routine ever again.

He followed me into the office, grunting a little as he picked up the sound system.

He'd never acted like the sound system was heavy before. Distracted, I raised my eyebrows in silent question.

"Heavy today," he muttered with a half grin.

"Uh-huh, let me see." I took the MegaVox case from him and lifted it with just two fingers. "No, it's lighter today, actually." Just to be sure, I opened the hard plastic lid and peeked inside. Yep, the fifty-pound MegaVox was still in there. Hmm, weird. Snapping the lid shut, I handed the case back, and he oomphed again.

"What's the matter, didn't eat your Wheaties this morning?" I teased as we headed down the stairs. But my mind was focused on yesterday's talk with Anne. She and I *had* to be wrong. Nothing about Tristan's facial expression or actions was anything like how Greg and the algebra boys had appeared. Still, Anne was more objective than me, and even she thought Tristan had to be gaze dazed. So he must be. Right?

"Didn't get much rest this weekend," Tristan replied. "Which reminds me…how's your dad taking the news that you won't be moving in with him?"

My brain blanked out again. "He's out of town for a while. But how… Did you talk to Anne?"

"No." He reached the bottom of the stairs, standing so close I had to tilt my head back to look up at him.

"Then how did you…?" The dream. Our minds really had been connected.

He smiled down at me, a soft smile that made me feel shaky inside. "I told you Friday night in our dream." He gave me a quick peck on my lips that robbed me of thought yet again. "Uh, not to sound less than manly here, but we should get moving before I drop this stuff. I swear it really is heavier today."

In stunned silence, I followed him out of the building. As we walked down the campus road, the wind made the woods at our right sigh and sway just like the trees had in our dreams together. I replayed every dream conversation we'd had, alternately fighting a blush or a groan at each thing I remembered saying to him. I would *never* wear just a T-shirt to bed again.

And then I remembered something else, and the words just blurted right out of me. "So you fought Dylan because of me."

"Yep. He was being an ass, saying stuff about you. He's lucky I didn't bust his lip while I was at it."

Which meant in a way, he'd lost the ability to play football for the entire last month of the season because of me. While the trees still blocked us from the view of the practice field, I reached over and wrapped an arm around Tristan's waist, giving him a long sideways hug. I felt him kiss the top of my head then murmur, "Like I said, I shouldn't have lost control. It was my fault for letting him rile me up like that."

Then the trees ended and we had to step away from each other and pretend we were nothing more than a head manager walking with one of her managers. It felt like I was ripping off my arm.

It took more effort than usual to hide my feelings for Tristan during practice. Every few seconds, my gaze strayed over to him. And every time I saw him, I thought about kissing him, dancing with him, lying on a blanket with him by a stream in my dream. Make that *our* dream.

I really wanted Anne and me to be wrong about Tristan being gaze dazed. Over and over, I compared his actions to the others' after making eye contact with me. They just didn't match. With Greg, I'd known almost right away that making eye contact with him had changed him. But the only difference Tristan had shown after making eye contact with me was his desire to date me. Even before our kiss in the uniform closet, he'd constantly found ways to touch me or be close to me. Granted, that might be a leftover effect from when we'd made eye contact in September. But he hadn't attempted to see me or even talk to me for weeks after the first eye contact. So how could he have been gaze dazed then?

Dimly I heard someone yell out my name. I glanced around for the source then jumped as someone shouted my name

again. It came from the MegaVox. I looked up at the bleachers to find an exasperated Mrs. Daniels staring down at me.
Uh-oh. No telling how long she'd had to yell to get my
attention.

Heat flared into my cheeks as I refocused on running the
music for the dancers. Crap. Had everyone on the team seen
me staring at Tristan?

Maybe he wasn't the only one gaze dazed around here.

I managed not to look at him again. But it was a constant
struggle.

Still lost in thought at the end of practice, I didn't say
anything as we walked together back to the dance rooms.
He waited in silence as I locked up the sound system in the
office closet. When I turned to face him, I found him leaning
a shoulder against the doorjamb.

"About our date tonight," he began.

"Tonight? I don't remember setting it for tonight." My
voice came out as a squeak. I stared at his nose so I could indirectly study the look in his eyes. Nope, he still didn't appear
possessed like the others had seemed.

"For our date tonight, I was thinking we should dream
connect again. Or at least try to."

I frowned and stared at the floor. "Tristan, maybe we
should just slow down and take a few minutes to really think
about this. We're talking about lying to our parents. A lot.
And often. My family is going to know if I lie to them. How
long do you really think we could keep this a secret? I mean,
I want to see you, too, don't get me wrong. But...aren't you
worried just the least little bit about the consequences if we
get caught?"

He frowned. "We won't get caught. Emily can make you
a charm to block your parents from reading your mind."

It wouldn't be my thoughts that would give away what

we were doing. "Oh, yeah? And is she also going to make a charm that will do something about my face? Because I don't know about you, but I'm a really crappy liar. They're going to be able to tell I'm lying just by looking at me!"

Smiling, he reached out to take my hand and give it a soft squeeze. "You worry too much. Parents aren't all-powerful. Emily and I get away with stuff all the time."

"Maybe you do. But I've never broken the rules before."

"Which is exactly what's going to help you now. They won't be scrutinizing everything you say and do. So just focus on something else when you're around them and don't worry about it."

The warmth from his hand flowed up my arm, soothing me. Then his thumb started caressing my skin in a small, slow circle, making it tough for me to think straight. Probably exactly as he intended.

I tugged my hand free and crossed my arms over my chest. "Tristan, be serious here. I don't want to hurt my family."

Sighing, he crossed his arms over his chest, too, and frowned. Rocking back on his heels, he asked, "Do you want to be with me?"

"I... Yes. But—"

"And do you think it's fair for our families or the Clann or anyone else to tell us who we can and can't be with?"

"Well, no, I guess not, but they—"

"No buts. I'm tired of others running my life for me. They've kept us apart for seven years. It's time we take back control over our own lives. Do what we think is right. Their issues are theirs, not ours. It's not your fault your family got kicked out of the Clann. And it's not my fault, either. So why punish us?"

I slumped, feeling his arguments physically wearing me down. Fighting him was hard enough. But standing up against both him and my own heart was starting to feel like an impossible battle. "Exactly how do you expect us to date in secret without someone finding out? Where would we even go on a date?"

He cocked his head in the direction of the dance room next door. "We'll always have the dance room. It can be our place. And we can dream connect. Every night if you want to."

I thought about his reputation for taking girls to restaurants, to the movies, to parties. He was talking about giving all that up and settling for dates spent sitting on a cold cement floor with takeout or only in our shared imaginations. Not that I'd mind. I'd take any kind of date with him I could get. But what about what he was used to? Wouldn't he miss all that while dating me? He deserved better.

I sighed, unable to escape my biggest worry of all. "Tristan, are you sure this is really you making these decisions?"

His eyebrows drew together in confusion, then he frowned. "Is this about the eye thing again? Savannah, that was over months ago."

"No, that was a week ago. In the closet, before we…" My face burned, and I couldn't finish.

"So you made eye contact with me again. No big deal. That was just some accidental spell you put on those boys or something. I would have felt it if you'd used any magic on me, and I haven't."

But it wasn't magic behind the gaze daze. Unfortunately, I couldn't explain that without also telling him about my vampire side. "What if it's not magic? What if it's something else?"

"Like what?"

I ground my teeth, at a loss for an explanation. "Just go with me here on this, okay? What if it's not like doing a spell or whatever, so you can't feel magic being used when I gaze daze someone? How close were you when I gaze dazed those guys in our ninth-grade algebra class?"

"I don't know, maybe fifty yards?"

"And how far away can you normally feel magic being used?"

"Depends on how strong it is. I've heard everyone on campus can feel it when my energy spikes." He grinned.

I tried not to roll my eyes. "So then either the gaze daze is a really low level of power use, or it's something that just can't be felt. Right?" Lord, I was so reaching here.

"Fine. Even if it is, I think I'd know if I felt differently when you looked at me. And I didn't."

"Then why did you act different? Why did you suddenly decide you wanted to be with me? You weren't even speaking to me before you fought with Greg."

"Savannah, my feelings for you have always been there. I've always needed to be with you. After you ended things with Greg, I just didn't see the point in fighting them anymore." He stroked my cheek. "It wasn't your eyes that made me want to live my own life for a change. Just you."

Oh, how I wanted to believe that. I leaned into his hand, feeling every muscle in my body relaxing against my will. I put up one last token argument. "Maybe I should move in with my father, after all. If I was gone, then you could know for sure whether you were thinking clearly or under the gaze-daze effect. And if it turned out to be the gaze daze, maybe with me gone it might wear off—"

"You do and I'll just have to find you," he growled, but his thumbs made a lie of his ferocious tone by softly caressing my cheeks. "And then it'd be all your fault for making me miss school."

He *was* pretty used to getting what he wanted all the time.

I could easily imagine him skipping school just to chase down some elusive girl. My lips twitched with the urge to smile.

"You want to know for sure I'm not under a spell?" he asked.

"It would be nice, yes."

"Then look at me."

I looked at his nose.

"My eyes, Savannah. Look into my eyes. And keep looking. See if they change like those other guys' did."

No way, I could *not* do it to him a third time. The effects would never wear off at this rate.

"Look at me."

"I can't."

"Look at me, damn it!"

Shocked, my gaze popped up to meet his against my will.

And it was Tristan Coleman staring back at me, with the exact same eyes I remembered from my childhood.

"Keep looking. Tell me if they change," he murmured.

I began to shake. This was too intense, staring into his eyes, searching them for signs that I was robbing him of sanity and free will like I'd done to Greg and the others.

The bell rang, signaling the end of first period. But neither of us moved. The seconds ticked by.

After another long minute, he said, "Well? Still me in there?"

I nodded, though I could hardly believe it. I had spent months getting used to the idea that every male I made eye contact with would go nuts. Yet here was Tristan, the one boy I wouldn't mind having for a stalker, and he didn't seem the slightest bit affected. Could he be wearing a family charm that protected him from the gaze daze? Were all descendants immune to it automatically? Maybe it was like their trying to read a vampire's mind…they had somehow built up a genetic defense against the vamp's gaze-daze effect?

I would have to ask my mom if she had ever been gaze dazed by my dad.

His hands slid down my shoulders and arms to hold my hands. "Then are we done arguing about this? Will you be my girlfriend?"

As if my heart had really ever given me a choice otherwise. Swallowing down a rising lump in my throat, I nodded and tugged my hands free so I could wrap my arms around his waist. I grinned, the rightness of this sensation making me wonder now why I had ever tried to fight it. He was right. The Clann's rules were stupid. If ever two people were meant to be together, we were it. And it was time we decided for ourselves for a change.

"Good." He kissed me, softly at first, then harder, gathering me against him until I couldn't tell who held who tighter.

He lifted his head with a gasp for air then grinned down at me. "Your gaze might not affect me, but kissing you definitely does." He stared down at me, and it was both terrifying and wonderful to stare back up at him. "Did you know your eyes turn silver when I kiss you?"

They should turn brown. He made me feel like I'd downed an entire pot of coffee when he kissed me. I was practically vibrating with energy.

Unfortunately, second period called, and life didn't revolve around kissing Tristan Coleman. Although I was starting to wish it did.

Tristan

I hadn't stopped grinning all morning. I flopped into my chair beside Emily in the cafeteria, and like a magnet, Savannah drew my gaze. She was so incredibly beautiful. And I was the lucky guy who got to kiss her. As I watched her standing in the food line, her cheeks turned pink. Could she feel me staring at her? Now that I knew she was a descendant by birth, I had a hunch she just might be able to sense my attention, after all.

"Okay, now I *know* something's wrong with you," Emily said.

"Hmm? Why's that?"

"First Dad finds you still passed out in the backyard at lunchtime on Saturday."

"I wasn't drunk."

"Uh-huh. Then you act like you're hung over until Sunday—"

"Can't be hung over if there's no booze or drugs involved."

"I tell you to go draw some energy from the ground—"

"Which I did, and it worked, thank you."

"And you seemed fine last night. But now you're flopping around like a rag doll again, only you're wearing a goofy grin."

"Hmm. You're right. I am pretty tired again. Think Mrs. Harper will mind if I sleep through Spanish this afternoon?"

She stared at me for a long minute with that frown she always wore when she was working on a problem. "Tell me something. You got home awfully late Friday night. You wouldn't happen to have gone on a date with someone after the game?"

"Yeah, actually, I did." Best date of my life, other than the dream one later that night.

"Would it have been with anyone I know?"

"Maybe. She's a student here."

"A Charmer?"

"Sort of."

"A redheaded junior who is *so off-limits?*" she hissed with shocked fury.

I cringed. "Maybe. Hey, did you know her family used to be in the Clann before her mom broke some rule and they were kicked out?"

She sighed and threw up her hands in the air. "You're an idiot. I knew you always liked her. But to actually break the rules and date her? There's a *reason* her family was kicked out of the Clann."

"Oh, yeah? And what is it?"

"I don't know. But it must have been huge for them to cast out her whole family. And now you tell me you're dating an outcast descendant, and every time you see her, you're weak afterward. You did see her this morning at Charmers practice, right?"

"Oh, yeah. I saw her." I grinned at the memory of our goodbye kiss. Make that kisses.

"What if she's draining you?"

My grin dropped straight into a scowl. Emily could be such a mood killer sometimes. "She's not draining me." Kissing Savannah was the best feeling ever.

"How would you know? Have you ever been drained before? You have no idea what it feels like."

Good point. Know-it-all brat. "And you do?"

She glared back at me. Ha! She didn't know what it felt like, either.

Which was all off topic anyways. "Look, Savannah wouldn't do that to me. Why would she? If she's got that kind of power, she could draw from nature just like the rest of us."

"Not if she was never trained to. What if this is her power's way of leaking out of control? Or what if this is part of the reason her family was cast out? They could all be power leeches. Or what if she's draining you as revenge for her family being cast out?"

"Enough with the conspiracy theories already. She's not like that. My being tired after seeing her is just a coincidence. You don't know anything about her."

"Not yet, I don't."

Good mood gone, I peeled myself from my chair. "I'm going outside for a while."

"Good. Do yourself a favor and do some drawing while you're there. And I don't mean the artistic type. I'll let you know what I discover."

Sisters. What a pain.

Still, Emily usually had good ideas. Maybe I would go sit under my grounding tree and draw a little energy from the earth like she'd suggested.

A few minutes later while leaned back against the tree in the biting-cold air, I heard the squeak of the cafeteria doors. At the same time, my gut and stomach ached from Savannah's nearness. Smiling, I snuck a peek at her.

She wore a matching smile as she emerged from the cafeteria with her friends. Then she looked my way, and the smile she flashed me was like looking directly at a summer sun at noon, lighting up the gray winter day.

And then she glanced past me at something. Her smile slipped, and her feet stumbled to a stop.

I looked behind me. Nothing there but an empty road, the practice field and the edge of the woods that circled three sides of the school grounds. What could make her freeze up like that?

Savannah

They were definitely staring at me. I wasn't sure how I knew this, but I did. And the longer I looked at the trio of adults standing at the edge of the woods behind Tristan, the more I could sense someone else's emotions…anger, curiosity, patient determination, fear, all roiling together in a dark, seething cloud against my skin despite my best efforts to shield against them. The emotions had to be coming from them. No one else nearby looked anything but happy.

Why didn't they ever blink? Or move?

I gripped my notebook, hugging it to my chest and stomach, my palms turning damp. Gut instinct screamed at me to run away. And yet my feet seemed frozen in place.

Why were they standing over there? And why were they staring at me?

From this distance, they looked like middle-aged adults, two men, one woman. Their faces watched me without any expression. The wind flipped the men's dark suit jackets and turned the woman's hair into a writhing black cloud around her head, yet she made no effort to push back the wild strands.

"Hey, Anne, do you know who those people are?" I jerked my head in the trio's direction, trying to act normal.

Anne glanced at the woods then gave me a blank look. "Who?"

"Those three people standing over there by the woods. At the edge of the practice field."

She continued to look clueless. But she was just messing with my head. Miss Always Practical Carrie wouldn't, though. "Carrie, do you know who they are?"

Carrie looked in the correct direction. "Where?"

"Oh, not funny, guys. The two men and one woman standing right over there." Feeling rude, I pointed anyway. Let the trio know I was talking about them. They'd been rude first by staring at me.

Carried stared at me, too, her blue eyes expressionless. "Sav, there's no one there."

"Oh, come on! Michelle, you see them, right?"

Michelle shook her head, and now all three of my friends were looking at me as if I'd gone nuts.

Maybe I had. I turned toward the creepy trio. Yep, they were still there, still solid and unwavering, and still staring at me. Goose bumps raced over my arms and thighs.

"Y'all *swear* you don't see them?" I'd meant to sound calm, but the words came out in a croak instead.

"I swear," Anne replied, and Carrie and Michelle nodded.

"Come on, let's…get to class," Anne muttered, grabbing my arm and dragging me away.

Lovely. As if I wasn't already freakish enough, now I was seeing invisible people. Either that or ghosts.

Thankfully, my afternoon classes were in the main building on the opposite side of the campus. Regardless, every crashing locker door in the main hall between classes made me jump.

And looming ahead after school was the usual Charmers practice. In the field right next to where those watchers had been standing.

Please be gone now, my mind chanted as I shuffled along the walkway to the sports and art building after the final school bell rang.

As I made my way up the cement ramp to the foyer doors, I glanced back at the woods. And stumbled. The trio were still there, and they were staring at me again. The woman's hair was impossibly tangled as the wind continued to whip it around her face unchecked. They looked as if they hadn't moved in hours and were perfectly capable of standing there until the end of time. Their seething mixture of emotions reached out like invisible fingers, spreading over my midsection like a malicious fog until I wanted to claw off my own skin just to get away from the sensation.

What did they *want*?

Panic rose, icy cold, starting in my chest and stomach then spreading out to numb my limbs. I clamped my teeth together and hurried inside. At Mrs. Daniels's office, I leaned against the doorjamb and slid down as my legs went weak with relief, my breaths coming out fast and short.

Oh, crap. I couldn't go back out there. I would have to walk right past them to get to the field. I would be within feet of them. They might jump out and grab me or something.

I'd have to miss practice today. I'd have to...

I didn't hear Tristan come up the stairs. "Hey, Sav, what's wrong?" He crossed the distance to me in three long strides then crouched down before me. His hands surrounded mine, the heat from his skin letting me know how cold I was.

"You'll think I'm crazy."

"Try me."

"There're these...people outside by the practice field. At the edge of the woods. Adults. Three of them. They keep staring at me. They were there at lunch, too, but my friends swore they couldn't see them. None of them could. How could they not *see* them? I think they're ghosts or something." The words poured out of me, my voice rising to a near shriek at the end.

"Okay, calm down. You say they were staring at you?"

How could I explain why the watchers freaked me out so much? "Yeah. But they're not blinking or moving or *anything*. They're like statues. Only their heads and eyes turn when I walk by." A sudden thought hit me. "Do you think the Clann sent them to spy on us? Maybe your parents suspect we're dating and sent them. But why not make themselves invisible to me, too? Wouldn't that make more sense?"

"Whoa, slow down." He stood and pulled me up with him. "If the Clann sent spies to watch me, which I doubt they'd do, they would make themselves invisible to everyone. Otherwise they wouldn't be very good spies, right?"

His calm confidence reached out to me like a soft, warm blanket. My heartbeat slowed down in response. Feeling stupid, I took a deep breath and tried to calm down. I was overreacting. "You're right. But why can't my friends see them?"

"I don't know. Why don't we find out if I can?"

It took several tries, but I managed to unlock the office closet so we could get the sound system and my trainer's bag. Then we made our way downstairs and out the building.

The watchers were still there. This time their eyes widened as if in shock. Proof they probably weren't ghosts. Ghosts didn't act surprised and weren't affected by the wind, were they?

"Are they still there?" Tristan muttered, looking in their direction.

I nodded, fear closing my throat again. He couldn't see them, either. Oh, crap, I really was going crazy.

"Well, they won't hurt you as long as I'm here." He reached out to hold my hand.

The woman in the middle lurched forward a step and hissed, but her companions grabbed her arms in restraint. Her fury washed over my skin.

I gasped and froze. "Let go of my hand. It upsets them."

He released my hand. "We're going to be late for practice. Why don't we go around the opposite side of the math building—"

As if they'd heard, the watchers turned toward the practice field. Then they took off, moving so fast they became three blurs. Holy crap, how could they *move* like that? They couldn't possibly be descendants, not unless they'd used magic to give themselves superpowers somehow. Then again, maybe that was exactly what they had done. After all, what did I know about magic and what descendants could or couldn't do with proper training?

Where had they gone?

The only thing worse than being stared at by three creepy watchers was not knowing where they were now. I jogged down the ramp to the road and past the math building. I was just in time to see the watchers' blurs streak alongside the practice-field fence before they stopped at the far end, becoming solid once more.

"Wow. They move fast."

"Where are they now?"

"Far end of the field outside the fence. And they're staring at me again."

His eyes widened. "Yeah, that is fast."

"You still can't see them, can you?"

"No. I'm sorry, I wish I could. Maybe if the Clann sent them then I could at least identify them."

A horrible thought came to me. "What if that's the point? Send watchers only I can see so I think I'm going crazy. Try to scare me away from seeing you."

We entered the field. I tried not to look at the watchers, but it was like trying not to look at a train hurtling toward me while I stood on the train tracks. Survival instinct demanded I glance their way every few seconds to make sure they hadn't moved again.

"Well, at least they're keeping their distance, right?" He helped me set up the sound system. "Just try to stay calm, and when I get ice in a while, I'll stop by the practice gym and ask Emily for advice."

"No, don't. Your sister will think I'm a nutcase."

"No, she won't. I promise. And if the Clann did send spies or someone to try to scare you, she can ask around without looking as suspicious as I would." He smiled. "Trust me, the girl is a mastermind. She can dig information out of anyone."

"Do *you* think I'm nuts?"

"I hope you are. About me, at least."

I managed a half smile. "Uh-huh. But seriously. Am I nuts?"

"Because of the watchers?" Crouching down beside me, he lifted his head, closed his eyes and pressed his fingertips to the ground. After a moment, the smile left his face. "No. Something doesn't feel right. And it's probably them."

CHAPTER 15

Tristan

It was a long hour and a half before practice neared an end and I could go for ice. I stopped by the practice gym first, interrupting the varsity cheer squad as I waved their captain over.

"This better be good," Emily said as she walked up to me.

"It is." I gave her a rundown of the problem and possible theories.

"Well, they can't be like us," she said when I finished. "We'd both feel it if they were using power."

"Then who are they?"

"You mean what."

A hundred childhood stories full of warnings against all kinds of scary things rushed through the back of my mind. "What are you thinking?"

"Shape-shifters. Vampires. Ghosts. Demons. Any of those would be able to move fast like that. Though shape-shifters can't make themselves invisible at all, so cross them off the list. And most descendants would be able to sense ghosts and demons almost like a use of power."

Which left vampires. Vampires here at JHS. Unbelievable. "What do they want?"

"Why don't you ask your girlfriend? Because I can guarantee the Clann would never have sent them. You know we don't mess around with vamps. They're magic leeches. Just because the Clann has a peace treaty with them doesn't make them any less dangerous to every descendant alive."

Our eyes widened in unison.

"Sav. She's a…" I started to say. Fear on a level I'd never felt before exploded inside me. "Emily, she's completely untrained. She wouldn't know how to protect herself at all."

"Be careful," she yelled as I sprinted out of the gym and back to the practice field. And felt my frozen mind kick into gear again when I spotted Savannah calmly sitting at the side of the field with a dancer.

"Hey. Where's the ice?" Savannah secured the dancer's bandage with a metal butterfly clip.

I leaned over and whispered against her ear, "Don't go anywhere or let them leave you here alone. I'll be right back with the ice. Promise me."

She nodded, her dark blue eyes wide even as she tried to fake a smile at the dancer she was helping.

I shot a warning glare toward the end of the field where I assumed the vampires were still lurking around. They'd better not even think about getting near Savannah while I was gone, or so help me, I'd stake every last one of them, and to hell with the peace treaty between our worlds.

Then I ran across campus to the field house. These would be the fastest bags of ice I'd ever thrown together.

I was on the last bag when Dylan strolled over to the locker-room doorway.

"Missing football so much you had to start hanging out in the field house?" he said.

Just what I needed right now. Normally I came here before football practice ended so I could avoid my old teammates. Talking with Emily and then running back to warn Savannah had thrown me behind tonight.

"Just helping out the Charmers," I said, shoveling ice into the clear plastic bag faster. Through the field house's open front door, I could see the campus getting darker as the sun set behind the trees and houses in the nearby neighborhood, throwing long shadows over the practice field.

"Rumor has it you're here every day now. That Colbert girl must be a pretty good—"

There was no thought. One minute I was shoveling ice, the next I'd dropped the metal scoop in the ice machine and had a softball-size fireball fully formed and rolling around inside my hand just waiting to be thrown.

A matching orb of energy slowly grew in Dylan's right hand. He growled, "Careful, Coleman. Wouldn't want you to lose your control again and get kicked off yet another team."

As ticked off as I was, part of me really didn't care what happened as long as I could shut him up once and for all about Savannah. But deep down inside, another part of me was yelling, *Don't be stupid, Tristan! This is exactly what he wants!*

Footsteps at the locker-room door only gave us seconds to snuff out the magic before Ron Abernathy walked in. "Hey, guys, what's up? Oh, hey, Tristan. Haven't seen you around much lately. How've you been?"

Still staring at Dylan, I muttered, "Okay, and you?"

"Not bad. Heard you were helping out the Charmers now. You lucky dog, getting to work with all those girls wearing nothing but leotards all the time. They got any more openings for managers? Might have to join the team myself!"

I forced a tight smile, though it felt like I was having to chip the expression out of stone to pull it off. "I'll let you know if any come up."

I was waiting for Ron to get lost so I could finally take care of an old problem here. But he showed no signs of leaving as he stood there watching us. Was he hoping to see us fight again, or trying to stop the fight before it began?

As the seconds ticked by in silence, the anger eased back down to something I could control again. This wasn't over by a long shot. Dylan would have to be dealt with eventually. He was like a bulldog once he saw something, and obviously he wasn't ready to let our issues go. But tonight, I had bigger problems to deal with.

Gritting my teeth, I turned away and finished filling the last ice bag, then closed it up with a metal twist tie. As I headed for the door, my arms filled with ice bags that did nothing to cool the blood still boiling beneath my skin, I told Ron over my shoulder, "See you later." He raised a hand in answer.

"See you later," Dylan said, his tone making it a promise.

"Looking forward to it." I smiled, and this time I didn't bother to try and make it look nice.

Once outside the field house, I took off at a jog through the fading light across campus to the practice field. By the time I got there, the team was still wrapping up practice. But now the sun had fully set. The field and surrounding track were lit by several stadium lights. But the wood-lined walk between the field and sports and art building had no lights at all. And after we got through that section, I would still have to get Savannah out of the building and across the dark campus to the front parking lot and her truck.

Once practice ended and she and I were headed toward the practice-field gate, I tried a different plan. "Listen, I think I should lock up the dance rooms for you tonight. Then you can go straight from here to your truck and home."

She glanced at me, then kept walking toward the campus road and the shadowed section by the woods. Hardheaded woman. "I can't. It's my job to make sure the sound system's secured and the dance floor's locked up. Our equipment costs way too much. We couldn't afford to replace it if it got stolen or damaged."

"I'll make sure everything is locked up properly."

"That's really sweet of you, but you have no idea how mad Mrs. Daniels would get if she found out I dumped my job off on you. Come on, let's get this done so we can go home."

Frustrated, I tucked the MegaVox under my right arm and carried the jam box using my right hand. I'd at least have my left hand free. I clenched it into a loose fist and willed a tiny flame to life inside. If anything came at us, I was as ready as I'd ever be.

Savannah rubbed her arm through her coat. "Hey, are you using…"

"Just keep walking please. I'll show you later, I promise."

Catching the worry in my tone, she nodded and walked faster.

As we drew closer to the dark section of the road, I put myself between Savannah and the woods at our left. For added measure, I guided her to the opposite side of the street, using the brick backside of the math building to help protect her. I also kept her moving at a near jog.

"Where are they?" I muttered.

She glanced behind us and whispered, "Still back at the practice field."

My ears strained for any little noise from the woods or behind us. The gravel crunched beneath our feet, seeming extra loud in the silence. In the distance, a girl shrieked then laughed in the front parking lot, making my muscles twitch.

Time stretched. The walk took only minutes, but it seemed

like hours before we made it past the woods to the cement ramp and then into the foyer. We were both breathing hard as we hurried inside. Now I just had to get her home safely.

On the way up the stairs, I showed her the flame inside my fist before I put it out. Then I told her what Emily had said.

Savannah turned pale. "But…they can't be."

"Trust me, Sav, vampires really exist." At Mrs. Daniels's office now, I stowed the equipment in the closet.

She frowned. "I know. But why would they be here?"

"You're still a descendant by birth. That means you can reach out and pull the earth's energy into yourself if you need to. That makes you like a big, limitless generator for vampires. They need energy. We've got it. Most of us know how to protect ourselves. But you were never trained. So the temptation must be irresistible to them."

Hands free at last, I walked over to hold hers. They were cold and shaking. *Oh, good job making her feel protected, Coleman.* "Hey, listen, you're going to be fine. Between your family's magic and mine, we'll have you covered 24/7. No vamp would try to attack you here with so many descendants around to witness it. And for the times when we can't be with you, your family can get you set up with some vamp wards for protection."

"No, they can't." Her eyes widened, as if she'd given away some secret.

"Why not? Don't they know how to make them?"

"No, it's not that. It's…we're…forbidden to do magic." She nibbled the inner corner of her lips, and I was a little distracted by the movement.

After a few seconds, I blinked and remembered what we had been talking about. "Okay, I guess that makes sense. No big deal, Emily should know how to make them by now. And until then, I can teach you how to make fire." I reached for her hand.

She jerked it away. "No, I can't!"

Huh? "Sure you can. It's one of the first things we learn how to do when our abilities start showing up at puberty. Just hold out your hand…"

She shook her head, her eyes wild and panicky.

A short laugh escaped me. "Come on, Sav. There's no reason to be afraid. The fire is a part of you, like a natural extension of your willpower. You just will it to life, like this." I held out my hand, willed the fire to life, and blue flame popped up from my palm.

She froze.

"Seriously, I promise you it doesn't hurt. And the Clann won't find out. I swear."

She stared off into the distance. After a long hesitation, she licked her lips and held out her hand palm up.

She stared at her palm. The seconds ticked by. Nothing happened.

"Are you picturing the fire coming to life in your hand?"

Her lips pressed together into a thin line as she gave a single, sharp nod. "It's not working."

Maybe the Clann had cast a spell on her family to somehow block their abilities. Sighing in frustration, I closed her hand. "Okay, don't worry about it. We'll just go with plan B and get some vamp wards from Emily. Until then, let's get you home."

She nodded, her eyes bleak. And she wouldn't really look at me. She was scared. And maybe embarrassed about the lack of magic abilities.

"Do we have any fundraisers coming up?" I asked, trying to refocus her.

"The Fall Ball on Saturday. After that, none for a while."

"And you'll be with me there. Okay, so we just need to worry about preventing alone time during team practices—"

"Um, you know, I think it's going to be okay, Tristan. Let me lock up, and I'll go home and tell Nanna about this. I'm sure she'll know what to do."

She finished her locking-up routine, her movements jerky.

As she locked the downstairs foyer doors after us, she murmured, "Maybe we'd better walk separately from here."

Was she crazy? "I don't think so. I'm not leaving you alone for those vamps to go after."

She frowned, her shoulders stiff as we hurried across the dark campus toward the front parking lot. At her truck, I leaned in through the open driver-side door, intending to kiss her cheek. She sucked in a fast breath and ducked back inside the truck. "Tristan…they might see us."

"Who?"

"The…" She looked at me for a moment, her eyes unreadable. "Anyone still on campus."

Before I could argue that we were all alone except for the vamps, she shut the door and started the engine. With a quick wave, she was gone, driving fast like she thought she could somehow outrun the vampires.

Savannah

Vampires had come to Jacksonville.

The thought pounded through my head the entire way home. On its heels came…*Why?*

Obviously the council had sent them to watch me. Which was probably why the term *watchers* had come to me in the first place. My father had used that term to refer to council spies back when I'd first started changing. But why had the council sent watchers? Because they knew about Tristan and me?

Well, if they hadn't before, they had to suspect now.

But if they knew about us for sure, why hadn't they done anything about it, instead of just standing around all day watching me? Wouldn't they have done something to stop us from walking together, something to make me get away from Tristan?

They must be there only to ensure that the peace treaty wasn't broken. Maybe they were waiting for me to lose control around him first, then they planned to step in if I attacked him or tried to drink his blood. If so, they were going to be disappointed, because I didn't have the slightest interest in his blood.

It was his heart I craved.

He had run all over the campus to get answers for me tonight, so confident that he could protect me from the vampires. And then he'd tried to help me learn how to create fire by magic, despite the rules forbidding it.

If he'd known I might be in the process of becoming a vampire and that I'd only pretended to try to create fire, what would he have done?

I had to tell him the truth. He deserved to know the risks. Especially since he was breaking the Clann's rules by dating me.

But if I told him I was a dirty half-breed, he might not want to see me anymore.

Although...we'd just started actually dating. Who bared their entire souls right after they started seeing each other?

I should wait awhile, see how long we lasted before I started sharing more family secrets with him. Tristan was notoriously commitmentphobic. He'd probably get tired of me like he had all his previous girlfriends and break up with me after a few weeks.

In the meantime, I would just have to be extra careful not

to let the watchers see us doing anything romantic together. Like holding hands. Or kissing. No hugs, either. Public dates were even more out of the question now, of course. As long as the vampires or anyone else could see us, it would have to be strictly a working relationship, nothing more.

Never mind how torturous that would be for me to endure.

I pulled into the driveway, parked behind Nanna's car and rested my forehead on the steering wheel. No public dates. No public displays of affection. No eating together at lunch or walking together between classes. How long would Tristan want to keep seeing me in a relationship like that? Did that even count as a relationship?

Tristan

I overslept the next morning.

"Mom's right, we should get you a doghouse." Emily kicked my foot. "You'd better get up. You're going to be late for practice."

Groaning, I dragged myself upright. Wow, I was wiped out, which might explain why I'd failed to dream connect with Savannah last night. I hadn't had enough energy for it.

"Do some energy drawing before you shower," she suggested. "And give you-know-who this to wear when you see her this morning."

A braided ribbon bracelet dropped into my lap. "Is this what we talked about last night?"

"Yep. It should work even if she gets it wet. So tell her not to take it off for any reason. See you at lunchtime."

"Thanks, Emily. You're the best."

"I know." Grinning, she went back inside the house.

Hmm, she was right as usual. I could use an energy boost. Quickly, I spread my hand out flat on the ground and drew up the energy into my body. But I pulled too hard, leaving a scorched hand shape on the grass. I winced, then shrugged it off. It would grow back. Eventually.

I rushed through my shower, deciding to go to school with wet hair so I wouldn't be late for practice. I barely reached the sports and art building before Savannah arrived.

From where I stood at the entrance doors, I could watch her every step of the way from the time she parked and got out of her truck until she reached the cement ramp. Watching her from here seemed a good compromise between keeping her safe and letting her have some freedom. Somehow, I didn't think she'd appreciate it if I gave in to the urge to hover over her every second of the day just to protect her from the vamps. Though denying that urge meant waiting for her with clenched teeth and a racing heart.

As she headed up the cement ramp toward me, she glanced behind her at the woods and turned pale. She started walking faster.

"Still there?" I murmured as she reached me and unlocked the doors with shaking hands.

She nodded, frowning and rubbing her forehead. She was even more pale than usual, too. She must not have gotten much sleep last night.

I waited by the hallway door upstairs until she finished her unlocking routine.

"Emily sent you something that should help with our problem." I walked toward her.

She grabbed the office doorjamb behind her. "Oh. Wow."

"Yeah. You feel the magic in it, too? Emily's really good. I don't know why Dad doesn't just train her to be the next leader of the Clann instead of me. But he's being old-fashioned. And hardheaded." Smiling, I held out the bracelet with both hands.

"Uh…what is it?" She stared at the bracelet, licking her lips.

"It's okay." I chuckled. "Hold out your wrist."

She hesitated then slowly lifted her left wrist. I tied it on with a quick double knot.

And she dropped to the floor with a loud smack. Son of a...

"Savannah!" Hitting my knees, I pulled back her hair from her face. She was out cold. I tapped her cheek and called her name again. No response. Panicking now, I tried again, but her head just rolled away from my hand. I put my ear near her nose and mouth. She was breathing but barely.

The bracelet. Something must have gone wrong with the spell. My fingers were suddenly too big, too clumsy as I fought the knot I'd created.

Get it off her. Got to get it off her. Now!

Finally the knot came loose. I threw the bracelet to the side, noticing a red welt around her wrist as if the bracelet had given her a chemical burn. She gasped like a drowning person resurfacing.

I lifted her head. "Savannah? Can you hear me?"

Her eyelids drifted open. "What..."

"You passed out. Are you okay?"

"I... Yeah." She struggled to sit up, pressing the heel of a hand to her forehead. "Oh, ow, my head."

Had she hit it on the floor? I carefully checked her skull but didn't find any lumps. I held her against my chest for a minute until my heartbeat slowed down and my hands stopped shaking. "Oh, man, I'm sorry, Savannah. Something must have gone wrong with the spell. I'll get Emily to fix it at lunch."

"What was it supposed to do?"

"It's just a basic vampire ward. The Clann parents give them to all the kids to wear until puberty. Then our power kicks in and we learn how to protect ourselves against vamps so we don't have to wear the wards anymore. I swear it shouldn't have done this to you."

She turned even whiter and didn't say anything as I helped her up. "Are you okay to walk?"

She nodded. "But I might have to ask for some help with my trainer bag today." She forced a smile, but her words came out a little slurred.

"No problem." Anything to make up for causing her to pass out like that. Just wait till I could get my hands on Emily. This better have been an accident. I pocketed the bracelet then loaded up for the trip out to the practice field.

We started to skirt the watchers' post near the woods, but she said the vampires were still keeping their distance and had moved away again.

I really hated not being able to see them for myself. Fighting an enemy blind sucked.

Savannah wore a frown throughout practice, and I caught her rubbing her forehead several times. She massaged her temples again at the end of practice as I put away the sound system.

"If that headache sticks around, promise me you'll take some aspirin," I told her.

With a weak smile, she nodded.

She winced as I kissed her cheek goodbye. Her head must really hurt.

Second-period English had never seemed so long. I spent the entire hour and a half wondering if her headache had finally gone away, and what in the world Emily had done to that bracelet. When the lunch-period bell rang, I was the first one out the door.

In the cafeteria, I grabbed Emily's elbow before she could take her seat at our table. "We need to talk." I steered her outside toward my grounding tree.

"What did you put in that bracelet?" I demanded once we were out of hearing range of the students at the picnic tables.

"Just the traditional vamp ward. Why?" Emily replied, her eyes wide with innocent confusion.

"It nearly killed her."

The color drained from her face. In a different situation, I would have enjoyed my know-it-all sister's look of shock. Right now, I just wanted to choke her.

"Tristan, that's impossible. I used the same spell every Clann parent uses on their kids for vamp protection. If it's safe enough to use on a toddler, it should be more than safe enough—"

"Well, it's not. As soon as I put it on her wrist, Savannah passed clean out and was barely breathing. I couldn't get her to wake up until I took the bracelet off her again. You must've screwed up the spell somehow."

Her eyes narrowed. "I never screw up spells. That's your department, little brother. Are you sure she didn't have an allergic reaction to the materials in the ribbons or something?"

I snorted. No one had an allergic reaction like that to freaking cotton. "Don't blame this on the damn ribbons. It was your spell work, and you know it. She didn't seem to want to put it on at first, either, like she knew something was wrong with it before it ever touched her." But Savannah had put it on anyway because she trusted me. Fury bubbled up inside me again, along with a slightly sick feeling. "She's an easy target for the vamps until we get her protected. You've got to fix this. Now."

"All right, pushy." She took the bracelet from me, frowning down at the ribbons. "Hey, did you get this thing anywhere near fire?"

"No. Why?"

She flipped it over so I could see the blackened side of the ribbons.

I swore again. "Savannah had what looked like a burn line around her wrist after she tried it on. Did you use any chemicals or—"

"No, it was straight energy and words, nothing else." She kept frowning, and she had that thoughtful look.

"What?"

"Come on, little brother. Time for research. You can help."

I followed her over to the tech building and into a partially full computer lab. Emily talked to the teacher for a minute then led me to two computers in an empty corner in the back.

"Grab a computer, pull up the internet and look up this word." She wrote the name *Lillith* on a slip of paper.

"Who's she?"

"The mother of all vampires. Now quit asking questions and look her up already."

Frowning, I pulled up the internet browser, waited for the Google search page to finish loading, then typed in the name. "What are we looking for exactly?"

"I'll tell you what to click on." Muttering about stupid, slow school computers, she followed her own directions.

We spent the rest of lunch period researching. When I didn't click on a link fast enough, she growled and took my mouse away from me so she could work both computers herself.

"We're going to be late for third period," I said after the bell rang, signaling the end of lunch.

"No biggie. The teacher here will give us passes."

An hour and twenty minutes later, just when I began to think we'd end up missing fourth period, too, she sighed. It wasn't a happy sound, though. "Found it. Read this."

I leaned over toward her computer monitor to read.

While the King James version of the Bible refers to Eve as Adam's first wife, ancient Hebrew texts state that Eve was Adam's second wife, created from his rib. Adam's first wife, named Lillith, was created by God from the clay of the earth just as Adam was. Because she was created in the same way as Adam, Lillith believed that she was Adam's equal. However, Adam believed he was superior to her, and this led to much arguing.

Lillith shouted out God's secret name, which gave her the power to fly away. Adam complained to God, so God sent three angels to bring her back. But she refused to return with them and threatened to become a plague upon mankind. So God punished her by killing one hundred of her children every day and creating a new wife, Eve, for Adam. In revenge, Lillith upheld her threat and became a demoness, seducing men in their dreams, harming pregnant women and babies, and drinking humans' blood. To replace the human children she could no longer create, Lillith also shared her blood with chosen human victims from time to time, thus creating the first vampires on earth. It is believed that these incubus vampires continue to exist in secret to this day.

When I was done reading, I was still confused. "Okay, what's your point?"

"Here's your answer. Savannah had it right the first time. Those vampires aren't here to leech off her. They're here to watch her. She's one of them." Emily looked at me, waiting for me to piece it all together.

"What? No, she's not. I've seen her mother and grandmother. They're both human. They're descendants, remember?"

"So she could be a dhampir instead."

I stared at her, one eyebrow raised. She realized she was

talking to someone who didn't spend all his time reading old spellbooks, right?

"Half human, or in this case half descendant, and half vampire."

Huh? "There's no such thing. Everybody knows vampires can't have kids."

"How do we know for sure? What if everyone just thinks that because most vampires can't stand to be around humans for long without draining them? What if Savannah's father is a vamp and he found some way to resist draining her mother?"

"Have you ever seen her father?"

Emily nodded. "I saw him once with Savannah at Chez Corvet's. He totally looked like a vampire." Chez Corvet's was the local Italian restaurant.

But I still couldn't believe it. Savannah, half vampire? I'd known her for years. Sure, she was pale and tended to sunburn every year instead of tanning. But that could be from her Irish roots instead. "We're talking about something that the Clann doesn't think is possible. And even if we go way out on a crazy limb here and pretend dhampirs do exist, that still doesn't mean she would have any vampire abilities. I've never seen her show any fangs or want to drink my blood or whatever."

"But you did say you felt tired after every time you see her."

I gave a half shrug. "Well, yeah. We kiss when we say hello and goodbye...."

Aw, hell. Vampires could take human energy through a bite or a kiss. Every descendant was taught that from day one.

Emily nodded, seeing the understanding on my face. "Like I said, she's draining you every time you two make out. You'll be dead in a week!"

Dragging a hand through my hair, I slumped back in

my seat. "I'm not that stupid. I know how to draw energy afterward, remember?" And Savannah's kisses were worth it.

She sighed. "Tristan, be smart about this. You've *got* to stop seeing her. It's the only safe thing to do. Otherwise—"

"No." I didn't even need to think about it. I didn't care what we'd been taught to believe as kids. Savannah wasn't a monster. She couldn't help what her dad was. She might not even know.

"Don't be stupid! Mom and Dad must know about this already. It's probably why her family was cast out. Our parents, the entire council, will *kill* you if they find out you two are involved. This isn't about some simple disagreement between our families anymore. She's one of *them.*"

"I don't care. It's too late."

She stared at me then groaned. "You fell in *love* with her?"

Why bother saying anything? She already knew how I'd answer.

"I've said it before, and I'll say it again." She closed both our internet browsers, her shoulders slumping. "You, little brother, are an idiot."

In this case, I had to agree with her. I was definitely an idiot. I'd fallen in love with the so-called enemy. But knowing that still didn't change my feelings. "What do I tell her? There's no way she knows about this."

"Tell her the truth."

"Are you crazy? I am not going to be the one to tell her something like this. How would you feel if someone told *you* this kind of stuff?"

"I'd think you were nuts. And if I did believe you…" She sighed. "I guess I'd freak out big-time."

"Exactly." Not to mention Savannah would probably want to break up with me.

Scowling, Emily held the bracelet between her palms,

closed her eyes and whispered a few words to remove the spell. I felt her power flare up over my skin, stabbing me with a thousand tiny needles over my arms and the back of my neck. Judging by the level of pain she was causing across my skin, I had to wonder again why Dad didn't just make her the next Clann leader. She obviously had the power for the job.

After a couple minutes, the energy died down and she handed me the bracelet. "Have her try it again."

"And tell her what?"

"That I fixed it."

I felt like I was holding a bomb. "Will it hurt her again?"

"No more than any other bracelet might. Though let me know if she still has a reaction to it."

"And if she does?"

She stood up and gave me a look of pity. "It would make things a lot easier for you two if she were just allergic to cotton ribbon."

"Emily said to tell you she fixed it," I said later that afternoon outside Mrs. Daniels's office as I held out the innocent-looking bracelet. "Want to try it on one more time?"

"Um…" Savannah chewed on her lower lip. "Are you sure your sister isn't trying to get rid of me?"

"Yeah, I'm sure."

She took a deep, shaky breath. "Okay, I trust you. Go for it. But if I conk out again, can you try to catch me this time? My right arm is already bruising up from the last try." She smiled and held out her trembling left wrist.

Her arm was bruised? I winced.

And yet I actually *wanted* her to pass out this time, messed up as that wish might be. Because if she did, then Emily and I were wrong about her being a half vampire. I would just have to be sure to catch her.

But when I tied the bracelet around her wrist, nothing happened. The knots tightened in my stomach.

"Whew! Okay, let's go to practice," she said, grinning with the relief I wished I felt as she unlocked the office closet and grabbed the equipment.

I followed her downstairs, guilt making me want to puke. I could only hope she would understand when she learned the truth someday. And forgive me.

CHAPTER 16

Savannah

November and December were two of the happiest months of my life. And all because of Tristan.

They were also the hardest, for the same reason.

I'd thought he would grow tired of me, find someone else. Someone he could publicly date. Like Bethany Brookes, who was constantly coming over to flirt with him at every freakin' practice. But even though he was polite, he never gave her much attention.

Whatever his reasons for being with me, Tristan found ways to make it work for us, from secret dinners and dancing in the Charmers practice room after hours, to sweet notes left in my locker when he delivered the Charmers game-day good-luck notes. And of course we could always count on dream connecting, which we did at least twice a week.

On every date, real and dreamed, he managed to pull me out of my shell. I'd never been much of a talker before, preferring to listen to others. But something about the way Tristan looked at me just drove me to chatter. Maybe talking was my way of fighting the urge to kiss him all the time, which tended to make him shaky on real dates and completely end our connected dreams.

Or maybe I was just trying to forget the fact that I still hadn't told him I might be turning into a vampire. Which was a debate-worthy topic all on its own, considering the vamp-ward bracelet he'd given me no longer affected me. So how could I really be turning into a full-fledged vampire?

But no matter how much I loved being with Tristan, it wasn't perfect. The council's watchers hadn't gotten tired of hanging around campus. They'd even started to spy on me at Charmers events. They scared me half to death outside the annual Fall Ball where, after putting up with Bethany Brookes's totally unsubtle flirting with Tristan all night, he and I had tried to sneak outside and have just one dance together. Only to have that dance cut short when I looked up and spotted the watchers spying on us from the parking lot. The only high point of the evening had been seeing Anne get revenge on Brat Twin Vanessa by arriving on the arm of her newly dumped ex-boyfriend, Ron Abernathy. Anne and Ron had further shocked everyone by coming dressed as a football player and a cheerleader. Only for revenge would Anne stoop to wearing a fake version of the enemy's uniform. The icing on the cake was how Anne actually looked better in the fake uniform than Vanessa did in the real version. Afterward, Ron began to sit at our lunch table every day, which made Anne smile a lot more than she ever had before.

But even with so much happiness in the air now, I couldn't completely forget that Tristan and I were breaking the rules every time we saw each other outside of school events. And to add to that pile of guilt, there were all the things that having to keep our relationship secret meant. Tristan couldn't take me to the movies or out to eat, couldn't sit with me at lunch, couldn't explain to his friends why he wasn't dating anyone right now. He couldn't even dance with me inside the building at the Fall Ball, because it was too easy for everyone to figure out who was behind each mask. So instead he'd spent the entire night working the concession stand with me and refused to go have a good time with everyone else.

Dating me must be really cramping his party-guy lifestyle.

By Christmas break, Tristan and I had been officially secretly together for two months. Less time than Greg and I had managed, and yet...

I was already completely in love with Tristan.

I must have always been in love with him, because admitting my feelings to myself now wasn't a discovery. It was more like how he said he felt when he did magic...as if I were finally relaxing a muscle I'd kept tensed up for years. Allowing myself to love Tristan was a relief, giving in to something I'd been fighting for far too long.

Just being around Tristan was a relief, an escape from the rest of the world and the future. When it was just me and him together, I forgot all the rules we were breaking. He made me feel normal, and good, and right.

When I was with him, I liked myself. And I knew exactly who I was.

But when we were apart, I remembered the world we really lived in, and it all came crashing down on me. I remembered that we were breaking the rules, and the people I was lying to, which only seemed to get harder to do with each passing day, and the things Tristan was giving up just to be with me. And when I remembered all of that, I didn't like myself much. When I looked in the mirror, I saw a weak, selfish girl who kept giving in to her emotions instead of doing the right thing.

When we were apart, I didn't recognize myself at all.

Something else that I remembered when I was away from Tristan was the continued absence of my father. My refusing to return his calls was way different from not getting any calls from him at all. Even when I'd refused to speak to him, Nanna had always mentioned when he'd called. But he hadn't since October. He'd warned me that he might not be able to contact us for a while, so I was trying hard not to worry about him. But he hadn't said he'd be out of touch for months.

Mom and Nanna didn't seem worried about his absence. They claimed the entire vampire society got together for some huge gathering every ten years or so, and that he must be busy helping prepare for this event. Yeah, right. What party, no matter how big, took four months to plan and kept you from checking on your kid once a week? Something was up. But until my father decided to share, I was in the dark and trying not to care enough to worry about him.

And trying not to let anyone see it, either. After all, how could I possibly explain?

Going to bed early on New Year's Eve, as I'd promised Tristan, was tougher than I'd imagined. Mom had made a point to be home off the road for a change and wanted to stay up to see the replay of the televised New York City ball drop at our local midnight hour. She even tried to bribe me with a bottle of sparkling apple cider, my favorite. So guilty I could hardly speak, I claimed I was too tired and went to bed right after the live ball drop at eleven o'clock instead.

The scene I found waiting for me in the dream made me temporarily forget the guilt, though. I'd landed in the middle of a city packed with a huge, noisy crowd. It was totally crazy.

"Tristan?" I yelled, though I had no idea how he could possibly hear me.

A broad aisle had been roped off in the center of the crowd.

Tristan walked along this aisle toward me, wearing jeans, a black wool coat and the blue-and-gold scarf and hat I'd spent four weeks working with Nanna to learn how to make him for Christmas. The knit hat hugged his head, making his hair peek out along the edges in little curls I wanted to grab and tug. The blue in the hat made his green eyes sparkle.

"What do you think?" He held his arms out wide.

"This is nuts! When did you learn how to do this?" We'd both always been able to imagine small changes into being in our shared dreams, but never anything on *this* scale.

"I had a lot of free time to practice on all those nights when we couldn't connect."

"Well, I am definitely impressed. But where exactly is this supposed to be?"

"Times Square in New York City, of course. Best place in the world to ring in the new year! Or at least as much of it as I can remember from last year's trip."

I looked around me again, this time slower and with even more respect. "Wow. This is all from your memory?"

"Yeah. Have you ever been to the Big Apple?"

I shook my head. The only traveling I'd done was when Mom had moved from New Orleans back to East Texas when I was two, plus short weekend trips for dance competitions with the Charmers earlier this month, which unfortunately Tristan's parents hadn't let him go on.

"Great! Then if I mess up anything, you won't know it."

I laughed.

He reached into his coat pocket then pulled out a cardboard hat and two noisemakers. "Let's party!"

After the current song ended, he said, "Your turn. Play a song we can dance to."

"Me? I can't."

"Sure you can. Just pretend you're listening to it on your iPod."

"Tristan, I can't do magic. I don't know how!" I probably couldn't even manage it if I really tried because of my vampire side.

"Sweetheart, you already are. How do you think we dream connect? If you couldn't do magic, I'd be able to see you in your dreams, but you wouldn't be able to see or hear me."

That made me blink a few times. I'd been doing magic for years and didn't even realize it?

Experimenting, I thought of a song, imagining it playing over some unseen speaker system, and it blasted out, scaring a squeal out of me. Laughing, Tristan grabbed me around the waist and spun me. "Keep it going!"

It was hard at first to focus on both the song and dance with Tristan. Humming the music helped. After a while, I got the hang of it and discovered I was actually pretty good at remembering all the notes of the songs on my iPod's playlists. Once I relaxed, dancing in the middle of Times Square with Tristan was an absolute blast and exactly what I needed to take my mind off all the fears and guilt that dogged me when I was awake. It was one of the absolute best moments of my life, even if it was only a dream and the noisy crowd around us looked suspiciously two-dimensional.

"Tristan, why are all these people flat like cardboard cut-outs?" I teased as he spun me out, twisted me, then tugged me back in to him.

His smile turned decidedly sheepish. "I only saw one side of them. I didn't really pay much attention to their backsides."

"Do your parents go to New York City often?"

"Yeah, usually every year for New Year's, at least. They like to check in on the Clann families there."

"Are there a lot of descendants there?"

He shrugged. "Maybe twenty or so. Nothing like East Texas. We've got just over a hundred in this area."

"So why didn't you go to New York this year?"

He changed the music to a slow song so he could hold me close. It took real effort not to melt into a mindless puddle. "What, and miss this with you? No, thanks. Besides, Emily wanted to go to some local party." He nuzzled the side of my neck with his nose, tickling a laugh out of me.

"And you? Are you missing any parties right now?" Ones he would be having fun at if not for me. Crap. As soon as the words were spoken, I couldn't get the thought out of my head again.

"Nope. I'm right where I want to be." He shivered in my arms.

"Cold?" I asked, distracted. Feeling a little naughty, I imagined gloves on my hands and grinned when they appeared. Then I pressed my gloved hands to his cheeks to warm them.

"In real life, yeah, probably. It was a little chilly when I fell asleep outside."

That got my attention.

"You're sleeping *outside*?" My voice rose to a shriek. I stumbled to a stop, making him trip over my toes. Was he crazy?

"I have to. It's the only way I can get around whatever spells my parents hid in my bedroom to keep us from dream connecting. But it's okay, I'm in a tent tonight. Next time I'll just have to remember to use a warmer sleeping bag."

This did not make me feel better. "Tristan, are you telling me that every time we dream connect, you're sleeping in your yard?" Where anything could attack him in his sleep. The nearby town of Palestine was notorious for both its dangerously aggressive wild hogs and its black-cat population in the miles of woods surrounding it; any of those animals could easily stray into our area. What if a crazed wild hog or a black cat found their way into the woods behind Tristan's house some night when he was sleeping outside and decided to attack him?

And even if that didn't happen, this was East Texas. The insects would eat him alive in the warmer months, he was risking getting sick or hypothermia in the winter and tornadoes were practically guaranteed in the spring. This went beyond nuts. Did he have a death wish or something?

"Would you quit worrying so much?" He gave my ponytail a quick yank. "I'm fine. Now look up, quick. The ball is dropping."

Frowning, I let him turn me around, hug me from behind, while he made the pretend ball of lights drop down to light the New Year's numbers. But inside, my organs seemed to be sinking an inch at a time right along with that lit ball.

All the things he was missing or enduring because of me kept adding up to a really long list. Why was he even dating me? I wasn't worth this much trouble.

"Hey, I've got an idea," he said. "Why don't you think of your New Year's resolution while I change things around here?"

I managed a nod and stared down at the ground. The sound of the crowd abruptly shut off, but I barely noticed. Beneath our feet, the cement and asphalt turned to moss.

"Okay, you can look now."

I looked up. We were in the clearing of our usual woods, but where our picnic blanket normally lay now stood a massive oak tree supporting a tree house. The same tree house from our childhood dreams.

The gnawing chill in my heart melted a bit. "Oh, Tristan. You remembered every detail of it."

"After you, my lady." He swept into a low bow before the ladder, which was actually just boards nailed to the tree trunk.

I climbed up and through the already open trapdoor then stood. "Is it bigger now?" My head should be hitting the ceiling, but it was nowhere near it. I felt like a little kid again.

He took my hand and led me to the balcony. "Yep, had to enlarge it. We're a heck of a lot taller now."

I returned his smile as I leaned on my forearms against the railing. The view was gorgeous from here. The moonlit forest surrounded us, stretching out in every direction like an endless ocean of swaying, sighing pine trees.

"It's beautiful," I whispered.

"But wait, there's more."

Booming erupted above us, followed by crackling. I jumped and looked at the sky with a gasp.

"Fireworks," he said with a boyish grin.

I laughed even as tears stung my eyes. "Very nice idea." Too nice. He was *way* too good a boyfriend for me.

He put an arm around me, letting me enjoy the pretend display in the sky for a few minutes. Then he turned me to face him.

"So have you figured out your New Year's resolution yet?" His voice was soft and even deeper than usual.

"Mmm, probably going to be the same as last year. Try to be a better person." And then some.

"Impossible. You're already perfect."

If he only knew. "And you? What's your resolution?"

"Hmm. How about to be the perfect boyfriend for you?" He whispered the words against the sensitive skin below my ear, making a shiver ripple over me.

"That's sweet." But all the kisses in the world couldn't distract me from the inescapable truth. No matter how right we seemed together, we could never truly be perfect for each other. Not as long as the rules and the rest of the world said we were supposed to be off-limits to one another.

Not as long as everyone thought I was a danger to him.

He searched my eyes. "Are you happy, Savannah?"

Tough question. The true answer was both yes and no. The more I was with him, the more I fell in love with him. But the more I loved him, the more I hated having to keep him a secret from my family and friends.

Still, he wanted an answer, and of course he expected it to be a happy one. "Why wouldn't I be happy? I get to date the sweetest—"

"Hottest?" he suggested.

I nodded. "Hottest, funniest—"

"Smartest?" Eyebrows raised, he lifted his nose in the air, apparently trying to look like some sort of genius.

"Most arrogant guy in our school," I finished with a laugh. Growling, he bent his head down and nipped my earlobe until I giggled.

"Who's also a good kisser?" The tip of his nose brushed a path over my cheek, his strong hands on my hips tugging me closer to him.

"The best," I corrected in a ragged whisper before he gave me a light kiss. We had to keep our kisses short and to a minimum in our dreams. Otherwise we tended to get distracted and lose the connection between our minds. Too many of our shared dreams had been cut short until we'd figured this out.

He pressed his forehead against mine and stared into my eyes, his expression solemn now and filling up the entire view before me. "I love you."

Something bubbled up inside me like a fountain of liquid sunlight. "Really?" I whispered, unable to stop a grin from forming.

"Yeah. Really."

"I love you, too, Tristan." And in that moment, they were the easiest, most natural words in the English language to say.

He tugged the rubber band out of my hair, setting my wild curls free so he could bury his hands in them. Then he kissed me, and I kissed him back, forgetting to keep it light, letting myself drown in the sensation of his lips moving over mine until the dream ended.

I woke up but kept my eyes closed, the memory of those three little words warming me from head to toe.

If only we could stay asleep and in our dreams together for the rest of our lives, my life would be perfect.

But gradually, maybe inevitably, the sensation of his kiss faded from my lips and an ache filled my lungs. Being with him felt so right. Until we were apart, when it all suddenly felt so wrong.

I loved him. Utterly. Completely. Totally. There wasn't a single cell inside my body that did not adore him. If he weren't in the Clann, he would be the single most perfect boyfriend imaginable.

But he was in the Clann. And worse, he was expected to become their future leader.

And I was a half-breed outcast.

And all the love in the world couldn't change those two facts.

Hot tears burned their way down my cheeks. I let them fall, too tired to bother wiping them away. No one could see me in the predawn darkness of my bedroom anyway.

What could I do to change things, to make it okay somehow for Tristan and me to be together openly? Could I talk to my father, maybe get him to convince the vampire council to change their minds? Could Tristan talk to his parents and the other elders in the Clann, make them see that they were wrong about him and me?

I rolled over, hugging my knees beneath the blanket Nanna had crocheted for me.

Who was I kidding? The Clann and the vampires had been fighting each other for centuries. Their hate and fear of each other had begun long before even Nanna was born. They hadn't changed their minds for my father and my mother. Why would they change their minds just because Tristan and I had fallen in love, too?

I remembered the way Tristan had looked at me in last night's dream, all the elaborate details he'd pulled together just to give us a perfect New Year's Eve celebration. The way he'd stared right into my soul and told me that he loved me.

Everything might change if he knew the truth.

What would he think if he knew I was half vampire? There was no telling what he'd been told all his life about vampires. At the very least, he had to have been taught to fear them, to view them as the enemy waiting for a chance to drink his blood and drain him dry.

He might start to see me that way, too.

Maybe if I loved him a little less, I could take that chance and tell him the truth. But I couldn't. I loved him too much to risk it. I never wanted him to question even for a second why I was with him or how I felt about him.

I just prayed that the adult descendants in the Clann kept their promise and never told him, either.

CHAPTER 17

Tristan

The new Charmers spring practice schedule was killing me.

Starting in February, for the next two and a half months, it seemed like the Charmers intended to eat, sleep and breathe preparations in the school auditorium for the team's annual Spring Show. In addition to their regular morning practices, afternoon practices had been extended from six to seven o'clock every evening, plus Saturday practices.

Savannah had put me on the stage crew with the other escorts and team dads. Unfortunately, they also took volunteers, including Dylan Williams this year. He was dating one of the Brat Twins, and no descendants were Charmers. So he must be volunteering either to annoy me or spy on me. Whatever his motives were, I was ready to kill him with my bare hands. And we were still only three weeks into the show preparations.

The jerk was always around, always watching. Every time I started to pull Savannah behind a prop or curtain for a kiss during the after-school practices, Dylan popped up with some request for help or a question for her. At least I still had the mornings with her, though.

Right now, that was *all* we had, since the spring weather was so crappy I hadn't been able to sleep outside in order to dream connect. Even morning practices didn't give us many chances to be alone together, because she worked mostly back-stage on the sound and lights while I was outside or in the gym helping build and paint sets. And every time I caught her upstairs in the mornings, either an officer or a manager was in the nearby costume closet.

We couldn't even risk dinner dates after practice anymore, because everyone started working in separate groups for the show's dance numbers, and they all left at different times.

Between the new practice schedule, the stormy weather and Dylan's spying eyes, my time with Savannah had been reduced to the ten short minutes we had alone together each morning before practice began.

I was slowly going insane.

Maybe if I'd never kissed her, held her, spent countless hours talking with her, our forced separation wouldn't be so bad. But I had, I was crazy about her, and…

And I flat-out missed her.

It was a Friday night. Everyone was gone. If not for her worries that we would be seen together, I'd have taken her out of town for a late dinner before now. I would have to find a way to change her mind about it tonight. After three weeks of practically no alone time together, she had to be going as crazy as I was.

Almost time to lock up for the evening. Finally. I checked the costume closet, turned off the dance-room lights and closed the doors. One less room for Savannah to have to shut down so we could leave quicker. I already knew where to take her to eat.

I headed down to the stage to collect the sound system, waiting as Savannah gathered up CDs and threw the stage's breakers. In the darkness broken only by her flashlight, the urge to kiss her nearly overpowered me. But I'd wait a little longer. Soon enough, I'd have her snuggled up against my side in my truck and on the way to a quiet, romantic dinner at a real table with real chairs and real food.

And maybe it would be enough to last me another week.

"Did you close up the dance room?" she asked as we reached the office.

"Yeah. Thought I'd save you some time. I think everyone's gone now anyway."

"Thanks." She locked the office closet. Then we stepped out of the room so she could turn off the lights.

As she locked the door, I said, "So listen, I'd really like to take you out tonight. There's this fantastic place about thirty minutes away, very quiet, cozy, good food—"

"Tristan, we can't. You know that." She turned to face me with a sigh.

I tucked a stray strand of hair behind her ear. "This restaurant's small, not as popular with the adults. I doubt we'll see anyone we know."

"You and the Clann know everyone."

"Not everyone. And I'll ask for a corner booth so no one will see us."

"I don't know."

She was wavering; I could see it in her eyes. "Please, Sav? I haven't seen you much for weeks." Smiling, I grabbed her and kissed her at the end of every sentence. "I miss you. I'm dying here. You've reduced me to begging."

"Tristan! Someone might see—"

I backed her toward the prop closet. "No, they won't. Everyone's gone for the night."

Suddenly, I couldn't wait. We could leave in a few minutes. First...

Reaching out blindly, I found the closet doorknob and pulled the door open.

"Savannah," I whispered against her lips as her hands stroked my neck, my shoulders, my chest. "I can't handle this, not seeing you."

"We see each other every day," she gasped.

"You know what I mean."

Backing her into the pitch-black closet, I shut the door behind us then lost myself in our kisses, not caring that I was growing light-headed and my knees threatened to give out. And then they did, but Savannah sank down to her knees with me, so it didn't matter. Nothing mattered as long as she kept kissing me. We were meant to be together. How could she ever doubt this?

A series of flashes broke us apart. My eyes flew open, only to be blinded by more bright bursts of light. A low whir and click followed each strobe. What the...

"Beautiful. Just beautiful," Dylan said in the darkness. "Honestly, I couldn't have staged the scene better myself." His voice circled around us toward the doors.

"Dylan, cut the crap. What are you doing?" I said.

One of the doors cracked open, spilling a bar of light over him. "You know, you almost make it too easy. I hated waiting all these months, but it was worth it. These pics are going to help me get you kicked out of the Clann, and maybe your dad, too. After all..." He smiled at Savannah. "We know how they hate Clann parents who can't control their...kids. And once your dad's gone, guess who'll be taking over?"

Dylan's dad, with Dylan next in line for the role.

Cold fury filled me, chilling me as I struggled to stand. I'd kissed Savannah too long, let her weaken me too much. My legs didn't want to lift me up. "I don't care. I never wanted to lead. And Dad doesn't have to lead the Clann to be more of a man than your entire family line combined."

"Famous last lines from the loser." Dylan ducked out the door and strolled away, camera and evidence in hand.

Great. Dad and Mom were going to be beyond ticked off this time. Using the wall, I staggered to my feet, Savannah helping at my side.

Then we heard Dylan's voice taunting from the top of the stairs. "I bet Savannah's family is going to love these pics. Should be some good ones for Grandma's scrapbook, don't you think?" He laughed, the sound echoing in the stairwell now.

She gasped. "Mom and Nanna...they're going to *kill* me."

Oh, hell. I had to get that camera. At least without it, it would be Dylan's word against ours. Shoving the closet door open, I stumbled out to the hallway then the stairs on legs that didn't want to respond. Dylan was already at the bottom of the stairwell.

I ran down the stairs two at a time, using the handrails on both sides to keep from falling down them instead. Kissing Savannah had taken way too much out of me this time.

But I had to keep going. And Dylan was running now, his sneakers slapping across the foyer linoleum. I pushed my body into a jog. I couldn't let him get out of sight.

He exited through the building doors.

I followed, gathering my will and remaining energy. By the time I got out the door, he was near the end of the cement ramp.

I focused on his back, and the energy burst out of me.

He flew three feet forward and down onto the cement stomach first. He lay there, apparently with the wind knocked out of him, giving me time to close the distance.

He rolled over. "Coleman," he gasped. "You...fight...dirty."

I straddled his chest and punched him across the jaw. As weak as I was, surprise was the only shot I had at winning this fight. "Where's the camera?" I checked his hands and pockets, then the ground around us. There, a few feet away.

Reaching out, I used my will to jerk the camera to me. It rose up then darted through the air straight into my outstretched hand. I flipped the door to the camera's compartment open and yanked out the memory card.

Pain exploded in my mouth and chin, twisting me around, and the card went flying out of my hand and into the grass on the side of the hill somewhere. Dylan hit me again, laying me out flat on my back as he got in two more hits. I had no energy left to fight or move or even lift my arms to block the blows. I had to draw some energy. The grass was only a yard or two from my outstretched hand. But I couldn't roll over to reach it.

He grabbed the camera, dug around in the grass, then looked up at the foyer doors and ran off.

CHAPTER 18

Savannah

Shock held me frozen for a moment. When I could move again, I ran down the stairs after the guys as fast as I could. Needles of pain burst over me as if I had run through explosions of fireworks, faded away, then returned. The guys were fighting with magic.

I shoved open the foyer doors and ran outside in time to see Dylan hit Tristan then grab the camera and run toward the front parking lot.

I started to go after him. But then I saw Tristan lying on the cement ramp. I ran to him instead.

He had a busted lip, his left cheek was starting to swell, and the knuckles on his right hand were cut and bleeding.

"Tristan, are you okay?" Kneeling, I lifted his head.

"Savannah, the grass…"

He didn't appear to be *that* beat up, yet he couldn't seem to move. Had Dylan used a freezing spell on him or something?

"Where are you hurt?" I asked, trying to stay calm. But my heart was screaming.

"Get me…to the grass," he whispered.

Huh? "I shouldn't move you."

"Please."

Maybe the cement beneath us was hurting him. I didn't understand, but it didn't matter. He seemed so weak. I'd do anything he asked as long as it helped.

Moving to his head, I grabbed him under the arms and dragged him backward toward the grass. I hadn't thought I'd be able to budge him. But it turned out not to be nearly as difficult as I'd expected. Maybe because he pushed with his feet to help.

As soon as I got him to the grass, my feet slipped on the wet ground. I landed on my butt. Good enough. I cradled his head in my lap. "Is this better?"

He nodded, spread his hands palm down on the grass and closed his eyes.

Prickling began along my neck and down my arms, faint at first, then growing more intense by the second.

"Ow," I gasped, rubbing my arms. It felt like a swarm of fire ants were attacking me.

"Sorry," he mumbled with a tired smile. "Had to get some energy."

"That's…you?"

He nodded.

"Oh. It's okay, then, keep going."

The prickling returned, grew, sharpened to tiny needles stabbing me all over. I knew what a pincushion felt like now. Gritting my teeth, I fought back a whimper. It would be over soon. Surely just a little longer…

He rolled up halfway, and the sensation stopped as if he'd hit a switch. Twin handprints of burned grass marked where his hands had just been. He turned toward me and cupped my cheek, his thumb stroking away tears I hadn't realized I'd cried. "I'm okay now, Sav. Sorry about that. Is Dylan gone?"

I nodded, leaning into his hand. I was just relieved that he was okay.

"Did he get the memory card? I dropped it around here somewhere."

I looked around us, but in the dark I couldn't see anything. "I don't know. I can't see it."

He cursed. "I should have held on to it—"

"He was hitting you. Don't worry about it." Gripping his wrist near my face, I closed my eyes. "You're okay. That's all I care about right now." I sighed through my nose then froze as my stomach grumbled. Something smelled good. Maybe it was Tristan's cologne.

"Are you wearing a new cologne today?" I said, drawing in more of the overwhelming scent.

"Uh, no." He sounded a little amused.

"Wow, you smell good."

"Oh, no, no more kisses tonight. That's what got us in this mess."

I should be upset at his words. But all I could focus on was how good he smelled. He seemed positively...lickable. I turned my face toward his hand still on my cheek, and the luscious scent intensified, making me want to moan.

I reached up to hold his hand and studied it. "Ouch. Your knuckles are bleeding."

"Yeah, I busted them on his face. Obviously not often enough, though. Listen, if he did find the memory card, I don't think he'll really send those pics to your family. His problem is with me, not you. He just likes to play head games..."

His voice faded away along with all other sounds except the solid, strong thud of his heart.

I brought his wounded fingers to my mouth and kissed a scraped knuckle. And the single most intoxicating, mind-numbing, soul-shattering flavor exploded across my tongue.

It was like red velvet cake, chocolate meringue pie, rocky-road ice cream and apple pie à la mode combined. But better. A million times better. I could live on this flavor for the rest of my life and die happy. I kissed the next knuckle on his hand, and the flavor filled me again, just a sip of pure heaven to tease and tantalize and drive me mad with need for more.

I could sell my soul without hesitation for a cupful of this taste.

"Savannah? Savannah!" Tristan pulled his hand from my grasp, and I nearly wept, the loss was that intense. The scent faded away, the taste on my tongue fast following it.

Despair swamped me, and I buried my face in my hands in an effort to hold it in. It was either that or scream from the emotion. I pulled in long breaths of clean air to clear my system of the druglike effects. But I couldn't clear out the memory of that smell, that taste on my tongue.

Slowly, reason seeped back in until I couldn't understand why I'd lost control in the first place. The memory was still there, but not the emotions, allowing me to think again.

What in the *world* had just happened?

"Savannah, are you okay?"

Was I? I'd kissed his wounded hand, and then…

I glanced at his hand, at his bloody knuckles. The taste in my mouth, surely it couldn't be…

A bead of blood still shone on his split lip. Unable to believe I was really doing it, I reached up, stroked a thumb over that glistening spot, then brought my thumb to my mouth. And like before, that same scent and taste filled my nose and mouth, drowning out every other sense, hollowing me out so nothing was left to take up room inside me. Clearing away everything I was, so only the craving was left. But this time, that craving was tainted by horror.

A nightmarish chorus of hisses, high-pitched like nails drawn across a thousand chalkboards, screeched from nearby, breaking through the mental fog and drawing my attention.

The watchers, just ten yards away on the opposite side of the road, bared their teeth and fangs at me. *Fangs*. Ohhh, holy crap.

I shot to my feet, and the vampires fled together in a blur.

"Savannah. What's wrong?" Tristan stood up beside me, the panic in his voice an echo of the fear pulsing through me.

"The watchers. They just hissed at me then took off."

"And before that? You completely zoned out on me."

"I…" I could *not* tell him about this, could never admit what seemed too horrible for even my own mind to absorb. "I…have to go home." Now. Before I did something way worse than just lick the blood off his fingers. I fumbled in my jacket pocket, found the team keys and all but threw them at him, afraid to get too close to him again. "Please lock up for me."

"You have to go home? Right now?"

I nodded, but even that tiny movement threatened to shatter my self-control.

"Well, at least let me walk you—"

"No! I can't. I'm sorry. I…" I could see a vein pulsing in the side of his neck, right there beneath the thin, breakable surface of his skin.

How easy would it be to cut that skin? Just a little nick, and then…

Oh, my God.

Unable to say another word, total loss of control seconds away, I turned and ran for my truck. The key scratched around the keyhole before I could get the door unlocked. I threw myself in, started the engine and caught a tear-blurred glimpse of Tristan running toward me as I sped away. He looked upset, confused, but okay.

He would be okay now. The watchers were gone. Tristan obviously wasn't weak anymore, judging by how hard he had been running after me. And since I'd left, he would be safe from me, too.

Tristan

It was a night for insanity all around apparently. I ran after Savannah, reaching the parking lot in time to see her truck fishtail out the exit in a flurry of spitting gravel and squealing tires. Wow, she'd gotten to her truck fast.

Slow down, Sav, please. I willed her to hear me. *You're going to get into a wreck if you don't.*

I'd have to go after her and make sure she got home okay.

Jogging back into the sports and art building, I crossed to the far end of the entrance hall and slapped a hand over all four light switches at once, plunging the foyer into darkness. I would lock the foyer doors, too. That should be enough to keep out any vandals. Later I'd come back, turn off the up-stairs lights we'd left on and grab our things. But only after I made sure Savannah got home safely.

Moonlight shone through the windows at either side of the foyer doors, lighting my way toward them. If I hurried, I might even catch up to Savannah before she got home. Then we could talk about whatever had freaked her out so badly.

A sharp sting stabbed at the side of my neck, and the world went black.

Savannah

I had to pull over. I couldn't see the road through my tears.

It had finally happened. I'd felt the bloodlust. That was the only explanation for it.

No denying it now. I was turning into a full-fledged

vampire. And that put Tristan in an incredible amount of danger. From me.

I didn't have any excuses anymore. I would have to break up with him. Tonight.

Fumbling with my cell phone, I finally managed to dial his cell. Only to reach his voice mail instead. I couldn't leave a message; his parents might hear it.

When I couldn't cry any more, I finished the drive home then trudged into the house.

"Savannah, your father finally called again," Nanna said as soon as I shut the front door.

"What? Did he leave a—"

"On the hall table by the phone."

I ran for the phone and number. Oh, *please,* let him have a solution for all of this!

He answered on the first ring.

"Dad!" The relief was so sharp it was almost painful, making me forget how much I wanted to hate him. I sank onto the edge of my bed. It would be all right now. He might still be a spy for the council, but at least he had the answers I needed to fix everything. "Oh, man, do I need to talk to you. Are you okay? I thought you'd be gone for weeks, not months."

"I am fine. And, yes, we do need to talk. However, it should be done in person. I am back in the States now. Can you meet me for lunch tomorrow at our usual restaurant? Eleven o'clock sharp. Be sure to dress nicely."

Dress nicely? He must have gone off the deep end while on his trip. And what was with the businesslike tone? "Um, sure, Dad. But you sound…weird. Is something wrong?"

"We will discuss it tomorrow. See you at eleven." He hung up.

I stared at the phone, muttered, "Yeah, I missed you, too, Dad," then ended the call. I don't know why I'd thought the conversation would go any better than that. After all, nothing had really changed. Just because I'd admitted I was happy he was okay didn't mean he cared about me now.

Exhaustion pushed down on my shoulders, making it hard to even breathe, much less deal with yet another problem tonight. Sleep. All I wanted was sleep. I would deal with everything tomorrow.

Flopping back on my bed, I flipped the comforter over myself, then fell asleep still dressed with all the lights on.

I couldn't remember my dream when I woke up late the next morning. All I could remember was that Tristan had been in it and trying to tell me something, but he kept disappearing in a haze the exact color of blood.

I didn't want to think about him or what happened last night. Or the color of blood. Normal. I would surround myself with the normal today.

I had to rush through a shower in order to get ready in time for the lunch meeting with my father. I threw on the only pantsuit I had and twisted my hair into a low bun. It was while I was dabbing on some makeup to partially hide my puffy eyes and red nose that Anne called.

"Hey, the girls and I wanted to know if you will come with us to Tyler today," she said. Her tone was a little flat, as if she already knew my answer.

"I really wish I could, but I'm meeting my father for lunch today, then I have Charmers Spring Show practice until late tonight."

"Yeah, I figured you couldn't," she muttered.

"Aw, Anne, don't be—"

"I know, I know. Don't be mad, and you'll see us next week in the cafeteria." She sighed. "We just kinda miss hanging out with you outside of school, you know?"

Lord, the guilt was just piling up on me lately. "What if

we have a group slumber party next weekend? I could come right after practice."

"Which lasts till what, nine at night on weekends?"

I winced. "More like ten or eleven."

She grumbled. "Nah, let's just wait till after the stupid show when you actually have time to hang out with your friends. That'll be in another month or two, right?"

"Anne—"

"I've gotta run. See you Monday." She hung up.

Feeling tired already even though the day had just started, I ended the call and went in search of my shoes. Obviously as soon as Spring Show season ended, I would have to make sure to spend more quality time outside of school with my friends.

Nanna must have heard me getting ready in the bathroom. When I came out, she had a cup of steaming tea waiting for me on the dining table. I didn't have much time, so I drank it standing up.

"Always in such a hurry," she murmured with a smile, shaking her head as her hands almost magically whipped a ball of soft pink yarn into the tiniest pair of baby shoes I'd ever seen. The daylight flooding in through the patio door made her silver needle flash, drawing my attention. Reminding me of the way the lights had flashed on Dylan's silver camera as he'd run off with it. "You look worried, hon. Is everything all right?"

I forced a smile. "Everything's fine, Nanna." I swallowed hard. "Um, did anyone call today?" *Like a really ticked-off descendant?*

"Like who?"

I shrugged. "Just wondering if there were any calls for me or whatever."

"No, dear, I don't think so."

I tried not to sigh out loud with relief. Dylan must not have found the memory card last night. Otherwise the Clann would be going nuts by now.

Frowning, Nanna glanced at the wall clock near the kitchen. "Aren't you going to be late for lunch with your father?"

I glanced at my watch. "Oh, crap! Okay, gotta run. Love you." I bent down and gave her a quick peck on her papery cheek. "Don't forget, after lunch, I've got Charmers practice till at least seven, maybe eight or nine. So I'll see you later tonight, okay?"

"Okay, hon. Love you, too. Tell your father I said hello."

"I will. Hey, nice booties, by the way."

She grinned, her face lighting up like a little kid on Christmas morning. "Why, thank you, dear! See you tonight."

I arrived at our usual restaurant, Chez Corvet's, faster than I'd expected. My father was already waiting for me at a white cloth-draped table in the middle of the mostly empty restaurant.

He looked the same as always, perfectly polished in one of his usual dark blue suits. And yet the way he stared at me today was different, colder somehow. The look definitely didn't invite any ecstatic, long-lost reunion hugs from me. Just seeing him staring at me like that reminded me why I'd given up trying to please him and refused to talk to him for months.

I sat across from him. After the waiter took my drink order and left, my father said in a voice so low I had to strain to hear it, "Can you hear me?"

The restaurant wasn't busy at this hour. Most of the lunch crowd wouldn't get here till twelve. Yet he acted as if we were surrounded by tables full of nosy eavesdroppers instead of empty chairs and one couple in a booth against the back wall.

Still, if he wanted to act mysterious, I guessed I could play along for the sake of getting some much-needed answers.

"Yes, I can hear you, barely," I whispered.

"Good. Keep your voice quiet just like that." He reached into his jacket's inner pocket and withdrew a black-and-silver flask.

"You carry around your own liquor?" I frowned at the flask as he reached for one of the empty wineglasses on our table.

His face remained expressionless as he slowly filled the glass with a dark red wine.

I sighed, getting impatient. Then a scent wafted over from the kitchen that made my mouth water. Oh, yeah, I'd forgotten to eat this morning. And last night, too. Well, I'd definitely be ordering whatever the chefs were making in the kitchen today. My stomach grumbled.

He slid the glass toward me. "Tell me, does this smell good to you?"

Huh? "You know I'm way too young to drink wine."

"I never said it was wine."

My heart skipped a beat. "Then what…" I stared down at the dark red liquid. "Oh." He was a vampire. Of course. So this was…blood. "It doesn't smell right." But it did smell… good. Ew, gross!

"You mean it does not smell like Tristan Coleman's."

I froze. He knew. Oh, holy heck.

I stared down at the table between us, my thoughts scrambling. I'd really hoped to leave my relationship with Tristan out of today's conversation and just focus on my latest changes instead. So much for that plan.

One dark eyebrow rose as he leaned back in his seat. "Tell me about last night."

"It sounds like you already heard about it. Did your council's other spies give you a call?"

"They did report to the council, yes. But I would like to hear your version of it. You two have been spending a lot of time together? Alone?"

It was either lie or tell the truth. And I was really, really tired of lying. After a long hesitation, I nodded.

"You care about this boy." It wasn't a question. My face must have already given me away.

"I'm sorry. I know I wasn't supposed to. I swear I tried not to. And I've been trying to break things off with him for a while now. But it's…it's harder than I thought it'd be."

"I know what that is like. I experienced the same difficulty with your mother."

His understanding tone surprised me. Hope flared too bright and quick inside me to be stopped. I gripped the edge of the table. "Would it really be so bad if I kept dating him? What if I swore to never, ever join the Clann?"

"They could still use him to manipulate you into helping them."

I closed my eyes, feeling my shoulders sag.

"And then there is the issue of the constant danger you pose to him. Every time you two are together, every time you kiss—"

"Kiss?" My eyes flew open.

He nodded. "Do you not remember? You also come from the incubus. We are able to take energy through a kiss."

I wanted to slap my forehead. I'd *completely* forgotten. So all the times I'd kissed Tristan, and I thought he was just joking around about feeling light-headed…

"And then there is the small matter of last night's events," he added.

I closed my eyes against the growing panic, trying to hold

down the sickening horror rising up in my stomach. "The bloodlust." No point denying any of it now. I was so royally screwed. "Is the council going to make me live with you now?"

When I finally found the courage to look at him, I expected him to be furious. Instead, a hint of a smile tightened one corner of his mouth. "You make such a thing sound like the end of the world."

I shrugged, too tired and defeated to think of anything polite to say. If I had to live with him, it *would* be the end of the world. Then again, it already felt like my life was pretty much over. I was officially one of the monsters now, complete with cravings for blood.

"Unfortunately, such things are not up to me to decide," he added. "Which is why we must leave soon. But first, look at me." He waited until I looked up at him in confusion. "Savannah, you will drink that now." He pointed at the glass of blood in front of me, all the while staring me down.

"Uh, no, thanks."

"Savannah, you will drink it this instant." His tone was weird, like he was trying to compel me to obey him.

"Look, I'm sorry, but I'm not going to drink that." He'd have to pinch my nose and force it down my throat first. I didn't care *how* much trouble I was in, I wasn't going to drink a whole glass of blood. I wasn't *that* far gone. Yet.

We stared at each other for a long, tense moment. Then suddenly he smiled. "That's my girl."

"Huh?" Were all vampires this moody and strange, or just him?

Still smiling, he picked up the glass and drained it. I actually had to look away in order to calm my gag reflex. Just because it smelled good didn't mean it was anything anyone in their right mind should be guzzling.

When he finished, he said, "You passed the test. Now we may leave."

Test? Like a pop quiz? I had to jump to my feet and practically run to keep up with him as he led the way out of the restaurant to the parking lot. "Hey, wait a minute! What test?"

He stopped by his car. "To see what vampire abilities you have now."

"Like?"

"So far, you are still immune to the elder vampires' ability to control fledgling vampires' wills."

Some vampire might be able to control me someday? I shuddered. To distract myself from that idea, I asked, "What else did you test me on back there?"

"You have a vampire's hearing, or you would not have been able to hear me at all. According to what the watchers learned from your friend Anne's mind, you have the ability to mesmerize human males with your gaze. Your physical abilities were nearly as advanced as a newly turned vampire when I saw you dance last spring. So you should be fully equal to a vampire in strength, speed and agility soon, possibly after your first feeding."

Feeding? I nearly threw up in my mouth.

"And though you may have experienced a bit of the blood-lust last night, you have not lost control over it as a newly turned vampire would. Most would not be able to control themselves so well, even around a normal human with injuries."

"I will *never* drink blood." Never mind last night. That was just a few drops. They didn't count.

All human expression left his face, showing the true alienness that I had come from. "If the bloodlust continues to strengthen within you, you may not have a choice eventually."

We'd see about that. "So what happens now? The council just keeps watching me?"

"I wish it were that simple. But you present a true danger to them now, even more so than before. The council insists on meeting you."

"Why?"

"Because of the bloodlust. You cannot be allowed to endanger our society's secrecy if you prove incapable of controlling it. The council must meet with you and decide what action to take."

"When?"

"Right now. I am to take you directly to the nearest airport, and from there, to their headquarters in Paris." He opened his car's driver-side door then stared at me.

"And if I don't want to go?"

He became so still he could pass for a statue. "That would... not be good."

Or what, the council would send someone to hurt Nanna and Mom?

Because I wanted to scream, I took a deep breath, held it for five seconds then let it out in a huff and yanked open the passenger-side door. "Fine, let's go. Seeing as how I obviously have no choice."

"Thank you."

On the way to the airport, I had to borrow Dad's phone because I'd left mine with all the rest of my things at school. I had to do a Google search for the dance-team director's home number before I could call her. "Mrs. Daniels, this is Savannah Colbert. I'm sorry, but I have a family emergency and have to go out of town for a few days."

"Oh, hello, Savannah. That's fine, I understand. Actually, I had intended to call you earlier today. Did you forget to lock the foyer doors last night?"

Huh? My mind was being pulled in too many directions at once. I had to blink a few times and backtrack to last night, which seemed a lifetime ago. "Oh. No. I had to ask Tristan to lock up for me because of the...family emergency. Did he turn off the lights?"

"The downstairs ones, yes. But the upstairs lights were still on this morning, and I found your and his things still there."

I cringed, closed my eyes and struggled for the strength to deal with yet another problem. "I'm so sorry that I couldn't take care of it myself. I'm not sure why Tristan forgot to lock up—"

"I understand, Savannah. I just wanted to double-check with you. I hope everything turns out well for you and your family. Please call me and let me know when you will be able to return to practice."

"Thank you. I will." I ended the call with a shake of my head.

Why would Tristan have forgotten to lock up? If he had the strength to run so fast after me when I left, then he definitely had the energy to at least lock the foyer doors before leaving. He knew that was our job now that we'd entered Spring Show season and had late practices every day. I'd explained to him a couple times how the janitors would no longer secure the building for us until after Spring Show weekend, when our need to use the building so late each night would end. He knew how paranoid I was about forgetting to take care of this, because then the school administrators would complain to Mrs. Daniels.

Had Tristan taken off after Dylan when I left and that's why he forgot to lock up?

"Do not forget to call your mother and grandmother," Dad said.

My heart still pounding with worry over Tristan, I numbly dialed the next number on my list and braced myself for a tougher sell on my upcoming trip.

"I do *not* want you to go with him," Nanna insisted after hearing about the trip with my father. "It's not safe."

I glanced sideways at my father, sure he could hear every word she'd said. "I don't think we have a choice, Nanna. Just...try not to worry. I'll stay close to him and out of trouble, and I'll be back in a couple days or so. I love you."

A long pause. "I love you, too, hon. Please be careful."

"I will."

I couldn't reach Mom, so I left a message on her cell phone. I could just imagine her reaction when she got it.

Then, even though it risked further ticking off my father, I had to call Tristan. When I got his voice mail, Dad glanced at me with one eyebrow raised in silence. I hung up without leaving a message. If Tristan had left his phone at home and his parents saw the missed call, at least they wouldn't recognize Dad's number.

Where the heck was Tristan?

We flew on the council's private jet, first to New York, where we stopped to refuel, then on to Paris. At first, I was too worn-out to want to talk much. But eight hours of endless worrying about Tristan, even while flying in a jet with a luxurious brass-and-white-leather interior, was enough to drive me crazy. Desperate for a distraction, I moved to the swivel chair opposite my dad's and cleared my throat to get his attention. There was still so much about the vampire world that I didn't know. If I was going to fully turn into one of them, maybe it was time for me to arm myself with as much information as possible.

He didn't seem annoyed as he lowered the newspaper he'd been reading. "Something you would like to ask?"

"Um, yeah." I cleared my throat, feeling more awkward than I ever had before. "Do you get paid to help the council?"

"No. Part of my punishment for defying them and marrying your mother is to help them in any capacity they deem appropriate now. Mainly, that role has been to provide them with updates about you and your progress in life."

"So your job really is to spy on me."

"Think of me more as your lawyer who meets on your behalf with the council."

"Which makes them, what...the court judge?"

"Consider them the government, police and the Supreme Court for all vampires. They create our laws, ensure our secrets are protected and rule over disputes among our kind."

"So when they say they want to meet me, this meeting—"

"Is a trial," he finished for me.

CHAPTER 19

Savannah

Great, now I was on trial. "Am I going to be back home in a few days?"

"I do not know. If all goes well, yes. I am trying to convince them that we have much to learn from you still. I have spent the last few months pleading your case to them."

He'd argued with the council...for me? Shocked, I blurted out, "Why would you do that?"

"Because you are my daughter. Why would I not try to protect you?" He said it simply, as if the answer was obvious.

"I...didn't realize you cared." I stared down at my hands in my lap. "I mean, all those volleyball games and basketball games...I asked you to come watch me play, but you never did. So I thought..." I lifted one shoulder in a half shrug.

"I was trying to minimize the council's spying upon you. Everything I see, they see. If you had begun to show vampire or magical abilities early in life, I did not want them to see it."

So all this time, he had been protecting me.

Except that still didn't explain his threatening Mom and

Nanna on the council's behalf. Unless… "At the restaurant today, you said elder vampires can command younger ones. Can the council command you?"

"Yes."

"Even completely against your will?"

"Yes."

"So when you passed on their threat to hurt Nanna and Mom if I didn't stop dancing…?"

"That was at their command."

My throat tightened. "What if I had refused to go with you today?"

"I am under command to bring you to them one way or another. If you had refused, I would have been forced to drug you. It would have hurt me greatly to do so. You are and always will be my child. But a command from the council is unbreakable and cannot be ignored."

I had to look away and blink fast as my eyes burned. I'd always thought he cared more about the council than me, that everything he did for them had been done willingly to earn their approval again. But if they had *forced* him to do it instead…

He was as much at their mercy as I was. And everything I'd thought about my father was wrong. Did I know him at all?

I had to take a few seconds to clear my throat before I could speak again. "So why don't they just command every vampire to follow the rules? Then they wouldn't have to worry about settling vamp problems or dealing with rule breakers."

"They like us to feel as if we have free will."

And yet the council could order vampires around like puppets if they chose, even as tools to be used against their own children.

I remembered everything I had accused him of, all the

times I'd refused to speak to him. Telling him he was no longer my dad. My hands shook. I pressed them against my knees to hold them still and forced myself to look at him. "Dad, I'm really sorry I made things harder for you with the council. And for giving you so much grief. Thank you for trying to protect me."

He nodded. Leaning forward, he rested a hand over one of mine. "I may be old, but there are still human emotions left within me. I am only sorry you thought otherwise of me."

In that moment, a heaviness inside that I'd long grown used to slowly began to lift, loosening the pressure on my chest. My dad cared about me. He'd fought the council for me. He was trying to help me now.

After a minute, he squeezed my hand then leaned back in his seat again.

I sat back, too, trying to smooth out the tangled mess of thoughts and emotions inside my head. So much was changing. It was definitely reassuring to know I wasn't alone here, that I had someone on my side to help me out. But it still didn't solve my biggest problem. How could I—we—convince the council that I wasn't a threat to them? And what would happen if we failed?

"Dad, are you still allowed to tell me the truth?"

"If I cannot, I am allowed not to answer you."

That would have to be good enough. "How much trouble am I in?"

"I convinced them before your birth that it was better to let you live and learn from you. But they only agreed because you were not magically trained, you stayed away from the Clann and you did not have the bloodlust. You did not pose an immediate threat to them."

And now I did.

They'd allowed me to live before. Now it seemed they might change their mind about that.

My mouth went dry, and I desperately reached for something else to think about. "So, um, you never told me where your...our...type of vampires come from exactly."

He sighed. "There are many different theories about our origins. We are not a race that has traditionally valued our own history. However, I have done my own research and found that we actually predate Adam and Eve's descendants."

Huh?

He told me then about Lillith, Adam's true first wife who ended up rebelling against God and becoming a demoness, as well as the mother of our race of vampires. She'd also gone around killing babies and seducing men in their sleep.

I thought of all the times I'd kissed Tristan in our shared dreams, unknowingly draining him of energy and life. I winced. "This Lillith sounds like a real role model for women. Did she eventually die?"

"No. She is still alive, sleeping deep beneath the Sumerian desert somewhere and awaiting the day she can seek final revenge on God."

Talk about not being able to choose the family we're born into. "Wow. Sorry I asked." I leaned back in my seat again, my stomach more knotted than it had ever been before, my head swirling with way too much information. I could definitely have lived without ever knowing about my blood ties to Lillith.

At least I knew one thing...Dad actually cared about me, after all.

He chuckled and reopened his paper. "You look tired. We have a few hours before our arrival. You should try to get some sleep."

Nodding, I reclined my chair and tried to relax.

When I came to in the plane, now dim except for a reading light above Dad, he closed and folded his newspaper then turned up the general lights. "Good, you are awake. We will be landing shortly."

Immediately, my heart began to race. Soon I would meet the control freaks who'd managed to reach out across an entire ocean and screw up my life. I wished they were on another planet instead of just another continent.

I wished Tristan could be here with me somehow. Or at least that I could know he was safe somewhere.

The plane stopped at the farthest hangar of the airport. A car with dark-tinted windows waited for us a few yards away. Once we were in the backseat, Dad held up a long, black satin scarf. A blindfold. "I apologize, but the council insists that this is necessary for their safety."

"Uh, okay." I held my head still while he tied the blindfold over my eyes then checked the edges to be sure I couldn't see out.

"Your hands may remain free as long as you do not touch the blindfold."

The car eased forward, and we were on our way. Great. My first time in Paris, and I wouldn't get to see a thing. Not even the Eiffel Tower.

It seemed we turned a lot, surely more than was actually necessary for the half-hour drive. Maybe they were trying to confuse me. I could have told them not to bother. I frequently got lost even with a map and a compass.

Then the car stopped.

Dad exited first then held on to my forearm to guide me from the car and beyond. I had a fleeting sense of a breeze ruffling the tiny hairs on my arms. Then a heavy-sounding door groaned open. We walked forward, and the breeze died away, replaced by chilly, moldy-smelling air.

We walked for what seemed like a long time, although it might have been only a couple minutes. The path had a wet-sounding hard floor and too many turns to count much less remember. We also went through a series of clanking metal doors others opened and closed for us. I sensed the guards we passed, the loss of sight making my emotional radar ramp into overdrive. Most of the guards projected boredom or mild curiosity. But none of them ever said anything. They must be using that vampire ESP stuff.

Dad stopped suddenly. Holding his mouth close to my ear, he breathed out in a rapid whisper, "I must warn you. In the beginning, the bloodlust is most often triggered by strong emotions. When you truly give yourself to the vampire side, only then will you find complete control over your needs. It takes fledgling vampires months to learn how to let go of their emotions in order to regain control. Some never do. But you *must* learn how to do this. Today. The council will have a surprise waiting for you to test your control. I am sorry, I did not know before we got on the plane, and then I could not safely warn you. So whatever you do, stay calm."

A surprise? What kind of surprise would make me want to just surrender to the vamp within? And wasn't that backward anyways? Wasn't it the vampire genes inside me that were causing the bloodlust? How could giving in to that side actually help me regain control over the bloodlust?

It didn't make any sense. And a tiny part of me had to wonder if this was some kind of trick to force me to finish the change into becoming a full vampire.

But if I couldn't trust my dad, I would have no one on my side here. I *had* to trust him.

With a frown, I nodded.

We started walking again in silence for a few more minutes, then paused one last time. Dad must have had to wait for permission to continue. With every second that passed, my nervousness cranked up another notch.

Finally, a loud, metallic groan signaled the opening of yet another door. We walked forward three steps, the sound of our footsteps becoming muffled on something soft and dry. Dad tugged on my forearm to stop me. I couldn't hear anyone nearby, not even breathing or heartbeats to signal we were with others now. But I could feel their emotions projected across my skin. They were nervous, angry, a little worried, but mostly afraid.

Afraid...of *me?*

The door clanged shut behind us, and Dad removed the blindfold.

Stay calm, I reminded myself, working to keep my breathing even.

I slowly opened my eyes, squinting a bit at the bright light in the room.

The council seemed to like the color red. The cement-block walls were bathed in it, and nine council members sat at a long, half-round table draped in a crimson-and-gold cloth.

"Honorable council, may I present my biological daughter, Savannah Colbert."

The members stared at me with faces like stone. But their emotions betrayed them, intensifying until I nearly gasped from their overwhelming flood of fear and curiosity.

"You have tested her, Michael?" the vampire in the center asked. His skin was as smooth and white as marble. His eyes, so light they appeared solid white except for their ebony pupils, never left me.

"I have."

Silence filled the room while they apparently read his mind for his report. I focused on not fidgeting.

"May I respectfully request that the council consider further discussing these deliberations out loud?" Dad said. "This would allow Savannah to follow the proceedings and elaborate on her abilities in her own words."

Yep, just as I'd guessed. They had been talking about me behind my back…right in front of me. The exact opposite of what the Brat Twins did to me in history class. Talk about annoying.

Another long pause, then the center councilman nodded. "We agree. Savannah, were you ever magically trained?"

"No. Even when it would have been helpful, my grandmother and mother refused. They promised everyone that they wouldn't." Thank goodness for it, too.

"Michael, you were not aware before that she has the bloodlust?" the council leader said.

"No, Caravass. I became aware of it when you did."

A ripple of alarm projected from the council.

"However, my memories today should have shown that Savannah was tested and is in firm control over it," Dad added.

"With regular human blood," Caravass corrected. "The watchers' report showed that she has no such control with regard to Clann blood. This is cause for great alarm. She cannot be allowed to violate our peace treaty with the Clann nor expose us to the world at large. If she cannot be controlled, she is a danger to our entire society."

"No, I'm not." I couldn't believe I'd had the nerve to speak up. No doubt any one of them could snap my neck before I even saw them leave their seats.

Caravass stared into my eyes. "How can you be sure of this?"

"Because I've been alone with a Clann descendant a lot over the last six months. I've had plenty opportunity to…" Feed? Drink from him? What was the right term? "…to bite him. But I haven't."

"Admirable control," Caravass said. "And yet you lost a little of that control when you actually saw and smelled his blood recently, did you not?"

I gulped. Just talking about it made the memory of that taste flood my mouth. "Yes. But that was my first time to ever feel the bloodlust. Now that I know what it feels like, I know I can control my reaction to it. And it's not like I actually bit him or anything."

"We desire proof. If you really believe you have complete control now, you will voluntarily agree to our test." Caravass waved a hand, and a guard at the right wall pressed a button. A smooth section of the wall slid away into a recessed pocket, revealing a window into what looked like a police interrogation room.

Handcuffed to a metal chair in the center of the otherwise empty, gray room sat Tristan, unconscious.

Against my will, I sucked in a sharp breath through my nose. *Tristan.* What had they done to him? Was he okay?

Dad might have warned me that Tristan was the surprise. The Clann would go crazy over this. I'd probably get blamed for it, too. Then again, if I'd never given in to the temptation to date him, he wouldn't be here in the first place. So I guessed it was my fault, after all.

"It is clear already that you do not have complete control around this witch boy," Caravass said.

"I'm half human. I care about him," I admitted in a whisper, tearing my gaze away from Tristan's drooping head.

"Emotions are a sign of a lack of control," a pinch-faced

councilwoman hissed. "We cannot afford to risk our entire society on a girl who cannot control her emotions."

"Especially when the cause for that loss of control is a Clann member," Caravass agreed.

Their collective fear rose, nearly suffocating me.

What a bunch of hypocrites! They weren't even going to give me a chance to prove myself. I had to say something. "Why don't you try me."

Dad stiffened. "I respectfully suggest that the test be kept within reason so as not to start another war with the Clann. Kidnapping their future leader could possibly already be construed as a violation of the treaty. It might be unwise to risk further provoking them."

Provoke the Clann further how...by *killing* Tristan?

The council hesitated, and I couldn't breathe.

"Agreed," Caravass said. "We will keep him alive for this test."

And afterward?

One step at a time, Sav, I told myself.

A guard outside the council chamber opened the vaultlike metal door behind me, and the inner guard stepped away from the window to lead me out. In silence, he turned to the left down a dim corridor that seemed to stretch forever in either direction. If I could get Tristan free, which way would we need to go? The place had seemed like a labyrinth on the way in.

We'd figure that out when the time came. If it did. First, I'd try to do what I should have been doing for months now; I would follow the rules.

After a few steps, the guard turned to the left again at a rectangular metal door. He reached under his jacket, withdrew a ring of keys on a chain and unlocked it. Then he stepped inside.

I followed him into the interrogation room. My gaze immediately snapped to Tristan, who was still knocked out. Part of me wanted to run over to him immediately. The other half of me was distracted by the emotions I kept sensing from the room we'd just left. On this side, the window looked like a mirror. I couldn't see my audience of judges. Yet I could almost pinpoint each council member's location through their anger, fear, worry and curiosity.

They were on the move for less than a second. Then the council stopped again by the window, gathering in a tight half circle only a few feet away. Probably so they could see me better when I failed their test.

The guard's face looked bored, as if to say this was nothing personal. Which was a lie. This was totally personal. And all my fault.

He reached inside his inner jacket pocket and took out two items…a syringe and a scalpel. The clear plastic protectors on the blade and needle made loud snicks as he removed them. The harsh fluorescent light overhead glinted off the needle and made the syringe's yellow contents glow.

I gulped, the air rushing in and out of my lungs in noisy gusts I couldn't hide within the silence of the cold cement room.

The guard stepped closer to us. My thigh muscles tensed, the instinct to fight pulsing through me, and the guard's eyes grew cautious. He knew I was desperate. But that didn't make me stupid. The guard was both a vampire and big, built like a linebacker beneath his badly fitted suit. And even if I could somehow fight him off, my audience of judges would step in to stop me.

Think straight, Sav, I told myself while I struggled to breathe. Time for logic, not emotion.

Okay. So we were in deep this time. But we weren't totally

doomed. Yet. The council had promised that I had only to pass one test, and then Tristan could go free.

An innocent boy who wouldn't even be here if I hadn't fallen in love with him. My fault he was in danger. If I'd only broken up with him...

No, no time for guilt right now. I had to focus on passing this test, and then we could go home.

Just one test to pass.

A test I was genetically destined to fail.

"What are those for?" I murmured, keeping my voice calm as I nodded at the tools in the guard's hands.

"They are your test." His French accent was so thick I could barely understand him. Then he pressed the scalpel to Tristan's neck.

Should I trust the council's promise not to kill Tristan? I searched the emotions in the other room but didn't sense any deception.

Holding my breath and praying I was making the right decision, I took two steps back from Tristan, closed my eyes and tried to calm my crazed thoughts.

Tristan's breathing changed, quickened and grew shallow. He was waking up. I glanced down at him. A bead of blood now welled from a nick below his jawline then trickled down his neck. Metal rang out against the cement floor. The guard had dropped the scalpel. I turned in time to see him backing out of the room, his hand over his mouth and nose as he tucked the now empty syringe into his inner jacket pocket one-handed. He wasn't even going to stop long enough to pick up the scalpel? Or was it that he wouldn't be able to endure the smell of the blood on the blade?

Lovely. So even the council's own vampire guards couldn't withstand the smell of Clann blood for long. And yet the council expected *me* to pass this test?

Maybe not. Maybe they wanted me to fail.

Well, they were about to be disappointed. I could handle this. After all, hadn't I sat in a restaurant with Dad and a full cup of blood right in front of me without a problem?

Then the scent of Tristan's powerful blood wafted toward me from both his neck and the scalpel. Oh, so *that's* why the guard had left the scalpel...to make the test twice as hard. It was working, too. Tristan's blood smelled so much better than regular human blood. Better than anything I'd ever smelled, really.

My mouth watered, and I took a step toward him before I even had time to think.

"Savannah!" he slurred, sounding drunk. He fought to raise his head as he squinted at me. They must be keeping some drugs in his system so he wouldn't be able to use magic and escape. "Oh, man, they grabbed you, too. Are you okay?"

I opened my mouth to reply, but no words came out.

He smelled so good, even better than I'd remembered.

"Sav? You look a little strange."

"You smell great." My feet were shuffling me right over to him. Was that a bad thing? It seemed only natural at the moment.

His sleepy, little-boy smile contrasted with the blondish-brown stubble on his cheeks and around his mouth. I wanted to run my hands over it.

"Uh, okay, thanks. Now are you going to free me or what?" He flopped his hands to indicate the handcuffs.

Mmm, yes, I should free him. I could use that scalpel to pick the locks. Then he could get up and wrap his arms around me, and I could stand on tiptoe and lick the blood...

Blood? Oh, yuck. Whoa. Wait. What was I doing this close to him? Only a foot remained between us!

I stumbled backward until my hands found the cinder-block

wall. I slid down the wall until my butt met the equally cold cement floor. But he wasn't safe enough yet. I could still crawl over to him. I pressed my knees to my chest and wrapped my arms around my shaking limbs.

Oh, crap. I *was* dangerous to him. This wasn't a dream or a nightmare. This was really me fighting my fully-awake self against the urge to drink Tristan's blood. And I didn't just want to drink a little. I wanted to drain him dry, to take every bit of his energy into me so I could keep him with me forever.

"Did they brainwash you or something?" he muttered, the words coming out more smoothly now. The drugs must be wearing off.

"No. I'm being tested."

"With what, the urge to free me?"

"It's okay. All I have to do is sit here and stay calm. Once the test is over, I'm sure they'll take you home. No one wants another war between the species."

"Species? What are you talking about? What species?"

"Ours. Yours and mine."

He stared at me. "You're making zero sense. Is this about last night?"

"A little, yes. Remember the watchers? They're with this… group. You could call them all one big family." A family of monsters. And I was one of them.

My feet slid forward as if they had a mind of their own. I dragged them back up against me.

"Vampires," he whispered.

I nodded and focused on trying not to breathe through my nose. But the room was small and the scent of his blood was rapidly filling the tiny space.

Whimpering, I pinched my nose shut with one hand, kept the other arm like a chain around my legs and closed my eyes.

Ah, better. But pinching my nose shut trapped the smell inside me so that it filled me up, tickling at the insides of my nose and throat.

"Sav, what is going on?" If he'd been rude or angry, I could have ignored him. But I couldn't block out that warm, low voice when it softly pleaded with me.

I had to tell him the truth.

"I'm half vampire." My voice came out flat, as dead as I felt inside, but it couldn't be helped. "My father is an incubus, a demon-vampire hybrid that can drink blood or drain you with a kiss. Apparently I can, too. It's the reason for my eyes changing color and the gaze daze. And why you feel weak after we kiss, and why we're drawn to each other...some sort of built-in suicidal attraction between the species." I looked at him, meeting his gaze, needing him to see the honesty in my next words. "I'm so sorry I didn't tell you before. I...I forgot about the draining-through-a-kiss thing. I thought as long as I never bit you, you'd be safe around me. I should have told you anyway, but I just wanted you to keep liking me."

I expected to find shock and horror in his eyes. Instead, I found...warmth. Caring. Impossible. He should at least be a little bit surprised. How many people heard their girlfriends announce that they were half vampire?

"You already knew, didn't you?" I whispered. "You knew and never told me?"

He flinched. "Emily and I guessed."

"How long?"

"When the bracelet nearly killed you."

"And you knew about the draining-kiss ability, too?"

He nodded.

He'd known for *months*. Months I'd spent feeling guilty for not telling him. And all that time, while I'd been kissing him, unaware that I was draining him, he'd known...and hadn't cared.

"Are you an idiot?" My arm loosened from around my knees. "How could you keep seeing me? *Kissing* me?" I rose up on my knees, so furious the cement didn't even hurt. "Do you have some kind of a death wish? Do you *want* to die?" I was nearly shouting now. And the angrier I became, the more irresistible he smelled.

From the other room came a heightened mixture of fear and the faintest hint of smugness. Oh, crap. I was giving them exactly what they wanted, losing control right before their eyes. Moaning, I pinched my nose shut again. Dad was right, emotions might make me more human, but they also definitely made the bloodlust worse. Calm, I had to stay calm. I sat back down against the wall.

"I didn't say anything because I love you. I didn't want you to run away from me, from us." The sadness in his voice created an echoing ache in my stomach.

He loved me. Even though he knew I was a dangerous monster.

I couldn't decide if I wanted to bite him, slap him or kiss him. "Do you know why we're in here? Why they kidnapped you? Because *you* are my test. There's a reason why the vampires are the Clann's worst enemy. That blood running down your neck is the ultimate test for me. You're the son of the Clann's most powerful family. They know you're like an addiction for me, the one person I'll crave above all others, even other descendants."

"Well, same here," he growled. "It doesn't matter what you are. Don't you have any idea how much I love you? How much I've always loved you? And I always will, no matter who or what you come from. So what if you take some of my energy when we kiss? Don't you get it? It's worth it to me, just to be with you."

He made craving someone sound romantic, like a symptom of love. The need I felt for his blood right now was anything *but* romantic. How could it be romantic to want to kill someone? A sharp laugh escaped me. "What we have here isn't love. It's just the monster's drive for survival."

He cursed and jerked at the cuffs, the tendons in his neck standing out. "Damn it, you're not a monster!" The blood dripped a little faster toward the collar of his shirt.

Oh, God. I couldn't do this anymore. His words, his voice and the furious ache within it, were ripping me apart. I couldn't talk to him, love him, want to hold him and want to drain him dry all at the same time. *This* wasn't love. Love was that sweet glow of warmth I'd always felt for him even when we were little kids. *This* was bloodlust. And it was threatening to destroy what little humanity I had left.

Maybe that humanity was the problem. According to Dad, there was only one way to end the torture here. Regain control over my emotions.

But could I really trust a former council member's advice?

"Sav, whatever you're thinking, don't do it," he murmured. "Don't pull away from me. I don't care what they said. You *know* what we have is real."

I gave him a sad smile, my decision made. "I'm so sorry, Tristan. For everything. But I promise it'll be over soon."

Then I closed my eyes.

I am an Ice Princess, I thought, reaching for that mask. The cold within answered, eagerly seeping over my face. But this time, it didn't stop there. Instead, it kept going, tightening my scalp, creeping down my neck and torso, spreading goose bumps along my arms and legs.

Oh, no. I'd gone too far, let it take over too much. I was drowning in the cold now, going numb from head to toe.

But then I realized…that numbing effect was exactly what I needed right now. Because if I was numb, then I wasn't having to battle the bloodlust. Or any other emotion. And that meant I was in control, not the bloodlust.

So I gave up, gave in to the vampire side that had been waiting there for me all along. I embraced that numbing cold, hugging it to me, using it to kill the emotions that had been wrecking my self-control and fueling the burning need for Tristan's blood.

Only then, encased in that imaginary block of ice, did the bloodlust finally fade away, along with all other feelings. And at last, I could safely meet his eyes again.

"I love you." His voice was a terrible combination of pleading and defeat. But it couldn't reach me now. I was safe behind the wall of ice.

Why had I fought my vampire side for so long? Emotions were the real danger, hurting me, distracting me, making me lose control. The cold was a sweet relief, offering me peace and calm.

I sat back against the wall, which seemed warmer than me now, laid my cheek against my knees and stared at the rusted metal door. "Don't worry. They'll come back soon to free us."

Both disappointment and relief floated from the council through the glass window. And yet still they waited. For my self-control to crack?

I closed my eyes and drifted on waves of numbing cold inside. It was strange, like how swimming in a winter ocean might feel after the first shocking sting went away. Did dying of hypothermia feel like this? Was it a comforting relief from the pain, a near-blissful release all on its own even before death approached? If so, maybe it wasn't such a bad way to go.

Part of me, deep down, said a crucial piece of me *was* dying. But the rest of me was wonderfully numb.

I even felt brave enough to take a short breath through my nose. Tristan's blood still smelled good, yet it couldn't get through the ice to trigger any emotions. I lifted my head and smiled. I'd done it. I'd beaten the test, withstood the temptation to kill the boy I loved...and all I'd had to do was stop fighting what I already was.

That sniff must have been what they were waiting for, because after another minute or two the door opened and the guard returned, still holding his wrist over his nose. He looked at me. This time, he couldn't seem to keep his face emotionless, his silver eyes wide with disbelief. "They are ready for you now."

Without looking at Tristan, I rolled up to my feet.

As I reentered the council chamber, that empty calm came with me, bringing clearer thoughts and understanding. I realized I wasn't afraid of the council anymore. Why should I be? Wasn't I one of them now, or nearly so? And wasn't that exactly what I'd always wanted, to truly belong somewhere? I nearly laughed out loud. How stupid of me, to always want what I couldn't have, when all along I'd had an entire world to fit in among if I just stopped fighting what I was. I had never been normal, never would be normal. I was a vampire in the making. There was no point denying it, and nothing I could do about it. So maybe it was time for me to learn to live with it.

"Impressive," Caravass said upon my return.

I dipped my chin in acknowledgment of the compliment. Ah, so lovely not to feel afraid anymore while facing the council. And now that I no longer had my own feelings clouding up my mind, I was free to concentrate on their emotions instead. The overwhelming majority of which was relief. But why were they so relieved? Because I'd passed their test and proved I wouldn't endanger their peace treaty?

Were they really *that* afraid of what I might do?

As the council returned my stare, I tried to imagine myself in their position. What must it be like, to be in charge of an international world of immortals, each one strong and blood-thirsty…? To know that my eternity would be spent trying to keep such a society secret from the world around us and at peace with the equally powerful Clann…? And then to be faced with such a mixed creature as myself, one that could potentially help or ruin us all…?

They must have wanted to avoid possible disaster and simply kill me as soon as I was born, if not before my birth. Yet they had agreed to let me live and see how I would turn out. And how had I repaid such a monumental risk on their part? I had threatened to expose them to the human world, secretly dated the future leader of the Clann for months and refused to even give them direct updates about the changes I had gone through.

Their methods were definitely medieval at times. They never should have kidnapped Tristan. But then again, we shouldn't have run around breaking the rules for months, either. So maybe Dad wasn't the only vampire I had misunderstood.

"We have reached our decision," Caravass said. "You do seem to have the bloodlust under control. For now. So you are free to go, but under a few conditions."

I raised an eyebrow in silent question.

"You must be taught the vampire rules and ways by your father."

"Of course." I would need all the help I could get.

"You will return here every six months to undergo testing. We want to stay abreast of your developments as a vampire, as well as monitor your magical power."

Now both my eyebrows went up. "Testing?"

One corner of Caravass's mouth tightened. "We will not be using a descendant for future tests."

I gave a single nod in agreement.

"And you must stop seeing the witch boy outside of school." Caravass tilted his head toward the still-uncovered window.

From the corner of my eye, I snuck a peek at Tristan, his shoulders slumped, his eyes dark and haunted. I looked away again.

"The only reason he has not destroyed us all is because of the drugs in his system at present," Caravass warned. "He is a danger to all within our world. You included."

Shouldn't that be the other way around? Weren't we vampires the danger? "So you still intend to let him live?" A tiny crack spread in the layers of imaginary ice that encased me.

"Your father has made a wise point. Harming this descendant would destroy the peace between ourselves and the Clann. But you must not be alone with him anymore. We cannot risk your losing control around him and single-handedly destroying the peace treaty."

I almost frowned, then stopped. No, I would not think about this. I already knew what needed to be done. "Agreed. But…may I have a few days to handle this in my own way?"

Silence filled the room as the council discussed telepathically. Then Caravass nodded. "Your father will keep you under close supervision until this is accomplished."

"Thank you."

"Meeting you has been…insightful." Caravass nodded at the guard, who opened the door for us again. "I hope to learn much from you and your developments over time."

I gave a short nod and followed Dad out of the chamber.

We waited in the dank hall as the guard entered the interrogation room. After a few minutes, he led Tristan out.

Tristan's wrists were still cuffed behind his back, but he seemed less sluggish now and able to walk fine. I carefully avoided looking at his face.

Dad put a blindfold over his eyes, checking around the edges to be sure Tristan couldn't see. He repeated the procedure with me. But then Dad did something surprising. He grabbed my wrist, tugged me over a few feet and placed my hand over Tristan's. Tristan's fingers immediately laced and locked with mine.

Had Dad done this to keep Tristan calm and cooperative?

Dad walked behind us, using gentle nudges on our shoulders to guide us back out of the tunnels to the street. The entire time, Tristan's heated grip on my cold hand never loosened.

The vampire inside me wanted him to let go. His touch created too much warmth, steadily melting the chill within me as Dad shepherded us out. How could I stay safe and numb when his skin was so hot against mine, nearly burning me from the contact?

At the car, we paused in the darkness while Dad removed Tristan's cuffs. As soon as we got into the equally dark backseat of the car and could remove our blindfolds, Tristan gathered me to him in a fierce hug.

Dad sat in the front with the driver and raised a black privacy wall between the two halves of the car. Only a small light set into each door panel provided a dim glow as the car began to move forward. Oh, of course. Being a vampire, Dad would be able to hear us if I lost control.

"Are you okay?" Tristan's voice came out muffled in my hair.

"Yes. You?" I felt as if I'd stepped into a bonfire. The heat from his arms around me, his thigh against the side of mine, his chest like a wall of warmth against me, was too much for the chill inside me to withstand. He bent his head toward me, and I barely had the strength to turn away at the last second so his kiss landed on my cheek instead.

"We'd better not," I murmured, everything inside me aching to do the exact opposite.

He chuckled. "Oh, yeah. At least not till we find somewhere for me to recharge, huh?"

I tried to swallow down the growing lump in my throat, my eyes burning as badly as if someone had poured chemicals into them. I pressed my face against his chest, focusing on the steady beat of his heart beneath my cheek.

He must have felt the tears soak through his shirt, because he reached up to thumb away a few. "Were you scared?"

That I was going to kill him? "Yes, terrified." I still was. Thankfully the guard had cleaned the blood off Tristan's neck before releasing him, or I'd be too afraid to risk being alone with him even now. Though every second we were together, I was still tempted to kiss him and drain him even further. So even now, he wasn't safe. Maybe the council had been too lenient in allowing me a few more days with him.

"Don't worry, Sav, it's over now. I'm just glad they let us go without hurting you."

I nodded and pressed closer to him, enjoying his touch for as long as I could. Because he was right…it was over. At least for us. He just didn't know it yet. As soon as our plane touched down outside of Jacksonville, I would keep my promise and break up with the only boy I had ever loved.

Until then, I would just have to hold on to every last second we had together and pray that it would be enough.

★ ★ ★ ★ ★

Crave Extras
Book 1 of The Clann
Playlist

CHAPTER ONE
"Invincible" by Muse (Savannah and the Brat Twins)
"Rollin in the Deep" by Adele (Savannah's issues at school)
"Superman" by Five for Fighting (Tristan's issues)

CHAPTER TWO
"Savin' Me" by Nickelback (Tristan worries)
"Your Star" by Evanescence (Savannah learns the truth)

CHAPTER THREE
"Hearing Damage" by Thom Yorke (Savannah's return)

CHAPTER FOUR
"Radioactive" by Kings of Leon (Tristan's training)

CHAPTER FIVE
"Everything Changes" by Staind (Tristan dreams of Savannah)
"Going Under" by Evanescence (After the recital)
"The Climb" by Miley Cyrus (Preparing for auditions)

CHAPTER SIX
"Bring on the Rain" by Jo Dee Messina (After the auditions)
"Mmm..." by Laura Izibor (Savannah's dream)
"Snow White Queen" by Evanescence (Savannah's phone chat with Dad)

CHAPTER SEVEN
"Say It Right" by Nelly Furtado (Savannah's first boyfriend)
"Impossible Dream" by Luther Vandross (Team theme)

CHAPTER EIGHT
"Leavin'" by Jessie McCartney (Tristan's jealousy)
"#1 Crush" by Garbage (Homecoming Dance)

CHAPTER NINE
"Stockholm Syndrome" by Muse (Breakups and fights)
"Falling Away with You" by Muse (Tristan's discovery)

CHAPTER TEN
"Sleepwalker" by Adam Lambert (Savannah's recovery, regrets and resisting temptation)
"Deep" by Nine Inch Nails (Facing off)
"Stop and Stare" by OneRepublic (Tristan's punishment)
"Iris" by The Goo Goo Dolls (Dream connection)

CHAPTER ELEVEN
"Good Girls Go Bad" by Cobra Starship w. Leighton Meester (At the Sonic)
"Crush" by David Archuleta (Joining the team)
"What I've Done" by Linkin Park (Family feud)

CHAPTER TWELVE
"Apologize" by Timbaland w. OneRepublic (Overdue apologies)
"Nobody Knows" by P!nk (Dancing in the dark)
"Secrets" by OneRepublic (Closet kisses)

CHAPTER THIRTEEN
"Try" by Asher Book (Date and dancing)
"Love Story" by Taylor Swift (Dream connection)

CHAPTER FOURTEEN
"Escape" by Enrique Iglesias (Gaze-daze discussion)
"Your Love's a Drug" by Leighton Meester (Settling in)

CHAPTER FIFTEEN
"Bounce" by Timbaland (Field house faceoff)

CHAPTER SIXTEEN
"Dear Life" by Anthony Hamilton (New Year's Eve connection)
"Anywhere" by Evanescence (Between love and guilt)

CHAPTER SEVENTEEN
"System" by Chester Bennington (Magic and mayhem)

CHAPTER EIGHTEEN
"24" by Jem (Going overseas)

CHAPTER NINETEEN
"Human" by Civil Twilight (The test)
"Letters from the Sky" by Civil Twilight (Leaving Paris)

Q & A with Melissa Darnell

Q: Where did your idea for *Crave* and The Clann come from?

A: I'm a huge reader of vampire and magic-themed romances, but I always found myself wishing that the heroine could be the vampire. Then, in 2008, I thought, wouldn't it be cool if she was the vampire, and the hero was a witch, and their two "species" were mortal enemies? Or even better, what if her family used to be witches, too, and her mother had a *Romeo and Juliet* kind of love story with her dad that produced an outcast who would later find herself in the same situation as her parents? From there, the idea of Savannah and Tristan just wouldn't get out of my head, and they've been there ever since!

Q: Savannah is a strong and admirable character who faces some really hard choices. What was your inspiration for creating her?

A: When I was a senior in high school, I began to have a lot of health problems and was diagnosed with lupus, an auto-immune disorder where basically my own immune system attacks itself. At the time, lupus was pretty much unheard of (and to this day I still run into health-care professionals who are unfamiliar with it), so it was hard for me to explain what I was going through and receive much understanding. It was a very lonely and alienating experience.

Being a teen is tough enough; you already tend to feel

like your parents just don't get you. Add to that an illness where your body turns traitor on you with some "weird" disease no one knows much about, and it's too easy to feel cut off from everyone around you. I wanted Savannah to go through something similar...going from "normal" to "freak" in less than a week, battling the feeling that no one around her can understand and wishing she could just be normal again, plus having to face confining rules that go completely against what her heart is telling her to do. In the end she'll find her strength and personal identity again, but it's going to be a long and emotional process, and one that I hope many readers will really be able to identify with and take hope and courage from.

Q: Sav's friendship with Anne is a source of joy and support for her throughout the book. What do you think is the essence of being a good friend?

A: Anne is based on my real-life best friend, who showed me the most loyal and true friendship imaginable. During tough times, when I was angry and scared and resentful of anyone who seemed to have it easier, she was there for me, continually reaching out to me. When your whole life seems out of control, an honest and true friend can anchor you to reality and help you see the bigger picture. Friends like that are absolutely priceless!

Q: You chose to tell *Crave* from both Sav's and Tristan's points of view. How hard was it to switch between them, and how was the experience of writing in Tristan's voice?

A: I really loved writing from both the male and female points of view. It was so much fun to see a scene two ways. When

I read or watch movies, I do the same thing...imagining what everyone is thinking at that moment. There can be a lot of hilarious confusion just from two people going through the same moment together yet having completely different ideas and understandings of it! I also really enjoy the fact that males and females can be so alike in some ways, such as in our hearts and emotions and needs, yet can think so differently and have completely opposite reactions. My only trouble was in keeping Tristan likable...growing up as a tomboy with three brothers and more guys for friends than girls gave me TOO much of an understanding into how guys think, and it's a constant fine line to make Tristan a realistic Southern teenage boy without making him unlikable!

Q: Dylan and the Brat Twins enjoy bullying Sav. Sadly, bullying is a problem for many students in schools today. Have you had experience with bullies, and do you have any advice for dealing with them?

A: As a teen, I actually experienced several of the incidents Savannah goes through in this book. I also know how angry I get at things that scare me. Unfortunately, I didn't have as clear an explanation as she does for the bullying. But at its heart, I think bullying comes from fear and insecurities in the tormentor's mind. Maybe they are going through really bad things at home, or learned how to bully others from their parents or family. In Savannah's case, Dylan and the Brat Twins are acting out of fear (and a little bit of unwanted attraction, on Dylan's part)...they know Savannah is dangerous, and that fear drives them to push her. If they can make her "crack" and show her dangerous side at school, then the Clann will be convinced to kick her out of Jacksonville and away from them.

Q: Tell us about one of your favorite memories from high school.

A: It's tough to choose just one favorite memory from high school. I loved the slumber parties and pasture parties my friends and I would have. I really enjoyed serving on the production staff of the annual creative-writing magazine... reading poems and short stories by my peers was such an eye-opening experience, because they gave me amazing insights into people who until then I couldn't relate to at all. But my single favorite moment was the day one of my essays actually made my senior English teacher cry. To be able to move even one reader like that is what makes writing and re-visions worth every second!

Q: We would guess that you've never actually met a vampire or a Clann magic user (but if you have, do tell!). How did you develop the mythology behind their paranormal abilities for *Crave?*

A: While I've never met a real vampire, I've often felt like one! My Irish ancestry gifted me with super pale skin that is next to impossible to tan but will freckle and burn in a nanosecond...not a great thing when you live in the land of the tan! I also have naturally pointy incisors that I used to get teased about in junior high...like Savannah's mother, I looked like a vampire when vampires weren't cool! LOL. I have pale gray eyes that actually do look more blue, dark gray or green depending on my moods and what I'm wearing. Plus, having lupus means that spending time in the sun can actually make me sick. So while I can't imagine wanting to drink anyone's blood, I can definitely relate to that alien feeling of physically not fitting in with others.

As for magic, seeing ghosts and experiencing bits of ESP does actually run in my family on my mother's side, so it wasn't much of a stretch to take it even further and imagine full-blown magic taking place!

Q: Tell us a little about your journey to publication. Did you always want to be a writer?

A: Ever since I taught myself how to read when I was four, I have been fascinated with books and the writer's ability to take their thoughts and share them with others. I have been writing ever since. And yet, there is something about writing fiction that requires a whole new level of courage!

When I was in the sixth grade, I submitted a poem that was chosen for publication in an international anthology. That same year, I also entered an essay contest and won a horse. Afterward, I had a lot of encouragement from family, friends and teachers to keep writing, and I wrote several nonfiction books. But I never believed I could become a published novelist and make an actual career out of it. It took meeting my husband and years of listening to his supportive nagging to finally get the courage to submit a story for publication seventeen years later!

Now I can't seem to STOP writing stories! LOL.

Q: What advice do you have for aspiring authors?

A: Believe in yourself. You hear this all the time, but it is absolutely true. If you can't *not* write, if it takes more effort to ignore the stories inside your head than it would to just write them down, then don't wait for others to tell you to go for it. Start writing! Then be prepared to revise, both before and after your story finds a home. Writing is a solitary pursuit. Getting published is all about teamwork!

Also, don't aim for perfection. If you're like me, you'll find yourself revising the same scenes or even the entire manuscript fifty times, just endlessly tinkering with it while trying to achieve some crazy idea of perfection. There's no such thing! Make it as good as you can *for now*. Learn something new from every story you write so that you're constantly improving and growing as a writer. Read bestsellers by other authors and pay attention to what you like about their stories, but don't ever feel like you need to write just like someone else in order to do well. The world needs more creativity and unique voices! Read the great how-to books on writing out there. But don't let the need for perfection or the fear of not being good enough stop you from actually sending that story out into the world. Do carefully consider what agents and editors tell you. If their suggestions make sense to you and your heart agrees, try them out, then wait a day or two and reread your story to see if it actually is better. If you absolutely can't stand the changes, follow your heart instead, but do at least consider why your editor or agent seems confused as to what you were going for and ways you can reword things for clearer understanding.

And finally, know the premise at the heart of your story! It will save you countless hours of misery and confusion both as you write your story and later during revisions. Hold true to the core point of why you want to tell that particular story, and it will give you clarity throughout every step of the process.

An exclusive excerpt from COVET
Book 2 of THE CLANN

The world hummed around us in our luxurious surroundings of white leather, exotic wood trim and gleaming gold accents. The boy I loved more than my own life sat beside me, a slight smile curving his lips, his arms wrapped around me. Protecting me even in his sleep.

I should have been protecting him instead.

He had to be uncomfortable, sleeping while sitting upright against the side of the private plane. I'd tried to get him to move to one of the reclining leather chairs when his eyelids had begun to droop. But Tristan had refused, claiming he preferred sitting on the floor so he could hold me properly.

And knowing what was coming for us, I'd given in. I wasn't too eager to let go of him, either.

One stray, golden-blond curl, rebellious like its owner, flopped over his forehead. Carefully I reached up and smoothed it back.

He sighed and snuggled me closer. Though I was practically already in his lap, my legs draped across his thighs, so I wasn't sure how much closer we could get.

I studied Tristan's face, relaxed and peaceful in sleep, and another tear slipped down the side of my nose. Stupid tears.

I hadn't managed to stop crying since we'd safely exited the council's underground labyrinth of tunnels. Knowing what I had to do for Tristan's own safety after the plane touched down outside of Jacksonville, I feared the tears would never stop.

So many perfectly logical and good reasons why I was all wrong for him, why I had to do what everyone else wanted and stop seeing him. My mind understood. Why couldn't my heart agree?

I closed my eyes and burrowed closer against him. I would do it. I would keep my promise to the council and to myself. Just...not yet. A few more hours while we were on this plane together, a few more precious memories to make before we landed so I would remember how it felt to be held and loved by him. How it felt to wrap my arms around his waist, feel his hard chest beneath my cheek, hear his heartbeat pounding beneath my ear. To feel safe within his arms, his strong hands holding me like I was a precious treasure...

"Savannah," a familiar voice whispered like an annoying mosquito near my ear.

"Mmm," I mumbled, wanting that voice to go away. Only one male's voice was welcome right now, and that one wasn't it.

"Savannah, wake up," Dad insisted.

Scowling, I cracked open one eyelid. Quieter than the sound of a breath, knowing his vampire ears would still hear, I sighed. "Yes, Dad?"

"We are an hour away from landing, and the pilot warned that we will be landing in bad weather. You should call your grandmother and mother and let them know." He held out his cell phone.

I took it, and he left again, disappearing toward the front of the cabin.

I tried to ease from Tristan's arms. But as soon as I moved, he woke up.

"Sorry," I whispered. "I need to make some calls. Go back to sleep."

"No, I'm okay." He tugged me back onto his lap, nuzzling my nose for a kiss. At the last second, I turned my head so his lips touched my cheek instead. He leaned his head back to search my face, his heavy-lidded gaze hurt and confused.

"We shouldn't…not until we land and you can draw some energy." His ability to pull up energy from the earth through direct contact with the ground was the only thing that had saved him a few days ago after too long a kiss with me and a fight with Dylan Williams. Otherwise he might have died that night.

He frowned but nodded, letting me up but holding on to my hand. His unusual need to touch me constantly over the past few hours made me wonder. Did he somehow know what the council had made me promise to do? Or had the council's test simply left him on edge and worried about me?

I moved to the nearby leather chair and dialed my home phone number one-handed.

The phone rang four times, then the answering machine clicked on. I glanced at my watch. It was 10:00 a.m. on a Sunday. Nanna, who my mother and I lived with, should be home and getting ready for church. Why wasn't she answering?

I tried again, thinking maybe she was in her room getting dressed. Again, I got the answering machine. This time I left a message.

Weird. Unease crept in as I called my mother's cell phone next. She was probably still on her latest sales trip.

Mom answered on the first ring, startling me. Unlike Nanna, Mom seldom had a signal while she was delivering emergency safety products and chemicals to forestry clients out in the fields and woods.

"Hey, Mom. Just wanted to let you know I'm okay and—"

"Savannah! Oh, thank God. I, we, your grandma…" Mom

sounded hysterical. "I was at a convention. I'm on my way home now. But I'm still hours away from Jacksonville and—"

My hands convulsed around both the phone and Tristan's hand involuntarily. "Mom? What's the matter? Slow down."

Tristan rolled up to his feet and moved to sit in the chair beside me, his thick eyebrows drawn together. He was a beautiful distraction I had to look away from, even as the strength of his hand kept me grounded.

"Sav, they took your nanna! They called me, and—"

"Whoa, what? Who took her?" Cold fear ran through my veins, along with disbelief.

"The Clann. They called me, asking about that Coleman boy as if I would know where he is. For some reason, they think you two are involved or something. I tried to tell them that was a mistake, that you'd never break the rules like that. But they didn't believe me."

I cringed and tried to tug my hand from Tristan's, but he simply encased my hand between both of his. The heat from his hands made me realize how cold I was becoming. A symptom of the vampire side within me kicking in. Not good.

"But they insisted he was with you," Mom continued. "I told them he couldn't be, that you were on a trip with your father, and they went crazy. They said they have your nanna, and they won't release her until we bring the Coleman boy back. I tried calling her, but she's not answering. They couldn't really have kidnapped her, could they?"

Holy crap. "Mom, hang on and let me talk to Dad."

Dad must have been listening in the front cabin, because he immediately joined us and took the phone. While Mom told him what was going on, I stared at Tristan and tried to absorb my mother's words.

"The Clann…they've kidnapped my grandmother," I told him, still in disbelief.

"They wouldn't do that," Tristan insisted, his full lips

pressing themselves into thin lines. "There's been some mistake."

I told him word for word what my mother had said. When I finished, he sat back in his chair, his normally tan face turning pale.

"I'll fix this. Give me a phone and I'll call my parents," Tristan promised me.

"Joan, we are half an hour from landing now. I will handle this and call you back when I have news." Dad ended the call then handed the phone to Tristan, his face as stoic as ever.

Tristan tried his father's cell phone first, then his mother's and even his sister Emily's. But no one answered. Frowning, he tried a few other Clann descendants' home and cell phones. No one was answering.

"I don't understand. Wouldn't they be waiting for your call?" I said.

"Yes. Unless…" Tristan looked away for a moment, then his gaze snapped back to mine, his jaw clenching. "Unless they're already meeting at the Circle and using power. It could block all incoming radio and cell-phone signals, if they've raised enough power together."

"Why would they raise a lot of power together?" I asked, not sure I really wanted to hear the answer.

Tristan stared at me, obviously unwilling to hurt me.

I couldn't look at him anymore, my throat so tight it hurt just to breathe. If anything happened to Nanna, if Tristan's fellow descendants did something to her, the fault would be completely ours. We'd broken the rules to be together. I'd thought the vampire council was our only real worry, that the Clann couldn't do anything more to my family since we were already cast out.

I was wrong.

★ ★ ★ ★ ★

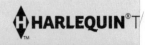